They are the Merricks,
two brothers and a sister, restless, daring, proud.
English by birth, they came to Scotland
with their father to occupy McClairen lands.
And there each would find a love as wild and glorious
as the Highland isle they claimed as their own.
Fia, the only daughter, is the ravishing one.
Raine, the second son, is the reckless one.
Ashton is the eldest son. This is his story. . . .

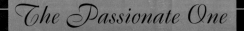

The Passionate One

"I STILL WOULD HAVE MY REWARD. WILL YOU KISS ME?"

She lifted her gaze; it became entangled with his as surely as the rose vine entangled with the yew at her back. "Aye."

Ash's strong arms reached past her, bracketing her head. He leaned forward and kissed her.

Her hands stole around his shoulders, pulling her body tight against his hard chest— He let her go.

Dazed, she stared at him. He stepped away from her, clasping his hands behind his back. Then he smiled and bent forward in a deep, courtly bow.

"I am well rewarded," he said. "I heard the others coming back. You'd best go. Now. Meet them outside the entrance. I'll follow later."

"But—" She stared at him without understanding, for he'd awoken with his kiss such feeling as she'd never experienced before. Never.

"Go." He was still smiling. "You see, you've won."

She turned away, gathering her skirts and bolting into the too bright light. And so she did not see Ash Merrick's gaze follow her, or see him take his hands from behind his back and turn them over. And she did not see the bloody hands that had been torn strangling the thorny vines behind her so he could keep from crushing her to him. . . .

ALL THROUGH THE NIGHT

Dell Books by Connie Brockway

McClairen's
Isle

~

The
Passionate
One

Connie
Brockway

A DELL BOOK

Published by
Dell Publishing
a division of Random House, Inc.
1540 Broadway
New York, New York 10036

ISBN: 0-440-22629-5

Printed in the United States of America

Published simultaneously in Canada

June 1999

10 9 8 7 6 5 4 3 2 1

OPM

For the nameless young dog killed in
Minneapolis, and for all nameless neglected,
mistreated, or abused animals everywhere.
God grant them safe haven.

Acknowledgments

Thank you, David, for listening way beyond midnight on so many nights, and thank you, darling Rachel, for never complaining about the thrice-weekly pizzas. Many thanks to my agent, Damaris Rowland, for her belief in me and to my editor, Maggie Crawford, for her talent and support. Thank you, Mrs. H. (AKA Christina Dodd), for always finding the weak spots and more important, always pointing them out. And finally, thank you, Anne Horde, a great sister-in-law, and a better friend.

Prologue

In 1523 the McClairen chieftain, Dougal of Donne, stood on northern Scotland's high headlands, looked out at a rocky island rising from the churning sea, and ordered a fortress built there. He had carefully picked this particular ground, it being an isolated, pine-strewn island connected to the headland by a single ramp of flinty rock more oft submerged than dry. No man would step foot on that isle without being seen and no army would cross that narrow land bridge if Dougal deemed differently.

Dougal designed the castle in the shape of a U, the short central façade facing squarely north against the sea while its two wings swept back, forming an open courtyard on the south. Below the courtyard he had a terraced garden cut into the rock where, protected from north gales by the castle's bulk, orchards and kitchen gardens could flourish, making the fortress proof against any siege.

For four years the proud castle gradually took form under Dougal's careful, albeit impatient, eye. Yet, for all its foreboding strength, Dougal did not stint on supplying his castle with creature comforts, blanketing the chill walls with thick tapestries, and carpeting the flag-stoned rooms with Oriental rugs.

When it was done, Dougal set off to bring back the inspiration for his work, Gordon McIntere's black-haired daughter.

He'd seen Lizabet only once before, on her thir-teenth birthday. Dougal knew that McIntere had planned to align his child with a richer clan than the McClairens. It mattered not to Dougal; he swore to have her whatever the price. He persuaded the old McIntere chief of the fervor of his suit with gifts and coins—and the sight of Dougal's seventy well-armed highlanders. Happily the wench had not yet married, though Dougal swore to his deathbed it wouldn't have mattered if she had. And so they wed and he carried her back to his island.

Legend says that on their arrival Dougal stopped some distance from the isle rising from a sea of mist, and pointed at the great castle, and vowed that once in those walls Lizabet would remain innocent of any man's touch save his own. The lassie's cheeks grew red on hearing her new husband's ardent oath, thus chris-tening the great, gray fortress with the unlikely name of Maiden's Blush.

Maiden's Blush she had remained throughout all Dougal's long life and that of his sons. Throughout the bloody sixteenth century not once did she fall to enemy hands—not even when Scotland's Queen Mary was beheaded.

The castle remained a loyal Stuart keep through the Hanovers' rule and civil war, and into the seventeenth century. When James II was exiled to France and the German George took the throne, her thick stone walls listened to a gathering of Highland chiefs swearing allegiance to the "king across the water."

Maiden's Blush herself kept George from seeking redress against the McClairens. The castle was impregnable. Any army attempting to take it by force was doomed to failure. It could only prove an embarrassment when it stood against the might of George's army—and held. Thus the crown never ventured and Maiden's Blush never fell, nor was she ever threatened.

Until, that is, one rare summer in the third decade of the eighteenth century when heather grew so thickly it hid the island's sharp old bones beneath a mantle of lavender flowers, and a gentle trade wind charmed a riot of brambled roses into bloom. That year Maiden's Blush housed a score of McClairens from diverse branches of that clan, all living under the care of Ian McClairen, Marquis of Donne.

Ian had come unexpectedly into his rank of chief. His three older brothers had died as a result of their part in the uprising of 1719. Colin, his younger brother, had gone to make his fortune in the East Indies, leaving Ian laird.

Ian never married. Instead, over the years, he gathered his clan in the castle. All of them were black-haired and fervent, with the McClairen knack for loyalty and the McClairen curse of bullheadedness. The youngest and prettiest of these was Ian's distant cousin,

Janet, whom Ian doted on as the child he'd never had. He would have given her anything in his power to give, anything she'd wanted.

She wanted an Englishman named Ronald Merrick.

Merrick was the eldest son of the Earl of Carr, the half-mad scion of an ancient Sussex family. He'd befriended one of the McClairen men in Edinburgh and come up to McClairen's Isle on the young man's invitation.

Ian had heard the rumors about his cousin's new English friend, that Merrick was profligate and ruinously extravagant, that he'd been in Edinburgh fleeing a huge pack of London creditors. But Ian, having more heart than insight, paid little heed to the tales. All young men, Ian reasoned, were wont to such excess if they lacked purpose, and everything Merrick said gave Ian reason to believe that the Englishman had found his purpose, the same one Ian owned, returning James III to the English throne.

Ian little suspected that Merrick had long been in the throes of quite a different driving passion, one far more compelling than any political loyalties.

Gorgeous, charming, and urbane, well-read and inbred, Ronald Merrick was a penultimate example of amorality. Yet Merrick was by no means the black sheep of his family. He was representative of that breed, being no better or worse, simply blessed—or cursed—with a spectacular combination of good looks and an agility of mind that allowed him to better serve his master—his own desire.

Merrick's desire was simple: He wanted society to bend its collective knee before him.

His self-absorption was unparalleled, his sense of

duty nonexistent. He served what best served his purposes and those purposes were whatever best served himself.

Of course his companions knew naught of this. To them he was simply a charming guest who had the devil's own luck with cards and a right handsome way with women.

But Fate has a fine sense of the absurd, she does. For though Merrick *wooed* the McClairens, thinking to cheat from them and their friends what Highland riches he could, he *won* Janet. Before he quite understood what had happened, he found himself wed to a rich, highland heiress. She was bonny and generous of heart and body and she adored Merrick. And if Merrick considered the world a penal colony and himself a prisoner barred from the center of his universe, that being London, at least he'd found himself a comfortable cell with a comely cell-mate.

The years passed and Merrick got two sons on his beauteous highland bride, so pleased with her that he almost forgot his purpose, his desire. Almost.

But one day as he rode into the courtyard, he thought how he would have liked to replace the central stone well with a marble fountain . . . if Maiden's Blush were his. A seemingly harmless, idle thought, but a seed of evil planted in a fertile bed swiftly bears poisonous fruit.

Thenceforth, each time Merrick entered the courtyard he would see some other item that he would replace or embellish or alter if it were only his to do so. Quickly other irritations chafed his never easy peace. Soon he could not dine without being acutely aware that the food he ate had been prepared to please another's palate, or that the dogs lounging in the hall were suffered there because another man willed it, or that the flowers spilling from the silver urns had been placed because of another's preference.

Envy grew in him like a canker, insidious and deep. It became so entwined in his every thought, so directed his every decision, that soon his hunger defined him. Not even his bonny bride could ease it.

He grew to hate the McClairens and all things Scottish, seeing them as manacles keeping him from his true desire. His eyes began to turn ever southward toward London, like those of a deserted lover pining for a former mistress. The newly rekindled desire burned in his imagination until it became an all-consuming conflagration. He needed to return to society. To London.

He kept the canker well hidden. Only Janet knew of it—and that only because she'd seen the cold distance in his eyes when he looked on their sons.

About this time, Colin McClairen, Ian's long absent brother, sent his wife and children to McClairen's Isle while he remained abroad. Ian offered them rooms at the castle but Colin's bride chose instead to live on the mainland.

Then, two years later in 1745, Bonny Prince Charlie landed in the north of Scotland. The McClairens rallied to him and were instrumental in his triumphant march to Edinburgh. They would have been instrumental in his even more triumphant march to London—but someone had betrayed their plans.

Prince Charlie was routed at Culloden and fled to France. Ian and his comrades were captured, taken to Newcastle, tried, and executed. Even Colin's sons were imprisoned while the Duke of Cumberland, who'd led the king's troops, swept through the Highlands like a burning scythe in a monstrous demonstration of merciless reprisal.

At first, Janet did not suspect Merrick of her clan's betrayal. But when he accepted Maiden's Blush from King George she grew uneasy. She fought to believe him when he told her that he'd accepted the castle because, as an Englishman, he could better hold it until, Colin, the new laird, returned.

Treachery had achieved what no amount of force could; for the first time in two centuries no male McClairen lived on McClairen's Isle. The new laird had not returned, and with no voice raised in their defense, his sons rotted in London's Tower.

Merrick commenced renovations on the castle.

Janet knew then, though she did not ask. She'd dared not. It was too late for Ian and his men, Colin's sons, but it was not too late for *her* children.

Or so she'd told herself.

For a time she grew more ill with her suspicions. Now, as twilight rolled across the North Sea, she turned from where she sat at the far end of the terraced gardens and gazed at the castle.

A wit had renamed it Wanton's Blush because of the embarrassment of ornamentation with which the old fortress had so lately been bedizened. It was an apt enough appellation. For centuries she'd worn the battered armor of a guardian; now she resembled nothing so much as a self-conscious and elderly bride. Decked out in fresh plaster, her dark bones covered in the tuck-pointed brick, her mossy roof replaced by gleaming slate, she'd been remade.

Even her ancient setting had been reappointed. The gorse and wind-stunted pine that had tangled like squabbling retainers at her feet had been replaced by curtseying ranks of tame gardens. Only the old kitchen gardens where Janet and her children rested remained intact. The stone walls still held the manacled limbs of ancient espaliered pear and apple trees, while thin onion stalks glowed fluorescent in the half-light, and marjoram and mint scented the air.

"Is it ours?" her eldest son, Ash, asked.

Lady Carr brushed the silky black curls from his forehead, a tender expression on her face. He was a beautiful boy and just coming into manhood, slender and elegantly fashioned.

"No," she answered. "We're just minding her a spell until Colin McClairen is free to claim her."

"Father says Wanton's Blush is his," Ash insisted in a troubled voice.

She must be careful of how she dealt with this. Of her three children, Ash was the most passionate one. He felt things too strongly; he saw things too clearly. No wonder his father avoided him. Ash had always been able to see beneath his father's thin veneer of charm to the emptiness within.

"She belongs to the McClairen, laird of the clan."

"Then where is he?" Raine appeared suddenly beside her, taking a combative stance.

Two years younger than his brother, Raine was already nearly as tall, answering Ash's fine-boned beauty with his own rough, elemental grace. He was her reckless one, impulsive and impetuous, capable of generosity as well as ruthlessness.

"Where is who?" At the sound of the smooth English voice, Ash stumbled to his feet.

A man moved down the marble steps toward them, sparkling like one of the marzipan fantasies the new French chef created. His coat was encrusted with gems, stitched with metal threads. Glittering gold lace cascaded from beneath his square jaw, and the white wig he wore shimmered with diadem dust.

Lord Ronald Merrick, now Earl of Carr. Until his father's recent death Janet hadn't even known Merrick's father had lived, let alone that he'd been an earl.

Carr arrived at her side, his expression becoming annoyed when he saw Fia asleep in her arms. "Where is the nurse?"

"I wanted to rock her to sleep myself, Carr. She's my own bairn. I don't need strangers to raise her."

"If you want to flaunt your coarse ancestors, so be it." Carr's voice was uncharacteristically indulgent. "But at another time. Our guests will be coming down soon and you need to get dressed."

"I am dressed."

Carr ignored her, peering instead at the little black-haired toddler she held. "You did well with this one."

Janet gazed down at Fia's creamy cheeks and pink rosebud mouth. Though just a child, even now one could see the beauty promised by the fine, regular features and dramatic coloring. Fia would be the ravishing one.

"Very well," Carr murmured. He glanced at Ash and Raine, a glance that did more to dismiss than acknowledge. "She'll have a thousand hearts laid at her feet—and her pick of a thousand titles," Carr predicted. "But not for a few years, eh?"

He flicked the edge of Lady Carr's plaid scarf with his fingertip. "Despite your mumbled bravado, my dear, you are not yet dressed. Did you honestly think I'd let you wear that McClairen rag to my ball?"

"I thought it was *our* ball," Janet said quietly.

"Why would you think that?" Carr's forehead lined with puzzlement. "I am the one who was lost to society, my dear. I am the prodigal whose return they've awaited, and you will not exhibit your political sympathies by wearing the McClairen plaid at my ball."

The wind ruffled the gold lace at his throat. "Such an act would not only be stupid, but dangerous. 'Tisn't that many years since the McClairen were ruled traitors. Or have you forgotten their fate?"

Beheading. No, she hadn't forgotten.

"Mother says Wanton's Blush doesn't belong to us," Raine interrupted suddenly, thirsty for his father's attention. "That it belongs to a laird."

"Does she now?" Carr queried, directing his sardonic smile toward his youngest son. "And were you so stupid as to believe her?"

Even in the faded light she could see Raine's skin darken.

"And what of you, boy?" Carr's probing gaze swung toward Ash. "Did your mother's prattle scare you? Did it offend you to think some unknown hairy-legged brute might someday stomp in and declare your inheritance for his own?"

"No, sir," Ash said.

"No?" Carr's brows rose. "Then you are a fool or a weakling." His smile never wavered; the gleam of amusement did not die in the brilliant eyes. "I despise both."

She did not know why he loathed his sons so. But he did. Each year more so than the previous one. Perhaps he hated them for their Scottish blood, or for having a stronger claim to Wanton's Blush than he, or simply for their youth and promise, promise he'd turned his back on years before. Only Fia seemed to have escaped his animosity.

"Sir, I only meant—"

"There will *be* no inheritance," Janet interrupted, unable to watch him toy with the boy any longer. "You've spent all my dower on tricking out Maiden's Blush like a cheap Vauxhall whore. And she *isn't* yours." The words came from her in a rush, long held, now finally spoken. "She belongs to the McClairens. You swore you'd plead Colin's case, explain that he wasn't even in the country when Ian plotted against the crown. But Colin is living like a pauper in a tumbled tower and you've done nothing to aid him."

"I've done what I could to deal with Colin Mc-Clairen." Carr's perfectly smooth face frightened her.

He'd done something to the new laird. She could see it in his eyes. A trembling began within her. She would have done anything for her children, anything. She'd held her tongue for their sake, but now, for the first time, she wondered if she'd done them a disservice. The truth might arm them better for the life they were destined to live than could her silence.

"Since the crown gave me Wanton's Blush—I do so enjoy that name—until its future is decided," Carr continued, "I shall make it tolerable. I daresay I shan't be here long. This evening's affair is important, a first step in my return to London. Know this, dear wife, I will use, I *have* used, whatever means necessary to see that I am restored to my rightful place in society."

Once she'd loved him and it was more toward that memory than the living man that she stretched out her hand. "You used to care for me, Carr," she murmured. "You had so much promise, such intellect and address, but it's been wasted!"

Carr's face rippled with violent anger. He grabbed her arm and dragged her upright. "It's late. You'll not wear that plaid."

She twisted. The sudden motion jerked awake the little one. Her plaid scarf ripped with a sharp sound. Fia cried out.

"I am the Earl of Carr. I have waited ten years for this night, ten years to begin my return to that strata to which I was born, which is my right. You will not do anything, *anything*, to jeopardize that."

He was flushed, furious. So, too, was she. She'd buried the truth from herself for nearly two years but she could do so no longer. The McClairen plaid hung in pieces from his fist, a fitting emblem of her clan's fate—shredded by Carr's implacable greed and ambition.

"Carr," her voice vibrated with her demand, "the truth. Did you sell my family to the English? Did you? Tell me!"

"Tell you what?" he hissed. "That superior men oft reach their goals by climbing atop the corpses of their enemies? Of course. Don't be naive."

"*Men?* Or you?" Lady Carr asked, in a low harsh voice though she knew the answer. She'd always known. "Did you betray them?"

"Get you to your rooms and get dressed, madame!"

"I won't," she said. "I loved you once, but no more. I won't betray my clan by living with their deceiver. If pride is the only legacy I leave my children, so be it."

"You may regret your words, madame." Carr flung down the scarf and snatched Fia from her, thrusting the little squirming girl at Ash. "Take her away. Take the other boy with you!"

"But—"

"By God, you will do as I say!" Carr's face grew mottled beneath the rice powder.

Janet's heart pounded with her body's intuitive terror. But her mind could not feel the fear, *would* not feel it. For too long she'd buried what she'd known, held her loyalty to her husband above the loyalty she owed her clan. No more. She would leave, take the children, go to her laird—

Raine had begun to cry silently. The tears on his cheeks caught the glint from the torches on the terrace high above.

"Please!" Ash pleaded. "Mother—"

She bent quickly, retrieved the scarf, and wrapped it about Fia's shoulders. "It's all right, Ash. Take Fia up." Her gaze found Raine, his fists balled, his chin thrust out. "Take your brother, too. Promise me you'll keep Raine safe, Ash. Please."

"I will," Ash's tears were flowing now. "I promise—"

Carr's palm jolted into the boy's back, sending him stumbling up the shell path. Ash caught Raine's hand and dragged him forward.

Carr turned toward Janet.

* * *

The cream of London's society had traveled Scotland's newly laid roads to see what the Earl of Carr had made of his unlikely acquisition. Now, as the party began, they descended from their rooms shedding powder and bon mots as they observed and judged the magnificence designed solely to impress them.

Within an hour the party was acknowledged to be a smashing success. Carr's guests were impressed, they were titillated, but best, they were amused. And Carr, even more gorgeous than he'd been a decade ago, held court.

Several there had known him in his last days as fashion's most disreputable and prideful leader. They'd whispered as his assets had been sold off and they'd stared at the packs of creditors waiting daily at the door of his town house. They'd nodded sagely when he'd finally fled the city rather than risk debtor's prison. They'd never expected to hear from him again.

But here he was, glowing with pleasure. He traded sallies, lavished compliments, and directed a league of servants to see that every desire was met, every courtesy extended, every convenience offered. He did so fine a job of hosting, in fact, that it was some time before anyone noted his wife's absence.

Finally an elderly roué mentioned this to Carr. Carr dispatched a servant to fetch his wife. The footman returned a short time later with the information that Lady Carr was nowhere to be found.

Carr went in search of her, his handsome face wearing the smallest degree of irritation. She was not in the gaming room. She was not in the ballroom. Neither was she in the Great Hall nor in any of the small antechambers.

The house was warm, Carr explained offhandedly. The crush, the excitement, the noise—she was, after all, unused to society. She might have gone to take some night air in the garden overlooking the sea. His companions volunteered to accompany him on his search.

The gardens were lovely. Paper lanterns had been strung along the perimeters and little candles flickered in the colored glass balls lining the footpaths. At the far end they found a gossamer scarf by an open gate.

Carr retrieved it with a dutiful husbandly cluck. His wife, it seemed, had an affinity for the sea. With a rueful shrug he turned back toward the castle saying that whatever his personal inclination, etiquette made clear that a party cannot have two absentee hosts.

Tipsy and amused and not at all averse to having a role in the little domestic drama, his companions pledged to find the errant lady. They lurched through the gate, laughing and calling her name, leaving Carr behind.

An hour later they burst through the terrace doors. Wigs askew, clothing in disrepair, they trembled on the edge of the dance floor, flushed and sobered and appalled.

The din of conversation faded. Slowly, every head turned toward them and then, instinctively, toward their host. Those closest to Carr stepped away, leaving him alone within a circle. Handsome head high, face taut with ill-suppressed emotion, he demanded an explanation.

"There's been an accident," one of the disheveled band exclaimed. "Lady Carr. She's fallen from the cliffs."

"Where is she?" Carr's body trembled. "Is she . . . alive? God, man, answer me!"

The man sobbed, shaking his head. "We saw her body on the rocks below. We tried to get down to her but it was no use. The sea took her."

Chapter 1

*L*ord Tunbridge was cheating.

In the dank, smoky back regions of Rose Tavern, the young bucks' festive mood had long dissipated. First their purses, then their jewelry, and finally their inheritances had bled into Tunbridge's hands. They sprawled in the malodorous abandonment only four days of fevered carousal can imbue, staring at visions of paternal rage, or worse, debtor's prison. There was nothing left for them to do now but wait for an end to their purgatory.

Because, though they knew Tunbridge was cheating—no one had so devilish luck—no one could say how. Certainly no one would dare make complaint to Tunbridge, an acknowledged duelist with an accredited five deaths to his record.

Only two men remained playing, Lord Tunbridge and Ash Merrick. A slack-mouthed wench snuggled on

Tunbridge's lap, her soft pink flesh glistening with the oppressive heat in the room, while outside a blustery, cold day reminded those abroad that winter had only recently ended.

Tunbridge ignored the doxie, his slim fingers straying like albino snakes amidst the piles of guineas and stacks of silver. It was not so great a heap as those that had already been won at that table, but it was a substantial sum, enough to recoup a decent portion of even the worst losses.

Tunbridge's cold gaze fixed on his opponent. Thus far Merrick had fared better than his companions. It was rumored he had arrived in London months ago, after a two-year stay as a guest in Louis XV's prisons, and had since seemingly fixed on making up for lost time.

London's rakehell cubs had taken him up immediately, as one would a new toy. And a prime entertaining toy he was. No man was wittier, no company more obliging, no guide in the ways of dissolution more knowledgeable. And no one was less bound by society's rules and had less care for society's opinions than Ash Merrick. But that was only to be expected.

Lord Carr was his father, after all, a man who'd been exiled to the Highlands rather than face his creditors and then been forced to stay in exile losing three rich Highland wives in short succession.

If Merrick was notorious, his father was infamous and the titillation of following so nefarious a leader had proven irresistible to the bored elite.

But if they adulated Merrick, it was a tainted adulation, well tempered with contempt. He was a no one. Prison fodder. His own sire would not underwrite him, and his mother had been a known Jacobite bitch. He lived by his wits on the fringes of society, and therefore, while being amongst them, he was patently not one *of* them.

More provoking, he did not want to be. And he did not care to hide that from them.

He allowed them to follow him; indeed, he encouraged them, holding wide the doors to a nether world of pleasure. Then he stood aside. Often he profited from a night spent gaming but they did not take exception, as his profit was never great enough to cause speculation. Besides, he earned their money in other ways, they reasoned, by showing them a London they'd never known existed.

Even now, even against Tunbridge, he'd only lost a few hundred pounds. Merrick rarely lost, so those capable of wakefulness, and thus malice, watched his imminent downfall with petty satisfaction. Except that is, for Thomas Donne, an obscenely wealthy, mysterious, and cursedly suave Scotsman—and some said Merrick's friend. Donne's lean countenance conveyed a wicked, subtle amusement.

Merrick, his lawn shirt open at his throat, his dark hair falling loose from its queue, sans wig, sans jacket, sans reputation, smiled obliquely and fingered the pearl-handled stiletto with which he'd been prying open nuts. His dark eyes, raised to catch Tunbridge's considering gaze, were vague and unfocused. Drunk. Tunbridge began shuffling the cards.

"Merrick," Tunbridge drawled, "I'm afraid there's no catching me this day. Another night is come and my taste for this sport wanes as my taste for another grows." The maid on his lap giggled. "What say we call quit?"

"Surely not yet," Merrick answered in wounded surprise. "You would not deny me the chance to retake what you've won?" The slight pause before he uttered the last word was less than a hesitation of breath. No one could say more and yet Tunbridge's face reddened beneath its sweat-streaked powder.

"Well, then, since there's just us two, what say to a game of piquet?" Tunbridge asked.

"Delightful," Merrick murmured, his attention fixed on raising the tankard of ale to his lips. Tunbridge cut the cards and Merrick did likewise, sighing resignedly when Tunbridge's king trumped his knave.

"Poor luck," Tunbridge said. "Doubtless you'll fare—"

The door leading to the public rooms swung open and a youth, dressed in the fashion of a courier, entered. He stood blinking in the smoky room, vapor rising from his wet cape. Spying Merrick, he picked a path over the outstretched legs of slumped bodies to Merrick's side and bent low to whisper his message.

For an instant Merrick's indolent gaze sharpened and the flesh seemed to cleave tighter to the well-shaped bones of his face. He held out his hand. With a furtive glance in either direction, the courier laid an envelope in it.

"I've your leave to interrupt play?" Merrick asked.

Tunbridge dealt the last of the five cards and shrugged. "By all means."

"My thanks." Merrick slid the stiletto's tip beneath the seal and flicked off the embossed wax. He opened the note and scanned the contents before crumpling it.

With a peculiar violence at odds with his gentle expression, he tossed it unerringly into the open fire. "It seems my services are needed. I must away."

"Ah well." Tunbridge commiserated with a small smile.

"But nothing is so pressing I need leave before the end of this game," Merrick added courteously.

Tunbridge's hands, hovering over the pile of coins, froze and for a second something in the atmosphere alerted even the least sentient to something potentially dangerous occurring in the room. Then Tunbridge's teeth flashed white in the dim light and he gathered his hand. "But of course."

He studied it awhile, allowing a small expression of satisfaction to play upon his lips before calmly discarding. Merrick shouted for the innkeeper to bring more drink and then, with only a glance at his hand, flung down eight cards.

So it went.

Each hand played slowly. Whatever Merrick had read in that letter seemed to combine with four days of relative abstinence to give him a powerful thirst. Aided by his fellows, encouraged by the constant refilling of his cup, he drank steadily and deeply. Between hands he peeled roasted chestnuts with his knife, muttering disconsolately as Tunbridge's point total grew steadily toward the hundred needed to end the game and take the ante.

With each hand, with each drink Merrick downed, Tunbridge grew more expansive and more contemptuous. His barbed goads grew sharper and his predatory smile flickered like guttering candlelight over his sallow countenance.

Finally, Tunbridge stood only eleven points from the win. He dealt. Merrick did not pay any great attention, being too busy draining the dregs of his ale into his mouth. Tunbridge's mouth pleated with satisfaction. He reached out to gather his cards.

And Merrick, with a speed belied by his clouded eyes, struck savagely, instantly, skewering Tunbridge's hand flat against the tabletop with the pearl-handled stiletto.

Tunbridge howled. The sound exploded in the thick, closed room, startling the sotted company to wakefulness. He clutched at the handle that stood quivering in the meat of his hand, swearing viciously.

Merrick rose, no hint of drunkenness in the graceful movement and swept the coins from the tabletop into his purse. Only then did he take hold the handle of the stiletto. For a moment his gaze locked with Tunbridge's.

"If there is no card beneath your palm, Lord Tunbridge, I must most sincerely apologize." With a savage jerk he freed the sharp knife from its fleshy bed. Instinctively, irresistibly, Tunbridge snatched his bleeding hand to his chest.

With a low laugh, Merrick swung around, pushed his way through the men lurching to their feet, and strode from the room. On the table behind him lay the bloodied ace of hearts.

Chapter 2

The day was glorious, spiced with the distant hint of sea marsh, the sky scoured clear blue and the forest minty green with new leaves. From beneath its canopy rode a group of young hunters and huntresses, brilliant in their velvet habits and flush with exertion.

At their lead rode a young woman with tanned, rosy cheeks and dark mahogany red hair lying damp upon her brow. A feather coiling jauntily from her hat teased the corner of her smile. Others were more seasoned riders than she, but few could match the pace Rhiannon Russell set.

Mounted at midmorning and having ridden without bothering to break for nourishment, they'd been unsuccessful this day, thwarted by the dry, crisp air and an old March hare who'd first led the hounds then lost them, streaking from a bramble thicket while the dogs milled wild-eyed in the overscented underbrush.

At the stables, the party dismounted as the kennel master collected the pack of lean-flanked quivering hounds. Yelping plaintively, Rhiannon's yellow gazehound, Stella, limped from the edge of the wood. With a laugh Rhiannon turned her horse and went to accompany the hound's limping progress. Stella was the last gift she was to have from her stepfather, and therefore doubly treasured.

"It's a worthless bitch," the kennel master said coming up the drive to meet her. "My granny has better eyesight." Her companions had by this time dismounted and were heading toward the manor where Edith Fraiser had promised their repast would be waiting.

"Aye," Rhiannon agreed, because she was a most agreeable girl. "Mayhap. But she's young yet and may prove herself worthy. Please? Take care of her?"

With a heavy sigh the kennel master agreed, for who could resist hazel eyes and the sweet request of one of Fair Badden's prettiest lassies? Rhiannon grinned her gratitude and dismounted, hurrying up the front steps after her friends.

At the door a young maid met her. "An English gentleman—a *London* English gentleman—" the girl said, "come to see you, miss." Her face was bright with awe, her voice hushed with the same.

Seldom did English gentlemen come to their small hamlet. More seldom still did *London* gentlemen make the trip to this rural outpost, for pretty though it undoubtedly was, it had nothing more to recommend itself than the prospect of its ownership, a prospect that never transpired as the land had been long held by others.

"I doubt he's come to see me, Marthe. I'm sure it's Mistress Fraiser he wants," Rhiannon said, unimpressed and uninterested, looking about expectantly for one tall, robust figure—Phillip, Squire Watt's youngest son.

"No, miss," Marthe insisted, recalling Rhiannon's wandering attention. "He come to see you. Not Mrs. . . . Ain't that right, Mrs. Fraiser?"

A stout, apple-cheeked woman with iron gray hair bustled down the hall toward them, adjusting the lace handkerchief tucked into her square décolletage.

"'Tis true, Rhiannon." Edith's round face was fashioned for complacence, not surprise. The line lifting her brow betrayed her amazement.

"But why?" Rhiannon asked.

"I do not know," Edith muttered and held out her hands.

Obediently, Rhiannon peeled off her yellow leather gloves, tucked them into her belt, and laid her hands in the older woman's. Mistress Fraiser turned them over and *tch*ed gently. "Dirty nails." She looked Rhiannon over with ill-concealed resignation. "Unkempt hair. Dusty habit. Well, it can't be helped. He's been waiting three hours already and it would be rude to have him wait longer."

Though she wanted to protest that her dishabille made her unfit to receive strange gentlemen, Rhiannon did not. She owed too much to Edith Fraiser to ever willfully contradict her, let alone refuse her directions. She'd come from the Highlands to Fair Badden a decade ago, a scrawny lassie fleeing the aftermath of Culloden, looking for some kinsman to shelter her.

Though Edith Fraiser was only a second cousin of

Rhiannon's mother, the Fraisers had taken her in. A successful and well-respected squire, Richard Fraiser ranked high in Fair Badden's countrified society. From the offset he'd treated Rhiannon like a daughter of the house, lavishing upon her every benefit of his wealth and prestige.

Their unstinting affection had harried Rhiannon's blood-soaked memories into hiding. Only at night, and then rarely, did phantoms stagger bleeding through a blasted, burning landscape, did uncles and cousins roar in torturous din as they sought to escape Butcher Cumberland's retribution against those who'd supported Bonny Prince Charlie. During the day, Rhiannon scarcely remembered her life before Fair Badden.

She lived in Fair Badden as though it had always been her home and she had always been accepted, at peace, content. Even her Highland brogue had disappeared over time. Then, ten months ago, Richard had died. Rhiannon and Edith clung together, finding in each other the slow healing only shared grief can offer.

Now Edith fussed over Rhiannon's hair, untangling knots and rubbing a smudge of dirt from her brow. That done she bussed Rhiannon warmly on the cheek, accepted a hug in return, and turned her by the shoulders. She gave her a little push.

"Along with you," she said, shepherding Rhiannon down the hallway. "Your friends will wait as long as there's ale to drink and cakes to eat." Her smile grew sly. "And your beau would wait without the lure of sweets, kisses being a sweet enough lure, I'll wager." She chuckled at Rhiannon's shy expression and stopped before the library door. "Go on."

"You're not coming in with me?" Rhiannon asked in surprise.

"No." A troubled thought shadowed Edith's soft features. "The gentleman asked to see you alone for a few minutes. He said he had news regarding your future.

"I'm thinking—that is, I'm hoping—he might be a lawyer sent from London with word of a lost entailment. Perhaps a little forgotten keepsake from your dear mother to act as a dowry. I only wish I had something more to give you myself, but it's all long since bespoke."

Rhiannon took Edith's hands. "You've already given me more than I can ever repay."

Flustered, Edith twitched Rhiannon's jacket shoulders into alignment. "Go on, now! I'll be here waiting when you come out." She opened the door and pushed Rhiannon inside.

A man sprawled in Squire Fraiser's favorite chair, one foot stretched out before him, the other bent at the knee, his fingers laced over his flat stomach. He gazed out the window, his face averted. All she could see of his head was a carelessly pulled back tail of coal black hair tied with a limp ribbon.

He wore a coat of deep burgundy velvet, a white linen shirt beneath it. Brussels lace fell gracefully over the first knuckles of his long, lean fingers, and more lace cascaded beneath his chin. His breeches were tight and made of tawny doeskin. His dark leather boots climbed past his knees and were folded in cuffs over his muscular thighs. The tip of his sword, sheathed in a leather scabbard and hanging from his belt, touched the floor beside him.

He would have been exquisite had he not been so disheveled. The burgundy coat was dusty and the faded linen shirt went wide of being pristine. The lace of one sleeve, delicate as gossamer, was ripped and soiled. His boots were stained and scarred and the scabbard containing his sword was likewise ill-used.

He did not look like any lawyer Rhiannon's imagination would have conjured.

A bit of pique flavored Rhiannon's curiosity. A gentleman—particularly a *London* gentleman—visiting the Fraiser's home should have stopped at The Ploughman's Inn to repair the damage travel had caused. But then, honesty goaded her generous mouth into a smile; a lady receiving a gentleman should have paused to repair the damage a hunt had caused.

He turned his head carefully, as if he were concerned to startle her and she thus knew that he'd been allowing her time to assess him. He looked tired, worn too thin and used too roughly. His eyes were jetty dark, the brows above slanting like black wings, but the skin beneath them looked bruised. He sported an old-fashioned clipped beard amidst the shadows of lean, unshaven cheeks, and his skin was very pale and very fine and somehow fragile.

Fleeting emotion, subtle and reserved, flickered over his aquiline features.

"Rhiannon Russell, I presume?" His voice was baritone and suave. He didn't bother to rise and his pose remained preternaturally still, like a cat at a mouse hole, watchful but not hungry—not yet.

"Yes." She became unaccountably aware of the hair streaming down her back, the sweat and grime from her leather gloves embedded beneath her short nails, and the mud splattering her bottle green skirt.

He rose. He was tallish and slender and his shoulders were very straight and broad. His mouth was kind but his eyes were not. His throat looked strong. The torn lace ending his shirtsleeves tangled in the carved gold setting of a great blue stone ring on his little finger. He flicked it away.

Even without the cachet of being a Londoner, the ladies of Fair Badden would have found him attractive, Rhiannon thought. Since he was from that great fabled city, they'd find him irresistible. Indeed, she herself could have found much to recommend in his black and white good looks . . . if she hadn't already succumbed to a golden-haired youth.

"You're not English."

"I am. A quarter," she said. "On my father's side."

"I wouldn't have guessed." Having spoken, he fell silent, studying her further.

She struggled to remember the lessons in courtesy Edith had instilled but none of them applied to meeting strange, elegantly shabby young men alone in her foster father's library.

"I'm afraid you have the advantage of me, sir," she finally ventured.

"Could I only be so fortunate as to claim as much with all my acquaintances," he said and then, "but didn't Mrs. Fraiser inform you of my name?"

"No," Rhiannon said. "Mrs. Fraiser has no head for names, unless they're the names of unscrupulous tradesmen. She only said that you'd come from London to see me and that you had news regarding my future."

"I am Ash Merrick." He sketched an elegant bow,

his watchfulness becoming pronounced now, as if his name should mean something to her, and when he saw that it did not, he went on. "The name Merrick is not familiar to you?"

She cast about cautiously in her mind and found nothing there to trigger a memory. "No," she said. "Should it?"

His mouth stretched into a wide grin. It was a beautiful smile, easy and charming, but it never quite reached his eyes. "Perhaps," he said, "since it's the name of your guardian."

Chapter 3

"*I* don't have a guardian," Rhiannon said and then, with her usual candor, amended, "I mean, not an official one. At least, none that I know of . . ."

She trailed off, visited by an imprecise memory. She was maybe eight years old, standing on the street of a strange city, squinting up at a door frame filled with beckoning light. The old woman who'd brought her had cold, gnarled fingers. They twisted round Rhiannon's wrist like ropy grape vines. A strangely accented voice spoke from within the warm, yellow light. "You want another Merrick, witch. Not Lord Carr."

She was to have lived with an Englishman. He was supposed to have been her guardian. She remembered the old lady saying so. She'd forgotten. But there'd been so much about those days and all the days preceding them that she'd forgotten. Flight and cold, fear and confusion, the days—weeks?—had bled into one long, seemingly endless nightmare from which she'd only awakened upon arrival in Fair Badden. Even when she tried to recall, it was insubstantial, flickers of sensation and images, more emotions than actual memories.

Rhiannon stared at the man arrayed in damaged elegance. Surely he was too young—"Are you Lord Carr?"

Once more the gorgeous smile lit his dark visage. "No. Lord Carr is my father. And you're perfectly correct if you're thinking him a negligent sort of guardian. He is."

She was unable to read the flavor of that amused estimation. His manner, his address, were nothing like those of Fair Badden's young men. "I don't understand."

"Neither do I, and I thought I had," he murmured, one brow climbing. And then, "I think Carr would like you to believe that he has simply misplaced you these past years."

"Did he?"

Ash Merrick's enigmatic smile spread. "I doubt my father has ever misplaced so much as a toothpick."

Each of his answers only provoked more questions, and each statement this Ash Merrick made only increased her discomfort. She once more felt she was standing at the door leading into that forbidden, enticing house. She was afraid to step over the threshold. It would cost her a price she could not name and was uncertain she could afford. And yet it beckoned.

"What is it you want, sir?"

"I? Nothing. I'm merely here to escort you to Wanton's Blush because *he* wants you, Rhiannon Russell."

"Why?" The sleek cat had tired of watching, he was playing with the mouse now.

"Your aunt was cousin to his wife," he said.

"*We're* cousins?" she asked. Impossible to believe that this black glossy creature and she were related.

"Oh, no. No. My mother had the distinction of being the *first* Lady Carr. Your mother was related to his second wife . . . or was it the third? Carr has an unhappy habit of losing wives to early graves."

"I see." But she didn't. With his explanation the exhaustion had returned to his dark, mobile face, touching her tender heart. "You've traveled a great distance, sir. Would you like something to drink? To eat?"

He looked up abruptly at the offer, his brows knit with surprise. "No," he said. "Thank you. We've business to conduct, you and I. Perhaps later."

"I don't understand," Rhiannon said. "Why now, after all these years has your father sent you to find me?"

"Unreasonable chit," Ash Merrick chided comfortably. "You are not supposed to ask questions. You are to fall into paroxysms of joy that Carr has deigned to offer you his protection . . . such as it is."

She studied him in consternation but forbore comment.

"What?" he queried when she did not reply. "No paroxysms? He'll be disappointed. But to answer your question, Miss Russell, Carr sends you the message that now that he has found you, he is willing—nota bene, my dear, he did not go so far as to declare his *eagerness*, merely his *willingness*—to accept his responsibility for you."

Her frown was severe, her concentration fierce. He

spoke obliquely and his manner was mocking but impersonal, as though the jest he saw was more at his expense than hers.

"And what do you say, Mr. Merrick?" she asked carefully.

"Miss Russell, a lady never puts a gentleman in the onerous position of making a judgment," he said. There was kindness—or perhaps pity—underscoring the ironical tone. "Particularly about his sire's motives. I never make judgments, Miss Russell, ergo I never misjudge. If I were following my own inclination, I would never have come here. I am only my father's agent. I do not question his edicts. I follow them."

His voice had grown terse. It was as if he'd decided to dislike her before they'd ever met. She could think of no reason he should do so—unless he resented his father's interest in her. Perhaps he was profligate and his purse light, she thought, eyeing his shabby raiment, and feared his father would be overly generous with his newly discovered ward.

The idea explained Ash Merrick's subtle antagonism and melted her earlier resentment. She could put him at ease. She didn't want his father's protection or his guardianship or his generosity. Nor did she need them.

"What did you do to your face?"

His question caught her off guard. He'd come closer while she'd been lost in thought. He grasped her chin, tilting her face into the shafts of late afternoon sunlight.

"My face?" Was he, too, going to scrub her cheek clean? She went still, embarrassed and unnerved and not at all certain it wouldn't be a touch thrilling to have this exotic, masculine creature offer so intimate a ministration.

At the wayward thought, heat climbed to her cheeks. "Forgive me, sir. We just finished hunting and I didn't have an oppor—"

"You received this wound hunting?" he asked incredulously, lifting his other hand and lightly tracing her cheek.

Warm little tendrils of sensation danced beneath his touch. His fingertips were rough, the knuckles large, and his wrists braceleted with old scars. No gentleman had hands like that. Not even a London gentleman. Particularly a London gentleman. Who *was* Ash Merrick?

Her gaze roved over his face as he frowned at the mark on her cheek. The lashes framing his dark eyes were as black as his hair, thick and spiky and long as a lassie's, and that was the only soft or feminine thing about him. This close, even his fashionably pale London skin seemed nothing more than a comely happenstance. The single purpose of that fine flesh was to shed water, avert wind, not to attract. Though it did that, too.

"Did you?" He released his clasp of her chin.

Ah, yes. He'd asked about her wound.

"No," she answered, no longer concerned with the words they spoke but rather with some other interplay occurring between them, some communication happening just beyond the scope of her mind to facilitate.

"Then how did this happen? One would imagine such a prize would awake the instinct to protect."

She did not understand. Her skin was unmarked by pox and not too browned by the sun, but no one had ever deemed it a prize. He looked into her eyes and his facile smile wavered and disappeared.

For the first time since she'd entered the library, Ash Merrick did not seem completely master of the situation. He drew away from her, looking puzzled, like the lad who has unlocked a secret drawer and found something he'd not anticipated and wasn't sure he liked.

"You were about to say?" His voice was smooth enough.

"Footpad," she answered faintly. "We were coming home from the neighbor's when we were accosted by a villain. He shot his pistols at our carriage as our driver whipped up the team. One of his bullets grazed me. As you can see, we escaped."

"Highwaymen? Here?" His tone was incredulous.

"Rare enough," she admitted. "But it happens."

He'd turned away from her and was rubbing his thumb along his dark, stubbled jawline.

"It looks worse than it ever felt," she offered, obliged by his obvious concern. His eyes slew back toward her, a flicker of astonishment in their dark depths.

"Ah . . . good."

"I'm afraid it will leave a scar, however," she added apologetically.

His expression grew bewildered. "Scar?"

"Yes."

"Nonsense. One won't even notice it," he dismissed the mark roughly.

It was gracious of him to reassure her—if that's what those grudging words had been an attempt at—but she really wasn't sensitive about her looks.

She knew her assets well enough and a two-inch line

traversing her cheek hadn't devalued their worth. Phillip certainly didn't seem to find her any less attractive . . . Phillip.

With a start she realized they had not yet finished discussing the reason for Ash Merrick's presence here.

"I appreciate your kindness, Mr. Merrick," she said, moving away from the magnetism surrounding him and taking a chair, "but you needn't worry about me. I am perfectly fine. I've been fine for over ten years and while I am . . ." she searched for some gentle way to reveal to him that his long journey had been unnecessary ". . . I am very warmed by your father's offer, I must refuse it. And your escort to his home."

"Offer?"

"Yes," she nodded, "of his guardianship. You see, I already have a wonderful family who have seen that all my needs have not only been met but are surpassed."

"I don't think you should view this as an offer, Miss Russell."

"No?"

"My father is determined you'll come live with him."

He simply didn't understand. His expression was cold, aloof, giving her a glimpse of the hard implacable will driving him. With a frisson of trepidation, she tried another smile. He couldn't very well kidnap her from her home.

"I hate to disappoint the gentleman," she said, "but as I've tried to explain, there's no need for him to assume his guardianship of me. Indeed, I would much oppose it. Mistress Fraiser, with whom I've lived these many years, is but recently a widow and I could not repay her loving care by abandoning her now."

"I assure you, my father will provide any accoutrements of wealth and privilege you should require," Ash Merrick said, his gaze on the ring adorning her hand.

"My affection for Mistress Fraiser is honest, sir," she snapped with uncharacteristic ire, stung by his inference that she wanted to stay here simply to keep herself well clothed. "My support of her is heartfelt. And I would not have you suggest otherwise!"

She took a deep breath, unnerved as much because he'd provoked her so easily as by his offensive suggestion.

"Perhaps Mistress Fraiser can ill afford the luxury of your heartfelt support," he suggested, looking pointedly at her pearl ring.

The notion of Edith Fraiser selling off the family silver to buy her a second-rate piece of frippery restored Rhiannon's usual good humor. This time her laugh was warm and spontaneous. "This ring and a piece of amber are all I have from my mother, sir, and its value is almost solely sentimental. I pray you only look about you. I assure you I am not causing Mistress Fraiser any financial hardship."

He made a cursory inspection of the room, tallying the fine furnishings, the ornate plaster mantel—Mistress Fraiser's pride and joy—the satin covered settees and silver mirror.

Then his gaze returned, once more, to her.

It flowed down her body and slowly, incrementally, roved back up her person, settling on the brocaded lapels of her hunting jacket. Her pulse quickened beneath that lazy regard, and her hand instinctively fluttered to her throat.

His gaze drifted up to meet hers, the dark centers of his eyes glowing like a hot cauldron of pitch.

"As good as anything you'll see in London, I'll wager," she said inanely, fingering the silk embroidered plaquets.

"Indeed." His voice was deep, heavy and smooth.

"It's French."

His mouth quirked. "I thought Scottish."

Her laughter was nervous. "Oh, no. You'll not find many Scottish fingers working over a piece like this."

"It *would* seem to require a more sophisticated hand," he agreed suavely.

"Yes." She nodded, knowing full well he was twitting her but unsure how. She smiled uncertainly. His lids narrowed, the thicket of lash hiding the brilliance of his eyes.

He hadn't looked the least reproachful when she'd snapped at him a moment before. There was not one person in Fair Badden who would not have looked shocked at having heard the sharp edge of Rhiannon Russell's tongue. There was not one person in Fair Badden who had ever heard it. She'd always been mindful of her debt of gratitude, careful never to give offense.

"I agree, Miss Russell, you've been well tended."

"Yes," she said. In a few minutes he would walk out of this room and ride away back to London. She didn't want him to go. Not yet.

"But being well tended isn't the only issue," he went on. "However tardy in his assumption of the role, my father *is* your legal guardian. He wants you at Wanton's Blush."

Wanton's Blush? She remembered that name. Her aunt had lived there. She froze. "In the Highlands?"

"Yes. Last time I was there, I believe it was in the Highlands. On McClairen's Isle."

The place name ambushed her from out of the past. Her heart leapt to her throat. Fear confounded her ability to breathe and she stared at him, stricken. He didn't even realize he was uttering what to her was a threat.

"And that," he stated, "is where you'll go and where you'll stay, until you marry or die or my father tires of this unprecedented whim to foster you."

"Marry?" Relief rushed over her. She would be able to thwart Lord Carr's demand. And if the smallest bit of regret tempered her relief, well, she'd already admitted to herself that Ash Merrick was fascinating. "Then we've no problem."

"Did we have a problem? I hadn't realized." He held out his hand, inviting her solution to the problem they didn't have.

"Yes, sir," she said. "I mean no, sir. We don't. Because, you see, in three weeks I'm to wed Phillip Watt."

Ash Merrick's hand froze in the act of reaching for her. Seconds clicked by as unreadable emotions flickered in rapid succession over his handsome, weary face. Then he threw back his head and laughed.

Chapter 4

The gentleman from London was laughing.

Edith Fraiser straightened from where she'd had her ear pressed fast against the door. She hadn't been able to discern much of what they'd been speaking about, but she could all too easily discern the timbre of that laughter. It wasn't *nice* laughter.

She pushed the door open and waded into the room amidst the rustle of her heavily draped skirts.

"My felicitations, Miss Russell," the dark young man was saying.

"Thank you." Rhiannon replied. Her glance at Edith was grateful and slightly bemused but free from any alarm.

Edith bustled forward. "Ah, Mr. . . . Mr.—"

"Merrick, ma'am. Ash Merrick." He executed a very nice bow. Edith beamed.

She was an uncomplicated and amicable soul, reluc-

tant to judge others unkindly, staunchly believing the
best of her fellow man. If Rhiannon hadn't taken umbrage at the man's laughter, then as far as she was concerned, no umbrage need be taken.

"Of course you are. And whom was it you said you
represent, Mr. Merrick?"

"He isn't a lawyer, ma'am." Rhiannon came to
Edith's side, hooking her arm companionably in hers.

"No?" Edith asked, unable to keep the disappointment from her voice. She'd had such hopes. "Then
there is no diamond brooch? Not even a wee entitle-
ment?"

Color flooded Rhiannon's tanned cheeks. "No,
ma'am."

"Brooch?" Ash Merrick questioned.

Edith turned to Rhiannon for an explanation. "Well,
if he hasn't brought you a brooch and he's no lawyer,
who is he?"

"*He* is Lord Carr's son, ma'am," Ash Merrick said.

Edith swung around at the silky pronouncement,
abashed by her momentary lapse of manners. She could
easily enough identify the source of steel in his tone; it
came from being spoken of as if he weren't present. But
where the amusement came from, she could not guess.

"And who is Lord Carr?" Edith asked. London gentleman or no, this young man had something about him
that made her uneasy, something more than sophistication.

"Lord Carr is Miss Russell's legal guardian," he replied. "I've come at his request to fetch her."

"What?" Edith gasped. Recollection brought with it
a surge of passionate outrage. "*Merrick*, you say?"

Rhiannon took her hand. "Ma'am, don't overset yourself—"

"Merrick!" Edith squawked, stomping forward and brought up short by Rhiannon's hold on her. "*Now* I remember where I know that name. 'Tis the name of that fellow who wouldn't take Rhiannon in when she fled Cumberland's men. Legal guardian, indeed. A coldhearted villain, sir!"

"Please, ma'am," Rhiannon pleaded. "Everything will be all—"

Edith spun around and hauled Rhiannon into a tight embrace, pulling the girl's face down against her soft plump neck, glaring at Ash Merrick above her hair. Poor, sweet motherless lass.

"A scoundrel, the man is!"

Rhiannon mumbled unintelligibly against her neck.

"An unfeeling knave, a—"

"I quite agree," Ash Merrick interrupted calmly.

Edith gaped at him, her arms loosening just enough so that Rhiannon's head popped up. She gasped for breath.

"Unfortunately his suitability as a guardian is not at issue," Merrick said. "Miss Russell's future is. Though, I must admit, it appears she's rather circumvented my father's intentions."

Edith eyed him warily. "Come again, sir?"

"Miss Russell tells me she's to be wed."

"Aye, she is." Edith's strong jaw thrust out combatively. If this fellow tried to stand in the way of true love's sweet course, he'd have to go through her to do it. "In three weeks time, right after May Day. She and Phillip Watt but I don't . . ." Realization dawned on her like a lightning strike. "Oh . . ." she crooned on a low exhalation. "I see. Aye."

"Yes," Rhiannon soothed. "It's all right, ma'am."

"That does put the mud in Carr's barrels, don't it?" Edith said to the gentleman. His expression had more than a touch of the complacent conspirator in it. "I mean, you can't drag a girl out of her marriage bed, can you?"

His answering smile was ambiguous. "Don't be too fond of that thought."

"Sir?"

"Of course he won't," he said pleasantly. "It would attract too much attention. No, my pater will just have to abandon his plans—whatever they might have been."

Edith released Rhiannon. The threat to her foster daughter having appeared and been vanquished all in the space of a few minutes, she allowed herself to feel magnanimous toward Carr's son. "You'd honor us, sir, if you'd stay for the nuptials. You bein' Rhiannon's *legal* guardian's spokesman and all, it would be fitting you be here in his stead to witness her marriage."

"Witness?" Ash queried. "Now there's one role I've yet to try."

"Oh do, sir."

Edith looked around at Rhiannon's unexpected support. The sunlight streaking in through the west windows set the lassie's mane aglow with highlights. Her cheeks were flushed with pleasure and the green in her hazel eyes sparkled like emeralds.

Looking at her, Edith thought she spied the vestiges of her bold Highland blood. She ignored the perception as unfair. Rhiannon had always been a dear, unassuming girl. The gleam in her eye didn't mean a thing except that she was courteous as well.

But what did the gleam in Ash Merrick's dark eyes mean?

Enough, thought Edith. She'd never been a fanciful sort and she wasn't about to become one now. What would a cosmopolitan gentleman find interesting in a simple country lass—even one as pretty as Rhiannon Russell? To hear their neighbor Lady Harquist tell it, pretty women stood ten deep in London's fashionable salons.

"We've room aplenty, Mr. Merrick," Edith said, determined to be hospitable. "Please stay."

Ash Merrick's smile caught her unawares. Lord, a man with a smile like that was a danger pure and simple, but the offer had already been made and she couldn't go back on it now.

"You are too good, madame. I accept your kind invitation. I'd be honored to join your prenuptial celebrations and stay to see Miss Russell safely wed."

An odd choice of words but Edith attributed it to London fashion. "Good!" She clasped Rhiannon's shoulder and spun her about. "You go have the maids fix up the master's chamber, Rhiannon."

"But Master Merrick will be hungry and our friends are—"

What had gotten into the girl to question her? thought Edith. Rhiannon always did what she was told. "'Our friends' will wait. The good Lord knows they always do. Spend more time loitering in my halls than their own! Be off with you. I'll see Master Merrick properly fed and introduced to your sweetheart, never fear. You join us after you've cleaned the stables from your hands and hair."

Without further protest, Rhiannon left, sending one last lingering look over her shoulder at the dark young man watching her so casually. Too casually. Once more a premonition threatened Edith Fraiser's complacence.

Edith Fraiser had been a beauty in her day, a country beauty but a beauty nonetheless. As much as she wanted to, she doubted that men from London were cut from so different a cloth as men from the country. Such determined nonchalance meant the same world round.

Happily, whatever this Ash Merrick's interest, Rhiannon's was fixed on Phillip Watt. Rhiannon was a loyal creature. There was no cause for alarm here and it might just benefit Rhiannon if Edith could enlist the goodwill of Lord Carr's heir. Perhaps a bit of a dowry . . .

With that thought Edith closed the door on Rhiannon's departure and turned. Ash Merrick eyed her with that touch of unsettling amusement, as if he knew full well what she'd been thinking.

"Mistress Fraiser," he said.

She made her way to the settee and dropped heavily into it. "She's a sweet-tempered girl, is my Rhiannon."

"Yes."

"And as biddable as a lamb despite her blood. Highland blood, you know."

"So I've been told."

"And a loyal girl, too. Faithful one would say."

"A veritable saint."

"No," Edith said consideringly. "Not *quite* a saint. You should see her on horseback, riding like a fury. I think she ran wild in those mountains of hers," she added thoughtfully. "And I know she's seen things no gel ought to see. Murderous things. It made her . . . I don't know."

She pulled at her hands, at a loss to describe the element of Rhiannon's character that had always eluded her. Not that it mattered. She loved Rhiannon without needing to fathom every aspect of her. And because she loved Rhiannon she would do her best for her.

Edith slapped her broad palms on her knees, her momentary and uncommon sojourn into introspection ending with a return to practicality.

"Will the Lord Carr be making some settlement on her, do you think?"

Ash Merrick's mouth curled in gentle derisiveness. "I very much doubt it."

"No?" Edith frowned.

"Not a farthing."

"Well, a fine guardian he's turned out to be. It's a blessing he didn't have her care earlier. She'd be dressed in rags if she'd been left on her own."

Ash cocked his head, studying her closely. "Would she now?"

"Ach, yes." Edith's head bobbed. "Poor lassie arrived here half-starved and white as a gull's breast, wrapped in her dead father's plaid."

"She has *no* property?" Ash pressed.

"Property?" Edith snorted. "A poor bit of amber and that wee pearl ring."

"Who brought her to you?"

"Some old hag." Edith dismissed the memory of the wizened, dirt-encrusted old lady with the fierce blue eyes. "Brought her to my doorstep but never set a foot inside herself. Delivered the goods, you might say, and went on her way."

"And she didn't leave any trunks or luggage with the girl?"

"Luggage?" Edith gave a bark of laughter. "My good sir, they *walked* here. Walked all the way from your father's house in London if I've the memory right. No, sir, they hadn't any luggage."

Ash's brows dipped in concentration. "What about family?"

Edith shook her head. "No, sir. Cumberland's men killed her only brother. Burnt in a croft with his uncle and all his cousins, so they say. Weren't even a body to bury."

No need to tell him that Rhiannon's brother may, just may, have escaped. The fellow was an Englishman, after all, and an earl's son, and there was still a price on the head of any clansman who had stood with the Pretender. Besides, they hadn't heard a whisper of the lad in all the years since Culloden.

She lowered her face and dabbed piously at her eyes before lifting the clear orbs once more to Ash's. "So you see, sir, the lass hasn't a thing to call her own. Nor any family to tend her. I'm only distantly related to her myself, you know. Not that I don't love Rhiannon like she were my own. I do. But love doesn't provide food or shelter, does it?"

When he didn't reply she pushed on, determined to make him, as his father's agent, see his duty.

"Master Merrick, let me be clear. I've no property of my own to settle on Rhiannon. I have the manor and the income from the land until I die because that's the way Squire Fraiser wanted it, bless his soul. But upon my death everything goes to my son what lives in the heathen orient and works for the East India Company." She included this last with undeniable pride.

"Really?"

"Yes. I was hoping what with Rhiannon being set to wed and all, perhaps you might enjoin your father to dower her a wee bit. Nuthin' grand, mind you. Just something to make the dear couple comfortable. Phillip, he's a third son and lucky enough that his father is willing to settle a sum on him at his marriage."

"Unusual. Most younger sons don't fare so well." His eyes were shuttered behind the thicket of dark lashes. His voice was as still as ice.

"Aye. But Watt dotes on Phillip. He's the child of his old age and he would not deny him whatever is in his power to give."

"But who would want an impoverished orphan for a bride?" he quizzed, his dark brows dipping.

"Any man what knows her worth," Edith said staunchly.

"But how is a man to discover that?" he murmured.

Chapter 5

"—if both men died, who paid the wager?" Rhiannon heard Margaret Atherton ask as, combed, clad, and freshly doused in rose water, she slipped unseen into the drawing room.

"The earl's widow paid," Ash Merrick said, "claiming it was worth the price just to see her husband finally complete a ride."

Scandalized laughter broke out amongst the group of Rhiannon's friends clustered at the far end of the room. Phillip; pretty, silly Susan Chapham; ripe Margaret Atherton; and steady, sensitive John Fortnum . . . every head was turned toward Ash like seedlings toward light. Even Edward St. John, the Marquis of Snowden's grandnephew—whose already generous conceit had been further puffed up by several seasons in London—hovered near.

"Ah! Here she is. Our Diana," John Fortnum cried upon spying her.

"*My* Diana." Phillip Watt broke from the group and came toward her, his face alight with possessive pride. Taller than any man in the room by half a head, brawny and robust and golden-haired, he was extraordinarily handsome. He caught her around the waist and lifted her above his shoulders, spinning until she gasped with laughter.

"Phillip!" she begged. "What will Mr. Merrick think of us? I doubt London ladies let their beaus toss them about like this."

"But I'm more than a beau, I'm a fiancé," Phillip said, smiling triumphantly. His blue eyes sparkled with proprietorship. "Mr. Merrick knows this is not London and if he thinks less of us for our country ways, then he's the worse for it, ain't he?"

"But Mr. Merrick does not think the worse of you," Ash said. "I think Mr. Watt is an exceptionally lucky young man."

"Well, whatever Mr. Watt and Mr. Merrick think," Edith Fraiser said, glowering from the doorway, "Mrs. Fraiser thinks it a right improper way to act and reminds Mr. Watt that she can still wield a switch with the best of them. If a man acts the bumptious lout, 'tis a lout's penalty he'll suffer!"

"Say not so!" Phillip enjoined, setting Rhiannon on her feet and striding through the room toward the door. There he gripped Edith about her ample waist and hefted her up and over his head. "'Tis jealousy that speaks, ma'am, and with no cause. Only your refusal to accept my hand forces me to make do with this chit."

The belligerent expression evaporated from Edith's

square face and her cheeks grew scarlet as she batted at Phillip's head, huffing insincere castigation. "Let me down, you young rogue! Let me down, I say. You best save these demonstrations of your manly vigor for your wedding night!"

The others broke into cheers and Phillip, grinning hugely, lowered Edith to the ground and swept a low bow before her. "I heed your sage advice, ma'am. Pray consider my . . . vigor duly hoarded," he said, his gaze fast on Rhiannon.

It was too warm a jest. Rhiannon's skin heated as knowing winks turned in her direction.

"What say you to that, Rhiannon?" Edward, ever the instigator, demanded.

"I? I know nothing of men."

Hoots met this demure evasion and Rhiannon, smiling with an uncharacteristic impishness, stilled her audience with a wave of her hand, aware of Ash Merrick's gaze resting on her with dutiful patience. She suddenly wanted to prick that indolent lack of expectation from his face, prove her wit was as sharp as any London lady's.

"But of beasts I know much," she continued, "and it is my observation that what a squirrel so dutifully hoards in anticipation of his winter bed, ends all too often nothing but . . . rotten nuts."

Laughter erupted in the room. Even Edith, after a gasped "Rhiannon!" broke into loud guffaws. And Ash Merrick's eyes, which Rhiannon had been watching, widened with gratifying surprise before he, too, joined in the laughter.

Only Phillip did not fully appreciate her wit. She was seldom forward, never ribald, and the look in Phillip's eye suggested he'd fostered a kitten and just discovered it was a fox. For an instant his handsome face soured before his innate good nature reasserted itself.

"Mr. Merrick!" Phillip called to their guest. "In London what would a man do with so saucy and bold a wench?"

"It depends—" Ash answered consideringly, coming toward Rhiannon. Once at her side he put his hand on his hip in the attitude of a connoisseur looking over offered goods. Her friends, alert to the fun, moved in, encircling them.

Slowly, he began walking around Rhiannon. She notched her chin up at an angle, her pert attitude delivering him a challenge she found herself incapable of explaining.

"Depends on what?" She refused to turn like some cornered hind. She did not need to. She could feel the heat of his regard as intensely as if he touched her.

"On many things." His voice was as smooth as French brandy warmed over a candle, intimate and close. His breath—surely it was stirring the hairs on the nape of her neck? Surely his lips hovered inches from her skin? He couldn't under Phillip's eye— He shouldn't—

She spun around. He raised his brows questioningly . . . from a good five feet away. Their gazes met and locked. Gray. Clear. Soft as an April fog, cool as a November sea. Impossible to look at anything besides those dark-thicketed eyes, to look deeper into their depths and find . . . Weariness. Such awful weariness behind the calm, pleasant façade—

"For instance?" Phillip prompted.

Ash's gaze broke from hers, severed like a spider's

strand by a razor's blade. "For instance," he said, "where in London 'the wench' is. There are different customs for different countries," he said.

"Countries?" Susan Chapham asked.

"Yes," Ash answered. "London isn't simply one great heap. It's an entire world with a myriad of tiny countries existing side by side, each barely aware of the other. Covent Garden and Seven Dials, Spitalfields and Whitechapel. In London's vast acres these are principalities ruled by kings and princes without so much as a last name."

"And would Rhiannon be a princess there?" Susan Chapham asked, and dissolved into giggles.

"I'd think she'd be a princess anywhere," Ash said with calculated charm.

"Well, then she best not go to London since it would mean a coming down in the world," John Fortnum stated.

"How'd you figure that?" Phillip asked.

"In three weeks' time, she'll be queen of Fair Badden," John offered.

"Queen?" Ash Merrick asked as the others laughed.

"Queen of the May," Susan explained, her tone resigned. "Three years running now. 'Tisn't fair."

"True enough," Edith cut in. "I don't see an end to it until the girl is wed and ineligible. Only virgins can rule on May Day, you know."

"No," Ash said. "I didn't."

"Never fear, Miss Chapham," Phillip said. "I can promise you Rhiannon won't be eligible next year. Or next month, for that matter."

The way he looked not at her, but at the group of

their friends, as though he spoke for their benefit more than hers, made Rhiannon uncomfortable.

"What say we get married earlier, Rhiannon, and give these other beauties a chance at the crown?" he asked, smiling.

The chattered gaiety faded in awed interest. The proposed marriage of Phillip Watt to Rhiannon Russell was the most extraordinary—and in some people's eyes the most foolhardy—piece of romance within Fair Badden's memory. Phillip's father, because he was enormously rich—and some said enormously dotty—had not only agreed to the wedding, but had settled enough money on his son so that Phillip could take the bride he desired and not the one he needed. And that woman was Rhiannon who, though pretty and darling, had no name, no family, and no dowry.

She could not help but leap at the chance to legalize her union early, before Phillip or his father came to their senses. They all looked at her, awaiting her flattered and hasty acceptance.

"No," Rhiannon said.

"No?" Phillip echoed.

Several jaws grew slack. Few people had ever heard Rhiannon utter that syllable, and never so flatly.

She fidgeted, her twisting fingers betraying an unease her cheerful voice did not. "I . . . I willingly if shamefully concede my greed. If there's any chance I should be fortunate enough to be May Queen again, I'll snatch it."

"But you'd be queen of my heart," Phillip said. "Is that not kingdom enough?"

Pretty words. A lovely sentiment. But Phillip's back was still to her and he had opened his arms in the direction of their friends, appealing to them, not her. Several nodded in agreement. If he had just looked at *her* when he said it . . .

Ash Merrick was looking at her.

Of all those present, he was the only one. He watched her intently.

Her heartbeat hastened. His regard was more than a summation of her physical self. He gauged her, weighing her reaction, studying her as if all his conscious thought were centered on her. She had never been the focus of such acute concentration. Not even Phillip's.

Phillip glanced over his shoulder at her, awaiting her reply. She should say yes. She should be grateful. She *was* grateful. Phillip could have chosen a gentlewoman, an heiress, perhaps even better, but he had chosen her. He represented everything she had ever needed. She would wed Phillip and be safe and happy in Fair Badden for the rest of her life.

But not yet. Not so soon.

"I have admitted my greed," she said, forcing a bright smile to her lips. "I cannot help it that I want both crowns."

Phillip blinked. Indeed, the entire party seemed nonplussed.

"If that can please you, Phillip?" she added faintly, suddenly despairingly aware of what she'd risked with her ill-advised teasing. For that was all it was . . . teasing. Of course she would marry Phillip. Tomorrow if he insisted. But deep within, a half-drowned Scottish-tinged voice begged different.

Phillip's face grew ruddy.

"Ach, you great oaf!" Edith suddenly barked into the quiet room, stomping forward to cuff Phillip smartly on the ear. He yelped and jumped back from her on-slaught.

"Have you no finer feelings? No dab of sentimental-ity?" Edith demanded. "Can you no see the gel wants her wee bit of courting and the trimmings of a fine and well-planned ceremony to mark the occasion of her wedding? None of your harum-scarum elopements for my Rhiannon. You'll wed her fit and proper. Not hieing off like some stable hand with his milkmaid, you great . . . *man*!"

The storm clouds lifted from Phillip's handsome face as comprehension took its place. "Is that it, Rhian-non?" he asked, his fond gaze just the smallest bit pa-tronizing.

Edith caught Rhiannon's eye, clearly warning her.

"Aye," Rhiannon said. "That's it."

"Well, then, you'll have the grandest wedding Fair Badden has ever seen!" With the pronouncement the men and women surrounded Phillip, clapping him on the back and calling loudly for drink to toast his mag-nanimity.

And Rhiannon smiled, and demurred, and accepted the ladies congratulations on wresting a feast from her bridegroom and the gentleman's appreciative sallies about knowing her own worth, and she lowered her eyes in embarrassment and did not look at Ash Merrick again. Because she knew he'd sensed her lie.

Chapter 6

*A*sh lay on his stomach beneath the bud-spangled limbs of an ancient elm. A fair breeze flirted with his cheek. Bees, woken to industry by spring's beckoning warmth, murmured in the clover. Beneath him a bed of fresh-sprung grass cushioned his abused body.

The months of drunkenness and debauchery had taken their toll. That atop two years chained to a French ship's galley as a "political prisoner."

The thought still provoked his bitter amusement. He'd never had the least interest in politics and neither had Raine.

He and his brother had stumbled into the trap the McClairens had set for his father in retaliation for his betrayal of them. The clansmen hadn't quite known what to do with Carr's evil progeny. Being McClairens and thus relentlessly faithful they couldn't quite bring themselves to murder Janet McClairen's sons. Though,

Ash thought with a twist of his lips, they'd come damn near three years before when they'd beaten Raine to a bloody pulp for supposedly raping a nun.

Ash's eyes narrowed. It still made no sense that they'd spared Raine after they'd captured him the second time. Though right at this minute Ash wasn't sure Raine would be grateful, because the McClairens, thinking to break Carr's back financially if not literally, had sold his sons to the French. They, in turn, had demanded a ransom from Carr.

A ransom that hadn't been forthcoming. Until Carr had capriciously decided to pay for Ash's release—but not Raine's. Carr's decision to leave Raine to rot still bit into Ash's heart like saltpeter in an ever-gaping wound. It, as much as anything else, compelled him beyond endurance and exhaustion to find the means to secure his brother's freedom.

Little wonder his health was depleted and near breaking. But though he was exhausted unto death, sleep was hard coming.

Even though he'd been in Fair Badden a week, he still felt as alien as if he'd been shipwrecked on Africa's dark coast . . . and just as wary. Fair Badden was simply too good to be real, particularly with what he knew of the world.

Yet at night he slept on a feather mattress with the sound of crickets clicking beneath his open window like the nervous worrying of papal beads in a novitiate's hand. Each morning he was greeted with smiles and pleasantries. Each day he drank sweet water from a deep, clear well and ate fresh bread, smoked meats, and farmhouse cheeses.

Each day Rhiannon Russell and Edith Fraiser divided homely duties between them: preparing confits and honey; distilling clover into a fresh, pungent wine; stitching sun-bleached clothing; and tending the rows of herbs outside the kitchen door.

He watched all this domestic harmony skeptically, looking for some sign of dissent. He did not find any. Though sometimes Rhiannon Russell would catch his eye and the tranquil submissiveness that seemed the hallmark of her character would be betrayed by a roguish gleam or a conspiratorial flash of a smile when one of his more subtle sallies blew far over the head of the worthy Mrs. Fraiser.

He wished Rhiannon didn't smile like that and that her eyes didn't gleam like that because, against all likelihood, Ash Merrick was charmed. And that surprised and alarmed him.

She was interesting. Lovely. And natural. And he'd had a surfeit of artifice.

More, she accepted *him*. As decent. As a gentleman. And no one here was wise enough or discerning enough to warn her differently.

Why should they? They were of the same opinion: the ambitious and self-satisfied Edward St. John; homely and sincere John Fortnum; all the eager lads who clamored for a story that they might taste second-hand London's dangerous habits. Even that great gold monolith Phillip Watt.

Restlessly, Ash rolled his tense neck, the movement releasing the grass's fresh perfume, a scent at variance with the darkening of his thoughts. Watt was heavy-handed and complacent and his status as fiancé had fired his ardor. Several times Ash saw the boy attempt to sweep the unwitting Rhiannon to some secluded enclave for a spot of slap and tickle. Or perhaps not so unwitting, Ash thought with a small smile.

That was part of her charm, after all, the flash of amused knowledge that leapt to her greening eyes when she blithely upset one of Phillip's amorous plans. She might be innocent but she was not gullible.

Neither was Edith Fraiser, the canny old cat. She'd certainly manipulated him adroitly enough.

She'd spent the week watching Ash. Every time he looked at Rhiannon, the old dame was looking at him. A few days ago, after sending Rhiannon on some errand, Edith had cornered him. Smiling and bobbing her head she explained that she was old and stiff and not nearly the duenna she need be. Therefore, she declared with impeccable reason, in Carr's stead Ash must be Rhiannon's chaperon.

The notion was so bizarre that he'd been blindsided into acquiescing. Since then he'd spent hours padding after the courting couple to see that Rhiannon's chastity remained intact.

In fact, that was what he was ostensibly doing now—chaperoning the happy couple. His orders were clear: Under no circumstances were Rhiannon and her swain to enter the yew maze, where "untoward" things might occur. He'd accepted with outward amiability but had taken himself off as soon as Phillip had steered Rhiannon through the maze's entrance.

For while he might enjoy letting down his guard and having these people assume him noble and gentlemanly, he wasn't quite ready to rap Watt's knuckles if they chanced too close to Rhiannon's breast. Because if he witnessed that, he would imagine his own hands brushing her velvety skin.

He imagined far too much regarding Rhiannon Russell.

He imagined her as he'd first seen her, flushed and pretty and awash with pleasure. Only in his mind her pleasure was sexual and the heat rising from her throat brought there by his touch. *His* hands had loosened her hair and *his* mouth had brought the full color to her lips. And *his* palm had molded to the sweet swells and lush line . . .

God, what was he thinking? He frowned, casting about for an explanation for this . . . fancy. He would not give it any weightier title.

The answer was simple: He hadn't had a woman in years. Upon his return to England he hadn't dared offend his newfound London "friends" by lifting their sisters' or wives' skirts. He wouldn't spend any of his hard-earned money on an expensive whore, or his health on a cheap one.

Of course he wanted the girl. He wasn't so used up, he thought angrily, that he wouldn't appreciate swiving a fresh, vivacious chit. He stirred uneasily.

Damn her for thinking him a tame and friendly sort. It irritated and fascinated him. How dare she think him better than he was? The only thing he'd ever been loyal to was his brother, and even that loyalty was blemished, for he could *not* quite bring himself to wrest Rhiannon from Fair Badden and deliver her to Carr and accept the money Carr offered for the job. Not even for Raine. Not knowing that once at Wanton's Blush she would in all likelihood die. All Carr's brides died.

Even closed, Ash's eyes narrowed in concentration. He'd assumed his father had sent him here to fetch another rich bride but Rhiannon had nothing. Less than nothing. Yet why would his father have sent him here otherwise?

Carr only concerned himself with that which brought him money or influence. He'd even let his youngest son rot in a French prison rather than pay his ransom.

Raine's ransom.

Ash's mouth flattened. It was the carrot Carr always dangled before him. How many times had his father cajoled and manipulated him with the promise of Raine's ransom? How many times had that promise been "postponed"?

If only Ash could earn enough money on his own. But each pigeon Ash plucked at the gaming table, each program he undertook to earn the fantastic sum the French demanded for Raine's life, brought him only marginally nearer that goal. As much as Ash hated his father, Carr alone had the wherewithal to purchase Raine's freedom.

But then, Ash thought bitterly, why should he? Carr had found a faithful puppet in Ash, one he could make dance with the tiniest jiggle of the strings. But when Ash had arrived here and discovered that his father's plans had been trumped by a country boy and his doting father . . . When he'd seen Rhiannon . . .

It was rare that Carr was thwarted. Ash would enjoy each moment to its fullest. And finally, with the familiar and poisoning vitriol singing in his blood, Ash fell asleep.

The black stone walls oozed cold, inky sweat. Chill seeped into the murky corridors. Ash slumped in the middle of the slanted stone floor beneath his prized rag of a blanket, capturing what warmth he could from his own breath, past shivering, merely enduring.

Behind him the cries and mutterings of the other prisoners faded. He tensed, waiting for the inevitable attack, the latest test of his waning strength, the newest contender for the stinking rag he himself had fought over. Animal and base, he strained to hear the muted approach.

There. A touch. Experimental and wary.

With a thick oath, Ash grabbed his assailant's shoulders and pitched him to his back. He threw himself on the prone figure. Snarling, he throttled him, meeting—

—Rhiannon Russell's panicked eyes.

With a gasp, he jerked his hands from her throat.

"My God." He'd nearly killed her. What had he become that even in his sleep he could kill? He struggled to clear his thoughts. He needed to say something, do something. He closed his eyes, dazed and sickened.

Cool fingers touched his cheek. Shocked, his eyelids flew open. She raised her other hand and with her fingertips brushed his mouth. Then gently, soothingly, she bracketed his face between her palms.

"It's all right," she whispered.

No fear. No indignation. No reproach.

Astounded, he realized she was *comforting* him. Comforting him with the marks of his hands still red around her throat. With his body heavy and penalizing on hers.

"It's all right, Merrick," she whispered.

She could not have done more or worse to him. With those simple words she robbed him of his half-formed apology, the explanation and excuse. She cut his soul from him, leaving him mute and exposed beneath her tender, pitying gaze.

She'd recognized him. Not his ruthlessness or the debauchery he'd so willingly embraced—those were still hidden from her. No. She knew something more profound: his vulnerability. His fear. Because she shared it.

She, too, had walked through nightmares. There was no other explanation for her immediate recognition, her spontaneous understanding . . . the succor she offered. She had mapped that same terror-filled geography.

He swallowed, breathing too hard, pressing his eyes closed against her pity. He didn't want this. He didn't want the connection. He wanted her body. Nothing more. And Lord, was it not enough?

Robbed of sight, he could only feel. She lay beneath him, supple and light-boned, locked into a parody of mating, her hips nested into his own. The image tormented him with its immediacy and impossibility. Blood surged through him, hardening him.

"It's all right," she repeated softly. "I have nightmares, too."

He opened his eyes and stared unseeing at her. She didn't understand. He didn't give a damn about nightmares. He wanted to press his bare flesh against hers, to feel her moving beneath him.

"Merrick!" Fear now. Clear, cold, recalling him. He couldn't have her afraid. It wasn't part of his plan.

"Merrick?"

"Aye." He rose unsteadily to his feet, attempting a smile, failing. "Aye. A dream."

He offered his hand and trustingly—damn her—she

took it. He helped her up. She should have leapt back, but she didn't. She studied him worriedly while he averted his eyes from her loosened neckline. It dipped too low over her breasts, her nipples inches from being exposed. Would they be pink and rosy or tawny and dark? Large or small? Would they pucker against his tongue—?

"I didn't mean to disturb you," she said. "I only . . . I saw you sleeping and"—her gaze fell to a hitherto unnoticed buttercup wilting in the grass at their feet—"Mrs. Fraiser used to wake me by brushing a flower across my face. She said the scent promised a pleasant waking."

"A pretty conceit," he said, finally producing an inane smile. She had no idea what he'd wanted. He fought to find the mild persona he'd adopted in this little rural community. He found it. "But I assure you, 'tis I who must humbly beg your pardon. Believe it or not, I'm not in the habit of throttling lovely young women who wake me."

"You were having—"

"There's no excuse for my behavior. Even in one's sleep manners are important and I believe strangling a woman would definitely be considered a breach of such. Don't you agree?"

A small frown puckered her brow. "Yes," she said, "I suppose."

"Where's your fiancé?" He looked away from the trap of her green eyes.

"He left." She began brushing the grass and twigs from her skirts as blithely as if nothing had happened.

"Without seeing you back to Mrs. Fraiser?"

"Phillip knew you were here," she said. "And some

of his friends were to meet at The Ploughman. He didn't want to keep them waiting."

Only a fool, he thought, would leave such as her for the company of fatuous, overindulged young men.

"Oh?" The sight of her long tanned finger combing bits of leaf from her hair captivated him. It had come free of its coil and fell in waves about her shoulders. Had his hands undone it? Had Phillip's?

"They were going to play cards," she said. "Oh, yes. He related an invitation to you to join them."

Cards? Fiercely, Ash forced his thoughts to the matter at hand. Rich, bored young men were meeting to game away their allowances. They wanted his company. Isn't that what he'd been maneuvering for? They could easily be induced to play for higher stakes and he could gain something from this trip . . . besides an unwanted passion.

Chapter 7

"*I* miss London terribly," drawled Edward St. John. "I don't doubt I shall go back for the season. A year seems a long time in the country. You've had a season, Phillip. Cut quite a swathe, I believe." His manner, though mild, hid a barb.

Phillip flushed slightly and quaffed the rest of his ale. He wiped his mouth with the back of his sleeve and motioned the innkeeper's son, Andrew, over to refill his cup. "Yes."

Edward turned to Ash. "I've met your father, you know," he said. "In fact, I spent two weeks at Wanton's Blush a few years back. Quite a fascinating man, your father."

They were ensconced in the only private room The Ploughman boasted. The others of their party had left. Only Phillip Watt, John Fortnum, St. John, and Ash remained.

"Isn't he," Ash murmured noncommittally. He was not surprised that St. John had found his way to Wanton's Blush. He wagered incautiously and ostentatiously. A plump little pigeon like St. John would certainly have attracted Carr's far-ranging notice.

"It made quite an end to what was a grand season." St. John looked around to make certain that his audience was suitably impressed. When no one responded, he finished scooping the small ante from the center of the table into his pocket.

Ash stretched out his leg, mentally tallying the wealth of jewels bedecking St. John's exquisite persimmon-colored silk jacket. It was amazing St. John had escaped Wanton's Blush apparently unscathed. Few did.

"You were regrettably absent, however." The little spark of malice in his eyes told Ash that St. John was well aware Ash had spent that season in a French gaol.

"I had prior commitments. Or rather, I was committed previously."

St. John burst out laughing and Phillip frowned, disliking being excluded from the joke. Men like St. John always enjoyed excluding others. Wearily, Ash waited for St. John to relate the amusing story of his incarceration.

How would Rhiannon react when the tale reached her? Would she find it vastly diverting to know she'd nearly been throttled by a gaol rat? Or horrifying? He was curious, he told himself, no more.

He glanced up to find St. John regarding him with a bland smile. Apparently he'd decided to keep the matter their little secret. Doubtless because as men of the world they understood the humor in his having been a prisoner while these country louts could never appreciate the jest.

Not that Ash appreciated it himself. But he appreciated men like St. John. They were so easy to anticipate. Ash nodded at him, promising himself that St. John would pay for his sport . . . and for reminding Ash of Rhiannon when he'd almost excised her from his thoughts.

"Your father, now there's a gaming man," St. John went on. "Unhappily for you, you don't seem to have inherited his luck with the cards. Happily for me, however."

"Yes," said Ash, "he's a rare devil all right." He plucked a wrinkled brown apple from the bowl at his side and began paring the soft skin with his stiletto. He was in no hurry; he had nowhere to go.

Today he'd primed the pump for his future gambling by establishing himself in the others' eyes as a fellow with questionable skill and no great luck. When he eventually left Fair Badden, his newfound companions would shake their heads over his belated good fortune, never bothering to tally the slow but steady stream of money that had made its way into his purse. No one would be the wiser. No one would be hurt.

He had to stay focused on that, on his hidden talents, on maintaining his persona as an entertaining companion, a bon vivant who tarried amongst them for a few short weeks.

"Exactly, sir," St. John said, "devilish."

"How did you meet Carr?" Fortnum asked.

"I was in Scotland staying at the home of some mutual acquaintances. He was there and invited me to stay at Wanton's Blush. How could I resist?" St. John held up his hands. "It's magnificent. A miniature London with all its varied pleasures."

"I didn't like London," Phillip Watt suddenly put in.

"Oh?" St. John asked, openly amused. "Pray tell, why?"

"Why should I go elsewhere for what I already have here?" Phillip leaned his great blond head back and beamed like some Adonis. "Fair Badden has everything I want."

Ash glanced at him. Doubtless within five years Watt and Rhiannon would have littered the rural landscape with little golden godlings and goddesses. Ash looked away. He'd always hated mythology.

"I have fine wine to drink," Phillip went on, winking at Ash in a friendly manner, "when the tide is right. Prime horseflesh to ride as well. Fine fellows to be my companions. And damn pretty girls."

"To ride?" St. John snickered.

"Aye!" Watt laughed, a shade too loudly.

Ash's wandering attention abruptly sharpened on Watt. The bloody fool would probably give Rhiannon a case of the pox on their wedding night.

"I agree with Phillip," John Fortnum put in. "Not about the ladies." His ears turned pink. "About the other thingies. I hear London is a dangerous place these days. Packs of young aristos roving the streets like mad dogs, assaulting good people. Damned impertinent."

St. John shrugged. "It's not as though violence hasn't found its way here. Watt's own bride-to-be was nearly killed not long ago."

Ah, yes, Ash remembered. The shallow furrow across her cheek. Another inch and the eye socket would have shattered, the clear hazel green eye rendered sightless.

"They never apprehended the man who did it?" he asked.

"No. He hasn't been caught," Phillip answered tersely.

"Shouldn't wonder that he will be soon," Fortnum said. "Stupid bugger."

"How so?" Ash asked.

"Well, look at who he picked to rob." Fortnum's face was alive with disgust. "An open carriage carrying two ladies on a fine afternoon. What did he hope to get? Tiaras?"

"I thought Mrs. Fraiser was well-to-do," Ash said.

"Aye," Fortnum answered, "she is. But she wouldn't be sporting what finery she owns in the afternoon. Maybe they do so in London, but in Fair Badden we keep out glitter for candlelight."

St. John, openly bored with the turn of conversation, picked at a hangnail.

"Perhaps he thought they carried deep purses," Ash suggested, his thoughts whirring.

"Why would he think that?" Fortnum asked. "Simple carriage. Unescorted ladies. What raises my hackles is that even after the driver whipped up the horses, the bastard shot at the ladies. He needn't have done that."

Ash allowed that he had a point.

"The blackguard had a mask on," Fortnum continued. "He wasn't going to be identified. If me and my dad hadn't been on the road and heard the pistol shot . . ." He trailed off, shaking his head.

Incredibly it sounded as if the carriage carrying Rhiannon and Mrs. Fraiser had been specifically targeted. Ash frowned.

He sighed gustily, as though the ways of evil men were beyond the ken of his civilized understanding, and rose from the table. Casually he collected his jacket and depleted purse. But as he took his leave of the others, he was already composing a letter to Thomas Donne.

Scottish expatriate, enormously wealthy, suave and perennially bored, Donne had little allegiance to anyone or anything. But he did have a supreme desire to find ways to fritter away the hours. He just might consider the challenge of finding out what he could about a Highland orphan interesting enough to accept.

The afternoon sun glanced off the whitewashed wall of the Fraiser's manor, warming the garden. On the grassy path separating vegetables from herbs, Rhiannon sat rolling Stella's silky ear between her fingers.

The young bitch yawned hugely, displaying large white fangs and a long, curling pink tongue. Then, grumbling, she stretched her great gangly body across Rhiannon's lap, moaned in contentment, and fell asleep once more. Rhiannon smiled. So fierce a bloodline this hound had, yet so tamed by simple kindness.

Like Ash Merrick.

For a moment, earlier that day, when she'd struggled beneath him, she'd been truly afraid. Yet when she'd called to him and touched his face he'd shivered, *shivered*. She wondered when last he'd been touched without violence or threat of pain.

Which was absurd. He was a London gentleman and a very handsome one at that. Many women must have explored the texture of his glossy black hair and ca-

ressed his lean, beard-shadowed cheeks. Yet, where had
those scars on his wrists come from? How to account
for them?

Disconcerted by her thoughts, Rhiannon fondled
Stella's other ear. The truth was she was drawn to Ash
Merrick. She should be ashamed. It smacked of disloy-
alty. Yet . . . well, what if she was?

What harm could it do? She was not so stupid as to
confuse fascination for some more permanent emotion.
She was simply intrigued by the discrepancies she saw
in him: the glib tongue and watchful eyes; the shabby
raiment and aristocratic manner; the fine-boned hands
with the battered wrists and callused palms. What
woman wouldn't be interested? That didn't mean she
would be anything less than a faithful and attentive
wife. When the time came.

As Phillip would be a husband. When the time came.

She knew Phillip had occasional assignations with
some of the village women. That they might not have
ended wasn't surprising. Phillip was gloriously handsome and genial and generous and—

"Rhiannon! Ah, there you are. Good." Edith Fraiser
came bustling around the corner of the house, her cap
fluttering in the breeze. She stopped by Rhiannon and
glanced around.

"He's not here," Rhiannon said.

"Good," Edith replied, nodding. And then, eyeing
Rhiannon suspiciously, "*Who's* not here?"

Rhiannon blinked in feigned innocence. "Who do
you *think* is not here?"

Edith blustered. "Phillip Watt, of course. Who did
you think I meant?"

"Phillip, of course," Rhiannon replied and then

ruined the virtuous response by laughing at Edith's doubtful expression. "Dear, dear, Mrs. Fraiser, your concerns are groundless—whatever they may be."

"You know me too well, Rhiannon Russell," Edith declared, spreading her skirts and dropping down beside Rhiannon like a roosting hen. She looked at Stella still snoozing contentedly. "Spoil that hound, you do. 'Tisn't natural. It's a beast, not a baby." A sly smile overtook the disgruntled expression on her face. "Soon enough you'll have your own babes and yon hound will be back in the kennels where she belongs."

"Never," declared Rhiannon. "I'm faithful, I am. Something you might recall," she added gently, "when misgivings send you flying from the house without your shawl."

"Humph," Edith said. "I see the way you circle Mr. Merrick. Like a shy colt spying an offered apple, wary but sure that the extended hand holds something sweet. Take a lesson from that colt, Rhiannon. More often than not the hand that holds out the apple is hiding the one what holds the noose."

Rhiannon laughed. "You are wise and knowing, but your imagination is running wild. I assure you Mr. Merrick has no desire to trap me with a noose or anything else."

Edith shook her head. "Can a girl raised in my house be so green? Must be so, for from the look in your eye I see you believe your own words. It's not that I don't understand the temptation of him. He's a fair way with him and he's rare pretty, too—when he's dusted off." She smoothed her skirts and released a gusty sigh. "I know you think I'm only a simple country woman and so I am—"

"No!" Rhiannon burst out. "I trust your judgment above all others. I look to you for guidance."

Edith straightened, smiling smugly. "Then be guided here, Rhiannon. Stay away from Mr. Merrick. He's dangerous."

"Dangerous? Isn't that perhaps a bit strong? He's affable and gentle and courteous and perhaps a bit more polished than we are accustomed—"

"Are you *arguing* with me?" Edith stared at Rhiannon openmouthed. She could not have been more surprised if the dog had spoken. Rhiannon never contradicted her. It was not like her to dig in her heels—except in matters of hunting and Stella.

Rhiannon's smooth brow puckered and her gaze fell in equal parts abashment and militancy. "Mayhap," she murmured, fiercely concentrating on plucking a burr from Stella's coat. "Forgive me."

Edith scowled. She knew what she saw and she saw a man whose gaze went dark and hot whenever it encountered the form of her darlin' Rhiannon. More worrisome still, whenever that same man was about, she saw a young woman not given to blushing turn the color of a red sunset.

But after hearing that tone from sweet, biddable Rhiannon, she knew that to pursue the conversation further was folly. She might be used to Rhiannon's amenable ways, but she'd also raised a strong-willed son. She recognized the obstinate set to Rhiannon's lips. It was only surprising that the willfulness most youngsters experienced in adolescence had in Rhiannon's case been so long delayed.

"I have a list here of the things that need doing," she said in a neutral voice. "It's going to be rare busy here about. There's the young people coming here tomorrow afternoon, and Lady Harquist insists we attend her annual ball." Edith sighed in exasperation.

Lady Harquist's husband had been made a baronet for his patriotism during the last Jacobite uprising. He'd never actually fought in any battle, but he'd supplied the local weavers with the free wool that was necessary to make uniforms for His Majesty's men.

Lady Harquist—nee Betty Lund—took her new position seriously. Thus each spring Fair Badden society enjoyed its one and only ball. It was no accident that Lady Harquist had set the date for her gala just before May Day.

She wished to contrast the rough-and-rowdy country entertainment with her own sophisticated party. Fortunately, Lady Harquist never realized she alone thought that in a contest between May Day and her ball, her ball prevailed.

"Who'll all be there?"

Edith glanced up at the innocent tones. "Everyone. Including Mr. Merrick, if that's what you're asking."

"Not at all!" Rhiannon's eyes widened. "You must try to overcome these prejudices."

"Hm." Edith studied the girl before turning her attention back to her list. "Then there's all the arrangements to be made for the wedding itself. Your dress isn't even half done and—"

"Oh!"

At the sound of dismay Edith's head shot up. Rhiannon scooted back and Stella's head landed on the ground with an audible thump. The dog cast an aggrieved look around and promptly went back to sleep.

"Hadn't we best make plans for the May Day first?"

Rhiannon asked anxiously. "I mean, the wedding isn't until after—"

"The day after May Day."

"Yes. Well. Still *after*. There's still much to do for Beltaine night. You promised we'd bring clover wine and we haven't even bottled it yet."

"There's enough to drink on Beltaine night without our adding to the general insobriety," Edith said virtuously.

"Mayhaps, madame." Rhiannon smiled and Edith felt her virtuous mien slip in answer to the girl's wheedling ways. "But would you condemn our neighbors to the aching heads and roiling bellies you know they'll suffer if they've only The Ploughman's vile bran ale with which to celebrate the eve of May Day?"

"Maybe they shouldn't drink so much." Edith sniffed and colored, conscious that she might have on one or two Beltaine nights imbibed a bit more than was seemly herself, but unwilling to admit it to Rhiannon.

"Ach, now, dear." Rhiannon reached over and tickled Edith under the chin, her smile conspiratorial. " 'Tis once a year we in Fair Badden have an excuse to play at being varlets and laggards and buffoons. The rest of the year we're too sober by half. What's a celebration without your good clover wine?"

The girl was right. Edith herself didn't want to get, er, *festive* on The Ploughman's rotgut ale, and intend to get festive she did.

"All right, Rhiannon," she capitulated with a grumble. "We'll bring the clover wine but if there were less celebrating on Beltaine night mayhap we mightn't have so many baptisms nine months hence."

It was true, particularly amongst Fair Badden's

younger, farming population. The old custom of young people pairing up and going off into the dark woods on Beltaine night to collect hawthorn blossoms often ended with the courting couple having an incentive to move past courting to the altar. Often that incentive was a babe.

"I wouldn't know about that," Rhiannon said. "I've been Virgin Queen of the Virgin May three years running now."

"You just make sure you *keep* running this Beltaine night, girl," Edith said severely. "At least until after your wedding."

Chapter 8

"*H*ide and seek?" Susan Chapham echoed Margaret Atherton's suggestion. "In the yew maze?"

She glanced around as she said it, an unnecessary precaution as Edith Fraiser had shepherded their parents into the drawing room where innumerable games of whist, coupled with matching glasses of port, would keep them busy all afternoon. "Dare we?"

The young men, reluctant to be caught instigating such naughty sport, remained mum but their smiles related their accord with the proposed entertainment. Only Ash Merrick remained uninvolved, his gaze distracted, his expression polite but bored. More than anyone Rhiannon had ever met, he provoked the mischievousness in her. She simply could not let him dismiss her and her friends.

"Why not?" Rhiannon therefore asked. " 'Twill be good practice for Beltaine. Mayhap we ladies will discover some hidey hole to keep ourselves safe from roaming males that night."

"And how do you propose to conduct the game?" Ash Merrick asked. He unfolded his whipcord length from where he'd been idly leaning against the maypole the villagers had erected that morning.

His time in Fair Badden had bestowed a tawny hue to his pale skin and since he so adamantly denounced wearing any wig, his hair, freshly washed, glistened like polished ebony.

"Everyone hides and one person tries to find them all?" Susan suggested.

"Sounds confounded tiring to me," St. John said, yawning behind his gloved hand.

"Have you a better suggestion?" one of the other young ladies asked.

"I do," Phillip declared. "The ladies hide and the last one to be found wins."

"But that isn't fair," Margaret said plaintively. "Rhiannon will be the last woman found. It's her yew maze, after all."

"Besides," John Fortnum said in his gruff, forthright way, "seems to me that since the men do all the work, the men ought to reap some sort of reward."

An inspired smile appeared on Phillip's face. "How about this? The gentleman who finds the last lady hidden in the maze shall be rewarded with"—he looked around—"a kiss."

The ladies tittered. The men grinned knowingly. And Ash Merrick leaned toward Margaret Atherton, saying something in a voice that did not carry. Something for her ears alone.

"Aye. A kiss it shall be!" Rhiannon declared.

"But Phillip knows this maze nearly as well as Rhiannon," Susan complained. "He'll be sure to win. . . ." And then, as realization struck her, "Ohh!"

Phillip's golden brows rose in feigned innocence. "I am sure Rhiannon knows hiding places I've yet to discover."

He was so sure of himself, thought Rhiannon, and the same quality that had driven her to support the game, the same thing that spurred her to race breakneck speeds when putting her horse to a hurdle, was pricked awake by his certainty.

She did indeed know a place or two Phillip had never discovered. Besides, Margaret knew the maze nearly as well as she, and from the manner in which she cast sidelong glances at Ash Merrick, she might well prove to be the last lady discovered . . . if Ash was the seeker.

Sure enough, Margaret lent her support to the proposal. "All right. I'm game."

"Indeed?" One of Ash's black brows climbed consideringly, a lazy sexual quality in his regard.

Margaret tittered unconscionably and Rhiannon felt her cheeks grow warm. She chided herself viciously. Why shouldn't he flirt with Margaret? He was unattached—as was Margaret.

She moved away from them, her feet carrying her swiftly as, with heated faces, the other young women in the party added their approval. As soon as it was decided that the women should have the count of two hundred before the men came to find them, they disbanded, multicolored skirts belling out as they fled amidst laughter into the maze's evergreen corridors.

As soon as she passed beneath the rose arbor that led

into the maze, Rhiannon broke to the left. Experienced hunters like her friends would drive to the back of the maze and scout for a hiding place there, amidst thick hedges in the densest part of the garden. But not her.

She would stay on a side path. After the men had passed, she would sneak back toward the front and the rose arbor she'd ducked under. There, the rose vine entangled with an ancient yew, hiding a little nook she had discovered years ago. Outside the maze she would be barely visible, but from within the maze no one would be able to see her.

She waited for the men to enter, her heart racing. She heard a muted hunting-horn sound and then the men crashing through the entry, calling out. Before long Susan Chapham's squeal of outrage proclaimed her the first woman to be found. Had it been Ash? Or was he seeking other quarry?

Cautiously Rhiannon peered around the corner. The only sound she heard was that of St. John's perennial complaints. She sped swiftly back toward the entrance. Crouching low, she angled her body sideways and pushed her way through the thick growth.

And then she was in.

She looked around. The very center of the huge yew had rotted away, making a small empty room with living walls. Slender needles of sunlight pierced the higher boughs, stabbing the earth with brilliant pinpricks. The tight, unfurled buds of the red rose adorned the dark green walls like rubies. Beneath, her feet crushed fifty years of accumulated yew needles. Their fragrance rose, sharp and pungent.

She hadn't been here for years. Not since she was a little girl, driven from her bed to hide from the redcoated devils who rode thundering through her dreams. Or had they been dreams? Memories most like, taking advantage of sleep's vulnerability to attack once again.

Thank God, she'd found haven. She'd found Fair Badden. She'd never have to face the landscape of her nightmares again. Ever.

She vanquished the memories, as she always vanquished the memories of her life before her arrival here. She would think of nothing unpleasant. She was playing a game on a lovely spring day and she was going to win. She could imagine Phillip's surprise when he strode confidently toward the bower he expected she'd be occupying only to find it empty.

She grinned. She would wait until he'd given up and then she'd walk serenely from the gate, stringing a chain of daisies as she came.

Ash Merrick might even smile.

Within a few minutes a triumphant call signaled the discovery of another lady and then another. Two more ladies had been flushed. Another cry and more laughter. That left only Rhiannon.

"She's here somewhere," she heard Phillip say from nearby.

"Aha, Watt! She's outmaneuvered you! Best think twice before marrying a wench what's smarter than you." It was John Fortnum.

"I'll find her."

But he didn't. A few minutes later Phillip called out, "There's nothing else for it, lads. We'll just have to drive her like a partridge. She'll be far back where the trees overhang the maze. Likely she's clambered up one and is swinging her legs overhead, laughing as we stumble about nose to the ground."

"Well, even if I don't win the kiss, you've just of-fered me reward enough to gain my aid," another man laughed. "Rhiannon Russell must have pretty legs."

Rhiannon's face grew hot.

"I'm for it, too!" John Fortnum answered, his voice moving off. "Lead on, Watt."

Rhiannon settled down to wait, leaning her head against the yew's shaggy trunk. It could take a goodly while before Phillip called quits. He was tenacious and he disliked being bested.

Perhaps it was the cool dimness chased with golden lights, or perhaps the hushed stillness, the rich damp scent of a hiding place, but soon her eyes drifted shut and she fell into a light, easy sleep.

"Tha thu agam." I have you.

Her eyes opened slowly, uncertain of what she'd heard. Gaelic. She hadn't heard the Gaelic tongue in ten years. She raised her head, her vision slow in adjust-ing to the sharp contrasting light.

Ash Merrick stood over her.

Sunlight dappled his broad shoulders, sparkled in his black hair. His head was cocked to one side and in the odd light she could not make out the expression in his dark eyes, though she could see clearly enough the dark lashes surrounding them, the shadow beneath the high cheekbone, the shape of his mouth.

"You spoke to me in Gaelic."

"Did I?" His voice was quiet. "I was raised in the Highlands, for all my English blood, you know."

"Aye. English . . . How would you . . . ?" She stuttered, stopped herself, went on. "I didn't hear you enter," she said, self-conscious beneath his mute appraisal. "How can that be? I should have heard the sound of yew boughs breaking and—"

"Easy, Miss Russell," he said. "I came in by the roses." He gestured toward a low opening leading to the grassy gardens outside. "I walked the outer periphery of the maze. Sometimes a man needs to stand back to see what's before him."

"Oh." She swallowed, brushing the hair back from her face. It didn't seem fair that he'd left the maze. It set unexpected anxiety shivering through her and she didn't understand why.

She tilted her head back. He bent down, startling her. She jumped a little. He went motionless for a heartbeat and then with a slow, wry smile, reached down and gently removed a sprig of yew from her skirts. Flustered, she brushed the needles from the folds.

"I've won," he said.

"Aye." She did not meet his eye.

"You didn't expect anyone to find you."

"Nay."

"You dislike it that I did."

"Aye," she replied sullenly.

"Why is that?

"I don't know," she muttered. "I'd hidden where no one would find me. I thought I was safe."

" 'Safe.' An interesting choice of words considering we were playing a game."

"It's a feeling, is all," she explained grudgingly. "I used to come here when I was just a lassie newly arrived from . . . newly arrived at Fair Badden."

"From the Highlands."

"Yes."

"You were what? Nine years old? Eight? Your family had fought for the Pretender, hadn't they?"

She nodded.

"Did you hide? When Cumberland's men came? Why? The troops didn't seek children."

"They sought anyone that wore a plaid," she replied in a hushed voice.

"And you hid in the woods." The words seemed to come from him without volition.

"Yes."

"And no one found you."

"Me or the old lady my mother sent with me." She hadn't ever told anyone of those days. Not even Edith Fraiser. She'd tried once, but Edith had tucked her shivering body onto her lap and told her to forget everything that had happened to her before she came to them.

Rhiannon had tried to do what Edith said. Like she had tried to do everything else the Fraisers had asked, to be good and dutiful and never give a moment's distress. Mostly she had succeeded. She could barely recall her own parents' faces. "We watched the croft burn."

He did not ask her to elaborate and for this she was grateful. But he understood. She could see it. Sense it. Following Cumberland's defeat of Prince Charlie's Highlanders at Culloden she'd lost everyone: father, brothers, uncles, cousins.

"Do you have family . . . besides your father?" she asked.

"A sister. A brother."

She nodded. "Where are—"

"Then you found your way here," he cut in. "But you still felt hunted."

"No." She shook her head. "Only sometimes at night. When the thunder came. I didn't want to be a coward and I didn't want to hurt Mrs. Fraiser's feelings—and they would have been sorely hurt had she thought I didn't feel safe in her own good home—so I'd steal outside and come here.

"No one ever found me. No one knew about it. I thought no one ever would—lest I told them. So it was safe, you understand. And now it isn't anymore, because you found me and I don't know that I'll ever feel safe here again." Or anywhere, she thought.

He studied her for a long moment before extending his hand as he had yesterday after wrestling her beneath him and making her aware of his strength, his tensile length, and his weight. He'd made her feel weak, vulnerable. Yet it was not a conscious aim of his. She could not fault him for making her feel that way, or in some odd way liking it. Because if she'd felt weak, he'd felt strong and she knew he would use that strength to protect her.

She placed her hand in his. Effortlessly, he assisted her to her feet. He stepped away.

"You should be safe. You should *feel* safe," he murmured, an edge of anger sharpening his tone.

"No matter now."

"I won't tell anyone about this place," he said. "In a few weeks I'll be gone and it will be your sanctuary once again." His words came rapidly, as though he must say them.

He didn't understand. Whether he went or stayed, wherever he was, she would always be cognizant of the fact he knew about this place. She would never be alone here again. *He* would be with her. But his impulse was kind and she could not rob him of that.

"Thank you."

"But"—he stepped nearer and she could see his chest rising and falling as though he'd been running— "I still would have my reward."

He stepped forward and she moved back until her shoulders pressed against the yew's green branches.

"An toir thu dhomh mo pog?" he whispered. *Will you give me my kiss?*

She lifted her gaze; it became entangled with his as surely as the rose vine entangled with the yew at her back. As steadfast and ineluctably. "Aye."

Slowly, carefully, Ash drew near her. His hands hung loose at his side, his eyes held hers. He angled his head and lowered his mouth until she felt his breath on her lips. Her eyelids fluttered closed. Their lips met.

As soft as summer mist. Delicately as dawn's first colors. Tenderly his mouth molded over hers, moved with breath-stealing sweetness and her own lips, readied for an overpowering assault, were conquered instead by exquisite gentleness.

He raised his arms and she, prepared to lean into his embrace, found that he did not embrace her at all and that instead his strong arms reached past her, bracketing her head, and finding purchase against the living walls behind her. He leaned forward, deepening the kiss.

She sighed, her head falling back, overwhelmed and shaken. She felt weak, her body drugged, her pulse erratic. Unsteadily she laid her hand against his chest for support. His heart beat thickly beneath her palm.

His mouth opened over hers, his breath stole between her lips. She could feel him, taste him, complex and exotic, spicy wine and fresh mint. The tip of his tongue gently lined her lips, coaxing them farther apart.

Her legs trembled. Her thoughts grew faint. All she was aware of was his mouth, his tongue gently playing, seeking the sleek lining of her inner lip, the tip of her own tongue. His heart thundered beneath her hand in an acute counterpoint to the leisurely intoxication of his kiss.

A sound rose in her throat. Her mouth opened wider. Her hands stole around his shoulders, pulling her body tight against his hard chest— He let her go.

Dazed, disoriented, lips sensitive and lush feeling, she stared at him. He stepped away from her, clasping his hands behind his back. His face was still. His dark eyes shuttered. Then he smiled and bent forward in a deep, courtly bow.

"I am well rewarded," he said. "I heard the others coming back. You'd best go. Now. Meet them outside the entrance. I'll follow later."

"But—" she stared at him without understanding, naive and stupid and ill, for he'd awoken with his kiss such feeling as she'd never experienced for Phillip Watt. Never.

Mrs. Fraiser had been wrong. Ash Merrick wasn't dangerous. He was courtly and genteel and his kisses were soft and stirring. Her feelings, *they* were dangerous.

"Go." He was still smiling. "You see, you've won."

She turned away, gathering her skirts and bolting into the too bright light. And so she did not see Ash Merrick's gaze follow her, or see him take his hands from behind his back and turn them over. And she did not see the bloody hands that had been torn strangling the thorny vines behind her so he could keep from crushing her to him.

Chapter 9

During the next week, Rhiannon saw little of Ash Merrick. Edith Fraiser needed her services in a myriad number of ways. Her foster mother sent her on lengthy errands to neighboring estates, occupied her mornings with overseeing the processing of spring honey, and decided now, of all times, to teach her the secrets of brewing a potent clover wine.

When Rhiannon did see Ash Merrick, perpetually on his way out to join the young men—of which Phillip was one—at some masculine entertainment, he was invariably polite and courteous but nothing more. He evinced none of the stunned bewilderment she herself so acutely felt, none of the sensual attraction she fought so hard to hide.

Their kiss meant nothing more to him than the meaningless prize it had been proclaimed. It was a simple meeting of lips, a casual misbehavior.

She only wished she could be so worldly and unaffected. But there had been nothing simple about her response to his kiss.

It had incited a maelstrom of emotions and sensations. The memory of it heated her blood, pooling a restless longing in her lips, her fingertips, her breasts. . . .

It frightened her. It haunted her. When she closed her eyes at night, Merrick's lean, hard form and dark-lashed eyes appeared with startling and all too revealing clarity. She'd been careful since to avoid his company.

Tonight, however, there was slim chance she would be able to avoid his company—or he, hers. Tonight was Lady Harquist's ball. She would have considered it the usual overpopulated, uncomfortable, and crushing affair it generally was, if not for the anxiety of wondering whether Ash Merrick would be there.

She assumed Ash had been included on the guest list but then, doubtless, even if invited he would decline. He had a more than adequate excuse; he'd brought no clothes fitting for a ball.

The thought brought relief at the same time as an acute, guilty regret.

Edith Fraiser had been right after all; Ash Merrick was dangerous.

"Begad, that creature you're riding is unfit to feed my dogs, Merrick!" Phillip avowed blearily.

Ash, jouncing along on a squat pony some distance ahead, clad in black silk, three quarters of his face covered by a mask, did not appear to have heard. The others in their party did. They raised drunken voices in boisterous concurrence. Even the gypsy rogues they traveled with had fallen prey to Ash Merrick's bonhomie. Teeth flashed beneath the fantastical papier-mâché masks as shouts in the Romany tongue filled the night air.

Phillip, in no mood to be ignored, spurred his pony forward. Far ahead of them, the Harquist manor blazed with light, a beacon in the dark.

"You're a right Mogul," Phillip proclaimed on reaching Ash's side.

Ash's dark gaze flashed sidelong but he simply smiled in that lazy way of his and took another swig from the leather skein bouncing on his hip.

When he didn't respond, Phillip went on. "Bedamned if this isn't a grand notion. Don't know why one of us didn't think of it years ago."

It was indeed a splendid notion, spectacular and hilarious. Earlier that day they'd been disconsolately draining tankards of ale at The Ploughman, complaining loudly about the deadly dullness of the fete they were obliged to endure that evening—Lady Harquist's spring ball.

Ash had been taciturn—an increasing tendency in the last few days. Even though Phillip had put himself out to entertain, Merrick was not to be cajoled. His obvious boredom had infected the others' moods, blighting their usual gaiety until a band of filthy, beggarly looking rascals had entered the inn.

Merrick's elegant head had lifted and he had watched them with more interest than he'd evinced all afternoon. A light of inspiration had slowly ignited in his silver eyes. He'd clapped his hand on the table.

"If the evening's entertainment promises tedium, my

dear sirs, you've but two course open to you," he'd declared. "You can forego it—"

"Not bloody likely," John Fortnum interjected disconsolately. "Me old pater would disinherit me if I gave the snub to Lady H."

"Me, too," Phillip confessed.

"Then you have only *one* option," Ash said impatiently. "*You* become the entertainment." He cast a knowing look in the direction of the foreigners. "Lest I be mistaken—and I am rarely mistaken in these matters—yonder sits An Opportunity."

Before anyone could protest, he had hailed the band's leader, Raoul, a gray-headed fellow as wiry as a river alder, to join them. Over the next two hours—and a keg of strong cider—Merrick had ascertained that the gypsies were in fact a troupe of acrobats and tumblers "what been hired to entertain at the big house."

Forthwith Ash had bribed Raoul with sweet words and sweeter coin into allowing them to join their company for the night, masquerading as fellow tumblers. So it was that St. John, Fortnum, and Phillip himself— as well as a half-dozen nameless rascals—were trotting down the road leading to Lady Harquist's, dressed in black leggings and shirts, faces concealed behind whimsical masks, drunk as lords, happy as angels, and as set on mischief as Satan's imps. All thanks to that infernally amusing and fascinating fellow at Phillip's side, Ash Merrick.

Phillip was dully aware he had a case of hero worship. Usually 'twas he, because of his height, his breadth, his looks, or his father's wealth, who attracted admiration. But Ash Merrick was utterly unimpressed by any of Phillip's attributes, having looks and address enough without seeking its reflection in others.

He was simply the damnedest, most dauntless, and most interesting man Phillip had ever met.

Phillip gazed blearily at his idol. Merrick was slender and hard as an épée. Even half-sotted, he fair stank of élan.

The thing of it was, thought Phillip, Merrick had the trick of making everything into a game. Take, for example, a few days ago when Merrick had suddenly announced that the local magistrates were old and blind and thus incapable of tracking down the rogue who had assaulted Rhiannon and Mrs. Fraiser. The task, he'd explained, belonged to young, sharp-eyed gentlemen.

Thus for the rest of that day and the next, Merrick had led his merry, confused companions over the countryside, interviewing hostelry workers, waylaying farmhands, searching for any clue as to the whereabouts of the highwayman.

They didn't find anything—of course not—but that wasn't the point, was it? The point was it had been fun. Exciting. Like this.

"I don't know that this is such a good idea after all," Fortnum called out from his position at the rear. The curling horns of his ram's mask bobbed in agitation. "There'll be the devil to pay when we're caught!"

"What are we to do with them, Watt?" Ash sighed. A feeling of pleasure suffused Phillip.

"I don't know," he said, trying to discern Merrick's desire.

"I suspect we'll just have to sweeten the game." Merrick placed a fist on his hip and eyed St. John and Fortnum severely. The wind ruffled his black locks and plastered his loose linen shirt to his chest. He looked every inch a black-hearted devil. There was about him a fateful ferocity that Phillip admired greatly.

"Let's see. How can we make this a worthy game for our friends here? You are betting men, are you not?" he asked.

Both men agreed.

"Ha! I knew I'd taken your measure right. Here it is, then. I wager that I can dupe everyone attending Lady Harquist's party for a full hour.

"And furthermore, I bet you that when my identity *is* finally divulged, not one word of censure greets that revelation no matter how crudely I misbehave, no matter how lecherous my leers, no matter how deeply I drink—and make no mistake, my dears, I intend to be very, very drunk." His smile was fierce and challenging.

"Oh, come now, Merrick," Fortnum sputtered.

"Ha!" St. John burst out. "I'll take that bet."

"Will you?" Ash tipped his head. "But I haven't said what the stakes are."

"What?" St. John asked.

Ash smiled. "Two hundred pounds."

Phillip caught back his surprise. Two hundred pounds was more than he'd ever wagered on a single bet before.

Ash's cool, mocking gaze scanned their faces. "I thought not," he murmured pleasantly. He took another deep draught from the wineskin.

"I say you can do it!" Phillip declared staunchly. Ash passed him the flask. Phillip slurped it greedily, eyeing his lily-livered companions scornfully.

"I'll take that bet," St. John finally said.

"Excellent, St. John," Merrick declared. "I knew *you*

were a game one. First, the rules. None of you, by action or word, must betray your acquaintance with any of Lady Harquist's guests. You must, on your honor, keep strictly away from those you call intimates, be they friend, father, or lover." His glance found Phillip. Heat rose to Phillip's cheeks. "Agreed?"

They all nodded.

"Good. Now, I'll want a sharp blade and a steady hand to hold a mirror."

"But why?" Fortnum asked.

Merrick laughed. "I fear overcoming the clue my beard provides would strain even my thespian skills," Merrick said. "Who can help me?"

It was one of the gypsies who found amongst his travel kit the means to rid Merrick of beard and moustache. Ten minutes later, the razor's sharp blade had revealed a square and manly jaw, a pair of deeply bowed and sensual lips. Merrick held the mirror up and gave a mocking laugh to his own reflection before pulling the black silk domino back down over his blacker hair and upper face. "Now, away my lads."

A short time later they were following Merrick down the cobbled drive that led up to the Harquists' manor. The weak moonlight washed over the contours of Merrick's thighs and shoulders. His hands were pale against the black silk cuff. Phillip quaffed more from the flask.

Who could possibly take exception to a man like Merrick? Yet, Rhiannon appeared to have developed an aversion to him. Odd. Especially since she had seemed to like Merrick well enough at first. But in the past few days Rhiannon had grown uneasy in Merrick's company, skittish. Through no fault of Merrick's.

Merrick was all that was pleasant and respectful to Rhiannon, even courtly. Perhaps he drank a bit much, and each day seemed to increase his thirst, but what of it? Phillip was perhaps imbibing more than usual, too. Especially now, with his impending nuptials closing in.

He twitched away the unpleasant sensation the thought awoke. Being a touch goosey about being leg-shackled was surely normal.

Rhiannon had best learn right now that Phillip was loyal to his friends and that his companions ranked high in his esteem. *Nothing* was more sacred to a man than his friends. They sustained and encouraged and understood him in a way a woman never could.

Phillip took another swig, arguing away his sense of unease. Rhiannon wouldn't interfere with him, he reasoned. It was why he'd settled on her for his wife. That and his father's prodding.

The old man had specifically chosen Rhiannon Russell as his youngest son's mate, explaining that Rhiannon was kind and loyal and grateful. She would quietly accept whatever Phillip did. She would not demand things a man could—*would* not give.

The old man was right. Rhiannon was the perfect choice for a wife. Besides he was fond of her.

Yes, it was time he wed. Though still young, he felt this subtle resistance to the idea of marrying grow each year. If he waited too long he might not be able to bring himself to do the deed at all—there was so much about living a bachelor's life that appealed to him. Freedom. Not being accountable to a woman for his whereabouts or his actions. Friends. And of course, he added as an afterthought, other ladies.

But he did want a family. He quite looked forward to having a couple brats, and the old man wanted grandsons, something his older brothers had yet to provide. Rhiannon would make a good mother.

As if he had read his mind, Merrick suddenly spoke to him. "Your darlin' bride-to-be is at tonight's festivities, is she not?"

"Yes."

"And any number of other rich young wenches," John Fortnum added. "Now that Phillip here is going all connubial, me dad's all in a lather for me to marry. Perhaps I should take advantage of this evening's sport to look over the prospects, unbeknownst to the prospects, of course. Just because Watt can sustain a penniless bride does not mean I can."

Merrick slew about in his saddle, peering at Phillip. "Just how is that, Watt? How came you to offer for the penniless, if lovely, Miss Russell?"

"Phillip here is proof of an old man's passion," Fortnum supplied before Phillip could speak. "And his father does therefore love him dearly. If it would keep Phillip in Fair Badden, his father would let him marry a tavern wench.

"A rich wife might want a London house. A well-connected wife might have family to visit on long extended trips away. Miss Russell has no reason to leave Fair Badden, nor any desire to do so."

Sober Phillip might have taken exception to such revelations, but he wasn't sober. He was deliciously drunk and surrounded by his bosom friends and on his way to a fine piece of sport. What and why would he keep anything private from these men?

"True," Phillip confessed. "But that's not the only

reason. Rhiannon's clever enough to spend the rest of her life being grateful to me for making her my wife." He grinned. "What other woman would have that sense?"

Chapter 10

They were rough, uncouth fellows. And they were exquisitely, hilariously, vibrantly alive. Fair Badden had never seen their like.

Other traveling performers measured Fair Badden's high society as the self-conscious, priggish band of yawners it was and suited their talents accordingly, somberly enacting philosophical vignettes or singing plodding chorales. Not these fellows. Rude and boisterous and bawdy, they had about them a joie de vivre that was infectious. True, the big silent fellow had no more important a role than letting his smaller fellows clamber over him, but he played the part of mountain well. Another masked man circulated through the room, snatching goblets of wine from Lady Harquist's guests' well-manicured hands and giving back salacious ditties in a high, inane falsetto.

They were unpredictable, thrilling, and novel. Even

the most consummate snob in Lady Harquist's company could not restrain an occasional smile at their antics. They sang ribald songs with leering enthusiasm, mocked their betters with uncanny insight, and quaffed expensive wine as though it were cider dregs. They tumbled and juggled, danced and somersaulted one over the other. Their short morality plays dissolved into delicious double entendres.

Rhiannon welcomed their vibrant company with relief, taking the opportunity to escape her unwelcome preoccupation with Ash Merrick by entering wholeheartedly into their heated word games. It was early yet. Not everyone had arrived. Cornered by a lean fellow in a black silk domino, she giggled, intoxicated by this unexpected freedom from her troubled thoughts.

"Ah, pretty ladybirds!" His voice was slurred and husky, and his thick French accent was so authentic one could not help but wonder if it were real. He peered owlishly at the young ladies tittering behind Rhiannon. "A full gaggle of them and all squawking love songs!"

He swept a crumpled tricorn from his head. A tight-fitting scarf of silk covered his hair. He bent over in so low a bow that his forehead nearly brushed the floor. Just as he was about to overset himself and crash face first into the ground, he snapped upright, blinking woozily.

Part of his act, no doubt, Rhiannon thought. Because though his voice was slurred, he moved with the grace of God's own fool, dodging the vases his fellow acrobats hurled at him, catching them midair, and sending them back. Through it all the inane smile remained plastered on his lower face. But behind the mask his dark eyes gleamed with feverish light.

"Here now, miss," he said snatching at Rhiannon and missing her by inches. Merrily, she danced out from his reach, twirling away in a cloud of jonquil-colored brocade. A tendril of hair escaped its knot and tumbled down her neck.

"Come, dearest. My haughty, devilish, quick-footed Mab," he crooned, reaching for her again. "You look an adventuresome wench, a curious kitten. I've heard it said that all 'ladies crave to be encountered with.' Admit it, sweetling, 'tis a fact that virgins dream of what a gypsy's embrace might be like."

A French gypsy who knew Shakespeare? Not likely.

Rhiannon snorted. "If I allowed your arms about me, sir," she said through her laughter, "I'd be wondering still."

His head swung up. A flicker of surprise appeared in his shadowed eyes.

"Oh ho! What are you saying, *mon amie*? That I'm not what I appear to be"—his voice lowered, became silky with innuendo—"or that *you're* not?"

Why, the audacious cur! The knave! Rhiannon thought in bemusement and could not help grinning at his audacity.

"Tinsel gypsy!" she declared.

"Downy child!" he returned in his low, rough voice, grinning drunkenly.

"I'm not so easily gulled." Rhiannon denied the charge of naïveté, placing her hands on her hips. She cocked a brow at him. "For have I not discovered *you*?"

She leaned forward, studying him closely, the marble smoothness of his blue-cast chin, the full sensual lips. They were unfamiliar yet . . .

"I know you," she murmured, mystified.

"No, Mademoiselle." He shook his head sadly. His dark eyes caught and held her own. "For how can you know me when I do not know myself?"

Around them the noise from the tumblers and jugglers dimmed to a hum. She was scarcely aware of her friends, moving closer.

Faithless flirt, she chastised herself hopelessly. Was it not enough that in her heart she'd betrayed Phillip with a black-haired Londoner, but now she betrayed both men to this . . . *actor* who had honed each slippery, honeyed word on a continent of twittering, blushing girls.

"Who *are* you?" she asked.

He shrugged. Stepped back. "Who do you want me to be? Tumbler?"

He folded at the waist and snapped suddenly backward, head over heels, landing lightly. Around them the ladies clapped. He did not acknowledge their applause; his eyes remained riveted on her.

"Minstrel?"

He withdrew a slender flute dangling from his belt and placed it to his lips. A frolicsome tune flushed from beneath his fingers. Once more the applause broke from the little group of watchers.

"Buffoon?"

He laughed, an unpleasant, helpless sound that caught at Rhiannon's heart, propelling her forward a step. He held out his hand, backing away as if her spontaneous movement somehow threatened him.

"No! Not yet the fool. Though there's always hope you'll witness it yet this night. You wouldn't want to miss it. I play that role best of all."

"Yes!" A young lady in an elaborate wig and diamond ear bobs cried. "Play the fool for us now!"

The tumbler's head turned toward the speaker. "Forgive me, *ma chérie*, but I must decline. That particular mask is threadbare, a shoddy, shopworn piece of work. Unfit for such exalted company. I'll retire and late this evening when you lay sighing upon some worthy"—he paused and the ladies gasped—"pillow, I'll mend it. When next we meet, I swear, I'll be a knave."

He stood rigidly a few seconds and then abruptly grinned. "But tonight I've a grander notion."

"What's that?" the girl asked, but he was not looking at her anymore.

His attention had returned to Rhiannon. Fascinated and charmed, she stayed though her conscience urged her to leave.

"Perhaps tonight I am . . . a hero? No?" He dropped to his knee and stretched a beseeching hand in Rhiannon's direction. "Chevalier? Knight gallant?"

She smiled and would have taken his hand but he snatched it away. He plucked a silver stiletto from where it was hidden in his boot and uncoiled with lethal grace. The knife flashed deadly in his hand.

"Or perhaps mercenary? Villain? Only tell me what you'll pay . . . and I'll tell you my price." His voice had gone flat, emptied. The tip of the blade moved in a threatening arc before the company of giggling women. It stopped at Rhiannon, held, wavered, and was abruptly snatched back.

"A rogue? Or a friend?" He flipped the stiletto into the air and caught it on its descent. Once, twice more.

He was breathing quickly now, each breath exposed by the clinging shirt, the rise and fall of his muscular chest. "A fribble? A blackguard?"

No drunkenness now marred his speech or clouded his bright eyes. He slunk closer to her, his feet sliding ahead of his taut body, his head angled away from her, approaching her like a feral dog.

"Only tell me what *you* desire, *mon coeur*," he said. "What do you want? I'll become it. Anything. It's what I am. What I do. My stock-in-trade."

His voice was hypnotic, base insinuation and bitter mockery underscoring a vast bleakness. The audience around them grew hushed. Margaret shuffled on her feet, her eyes darting nervously. The smile of another bewigged young lady remained fixed on her face like a beauty mark she'd forgotten to take off.

And then the moment was gone. The dark tumbler flung himself back and away.

"No suggestions?" he complained. "You'd leave me to my own devices? My own imaginings? Not a safe place to leave a man such as me."

He sighed heavily. "Then I'll be a juggler. *Here*, my friends, to me!"

At his call several of his fellow acrobats abandoned their pursuits. He called out again, raised his stiletto, and flung it over the heads of Lady Harquist's guests. As one, the guests ducked and shouted in alarm. The blade whistled high above their elegant coiffures, their feathered, puffed, and swollen wigs.

A short, bandy-legged fellow perched atop the giant's shoulders cackled gleefully and caught the dark tumbler's missile. Magically, its twin appeared in his other hand. With a hoot, he hurled first one then the other back at Rhiannon's would-be hero.

He caught them both and sent them chasing one another in an arc above his head. A third knife joined them, and then a fourth, as the other members of the troupe sent their blades spinning and flashing toward the black-clad figure.

Effortlessly he caught and added each to the sparkling, glittering circle of death that flew above his head, occasionally plucking one from the circle and sending it out amidst the party, only to have it returned seconds later chased by a new one. The company held their breath, clasping their gloved hands to their mouths in fascinated terror.

He made it look so easy, so effortless. But Rhiannon, standing closest to him, saw the sheen break out on his closely shaven chin and exposed throat, witnessed the intensity with which he watched the tumbling blades fall toward him, an intensity at odds with his easy banter and fluid movements.

Now, released from his attentions, the niggling impression of familiarity returned to tease her. The lean, hard acrobat's body hidden under dusty, ill-fitting finery, the supple grace, even the choice of words, though spoken in an accent . . .

Her gaze flew toward the young giant standing currently unemployed and idle against the wall. His mask had gone askew. One bushy golden brow appeared in the jagged eyehole.

Phillip?

Her head snapped around. The juggler had reached above his head to catch a knife thrown a shade too high. The cuff slipped up his arm.

A thick, pale rope of scarred flesh decorated his wrist.

"Merrick?" she whispered, jerking forward.

From the corner of her eye she saw a silver gleam, then heard a thunk. She wheeled about. Behind her a stiletto vibrated in the paneled wall.

Exactly where she'd been standing.

Chapter 11

Rhiannon stared at the still quivering blade. Some hand had grown sloppy with drink, she thought breathlessly. Had she not moved . . .

Ash tore off his silk mask, looking beyond her, his gaze hunting through the assembled crowd. A gasp followed his revelation and was pursued by the rumbling of a hundred voices.

"It's that Merrick fellow!"

"Merrick? The fellow staying at the Fraisers'?"

"Merrick. Ash Merrick. Carr's son—"

A flicker ignited in the cool depths of Ash's dark eyes as he searched the faces turned toward him. He was not drunk, he was pretending, Rhiannon thought. And all those things he'd said, all those words he'd played upon . . .

"What sort of a game is this?" she heard Edith Fraiser exclaim. The company parted and she sailed forth, her skirts bunched in fists on either hip, her face rouged with concern. Purposefully, she stomped toward Merrick, bypassing the knife without a glance.

With a start, Rhiannon realized that her foster mother, as well as the vast majority of those present, was unaware of how close that blade had come to separating Rhiannon's spirit from her flesh.

"Is that really Mr. Merrick, then?" Edith demanded.

"Aye, madame," Merrick murmured in a low, distracted tone. "And I, too, would like to know what game this is."

He turned and suddenly his face wore a lopsided smile. "Ala*th* . . . I mean alas . . . I am revealed!" he called, bowing inelegantly. "And since *I* am revealed, I insist my cohorts suffer likewise. Unmask! Unmask!"

With a drunken shout, Phillip tugged until his mask came off. "Me, too!" he cried jubilantly. "Revealed, that is!'

The others followed his example. Around them, Lady Harquist's astounded guests stared, snickered, smiled, and finally laughed. Even Lady Harquist, seeing how well the fake acrobats were received, allowed herself a moue of self-congratulation.

True, a few ladies sniffed—these, confirmed sticklers—but overwhelmingly the crowd approved. A spattering of applause even broke out and Phillip's father, hunched and crippled with gout though he was, banged his cane upon the floor in approval.

"This your doing, Mr. Merrick?" the old man demanded. "Good for you, sir. Our society is grown stale of late. We're wanting a bit of piss to shine the pewter!"

With a debonair swoop of his hand, Ash saluted the crowd and then ruined the gesture by staggering sideways and tipping into the wall. His shoulder hit the paneling with an audible thud. He stayed there, canted against the paneling, his face six inches from where the knife protruded. He cocked his head and studied it.

"What's this? What's this?" he muttered.

He was drunk after all, Rhiannon thought and then castigated herself for being disillusioned.

So? She'd mistook a spark of reflected light in his pupil for keenness and the candle-made shadows beneath his cheeks for taut alertness. She'd supposed his words filled with meaning when they were filled only with mead. She averted her eyes from him. They felt hot and she would not cry. She had no reason to cry.

Ash craned his head around and, seeing her, smiled stupidly. She winced and then, realizing how unfair she was, forced a smile. It was no part of his fault that she'd dressed him as her knight and that the shining armor did not fit.

His expression betrayed a momentary puzzlement and then he pointed at the knife. "You were standing here, weren't you, Miss Russell?"

"Yes," she answered. "What of it?"

Curious partygoers, finally alerted to the presence of a knife in their hostess's linen-paneled wall, had gathered in a loose semicircle around them.

"He thinks someone hurled a knife at Miss Russell," a lady said.

A snort of masculine contempt. "Some bungler missent it. Accident."

"Probably one of Watt's fool friends," an older man declared. "Not a grain of sense amongst the lot."

A low murmur rippled through the assembly.

"What's that Merrick fellow doing now?" a lady near Rhiannon asked.

"Who cares? Just let him stretch the cloth tight across those shoulders once more and I'll be counted content," a low feminine voice whispered in approval.

"Handsome creature, is he not? Dark as a storm-tossed night," another lady concurred.

"Aye and I'd be tossed right enough . . . if I could arrange to meet him of a night," came the throaty rejoinder.

Rhiannon bit back a reply. It was no concern of hers what these trollops thought. Ash finished his scrutiny of the stiletto and turned. His gaze lit on her.

"Begad! I have it!" he declared with an air of sudden inspiration. "Someone here has mistook this tasty morsel for his dinner!" He pointed at her. Dozens of eyes followed his gesture with amused interest.

He clucked his tongue. "Now what knave would seek to use a knife on what is so clearly . . . finger food?"

Heat raced up Rhiannon's throat and burned in her cheeks. Several of the men caught back their laughter, and smiles were traded behind the shield of lace handkerchiefs and widespread fans. He was easing the tensions that had grown in the overheated room, Rhiannon realized. Relaxing them. Why?

"Come now," Ash said, "someone must claim this knife. Where did it come from, friend rogue?" He hailed the wiry acrobat who'd clambered on Phillip's shoulders.

She'd forgotten Phillip. She looked around. Her fiancé was no longer sitting on the floor. He'd disappeared.

"I do not know where that comes from," the gypsy answered. "I was concentrating on the knives. *My* knives. That sticker isn't a Romany blade."

Ash jerked the blade from the wall. "True," he said. "No gypsy threw this pretty steel."

He ran his fingertip along the blade, testing the edge. He withdrew a finger marked with a thin red line.

"And as we all can attest, the only reason a blade leaving a Romany hand would hit this wall is because that is where the gypsy wanted it. Why would one of them do that, do you suppose? It's a far bit too early for them to be expressing disappointment in the tips."

Laughter met this unassailable observation. Merrick sighed gustily, squinting at the knife. "Whose then?"

He lurched toward Rhiannon and without warning grasped her upper arm, pulling her near. His grip was strong; his body exuded the remnant heat and scent of his exertions. Earthy. Masculine.

His dark face moved close. His rum-soaked breath sluiced over her face. She should have been disgusted and part of her was, but another was not. Another part of her wanted to discover if his mouth tasted of the drink, if drunk he could still make her knees grow weak with his kiss, if his body was as hot as it seemed.

"Who do you think flung that knife, miss? And why? Did someone think to make symmetry on that lovely face of yours with a twin scar?"

"I'm sure it was an accident." She pulled back; it would be too easy to lean forward.

"Aye. Accidents."

"Here now, Merrick!" Phillip's loud salutation broke over their heads like a thunderclap. He appeared behind them, towering over them like a convivial giant.

He swung one of his huge arms around Rhiannon's shoulders and another around Ash drawing them both together in an embrace that brought them within inches of each other. "It won't do any good, Merrick!" he said, fondly ruffling Ash's black hair.

"What won't do any good?"

"Fussing over that damned sticker won't divert anyone's attention from the fact that you owe St. John two hundred pounds!" At this, Phillip crowed with laughter.

"That's right, Merrick," St. John said, making his way toward them. "Your disguise didn't last the hour you promised."

"What's this about a bet?" one of the gentlemen asked.

"True, sir," Phillip said. "Mr. Merrick here bet St. John that he could cozen you all into thinking him one of these gypsy knaves for just as long as he wanted. Well, he lost and now he can stay and take his comeuppance."

Phillip exerted another powerful squeeze on his hapless prisoners. Ash was no proof against Phillip's strength. He stumbled toward Rhiannon who, manhandled in a like manner on Phillip's other side, toppled forward. Ash's hands flew out, catching her around the waist and steadying her.

His touch set her afire. She swallowed, willing herself not to react, not to flush, not to melt.

Even through the thick satin material, his touch burned her. So little a thing, so harmless, and yet, it stirred her blood, incited riotous visions. Visions she had no right entertaining.

She was worse than any flirt; she was a right molly, a

slut, but that knowledge did not stop her from hating it when he took his hand away. She looked around in a panic, anywhere so she wouldn't have to encounter his eyes, and found Phillip watching her.

"*Th*ass right." His handsome golden head bobbed with soggy approval. "Make up. Be friends."

"Why should they?" St. John's humorous voice intoned. "She's the author of his loss. 'Twas she who called out Merrick's name. She revealed him."

"Did she, now?" Phillip asked, eyeing Rhiannon proudly. "What do you think of that, Ash Merrick? I think I ought to collect half the winnings."

"Not bloody likely," St. John said before Ash could answer. He leaned in close, his mouth inches from Rhiannon's ear, but though he whispered close to Rhiannon 'twas Ash his gaze fixed on.

"Best watch that girl, Merrick," St. John advised. "She'll be the ruin of you."

Ash blinked at St. John, a vague smile on his handsome face. "Unless I'm wrong, I believe she already has been."

He smiled throughout the rest of party. He smiled as he drank his way through an additional two bottles of port and he smiled as he traded suggestive sallies with Margaret Atherton. He smiled as he danced and he smiled as he counted out two hundred pounds into St. John's plump, gloved hand. And he smiled, by God, as he saw Rhiannon's confusion become disappointment then hurt.

When dawn stained the sky with her orchid-colored blood, he smiled and accepted Lady Harquist's offer of a bed. He was smiling as he staggered from the salon, and when he turned the door handle to the bedchamber, he was smiling still.

Because while tomorrow his obligation to his brother might make him a cheat or a thief or even a murderer, here, tonight, in this place, he was a congenial rascal, a bon vivant. A smiler.

But when the door shut behind him and he leaned his head against its panels, his smile died. He'd lost two hundred pounds because of her. Raine rotted in a French prison and he played fast and loose with money that could buy his freedom. And why? Because someone had thrown a knife too near her and he'd immediately concluded that her life was in mortal danger and he must save her, revealing himself—and losing his bet—in the process. At least he'd had enough presence of mind to mask his concern beneath a façade of drunkenness.

He should be strung up and gutted. One minute of lucid thinking would have shown that it *had* been an accident just like the highwayman having targeted Rhiannon's carriage had been simple ill luck.

Ash had searched the countryside without finding a trace of the robber. And the reason for that was simple: He'd found none because the bounder had fled. There was no malevolent assassin lurking about waiting for the opportunity to kill a penniless girl.

Ash sneered. Either the two accidents had been just that, unconnected misfortunes, or someone in Fair Badden wanted Rhiannon dead. And who would that be, and why?

He was the worst kind of fool, one who needed to romanticize simple lust. He'd spent most of the week trying to get drunk enough to lose his erection. It hadn't worked.

He closed his eyes, willing the liquor in his blood to erase the taste of her soft mouth, the fragrance of her dark hair. . . . Six more days. Then she'd belong to that big, congenial boy.

Ash's hands clenched at his side, as he forced one last smile around his teeth. He had to get out of here. He had to get out of this damnable place, these terrifyingly defenseless lambs. The wolf should slink back to the black forests and leave the sheep wholly innocent of what had, for some short weeks, moved undiscovered amongst them.

He could leave now. There was no real reason for him to stay. He pushed himself away from the door. He *would* leave now.

Except that someone *had* thrown that knife. At her heart. He knew it.

He twisted, pounding his fist against the door. The stiletto had impaled the paneling at chest level. It stood at right angles to the wall. Someone had hurled it with deadly speed and precision.

He cursed roundly and viciously, but in the end it didn't affect his decision. He'd stay until she was another man's concern, another man's responsibility.

Another man's.

Chapter 12

*E*dith Fraiser sat on the bench outside the kitchen door, the gay ribbons that would adorn Rhiannon's May Day dress spilling over her skirts. She peered at the horizon. Dark weather was coming. Not today or this night, thank the Lord, which was Beltaine Night. No one enjoyed a soggy Beltaine. But perhaps tomorrow—which would be a shame as a soggy May Day was almost as sad.

She wiped her damp forehead, wondering if it really was as unseasonably warm as she thought or if her own frets and stews only made it seem so. She glanced at Rhiannon who, with Stella in attendance, was busily plaiting wild anemones into a maypole garland.

Two more days, Edith thought, returning to her task. It would be all right, after all. Two more days and the wench would be safely wed.

For a bitter moment there at Lady Harquist's ball

Edith had thought for sure that the dark Londoner was simply going to pick Rhiannon up and carry her off like some rogue medieval knight come looting. The man certainly looked the part with his black good looks and the tension vibrating in his lean figure.

But nothing like that had happened. Not only hadn't he carried Rhiannon off, he'd paid scant attention to her for the rest of the night, and the days and nights that followed.

Perhaps she was simply getting fanciful in her old age. What with the strain of praying Squire Watts didn't change his mind and withdraw his consent to the marriage and hoping Phillip remained resolved to wed, was it any wonder if she was a wee bit overprotective?

But now she could relax. Tonight all Fair Badden would turn out for the Beltaine Eve festivities and Rhiannon would be under the watchful eye of not only herself but the entire community. Then tomorrow was May Day with its innocent—and blessedly sunlit—pleasures and the afternoon hunt Squire Watt had arranged as a special wedding present to the bride, the last hunt of the season. Rhiannon would never miss a hunt.

And then . . . Edith clipped off a length of bright red ribbon and pleated it into a fat rosette to affix to Rhiannon's skirts. The next day Phillip and Rhiannon would wed.

She sighed gustily, drawing a glance from Rhiannon. She smiled fondly at the girl. True to her sweet nature Rhiannon returned the smile twofold. Edith bent her head over her sewing, nodding happily.

Aye, she could relax.

* * *

It was Beltaine Eve, and Fair Badden's marketplace overflowed with revelry. Stalls and carts, piled with toys, confections, and trinkets lit by rush torches and lanterns, cluttered the cobbled square. In the center of the square the traditional Beltaine fire was being erected. Flowing around the unlit fire and hapless staggering of goods, all manner of people milled and jostled, trading smiles with egalitarian abandon.

True to its ancient traditions, the May Day celebrations stripped each resident of Fair Badden of office and status. Manor-bred mingled freely with baseborn. Peasant and aristocrat alike had dressed in simple country garb sewn over with bright ribbons. Bells tinkled, dogs yapped, and the pennants snapped from atop the four corners of the open-sided pavilion set at the square's far end.

Under this tent's billowing canopy stood a huge plank table, its surface sticky with spilled ale, honey cake crumbs, and cheese rinds. Beneath the table a young gazehound bitch scavenged tidbits.

Rhiannon Russell, Queen of the May, drunk as a lord and teetering like an unfledged owlet, dug her bare and dirty toes into Stella's silky fur. Beside her was her lady-in-waiting who—for reasons Rhiannon could no longer fathom but which she distinctly remembered having been hysterical about some hours earlier—was a brown cow named Molly. The lady-in-waiting stretched out her neck and tried to snatch the royal tiara off the royal brow. With a frown, Rhiannon rapped the cheeky wench across her broad brown nose, the movement upsetting the balance of her clover blossom crown.

"King" Phillip, slumped on the oak keg throne next

to hers, roused himself enough to grab hold of Rhiannon's crown and jerk it from Molly's mouth. Having successfully attended to his consortly duties, he lapsed once again into his former vapid, grinning state.

Rhiannon studied him with soggy affection. Good ole King Phil. Steady, handsome, dependable, undemanding, sweet King Phil. She smiled at him. He didn't notice.

She slouched back, feeling magnanimous and sentimental and overheated. Around her the "court" buzzed and murmured, drank and sang. She knew them all. Every one. This was her home. These people were her family. No matter what ghosts called to her spirit from their graves—and what man called to her other far more earthy parts—here she was loved and respected and safe.

An unsteady hand reached over Rhiannon's shoulder and slopped May wine into her goblet. Her *royal* goblet.

"To the good people of Good Badden. Fair Badden. Not so Badden," she declared. Gripping the cheap pewter cup with both hands, she tossed the contents down her throat in one long, noisy gulp.

"Long live Queen Rhiannon!" the crowd yelled.

"And her king. Don't forget the king." Phillip announced, a spark of consciousness brightening his eyes.

Not that they needed brightening. Phillip had truly bright blue eyes. Very beautiful. Really nice. And she was lucky—no, Rhiannon thought earnestly, she was *privileged* to be the woman who got to marry them . . . him. She reached over to refill her goblet.

Phillip smiled vaguely at her, as if he couldn't quite place her in his memory but knew she had some status nonetheless. "Pretty Rhiannon. Pretty Queen," he muttered fondly. "Favorite of everyone. Fellows all envy me."

Abruptly, he linked a giant paw around the back of her neck. Toppled from her throne by Phillip's enthusiasm, she flung her arms around his neck to keep from landing on her bum. The room exploded with hoots of approval as his mouth came down on hers in a loud, wet smack.

He kept kissing her. Demandingly, forcefully, and oddly passionlessly, and Rhiannon, woozy and complacent, allowed it. Finally he released her.

"You'll make a good Queen won't you, m'dear?" he asked.

He patted her cheek awkwardly, his expression begging for reassurance. His sudden insecurity caused acute and lethal guilt to eat its way through Rhiannon's agreeable alcoholic haze. Unable to meet his anxious gaze, she glanced away and so caught sight of a dark, masculine figure disappearing abruptly into the darkness beyond the pavilion's lights.

It wasn't him. It wasn't Ash.

"We'll live here and be hap—content. I'll be a good husband," Phillip was saying. "You couldn't do better."

He was right. She was marrying far above her station, better than anyone could ever have expected. And she *would* be . . . content. Then why was she still staring at the place where the dark figure had disappeared?

She glanced at Phillip but he had already slouched back on his throne, his eyelids falling over his gorgeous blue eyes. A second later he was snoring. She slipped from his lap, regarding him ashamedly. Every time Ash Merrick was near, she forgot her soon-to-be groom.

Drat Ash Merrick and his flashing smile and his cautious eyes. Drat his hard body and his soft mouth. Drat a man who made the very word "content" seem a laughable, pallid notion. Drat him for taking that wagered kiss. Drat him for stopping at that.

Where the devil was the man? Rhiannon glared at the crowd about her. He was a guest in her foster mother's home. He'd been invited to take part in the festivities. He should be here.

"I'm Queen, aren't I?" she demanded of her heifer-in-waiting. In answer, Molly once more plucked the crown from her head. Rhiannon let her have it. "What good's a crown if the wearer doesn't rule?" she asked loudly.

The crowd looked up at her outburst, primed for play. If their queen had a game in mind, they were all for it.

"If I'm Queen, I should be able to make laws, shouldn't I?"

"Aye!" A chorus of voices agreed. "Aye, you're Queen! What law is it you're wanting to make?"

"I want . . . I want every one of my loyal subjects to bend his knee before me, er, us, and swear his fealty."

The crowd, amused and rowdy, traded glances and shrugged. "We already done that."

"No, you haven't," Rhiannon corrected them. "Not *all* of you."

"Who ain't performed the proper respects?"

"The Londoner. Ash Merrick," she announced darkly.

"Why, that's right," John Fortnum said in the amazed tones of discovery. "He hasn't been round most of the day. The maggoty knave didn't even attend the coronation!"

"Well, we'll set that to rights," announced a burly "knight," "won't we, lads?"

At this, those still capable of action streamed from the pavilion, dispersing into the crowds outside. Fired by alcohol, they swept through the market, calling and clamoring for "the foreigner, Merrick."

As the hunt progressed, those who had no part in it began shouting for the King and Queen of the May to come to the Beltaine fire and leap across it. It was a custom as old as Beltaine itself, a pledge sealing a couple's matrimonial fate. The call gathered force until it could no longer be gainsaid. The revelers entered the pavilion, snatched Rhiannon and Phillip from their thrones, and carried them out into the night to the fire's side.

At the same time, the hunters finally met with success. They found Merrick at The Ploughman, wiping the froth of ale from his upper lip.

"Merrick!"

Gleefully they encircled him. He turned tiredly.

"St. John," he said. "I'm not in the mood, boy."

St. John's eyes widened in mock despair. "He says he's not in the mood," he told his fellows. He looked back into Merrick's eyes. "Too bad, old fellow."

"What's this all about?"

"You're wanted at court, Merrick. A royal decree."

"Oh?" Merrick turned his back on them, motioning the ale seller to draw him another tankard. "What for? Does His Majesty need instruction in seduction? I'm afraid I have no advice to offer."

He took a deep draught of ale before placing the

tankard with telling precision back on the counter. "From what I saw, he looked like he was doing fine. The royal wench was warming his lap and her royal mouth was encouraging his ardor. It all looked most promising. But then, I've never enjoyed spectator sports. Mind you, don't let that stop you, lads."

They jeered and winked at his insolence. Then, before he could resist, they'd surrounded him and tied his arms behind his back. With much laughter they shoved and cajoled and half-carried him back to the May Queen.

They found her standing before the bonfire, weaving slightly. At her feet sat Phillip, sunk in drunken fascination with the recently ignited fire.

"Queen Rhiannon!" they called out and, wresting Merrick from their midst, shoved him before her and stood back, well-pleased with themselves.

She stared at him in surprise, having forgotten she'd sent these men to return with him. His hair tumbled over his brow; his expression was unreadable.

"Here he is," St. John declared.

Ash tilted his head to the side, regarding her intently. Dear Lord, why had she drunk so much of that clover wine?

She steeled herself. It was too late to fret over how much she'd imbibed. Besides, she felt daring, and why shouldn't she? He'd befriended her and then abandoned her. He had dallied with her and then ignored her. Why, he had caused her to betray a husband she did not yet have!

And the memory of his kiss played havoc with her body.

"Well, Your Majesty?" St. John said, his brows climbing. "You wanted him. Here he is. Now what?"

She swayed slightly, the taste of wine thick on her tongue, the crackle and pop of the green-wood fire masking the buzz in her ears.

"Your Majesty?" John Fortnum's voice. Reminding her of her role. She was Queen.

"Be you Merrick of London?" she asked.

Ash eyed her guardedly.

"Answer her and it'll go well with you," John Fortnum promised kindly. "She's a most munificent ruler. Perhaps she'll knight you."

Merrick smiled, his face turned away from her and toward the crowd. "Fortnum, if your tender treatment of me is a sample of her munificence I'll have to refuse any further samples. I may not survive a knighthood."

The men and women laughed in appreciation. Rhiannon scowled.

She did not want him charming them; he charmed too easily by half. She would not allow him to turn this into a marketplace for his charisma.

"You'll have no offers from me gracious or otherwise," she declared loudly. She held out her hand and motioned for the wine bottle a lass near her held. With a grin the girl handed it to her.

Eyes locked on Merrick, she moved toward him, her hips swaying slowly, provocatively, her lids heavy with wine and the yearning he'd incited and would never satisfy.

She halted within arm's reach, close enough that he could not help but see her. Only his eyes moved, rising slowly to meet hers from under dense, black lashes.

"Lord, but you are exquisite." The words seemed torn from his lips, a spoken thought not flattery.

She tipped her head back and drank deeply from the bottle. False courage, she knew, but any courage was welcome when a woman was faced with Ash Merrick's dark and passionate eyes.

"What do you want of me? Whatever I own is at your disposal." One side of his mouth lifted in a crooked grin. His gaze held hers. "Whatever skills I possess are yours to command."

"Not enough," she breathed, stepping closer, vaguely conscious that she skirted too near the fire, both figuratively and literally.

"Really?" His tone was mead infused, intoxicating and low and sweet, pitched for her ears alone. "What queen could ask more of her subject? And what would that be?"

She hesitated, craven and coward that she was, afraid to tell him the truth.

"Only say it and I will give it to you."

She tore her gaze away from his, raised the bottle to her lips, and took another draught of bravado, an increment away from declaring what she did indeed want of this man. But then she would lose all that she'd spent years in attaining. She took another drink. It burned going down.

"Yes?" he prompted, a tense note hidden in his gentle cajolery.

"Your regard," she burst out and then, "your note. Your attention."

Fearful of how revealing her words were, she straightened, forced a laugh between her stiff lips. She lifted her goblet to those watching. "A Queen's due from her vassals."

"Here! Here!" the crowd responded.

"But I'm not your subject, madame," Merrick reminded her gently. "I'm a foreigner, a sojourner, an alien. I'm not one of them." His eyes flickered over the crowd. "But then, neither are you, are you . . . Your Majesty?"

She froze. With so few words he named her an outsider, an imposter, an orphan. Abruptly the focus of her concern shifted. A trembling of fear began in her heart and lungs, filling her chest.

She fought the sensation. She *did* belong here. She'd done everything, become everything anyone could want. She'd lost her accent, even her memories. All of it done so that she could stay. She had purchased her right to be here and she had paid for it with the coin of her heritage.

Beneath her feet the earth seemed to rise like the arching back of a cat. Ash was watching her.

"Sir." Her voice sounded faint, distant. "You are in my kingdom. You will demonstrate your fealty."

"I've had enough games, Rhiannon."

His voice was pitched so only she could hear him, and yet she lost the meaning of his words, it so unnerved her to hear her Christian name for the first time from his lips.

She tried to focus but the earth was dipping dangerously and the fire was stretching toward her. He was too close. He was always too close—or too far. Out of the corner of her eye she saw Phillip stirring.

"Rhiannon? Why's Merrick got his hands tied up?" Phillip lumbered to his feet. Oh, God. She'd forgotten him again. She closed her eyes and immediately felt the effects of Edith's clover wine. "Rhiannon? Merrick?"

Her husband. Her lover. Safety. Danger. Home. Refuge. Outsider. Her eyelids fluttered. She swayed.

"What are you doing to Merrick?" Phillip shouted in a bewildered voice.

She heard a crash behind her, from Phillip's direction. The crowd erupted in a cacophony of alarm. She started to wheel around but the movement sent her spinning madly, the world darkening.

"Catch her, you fools!" she heard Ash shout and then the ground rose up like a blow.

Chapter 13

*W*att had either sprained his ankle or broken it.

He'd launched himself through the boughs waiting to be fed into the fire and caught a foot. He landed in a heap of wide-eyed disbelief. With the simple conciseness of the very drunk he'd then announced that he was hurt and proceeded to apologize to Rhiannon explaining that he would not be able to jump over the bonfire and seal their betrothal. Since Rhiannon was sagging unconscious in John Fortnum's arms, she did not respond.

Phillip's friends turned their attention to consoling their King. With a huzzah, they hefted Phillip above their heads and took him back to the pavilion where he was duly splinted, saturated with drink, and finally propped on a chair.

Ash witnessed it all with a mixture of anger and

helplessness. He had no right to hold, administer to, or even touch Rhiannon. He hovered until Margaret Atherton took charge of Rhiannon, then he found his way back to the tavern where he spent the next several hours. But the thought of Rhiannon being untended and vulnerable during the rest of this night of free-for-all carousing prevented him from drinking and preyed on his imagination until it became an obsession. Someone *had* shot at her. A knife *had* nearly pierced her chest. A night like this would present the perfect cover for an attempted murder. . . .

The blasted witch had coiled herself into the tangled mess of his life, and like a knot, she would not come free. Not unless she was cut out, which marriage to that golden-haired oaf would certainly accomplish.

But for tonight . . . Ash slammed the half-full tankard down on the counter. Damn it to bleeding hell! She was likely sitting on Watt's good leg, purring in his arms, as he stood here poleaxed by misguided fear.

But what if she wasn't?

He pushed the tankard away and stepped over several bodies sprawled senseless on the floor, heading through the door. Outside, a few knots of women and men still clustered about the grounds. Few young people were present, however, and Ash remarked it uncomfortably. Where had Fair Badden's youth gone? He scanned the area for Rhiannon and spied Edith Fraiser sitting with her eyes closed, the hound Stella resting her heavy head on Edith's lap. The marketplace was much quieter than it had been a few hours earlier and it wasn't even midnight.

At the end of the square Ash found an old man gazing at the moon and smiling, a look of fond remembrance on his seamed, leathery face. Ash asked him where everyone had gone and why they'd abandoned their revelries so early.

The old man snorted and after shaking his head in a profoundly pitying fashion, explained to Ash that the revelries hadn't ended, they'd simply been transferred to a more private setting.

Over the course of the last few hours, it would seem, the younger girls had gone into the woods to gather hawthorn blooms to ensure good luck for the coming year. But the shawls they carried on their arms and the back-long glances they'd sent the young men who watched them go were invitation to another sort of hunt, the old man explained with a chuckle and a wink.

The young men hadn't needed any prodding to follow after, stepping into the forest's dark embrace to seek another embrace entirely. Not that all the young women were so inclined, the old man hastened to point out, but if a lad were lucky . . .

Ash left him, his thoughts haunted by images he could barely tolerate.

Were Watt and Rhiannon among their numbers? Ash wondered. Was she straining beneath him right now?

His hands flexed at his sides and his eyes glittered like flawed diamonds, a black carbon core corrupting their brilliance. A peel of raucous male laughter coming from the pavilion drew his attention and he turned in its direction.

Inside, Watt sat on his throne, his lower leg padded thick and stiffly bound to a board. Immediately the tension drained from Ash. Of course Watt wouldn't be with Rhiannon. He couldn't even follow her on that leg. Watt's ever-present coterie of friends was with him. They were arguing over something. When the company saw Ash, several flushed guiltily, except for St. John who grinned like an evil gargoyle, winked at his fellows, and clapped Ash on the back.

Ash was in no mood to play St. John's cat's-paw. Or to entertain and charm. He looked around for Rhiannon. She was not there. She must have gone home, though it was odd she'd left without Edith.

"Gads, I'm glad you're here, Merrick! *You* of all people must know the song." St. John laid his arm over Ash's shoulders. "Popular a few years back. I heard it in the Highlands, matter of fact."

Phillip looked away, his face turning dusky red.

"We know the front part but can't figure out quite how the bloody thing ends," St. John went on. "Here. Tell us."

Ash narrowed his eyes on the group. One of them tittered and hid his lips behind his palm. Another's eyes went wide as he struggled to contain his amusement, and suddenly Ash knew the song they'd been singing. It had been popular some years back, soon after the incident that had inspired it. Ash's mouth went dry.

"It's a thing called 'The Ride of the Demon Brood.'" St. John smiled.

Ash struggled for composure. He'd disparaged these men for being naive and unaware. God, how the fates must be laughing at him. He'd assumed that here, in this tiny outpost in nowhere, here at least he would escape his notoriety. With empty eyes he gazed at St.

John's puckish countenance. He wouldn't give him the pleasure of seeing how well he'd scored, how sharp the knife, how raw the wound. He was far better at hiding pain than this man could imagine.

And as far as the embarrassment St. John obviously hoped to provoke in Ash if St. John thought some antique ballad could bring shame to a name that had no understanding of the concept . . . the idea wrung a laugh from Ash's throat, startling St. John.

"Why, certainly," he declared hoarsely. "What lines were you having trouble with?"

The other men had sobered and were regarding Ash warily.

"No one recalls?" Ash asked lightly. How to tell them. Part of him wanted to explain, to insist they believe him if he claimed the ballad a lie, a piece of propaganda, a hideous hyperbole of the truth. But what difference? His past had taught him that people wanted to believe the worst. So be it.

"Then let us recap. The story goes like this: In order to save her brothers' lives, a Scottish lassie must prevent the ragged remnants of her clan from hanging the worthless youngest son of the Demon Earl.

"The lad is accused of raping a novitiate and the clan's call for his blood is well justified. But the poor girl's brothers languish in London awaiting trial for their part in the uprising of forty-five." Ash grinned savagely.

Raine hadn't raped that girl. Ash had never asked but he didn't need to, he knew his brother. He looked around at the rapacious faces. They hung on every word, unhappily transfixed by the sad, sordid tale.

"I swear I have told this story so often I have managed to encapsulate the entire tale in a fifth the time it takes to sing the damned thing!"

His sweeping gaze caught and held each man present. They squirmed uncomfortably.

"Let's see, where was I? Oh, yes. Our pitiful heroine. Eight? Ten years old? And all this drama to contend with. The thing of it is, the thing that breaks the heart, is this: That very night while her father is away pleading for his sons' lives the girl's mother has died in childbirth.

"Now, if her clansmen kill the English Demon Earl's cub she can kiss adieu to any hope that King George will be merciful and free her brothers. Is it any wonder she makes such an effort to halt the boy's lynching even though he is her enemy?"

In his mind's eye he could still see that raggedy girl-child, her thin white arms wrapped tightly about Raine's throat, her gold hair streaming down her night-gown, her bare feet sunk in the ice- and mud-rutted road. He wanted to tell them that she'd been the only spot of mercy in a night black with vengeance and retribution. That he'd ached even then for that child. That he'd regretted what had happened.

But they wouldn't understand the choices he'd made, they'd all made, all the actors on that cold, winter stage. They wouldn't believe him and he wouldn't allow anyone to dine on his grief.

He continued. "Well, the lass prevents the bloody deed by flinging her arms around the bound boy, shielding him with her own wee body—and I say the tale would have been a sight more interesting if the girl had been sixteen rather than ten but then Highlanders are an odd breed. Anyway, while thus, the Demon Earl himself rides up, a hundred redcoats with him. At his side are his devilish eldest son and, behind, watching, the little black-haired witch who is his daughter."

"Aye, that's the spot we'd gotten to," a slurred voice called from the shadows.

"Is it?" Ash queried, fighting the revulsion threatening to overwhelm him. He would not succumb. Not in front of St. John and some of these others.

A few of them shuffled, miserably wishing to be elsewhere but held captive by his recital of the old tragedy.

"Go on," St. John urged and then added, "if you've the guts."

"Allow me to satisfy your . . . thirst for knowledge. I will recite," Ash said, shifting a leg forward, placing one hand on his hip, and spreading the other across his chest. His heart pumped dully beneath his palm.

The theatrical stance, the melodramatic timbre of Ash's voice mocked the listeners, openly chastising their prurient fascination; and they resented it. They'd counted him a friend and none looked more aggrieved at his defection than Phillip. Ash began to recite:

With rapier drawn, the eldest son
Dragged his brother up before him.
And brandishing his blade, death he gave
To the men who barred his way.

Blood bloomed thick on the hoary ground
As Scotsmen were mowed down.

Like a sickle cuts through wheat,
They died as one, the clan complete.

When all about had silent grown
The laird's young orphaned daughter moaned.
And the Demon Earl kneed his stallion near
And bending low, lent his ear.

"Why saved you my worthless son from death?"
He queried low, beneath his breath.
"To save my brothers," she replied.
"Whom George would kill if your son were to die."

The Demon Earl then laughed,
A sound so wicked, the redcoats gasped.
"John of McClairen's head now sits on a pike,
Set above Temple Bar last night."

The words clogged his throat, damning and true yet a truth without honesty. The ballad did not tell how sickened he'd been by his act, how savagely the clan had beaten Raine, the number of soldiers who died in the confrontation.

"Do you want the rest?" he asked, praying they would say no. "Some versions tag on a rather tiresome denouement."

"Is the song about you?" Phillip whispered. "Is it true?"

"True?" Ash asked. Would they believe him if he said no? He wouldn't risk being doubly hurt by his recitation. "Dear me, no. I can attest to the fact that my father is no demon. All too human, just lately evincing signs of gout—"

"Did it happen that way?" John Fortnum's honest, homely face was etched with sadness.

"Yes." His anger died on seeing the shocked misery of the listeners, leaving behind only self-disgust. They'd not known what they were doing. He had. He'd punished them for his own past.

"Rhiannon will be so hurt," John murmured. "She thinks you're such a nice gentleman."

She was worth any ten of them. And they didn't know it. They had no idea they harbored a refugee. Good, obedient Rhiannon Russell. Willing to trade her freedom for sanctuary. Yet beneath that dutiful exterior lay a core of tempered metal, forged by war and its aftermath. But never tested. Hidden here, instead. Like a Spanish blade that is packed in wool and tucked away in an attic chest. He turned, suddenly exhausted, and started to leave.

"Best she didn't stay to hear this," Phillip said mournfully. "Best thing she went off to collect flowers."

Rhiannon was *alone* in the woods? Ash wheeled around. He strode back to Phillip's chair, grabbing him by his shirt and hefting him half out of his seat. "What did you say?"

"Lemme go," Phillip cried. "Don't mind tellin' you you're disappointin' to me. First I find out you're some sort of a demon-spawned murderer and now you're being flat-out offensive." He batted ineffectually at Ash's hands.

Ash shook him. "Didn't she go home?"

"Course, not! She's Queen of the May. Went to pluck posies in the forest—"

With an inarticulate sound, Ash dropped Phillip back in his seat. Rhiannon was alone in the woods after someone had flung a knife at her but a few days earlier. Without another word, he left.

Chapter 14

*I*t was too nice a night to go home, and there was no one to go home with, but most important Rhiannon didn't know which way home was. The basket hanging from her arm banged against her hip as she walked. Only weak moonlight illuminated the forest floor, and a rising, drifting mist obscured any familiar landmarks.

Rhiannon hesitated and drew to a halt. Perhaps she should have stayed in the square and found someone to help her take Edith home. But she was Queen of the May, Virgin Queen of the May, and the Virgin Queen of the May always, *always*, spent Beltaine night gathering hawthorn flowers for her May Day coronet.

Of course, the Queen of the May also always went into the woods knowing that the King of the May would be in hot pursuit. Traditionally the Queen then spent the night fending off the King's advances so that the next day when she was crowned with those pure, white hawthorn blooms the knowledge that she was just as pure kept her from blushing. And that was important.

Wasn't it?

Not that Phillip had ever pursued too hotly or pushed too heavily. He was a gentleman, after all.

But then again, in past years when they had been king and queen, they had not been betrothed. Tonight Phillip might have pressed his suit and she, bedeviled by unfamiliar urges, might have been receptive. But then he'd gone and broken his ankle.

She gazed glumly down. Unfortunately, just because the King could not fulfill his role, did not mean she was exonerated of *her* obligations. And, by the Virgin, hadn't she done a ripping good job of it? Over a hundred damn flowers filled her basket.

Realizing her profanity, Rhiannon frowned. She was a good, decent young lady. She had been ever since she'd come to Fair Badden. But lately she didn't feel very "good."

She didn't understand what was happening to her. She seemed to always be edgy and irritable. The constant need to be "good" had begun to chaff—even with Edith Fraiser. Only with Ash Merrick did she feel truly at ease.

Perhaps it was because she owed him nothing, no debt of gratitude, no unspoken vow of obedience. Not that she didn't *love* her life here, and Edith Fraiser, and all her friends, but sometimes it was hard to discern between love and obligation. She was more . . . natural in Ash's company.

And more likely to do abominably stupid things.

With a groan, Rhiannon closed her eyes. She would

never have believed herself capable of such outrageous
behavior. Ash Merrick had always treated her with gentlemanly courtesy—even in his kiss. In return she'd had
him hunted, tied, and brought before her like some
criminal. Then she'd proceeded to fall over in a
drunken stupor. How he must loathe her.

She hastened forward as though she could outdis-
tance her memory, humiliation burning her cheeks.
She'd gone some distance when off to her side came the
muted sounds of dalliance, pleading and private as a
novena.

The sound stopped her as effectively as a stone wall.
She strained her ears, listening, swaying slightly on her
feet, as the effects of Edith's clover wine had not yet
fully left her. She couldn't see a thing. Darkness and
mist combined to hide the figures making those earnest
sounds.

She didn't dare venture farther and risk stumbling
onto a tryst. What if it were Margaret Atherton and—

She wheeled around, her head spinning, and began
retracing her steps. She'd almost reached an ancient,
spreading hawthorn when a muted giggle reached her
ears. Once more, she stumbled to a stop.

More lovers? she wondered in despair. The soft provocative laughter moved off but because of the fog, she
was unable to tell in what direction. With a sound of
frustration she sank to the ground beside the tree's
great trunk.

Stupid Beltaine customs.

She would just have to stay here, until the mist lifted
or the moon grew stronger or some friendly woodland
sprite took pity on her and led her out of this fantastical

world of blue shadows and earthbound clouds, ghostly
luminescence and heady night-born fragrances.

She leaned her head back against the tree trunk and
closed her eyes, letting the magic of the place bewitch
her, creating fantasies she had no right entertaining,
things she'd fought against but now, here, she found
impossible to resist. She forgave herself.

It was Beltaine night, after all, and she was alone and
she did not want to be the Virgin Queen of the Virgin
May. She wanted Ash Merrick.

The moments grew one into another. The moon
rose with benign leisure as images of a dark, angular
face and a hard lean body filled Rhiannon's thoughts.
He was like Oberon, she thought, king of the sylvan
spirits. Aye, Ash Merrick would make a fit sovereign of
dark enchantment. He'd come silently, materializing
from the shadows, a spirit of pure desire conjured into
flesh—

"Rhiannon."

She opened her eyes, gazing at him without surprise.
"*Oberon*," she whispered. Dark forest prince, black
light-devouring hair, and eyes gilded like steel.

He'd been on one knee beside her but now he slowly
straightened. The mist swirled in agitation as he rose,
slipping from his shoulders like a fairy's cloak and leaving a dusting of moon-silvered moisture on his pale
skin.

"Ash."

She sighed, entranced and warmly intoxicated—by
wine and want and by the beauty of him. She smiled
and he stepped forward as though drawn. A light laugh
escaped her with the thought that she might draw him

with her smile. But she did not believe it and her smile turned sad.

"You're safe," he said.

"I'd thought so," she answered, not yet willing to cede her dreams to reality. As long as they stayed here in this little island surrounded by mist and magic he was hers. And wasn't that what Beltaine was at its core? A night of abandonment . . . to dreams and wishes, wants and hopes? And she had never before taken advantage of its magic. She deserved one Beltaine night.

"I'd thought I was safe," she murmured again. "But now, I'm not so sure."

He tilted his head and the movement placed his face in shadows so that when he spoke his voice seemed disembodied, carrying through the moisture-laden air with startling intimacy. "Why is that?"

"You're here and so too am I and I doubt much whether that is a safe thing," she answered simply.

She heard him catch his breath. "Do you fear I would hurt you?"

"Never."

A short telling pause. "Unwise, little Titania."

Titania. Oberon's queen. He might have read her thoughts.

"Unwise for whom?" she asked gazing into the dark shadows that hid his expression.

"Exactly."

His shirt rose and fell in deep, increasing measure but in no other way did he move. Intuitively she knew he would not make a gesture nor say a word, that he was forcing her to decide what next happened.

Two days hence and she would be married and belong to another. Two nights hence and he would leave.

It was Beltaine, she told herself with frantic insistence. Beltaine existed apart from the rest of the year. Its revelries were above the laws governing the rest of the days and weeks. No one was held accountable for what they did on Beltaine night.

The rest of her life she would be another's but not tonight.

She wet her lips with the tip of tongue, her fear of his rejection nearly paralyzing her, her mouth dry. She didn't know what to say, how to win him and he stood so silently, an attitude of fearful expectancy about him.

Instinctively and utterly without design she leaned forward, her head lifted, and she raised one hand, palm up, in supplication. "Please."

She saw a light shudder pass through his body.

"Please, Ash."

Abruptly, as though some cord binding him had suddenly been severed, he surged forward and dropped heavily to his knees beside her. Roughly, he pulled her up and into his arms. His mouth fell on hers with undisguised urgency. He bent her over his arm, holding her there.

With a sob she wrapped her arms around his broad shoulders, holding fiercely to him. He rained kisses on her mouth and cheeks, hungry kisses, desperate kisses, kisses long denied and passionate. His free hand moved, roving over her body in trembling haste, as though collecting the measure of her, the feel and form of her—a blind man learning to see.

She cupped his jaw between her hands, hoarding each sensation—the rasp of his beard against her palms, the silky coolness of his hair between her fingers, the hard angle of his jaw.

His tongue moved insistently against the seam of her lips. She opened her mouth and the warm tip delved deep within. Her head spun.

Her hands skated down his strong throat to his collarbone and beneath the loose shirt to his heated flesh. Sinful, satiny skin. She wanted more, she wanted to arch her body against his naked flesh like a cat.

She pulled at his shirt until he became aware of what she wanted. He broke off the kiss. Her head fell back into the lee of his arm. He stared down at her.

"We're near a place where there is no return," he said, his breathing ragged. "I am not a nice man, Rhiannon. I've little honor and less restraint. This is the extent of both noble traits. From here out I will take whatever I can, whatever portion you'll allow even knowing it was never meant to be mine."

His face was set, and his words were brutal and honest but she didn't want to listen, hear, or heed them. She touched his cheek. He turned his head and pressed a hot kiss against her palm.

"It's Beltaine night," she whispered hoarsely. "Nothing we do tonight counts against the dawn."

For one long second he looked down at her and she thought she saw a wound within their silvered depths. He smiled with terrible resignation. She opened her lips to ask him why, but he set his finger against her mouth and hushed her, easing her down onto her back and straightening up on his knees. With one smooth, economical movement he grasped the edge of his shirt and peeled it from his body. She stared in awe at the masculine beauty he revealed.

The moonlight outlined the hard ladder of his ribs and played with intimate sensuality over the muscles of his chest. Dark hair covered his breastbone in a triangle and more dark hair grew low on his ridged and taut stomach, disappearing beneath the waistband of his breeches.

His arms were long, the biceps well developed, his wrists supple and powerful beneath their scars.

Slowly, his eyes never leaving hers, he put one hand then the other alongside her hips, tipping over the basket of hawthorn blooms as he did so and scattering the shadowed ground with white petals. He lowered himself until his chest just brushed against her.

"Nothing counts," he whispered hoarsely and then his mouth claimed hers.

He hadn't lied to her. There was nothing of restraint or composure in his actions, nothing courtly or obsequious in his manner. He quite simply, quite ruthlessly lay siege to her senses.

One arm snaked beneath her, hauling her up against him as the other hand reached between them and jerked her bodice down, exposing her breasts. He lifted his head, something feral and possessive in the gaze that met hers. She should have been afraid of his ill-contained violence, but she wasn't. She drew a deep shuddering breath and her breasts grazed his chest.

He looked down at the dark puckered tips, smiled, lowered his head, and licked a nipple.

She gasped, embarrassed and panicked by the unfamiliar sensations that shot through her. She grabbed handfuls of his long dark hair in her hands, trying to pull him back. He ignored her, taking the hard nub deep into his mouth, until it grazed the back of his tongue. He drew hard on it, suckling her with devastating deliberation.

Her gasp turned into a moan. Sensation after sensation assaulted her untried body, pulled chords of response from her nipple to a point between her legs. Her fingers loosened in his hair. Her back arched. With a sob, she silently offered more of what he'd so roughly taken.

The sound seemed to set a spur of need through him. His hands traveled down over her quivering belly to the waistband of her skirts. He grasped bunches of the cheap material, rucked it high above her thighs, all the while plying her breasts with his attentions, dazing her with physical sensations she'd never imagined existed.

Dimly she became aware of cool night air tickling her thighs and whispering gently over the down-covered vee at their apex. Reality spun into focus with a shattering jolt. She snatched her hand down to cover herself.

He grabbed her wrist, easily pulling it up and away and pinning it beside her face.

"Ash—"

His lips found hers. His tongue plied the interior of her mouth with deep, rich strokes. He nudged his knee between her legs. Reflexively, she clamped them together.

He would have none of it. He forced his knee between her legs, spreading them apart, and at the same time she felt his fingers there, at the very entrance of her body. Mortification brought a strangled sound to her throat.

"It doesn't count," he muttered against her lips. His tone was dazed and dark and bitter and lost, but his mouth was sweet and pleading and tender.

Gently he caressed her mound until he found the sleekness beneath. She jerked, but the movement only moved his fingers deeper into that nether cleft. The trembling that had begun deep within her spread and centered there. She moaned as he rubbed and fondled her.

Her legs went lax with the exquisite sensations he roused. He cupped her mound, his callused palm pressing tight against her as his fingers gently eased into her very body, stretching, testing—driving her mad. She had no idea her body could be played like an instrument, that so much pleasure could center in as small a nubbin as the one that Ash caressed with such mind-wrecking genius.

And it wasn't enough. She shuddered with the unsatisfied craving he'd inspired. Her hips lifted, instinctively trying to force a deeper contact.

He stopped. She sobbed and he covered her mouth with his own, drinking her need as though it was an opiate. Then the heel of his hand moved against her, building the sensations all over again, carrying her toward the brink of that unnamable place. Dimly, she heard her own ragged breathing. Her eyelids fluttered, shutting out the night sky above—

He stopped again. She sobbed in frustration, clutching at him.

"Aye, *daor*. Want and want more and then maybe you'll begin to know my own desire." His fingers moved deep within, his palm rubbing quicker and quicker. There. Nearly . . . almost . . . !

Gratification exploded within her, bringing with it crescendo after crescendo of pure, physical pleasure. Her back arched, pulled taut by her crisis, her limbs went rigid, her hands clutched into fists. And then it was over, the tension seeping from her, leaving her sated and spent.

She felt him ease his fingers from her. Weak and shaken, she opened her eyes. A crooked smile twisted his sensual mouth. A mouth she could not for the life of her look at without wanting to kiss.

"It's all right, Rhiannon." His voice was soft, gentle. "It truly didn't count. You're a virgin still."

She barely heard him. Dear God, she must truly be depraved. Because simply looking at him, the darkness and light molding to his hard body, the moonlight trapped in his dark-lashed eyes, caused desire to pool anew in her breasts and lips and between her legs. She struggled up, heedless of the cool air on her naked breasts or her hair tumbling down her back. Her eyes riveted on the bemused expression that was slowly replacing the gentle mocking one he'd worn.

She stretched out her hand and touched his throat. The skin was hot and damp beneath her fingertips—as though he'd exerted himself in some arduous test. Her touch moved slowly downward. His muscles tightened reflexively beneath it. She covered his heart with her palm, her hand riding the heavy rise and fall of his chest.

She *needed* him. A piece of the heart he held so carefully apart. Once again she had no words for what she wanted or why, having never allowed sentient thought to frame the words.

"Please, Ash."

A hoarse sound, brief and heartbreaking. Anger or regret? She could not say. But then, without a word, he swept her into his arms and snatched his cape from the ground. He rose and carried her out from under the dark moon shadows cast by the hawthorn's boughs. She wrapped her arms around his throat and rested her cheek against his chest and listened to the deep, even beat of his pulse.

He carried her out into a grassy clearing bathed wholly in soft light. He spread his cloak and laid her gently down. With unconscious grace, he lowered himself beside her.

"Can something that does not exist be killed?" he asked her, gently stroking the tangled hair from her brow.

"I don't understand," she murmured. His fingers moved lower, brushing over her breasts. The tips budded beneath his teasing. She could not think when he touched her like this. But hadn't that been her goal this night? Not to think? Hadn't she told him that?

"Look there," he said in a low ragged voice, sweeping his arm out over the moon-bathed field. "If I am Oberon, then this is my dawn. This is my moontide noon, and here . . . it counts." He said the last savagely, intently.

Something elemental and vital seized at her emotions, demanded recognition, but then he rolled his hips into hers, driving all thought from her mind.

His member bulged against her mound, provocative and erotic. He rocked his hips against her, and desire, so lately sated, bloomed again, this time ripe and mature. She gasped in startled pleasure. He met her gaze as he bunched her skirts about her waist and gripped her thighs, moving them apart. Something hard and masculine touched her center.

His gaze did not release hers. His mouth was tense

and hard, his eyes gleaming as he held himself still, letting her accustom herself to that part of him. She moved and the thick knob rubbed deliciously against her, dragging little moans from her.

Helplessly, she pulled his head down to hers and opened her mouth, hungry for his kiss. Wine. Cinnamon. Heat. Her head spun and whirled, her senses flashed and floated. She wanted to be absorbed into his hard body, to meld herself with his strength, burn with the passion she sensed he trembled on the brink of unleashing.

He slid his hands behind her knees and lifted them over his hips, poised in the very entrance to her. Then he slipped his palms beneath her buttocks, effortlessly lifting her. His erection rubbed wet and silky between the soft folds. She squirmed, her breath hitching in her throat at the promised pleasure.

He closed his eyes. His lips curled back from his teeth, clenched tightly together. She watched him, wanting more, wanting all of him.

"Please, Ash."

Moisture beaded his brow. His skin was dusky, his eyes savage.

"Moonlight doesn't make this any more real, make it count for anything more," he said. "It's madness to want things you can't afford, and I can't afford you." His words tumbled out in a rush, violent and inarticulate. He dropped his head and kissed her again, deeply, passionately before lifting his head. She returned it desperately, uncertain why he'd stopped, what she'd done.

"I want you, Ash. I *need* you. *Please* want me."

"Need." His eyes were dazed. He shook his head.

He gripped her hips and pushed into her, stretching

her. Impossibly big, impossibly hard. His expression was taut, his eyes lost in the shadows created by thick lashes. His hair fell in a black unkempt mane about his throat. Sweat gleamed on his bunched shoulder muscles and straining biceps. Her fingers dug deeply into his trembling arms, trying to find purchase against the torrent of sensation buffeting her.

"No going back," he whispered hoarsely. "No second thoughts. Open your legs wider. Yes. There."

A sharp, brief pain. She gasped. He grated out a sound against the back of his teeth, a curse or a prayer.

He filled her, deeply and utterly, and held still, his arms faintly trembling, sweat coating his chest. Slowly, pleasure returned, then more spiraling waves of pleasure. Nothing had ever felt so good. He moved. A rich, thick slide of silken steel. He retreated. Again. A hard, slow thrust.

Her world spun with heady gratification. Instinctively she met the next thrust. And the next.

"Yes," he breathed. "Yes."

He rocked into her and she clung to him, riding the increasing tempo of his thrusts.

"Slowly, *eun*. Easy."

But it wasn't easy! It was hard, passionate work. Her heartbeat thundered. She panted. Struggling to reach that point again, she whimpered as it danced just beyond her reach. He grasped her buttocks, driving deeper.

"*Thoir dhomh*," he demanded. *Give to me.* "*Gabh, me eun.*"

There. There. And there. Light and dark careened and splintered as pulse after pulse of exquisite, wrenching pleasure beat through her, in her, to her very core. She sobbed with the exquisite release of it.

Then his arms clamped tighter about her. Again he drove into her body. His head snapped back and he lifted himself up on his arms. His hips ground against her own. A deep, body-wrenching shudder racked through him.

And when it was over, his head fell against her damp throat, his breathing harsh in her ear.

"Damn the dawn," he ground out in a thick, dazed voice. "Damn the bloody dawn."

Chapter 15

*B*eltaine night slipped away, its shadows replaced by the bright raucous colors of sunrise. The freshening wind whipped color in the wan cheeks of maids and boys for whom a night of revelry was no excuse for sloth. By noon even the privileged had awoke, emerging to resume the business of celebration. By midday most of Fair Badden had once again congregated in the town square around the gaily decorated maypole, waiting for the next round of activities.

Not all, however. At the Fraiser's house, Ash Merrick sat at the long, scarred kitchen table, a mug of milk cupped between hands that unaccountably trembled. He grimaced at the white liquid.

Milk, for God's sake. He really had forgotten who he was. Last night he'd carried Rhiannon's slumbering form back to her room and left before Edith Fraiser scurried back to find Rhiannon's bed empty. It was a small enough act of kindness and one he owed her after having taken her maidenhead on the day before the eve of her wedding.

He drew his hand across his face. He hadn't intended to take her.

Or had he? He still couldn't believe he'd succumbed to the misguided impulse to find her and keep her safe from predators—two-footed as well as four. He'd found her all right. Half lying against a tree, her head thrown back, and her long, delicious throat arched as if for a lover's kiss.

But it hadn't been the sweet abandonment of her pose, or the swell of unbound breasts, or even the length of exposed thigh that he had been incapable of resisting. No, 'twas her feet that had overset every last shred of decency in him.

Bare and elegant, long and slender, they'd emerged from beneath the garishly decorated milkmaid's skirt. Though the pink soles of her feet were stained with grass and dirt, the nails of each small toe were nonetheless clean, glinting in the moonlight like abalone shells.

He would have bet his last penny that not one other of Fair Badden's young ladies pretending to be simple country lassies had gone unshod. Only Rhiannon Russell had kicked off her shoes and felt the grass springing wet and fresh between her toes. The hint of wildness, the suggestion of a sybarite waiting to explore a sensual world, had filled him with lust.

He'd wanted her more in that moment than he'd ever wanted anything before. He wanted to be the lover she arched her neck for. Every other consideration had evaporated before that sudden, single-minded intent.

So he'd set his mouth to the base of her throat and

felt the pulse quiver like a wild bird in a trapper's palm, sealing their fate. Because once he'd touched her, there had been no turning back. Whatever brief prick of conscience had begged him not to deflower a virgin before her marriage had been devastated by the answering ardor of her mouth. Her strong young body had surged upward to meet him with beautiful abandon, wrecking his tepid scruples, a battering ram destroying a straw hut.

His futile attempt to demonstrate his self-control had never been more than a bluff. She'd only to whisper "please" for every other consideration to burn to cinders before their cumulative need.

She'd been more honest than he, he thought with a wry smile. For at least she'd known that their pleasuring of each other had been a night-bred thing. Not real. He closed his eyes. She'd said it wasn't real. He must remember that.

Indeed, morning would doubtless erase the easy truce she'd made with her conscience. Now it was time to pay. One always paid.

She would be filled with condemnation, as well she should be, for on her wedding night there would be questions, and Rhiannon, honest, damnable Rhiannon, would answer them and ruin herself in the process.

He scraped his hair back from his eyes and stared out of the kitchen window. Rhiannon's big bitch, Stella, lay idly regarding a rabbit munching Edith Fraiser's comfrey plants. Ash watched her, remembering Rhiannon tenderly stroking the useless monster's ears. Smiling. Relaxed and happy. She should always be thus. His hands tightened around the mug.

He would have to stay until after Watt had married

her. Because though Ash could offer Rhiannon nothing of himself—having nothing worth offering, not even the decency to resist the bride of a man who considered him a hero—at least he could offer her the protection that fear inspired. That, at least, was one thing he owned: the ability to instill fear. Today he would find opportunity to explain to Phillip in very clear, very explicit terms just how dangerous renouncing Rhiannon Russell would prove—

"Ash."

He closed his eyes a second. He should have known she wouldn't avoid him, that she would confront her seducer rather than avoid him. These people didn't understand her at all. They did not understand that though she had been subdued by wounds garnered at Culloden, it was not in her nature to be subdued. He plastered a suitable smile on his face—nothing too intimate, nothing too cavalier. The smile of a lover who didn't count. He looked around.

Her satiny skin appeared more delicate than he remembered, and the sunlight revealed violet-tinted stains beneath her eyes. They looked greener today, her hair darker.

"Rhiannon. Miss Russell." He held up his hand, offering her the choice of what she would have him call her.

She frowned and skirted the room, moving to the window and a ceramic vase filled with wild anemones. She touched the rosy petal delicately—like she'd touched him last night.

"This is so hard," she murmured.

In profile her hazel eyes looked glassine and brilliant. Tears? Yes. Of course there'd be tears. He steeled himself because there was nothing else he could do.

"It was wrong."

"Yes." Wrong, right—when had either made any difference to him? He gazed at her, tired beyond endurance. "It was wrong."

"I'll make him a good wife, you know." She glanced sideways, to see whether she'd convinced him. "I will. I know what we did last night was a sin and I know that you are Phillip's friend—" God help him before he laughed or sobbed, the pretty naive wench. Did she not understand even yet? "But I must ask you . . . no, I must beg you, please do not tell him."

He exhaled in relief, tension draining from his body. Good. She'd resolved to hold her tongue, the only thing she could do if there were any chance at all she would escape last night without consequence. She was still intent on marrying Phillip and that was just as it should be—and this odd sense of betrayal? Nothing.

Phillip could give her so many things and he could only give her—*passion*. Why, in some twisted greedy corner of his heart, did that seem to him enough when he knew, rationally, logically, it was not? "Yes. I mean, no. I won't."

"Swear it." A pleading note softened the demand.

"I swear."

She turned toward him, the movement swinging the soft waves of her unbound hair to settle over her shoulder. It was like a cloud of silk, he remembered. But why unbound? Ah yes, she was Queen of the May.

"You don't know Phillip as I do and I . . . it's not that I think you would purposefully hurt him but if you felt bound by honor to tell him he would feel obligated to call you out. He mustn't be hurt." She held out a hand in an impulsive gesture of appeal.

"Of course."

"You must understand, it's best if I—"

"You don't need to say another word," he broke in softly, unable to listen to more.

"Thank you." Her smile was sad and grateful. After what he'd done to her, she gifted him with that wholly beautiful smile because—his eyes widened in shocked recognition—because she believed that he felt the same. That he *cared* about Phillip Watt! *Because he was a gentleman.*

The enormous irony of it, her horrendous mistake, hit him like a blow. He looked away.

Enough of this, he thought, suddenly savage. *I'm sick to death of carrying the weight of her good opinion.*

He would tell her he didn't give a damn about cuckolding her betrothed. He'd tried to tell her of his true nature last night. Perhaps he should try again, disabuse her of her provincial notions regarding his gentlemanliness, show her just whom she'd lain beneath last night.

He'd only cared about one thing: spending himself between her thighs. He still only cared about one thing, as evidenced by the hardening of his loins as he looked at her.

Yet, somehow, this little thing—her wrong-headed belief that he would act chivalrously, that he was, in fact, better than he was—kept him from speaking.

"You are hurting," she said. She moved from the window, slowly diminishing the space between them. He held his breath, willing her to stay put. She didn't. "I can see it in your eyes. I am so sorry."

Why was she saying this? What was she doing to him?

"It was . . ." Whatever she'd been about to say died on her lips. A sad, lost smile gently turned the corners of her mouth, like an echo of innocence. "Oh, Ash. I know it is wrong, more wrong than anything I have ever done, but I cannot regret last night."

Utterly destroying him.

"I will keep the memory of it," she went on inexorably, softly singing her way to the very core of him with her lethal words. "It may seem to me now a meager sort of thing, a memory, but in years to come I am sure it will— Please," she moved a step closer. Uncertainty clouded her expression, a quavering note of abashment colored her voice. "Please, won't you kiss me good-bye?"

He stared at her, unable to speak.

She must have taken his silence for acquiescence. Hesitantly she rose on her tiptoes and brushed her mouth over his. But in forming the word "good-bye" her lips lingered an instant too long. Long enough for the stunned paralysis to leave his limbs, long enough for him to snake his arm around her supple waist and pull her closer, deepening the kiss into something darker, stirring . . . infinitely more satisfying.

She kissed so sweetly. So tantalizingly. Her mouth was fruit, delicious and succulent, and he was starving. Had been starving for years. Hungrily he traced her lips with the tip of his tongue, slipping into the sleek, moist interior. Her tongue fluttered against his and he stroked it lavishly, deeply.

With a sigh of defeat, she wrapped her arms around his shoulders, tipped back her head, and surrendered.

She kissed him—Lord, how she kissed him—with all the longing of a tragic, final leave-taking: yearningly, tenderly, despairingly. He cupped her delicately molded skull between his palms, combing back her silky, dense hair, mouthing soft, incoherent words of ravishment and seduction. Desire coiled and sprang, confounding him with its power.

She withdrew from the kiss and he followed her retreat. He lifted his free hand and rubbed the pad of his thumb back and forth against her lower lip. His body shuddered with the restraint he exercised. "Rhiannon . . ."

With a sudden, hopeless sound she dropped her hands and pushed against his chest. She broke free of his embrace and twirled. He heard the swish of her hem, the rapid tattoo of her fleeing shoes, and the breathy echo of her sobbed "Good-bye." By the time he looked she'd disappeared through the kitchen door.

He slumped against the table, groping for support, realizing what she thought. She thought him her lover, her tender, considerate companion in guilt and that kiss had been his severance pay, a memento. His lips curled back.

Absurd. Horrifyingly naive. Unendurably so.

He'd bedded the wench. He'd had what he'd wanted. It was past time he remembered why he was here and where he was going. He should be in London, at the gaming tables, working for Raine's release, not here, lusting after some wench who had a wrongheaded notion regarding his nobility.

His fists clenched at his side, the thick scar tissue glistened like white. He stared about the kitchen as if looking for a means of escape.

He must think of Raine. He'd promised his mother he would keep him safe, and right now he didn't even know whether Raine was alive. Abruptly, Ash swept the mug of milk from the table, shattering it. Like the reproachful stain of a maiden's lost virtue, the sweet milk spread across the tiles and seeped into the earth between. Tainted. Lost. Gone.

He strode from the kitchen, out into the backyard, and to the stable, calling for the boy to saddle his horse.

The town square hummed with drowsy activity, the bright streamers bedecking several pink-cheeked lads and lassies attesting to the fact that the maypole dance had recently ended. Watt and his cronies had gathered around a square table in front of The Ploughman.

Good, Ash thought. With very little effort he should be able to repair the damage done by his ill-advised recitation and St. John's gossip. They were a provincial, gullible lot.

A vague sense of self-disgust crawled up Ash's throat. He swallowed it down, like he had every bit of vileness in his life, accepting it whole. Watt wanted to like him.

Deliberately he forced his gaze past Rhiannon, sitting on the ground beside Watt, fussing over his splintered leg. Watt covered her hand with his great tanned paw, leaning over to speak earnestly. They were absorbed in each other, deaf to all others, but Ash's ears were damnably acute.

". . . of course you must ride this afternoon, Rhiannon," Phillip was saying. "I refuse to allow you to stay back because of my injury. Besides, Father arranged this hunt particularly for you. Really, Rhiannon, you must go. I insist on it!"

She dashed the back of her free hand across her cheeks, ridding herself of tears. Ash clamped down on his insane impulse to snatch her up into his arms and kiss the tears from her face.

"—really are too kind, Phillip," she answered. "I don't deserve you."

Phillip awkwardly patted her cheek. "It's all right. Nerves. A day before our wedding and all."

She colored violently, and pulled her hand from under his. Ash saw the moment in which her honor extinguished her common sense. "Phillip, I have to tell—"

She mustn't do it.

"Watt!" Ash hailed.

Rhiannon glanced up. Her mouth looked bruised.

"Miss Russell." Ash nodded his greeting. "Are you not going to join the delightful game Miss Chapham has arranged?"

He smiled brilliantly. She needed a few lessons in deception. She'd best learn them soon. *Before* she entered Phillip's bed. He swung his glance back to Phillip. The blond giant regarded him sullenly.

"Watt," Ash said, "if you don't take a care to warn visitors of the potency of your village scrumpy, you'll end up with a great line of dunderheaded knaves queuing up before your magistrate trying to account for their idiocy."

The hurt somewhat evaporated from Watt's expression, but the wariness remained.

"I barely recall what type of an ass I made of myself last night," Ash said with winning candor, "but I'm sure it was a large one. I'm liable to lay claim to all sorts of crimes when I'm in that state. And make promises I can't keep and swear allegiance I have no intention of remaining loyal to. Forgive me?"

He ignored the hurt in Rhiannon's eyes. Of course she would think he was addressing her.

"Pay it no mind, Merrick," Phillip said, clapping Ash on the shoulder. "And never mind what was said or sung or . . ." he blundered on, "whatever. Fair Badden's scrumpy has caused the best of us to make ridiculous claims. And," he shot a dark look at St. John, "there are those who will always derive pleasure from carrying tales. Whether true or no."

"You are too kind," Ash murmured.

"Here. Sit by me." Phillip waved Andrew, the innkeeper's boy, to bring another chair. Ash sank into it. Rhiannon scuttled away from him.

"I say, what's that they're playing, Miss Russell?" Ash asked pleasantly, needing an excuse to look at her, to examine just how deep he'd driven the spike.

"Blindman's Bluff," she said, eyes lowered. "Would you care to play?"

He stretched his long legs out in front of him. "Dear me, no. Wouldn't know how."

"But everyone knows Blindman's Bluff," she said.

"Not me," he said. "There was no nursery where I grew up. No playroom. No classroom. Not a nanny or a governess. Only a twisted, misshapen old nurse that worked cheap and was for whatever reason loyal to my mother's family name."

As soon as the words had crossed his lips, he regretted them. Rhiannon had gone still, her face numb.

He glared at her. She'd bewitched him, forced confidences from him that he had not intended to give, brought a ripple of unease to the smooth tableau he'd been working to create. He sought to regain lost ground.

He shook his head. "By Jingo, one must tread carefully about you and your softhearted bride, Watt. I can understand her frailty, being country bred and lacking wisdom in the ways of the world and worldly men." *He must not look at her.* "I didn't mean to suggest I did not play games as a child. We played aplenty."

Desperate games. Feral games. His father had been a master at teaching them.

"Mostly games of chance. Inveterate gamblers, we Merricks. Same with your people I imagine, eh, Watt?"

"Yes. Indeed," Phillip blustered.

"Now, tell me about this Blindman's Bluff. Can one bet on the outcome?"

"I suppose," Phillip said consideringly.

"I'll wager you a shilling to a crown that Margaret Atherton is the first to be caught," he said to Watt, avoiding Rhiannon's eye. There was still something to be taken from Fair Badden. Even if it wasn't the thing he wanted.

Rhiannon rose to her feet. She hesitated, uncertain of whether she ought to stay, but Phillip had forgotten her and Ash would not look at her. She walked away, silently praying her trembling legs would hold her until she'd rounded The Ploughman's corner and found the bench set against its sunny outer wall. Her knees did not betray her but the moment she stepped in front of the homely bench they gave out and she sank down, finally finding a moment of privacy in which to try and sort her wild thoughts and indiscreet heart.

She couldn't stop shivering, a deep shudder that began inside and worked its way out. She knew its source. She'd betrayed Phillip and the guilt of it was eating her from the inside out.

She buried her face in her hands. Tears sprang to her eyes and washed down her hot cheeks and she cursed herself roundly for it. Tears did no good; guilt did less, for neither could call back last night and let her replay those fateful hours. Even if they could, she was not sure she wanted those hours altered.

Except he did.

She saw it in his cool dark eyes this morning in the kitchen and heard it in the veiled warning he'd issued her with his words about "worldly men and naive country lasses." She scrubbed at her eyes and pressed the heels of her hands against her temples trying to think, to make some decision.

Clearly she had to tell Phillip what she'd done or she'd become so shaken by the keeping of this secret that she'd fly apart. Twice now she'd tried and twice Phillip had managed to stymie her. It was almost as if he already knew what she would say and feared it and sought to keep her from telling him. She twisted her fingers in her lap.

Nonsense. It was only her own wishful thinking. How much easier this would be if she could convince herself that Phillip was best off not knowing. And she could, with very little difficulty, convince herself of just that. She knew Phillip had no great love for her, that he'd chosen her as his bride because she was biddable and undemanding. He'd even told her once that his father had quite succinctly pointed out her suitability to be Phillip's wife because she had no aspirations to live anywhere but Fair Badden, no inclinations to travel, and no social ambitions regarding the London season.

And the old man had been right. She and Phillip were perfectly suited. She did not want to leave Fair Badden. It was lovely, quiet, and safe. Just the thought of venturing elsewhere added ripples of panic to her shivers of misery. Out there—bad things happened.

She should have thought of that before she'd risked her future—the lovely, genteel future that even now was still within her grasp—on a night of surrender to her long-buried passionate nature.

Time to bury that nature again. Deeper this time. So deeply that it would finally die, never again to be resurrected.

An involuntary sound of anguish escaped her lips. Unsteadily, she stood up. She couldn't think anymore, each thought circled back onto itself, a snake eating its tail. She felt dazed and frightened. The light glancing off The Ploughman's whitewashed wall dazzled her eyes and she looked away. She mustn't think anymore.

She saw Edith Fraiser moving gingerly across the town square, a thin envelope in her hand. Behind her one of the men held a brace of hounds straining at the leash.

The sight instantly calmed Rhiannon, releasing the poisonous tension coiling within her. *The hunt.* The hunt would clear her thoughts and sweep the confusion from her heart. A race with the wind that would leave behind every vestige of her life, every concern, obligation—and betrayal. Aye. She'd follow the hunt.

*   *   *

Ash flicked the envelope Edith Fraiser had given him beneath his chin as he watched Susan Chapham being blindfolded.

He should be quite pleased. His purse was nearly fifty pounds heavier; he'd reestablished himself amongst these well-fleeced sheep as a harmless lambikins; and he'd kept Rhiannon from running to Phillip in full mea culpa cry before her wedding.

He *was* quite pleased. This feeling of heartsickness was simply the result of too much country. A surfeit of vegetables. Too much sun.

He opened the envelope, and glanced at the signature. It was from Thomas Donne. Ash's interest sharpened as he read. The letter suggested a reason for the attacks on Rhiannon—an improbable conjecture, but a reason nonetheless. He frowned.

It had been his plan to leave soon but because he owed the lass some small part of his consideration he would wait around and play watchdog. All would come right, for then she would once and for all be Phillip Watt's concern.

And if he could not account for the hurtful rhythm of his heartbeat, he did not try.

Chapter 16

"Go on without me. I'll just stay back and enjoy the day," said Ash Merrick from atop the back of his steed.

The two young men he addressed, the last members of the hunting party to mount up, regarded him dubiously. Ash waved them off and watched them go, his smile dissolving. He wasn't about to inform them that for him those years a young man dedicates to refining his hunting skills had been spent in a dungeon.

His gaze picked out Rhiannon Russell's figure. Clad in midnight blue velvet that turned her roan tresses incandescent, she lagged near the rear of the group rather than the front where he would have expected her.

Behind her, Stella darted into a patch of bushes. Rhiannon called out to her. With a crash the hound burst from the tangle of brush, tongue lolling, tail wagging.

Would that all curs be so well favored, Ash thought. The other hounds barked and danced at the end of leashes, waiting for the Master of the Hunt to loose them to the trail, but Rhiannon's dog enjoyed its freedom. And Rhiannon's love.

He frowned and pulled Donne's letter from his waistcoat pocket, scanning the missive for the portion that had made him reconsider leaving:

—if this man in the French islands is, indeed, Miss Russell's long-lost brother, should he die without wife or brat his plantation would revert to his next of kin. Since she is Scottish, Miss Russell would be next in line, even though she is female. We Scots are so barbarously nonpartisan with regard to women, aren't we?

However, should Miss Russell wed one of your Englishmen, her property becomes his. Someone might take exception to this. I think I would make some inquiries about Miss Russell's extended family.

But all this presupposes a brother precipitously restored from the grave and just as precipitously returned, as well as a secret family member plotting from the shadows.

Instead I would look for a potential murderer in Miss Russell's jealous rival or some person harboring a grudge. If Miss Russell has trapped herself a groom by becoming enceinte, I would say look there. Or perhaps the elder Watt cannot abide the thought of a Jacobite daughter yet dares not risk alienating his son by refusing to countenance the marriage?

Now, enlighten me as to whether those rural strumpets know any interesting tricks that have eluded their urban cousins—

Ash refolded the vellum and pocketed it. Interesting. He hadn't realized that the Scots laws governing inheritance were so different from the English. Certainly a molasses-producing plantation would be prize enough to commit murder for.

No wonder Carr wanted to marry Rhiannon.

But as Donne suggested, the tale of the long-lost brother did seem unlikely. Perhaps Rhiannon had beaten out other favorites for the Watt name but he'd seen no show of animosity amongst her friends. He, above all others, knew that Rhiannon had not trapped Watt into marriage by conceiving, and Watt's father had apparently handpicked Rhiannon to be Phillip's wife—

A thought niggled at Ash, impressions, chance phrases. He sifted through them, scowling in concentration. Phillip. Handsome, athletic Phillip. Always surrounded by his boon companions. Gruffly boastful of his romantic conquests. Yet in the month since his arrival not once had they sought out women of easy virture. No one had even suggested it.

If Phillip had not wanted a bride . . . if there was in him something that resisted yet could not be voiced . . . if he feared a wife might expose something he wanted left alone—

Ash shook his head. He was being overly imaginative. These incidents were just what they seemed. Still, the hunt setting with everyone tearing off would present a prime opportunity to manufacture yet another "accident."

He touched his heels to the gelding's side and loped off in the direction of the disappearing hunters.

Rhiannon's heart was not in the hunt. Always before when she'd needed to escape, the hunt offered her the opportunity.

Not today. She reined her horse at the edge of a thick copse of hemlock and watched the others hurdle down the steep embankment after the pack of trumpeting hounds. Absently, she looked for Stella's rangy form and when she could not find her, she smiled wanly.

The dog was a disaster. She'd rather chase squirrels then add her voice to those of her littermates. Three times already today Rhiannon had had to call her from her own doggy pursuits and lead her back to the pack. It was becoming increasingly obvious that no amount of cajoling or scolding was going to turn Stella into a decent gazehound.

Rhiannon nudged her mount forward, riding along the fringe of the woods, listening for the telltale sounds of a dog playing.

The minutes ticked by, becoming half an hour and then an hour. Rhiannon began to grow concerned. The other hunters had long since disappeared from view and the sun's rays slanted across the long forms of oak and larch. Soon it would be dark and Stella would be lost.

Rhiannon lifted herself in the saddle, calling out and

listening. Nothing. She turned the horse back and re-traced her route, certain now that Stella had gone east rather than west as she'd assumed. Her raised voice sharpened with fear when she heard a sudden high-pitched howl.

She moved toward the sound, into a dense tangle of overgrown shrubbery that formed a wall along the forest's edge. She dug her heels into her mare's flanks, but the horse shied from entering.

Another yip dissolved her caution. She set her whip against her mount's rump and the skittish horse gathered its haunches beneath it and plunged into the thicket. Immediately vines and brambles caught and tore at Rhiannon's hair and face. The mare neighed in distress, jumping and lurching in fitful forward motion through the net of bindweed clutching at her legs.

Rhiannon held her arm up, warding off the worst of the nettles and barbs. Fifty yards, and then seventy. Several slashes sliced through her skirts and sleeves. A new fear took hold. Her horse could be blinded by such savage growth.

She reined in. The mare thrashed her head back and forth, fighting the bit in her mouth, frightened by the unseen enemies pulling at her legs. Rhiannon could no longer hear Stella. She searched the area for easier egress. To her left and farther in she made out a patch of light through a low, thin corridor: a deer trail. She pulled her mount's head around, crooning encouragement.

The horse blundered onto the trail, her flanks twitching with excitement, her ears flat against her head. Rhiannon raised herself in the stirrups to see where the trail led. A rabbit darted from beneath the ferns, shooting across her horse's path.

It was too much for Rhiannon's frenzied mount.

The mare bolted, catching Rhiannon unawares and snatching the reins from her hands. Free, the horse raced like a devil fleeing hell. Rhiannon threw herself flat along its outstretched neck, snatching unsuccessfully for the reins streaming along its withers.

Clots of black earth spun from beneath the mare's hooves. Green and gold, light and dark passed by Rhiannon's face in a stampeding blur. Without foothold or handhold, her velvet habit became a slide. She skittered in the polished leather saddle. One sharp turn, a sudden stop, and she would lose her grip. She buried her fingers in the mane, crouched over the mare's withers, and prayed.

A shout ahead. A crash. The thunder of pursuing hooves. Her horse veered, hurtling her forward—

A strong arm snatched her from the saddle. Her back slammed into a hard body, her hips banged into a thigh. She twisted, clutching wildly. The arm around her yanked her up and settled her between hard legs.

Ahead, her horse's low bunched hindquarters disappeared. The black-gloved hand before her drew back on the reins of the horse. She slewed around to face her rescuer knowing, certain, yes . . . Ash.

"I thought you were supposed to be some sort of bleeding Diana!" he shouted angrily.

"What—"

"You! Everyone says you ride like a centaur. I've seen better riders on a costermonger's cart!"

"I lost my reins," she whispered, stunned by his anger.

"Lost your *reins*? Damnation!" His arms tightened around her. "The middle of a poacher's trap is not the place to lose one's reins. Or didn't your equestrian instructor teach you that?"

"Poacher's trap?"

She blinked up at him, confused and disoriented. Heat and power radiated from him, soaked through his shirt, warming her, bracing her.

"Yes. Poacher's trap. The bloody deer run is ringed with razored barbs. If you had made it down the chute—"

His eyes glittered as he stared over her head. His voice was a dangerous thing. Beneath the blue-black shadow of beard his jaw hardened.

"What the hell are you doing out here, anyway?"

"Stella." She remembered suddenly. She pushed at his chest, scrambled to free herself of his implacable grip. "Stella!"

A thready howl answered her call.

"Please!" She grasped his arms. Muscles bunched beneath her fingers. "Please. She's hurt. Can't you hear?"

His gaze locked with hers. Abruptly, he swung her to the ground, one hand still imprisoning her wrists as he followed her.

"I'll go. Wait here. Hold the reins. *Keep* holding the reins."

"Yes. Please. Thank you—"

He'd already gone, moving with catlike grace down the leaf-canopied trail and disappearing into the flat disc of sunlight ahead.

The moments extended in thick, heartbeat-accented measures, one after the other. A branch snapped nearby and a covey of partridge flushed, air trembling beneath their wings as they broke skyward. Rhiannon waited. A high-pitched yelp jerked her to the end of the reins tethering her to Ash's sweat-foamed horse.

"Ash!" His horse snorted at the sharp tone and danced backward. "Ash!"

"Yes."

She peered down the trail and saw a dark masculine figure break from the light and stride forth, carrying a huge animal in his arms. She knotted the reins to a sapling and flew down the trail heedless of Ash's barked order to stay.

She had almost reached them when she saw the blood. It ringed the dog's neck with a crimson collar and streaked her hindquarters. One hind leg dangled awkwardly from Ash's clasp.

"Stella," she whispered.

The dog lifted pain-filled amber eyes and whined. Gingerly Rhiannon stroked the silky head and worked cautious fingers through the sleek coat. Her fingers grew wet with blood.

"What happened?"

"She was in the middle of the trap. Couldn't get out."

"Will she be all right?"

He didn't meet her eye. His own face was flushed, his eyes hot. "Her leg is broken."

She spun around and returned to the tied horse, calling over her shoulder. "We have to get her back. Mrs. Fraiser can set the bone of any man or beast."

Ash followed her. "Mount up, Rhiannon. I'll hand her up to you. Keep her still as possible."

Rhiannon clambered astride. The horse shifted but did not shy when Ash lifted Stella up onto Rhiannon's lap. The dog whimpered and Rhiannon whispered soft comforting words, painfully aware of the dangling leg.

Without a word, Ash took the reins and led the way back up the narrow path. They emerged at the far end of the thicket, a good distance from where Rhiannon had entered. She looked down at Stella. The dog panted shallowly, her eyes half-closed against the pain. Blood stained Rhiannon's skirts.

"How long will it take to bring her to the Fraisers'?" she asked Ash.

"Two hours. Maybe less. I don't want to—"

"Hallo!"

At the sound both Rhiannon and Ash looked up. A pony cart was jostling its way along the forest track toward them. Phillip drove it, his splinted leg resting on the front axle. "Hallo!"

"Thank God. We can rest Stella on the seat beside him." Rhiannon lifted her arm, waving wildly. "Here! Phillip! Here!"

Ash remained watchfully silent as Phillip pulled up beside them, his grin fading to an expression of concern. "What is this?"

"Stella has broken her leg and lost a great deal of blood. Oh, Phillip. You must drive her back to Mrs. Fraiser's."

"Of course," Phillip said, shifting to the side of the cart. Wordlessly, Ash took Stella from Rhiannon and placed her alongside Phillip.

"I'll see her forthwith to the manor," Phillip promised, his big hand on the dog's head. In that moment Rhiannon felt sick with gratitude and affection and guilt. He was such a good man. A decent, kindhearted man. "Rhiannon, you ride along behind me. If Stella grows restive she'll need your voice to calm her."

"Stella won't grow restive. She's lost too much blood," Ash said, breaking his silence. "Don't get down, Rhiannon. You're staying with me."

Rhiannon, in the process of alighting, froze. "Phillip is right. I can help Mrs. Fraiser—"

"No," Ash said, approaching his horse. Before she realized what was happening, he'd grasped the back of the saddle and swung up behind her. One strong arm wrapped around her waist, pulling her tight against him, imprisoning her there. "You won't be going back to Mrs. Fraiser's. Now or in the foreseeable future."

"What the hell is this?" Phillip demanded. Pain and betrayal filled his handsome countenance. "Rhiannon? Is this—is he what you've been trying to tell me? That you and he—? You bastard!" Phillip erupted. "You bloody bastard! I thought you were my friend!"

A cold, acid bath of fear gripped Rhiannon. Stunned beyond coherent thought she twisted in Ash's grip. "Ash, you can't. You can't do this." She tore at the arm imprisoning her. She might as well have been clawing at iron manacles.

"Why are you here, Watt?" Ash's voice, so close to her ear, came deadly and soft. "This isn't the course the hunters followed. The only thing here is a poacher's trap, set to catch a young girl and baited with a tortured dog."

"What?" Rhiannon gasped.

"There's nothing in that trap that would break a dog's leg," Ash went on. "Someone broke her leg on purpose and then twisted it to set the hound howling so that its fond mistress would follow the sound."

"No one would do something so vile!" Phillip declared. "You're mad to suggest it."

"Am I? Why all these accidents? How many times in the past month has Rhiannon nearly been killed? How many times were you there?"

"Rhiannon! You don't believe this madman, do you?"

"No!" she shouted. "Ash, I don't know what you're about, why you're saying these things. You can't mean them. Phillip couldn't have done this. His leg is broken. Only think!"

A low, nasty laugh tickled the hairs by her ear. "So innocent. It has its appeal, I'll admit, but *you* think, Rhiannon. The trap could have been laid a long time ago. A contingency plan, eh, Watt?"

Phillip rose awkwardly. His face suffused with color. "Let her down! You have no right—"

"I have every right and you might be so good as to inform Mrs. Fraiser of such so that she does not set any of your local magistrates after us."

Phillip sank down on the seat. "What do you mean?"

"I have letters naming me Lord Carr's agent, with the legal right to act in his behalf. And as Rhiannon Russell's surrogate and oh-so-legal guardian, I'm exercising those rights. There are new laws, Watt, making it illegal for a woman to wed without her guardian's consent before she reaches the age of twenty-one. I believe Rhiannon is younger."

"No!" Each calm, cold word sounded a death knell to her future, her life. Ash Merrick was snatching it from her. All of her life she had been ripped from those she loved, fled or chased or taken away. It was beginning again. No choices. Simply robbing her of her right to make her own decisions.

Wildly, she twisted in Ash's hold, fighting him. "No!"

"For the love of God, man," Phillip pleaded. "Can't you see she's frantic? Let us go back to Fraiser's. Discuss this. Whatever you and Rhiannon have done—"

"What we have done?" Ash laughed harshly. "I have *had* her, Watt! I've taken her maidenhead. Don't you understand? She's no longer a virgin bride. You won't marry her now. No one would expect you to."

Rhiannon hissed with fury at Ash's betrayal. He'd promised! And he'd not only lied, but was deliberately provoking Phillip, taunting him.

Savagely she wrenched around in Ash's arms, scoring his wrists with her nails. He did not even counter her frantic clawing. There was nothing malleable or soft in him.

"If you are trying to assuage your guilt over abducting her, it's not that easy, Merrick." Phillip's face was pale, white lines bracketing his nostrils, his jaw trembling. "We can still marry. Other brides have not been virgins. Leave her here, Merrick. I assure you, no one will call off the wedding."

"You leave me no choice but to take her," Rhiannon thought she heard Ash say under his breath. His horse danced sideways.

"You cannot simply steal her like this," Phillip said.

She felt more than saw the curl of Ash's lip as he turned his horse away and set his heels to its sides.

"Oh, but I can."

Chapter 17

$\mathcal{L}$ate that afternoon in an unnamed hamlet thirty miles west of Fair Badden, a single horse rode into the yard of the local blacksmith. It carried a dark man riding behind a tousled young woman. The smithy abandoned his bellows, wiping his own hands on his leather apron. He did not like the looks of this pair.

First off, they were quality. Dusty quality, sweat-stained and travel-worn quality, but quality nonetheless. But, it weren't that they were quality alone that set a nerve twitching beneath the smithy's eye. It were that they were quality on the run, and running hard from the looks of them and their barrel-chested, lathered horse.

The girl looked exhausted. The man, a hard and tensile-looking creature, took no note of his companion's condition. He dismounted, leaving the girl sagging in the saddle.

The smithy, a fond father with daughters of his own, moved forward until he saw the sparkle of fury in the girl's bright eyes. A lovers' spat, perhaps, thought the smithy. Perhaps his interference would not be appreciated. Though if his lover had looked at him like the girl glared at the man's back, he'd have looked elsewhere for his sport no matter what the lure of reddish hair and a full bosom.

A glance at the watchful way the dark man waited— limbs balanced just so—added its counsel urging the smithy to mind his own business. A nasty-looking customer, the stranger.

"I need a horse." The man pointed at the roan mare fenced in the yard beside the smithy.

His speech marked him a city man, as did his tight breeches and the pearl blade handle protruding from the folded edge of his boots.

"And a saddle, too. Not a lady's saddle. I'll pay in coin," he said and named a sum far exceeding the worth of either horse or leather, and the smithy, what with all those beloved daughters, abandoned chivalry in the interest of practicality. Daughters liked dresses.

The smithy caught the mare and tied her at the fence before fetching an old saddle from its peg.

"May I get down?" he heard the lass ask. From the stilted sound of her voice and the blood rising in her cheeks, the smithy guessed she disliked making the request.

The man studied her a minute. She lifted her chin defiantly. Proud lass. Foolish lass. The man's mouth tightened but he went to her and without word or warning plucked her from her perch.

"No." Her single word was denial—repudiation and calm, frigid command. "Don't touch me."

The man's narrow face dulled with color but he did not set her down. He swung about, the lass in his arms as stiff as a paste doll.

"You'll go round back there," he said to her. "And you'll come back before the mare's done being saddled."

He set her down, stepping back before she could push him away. She yanked up her heavy skirts and paced off behind the smithy, her hem swishing angrily.

"Yore wife?" the smithy asked, pricked again by the unwelcome call of gallantry.

"Don't think of interfering, friend," the man advised. "It will only get you hurt."

The smithy could fair believe that but still if the lass needed him . . .

The young woman reappeared a minute later and watched while the smithy finished cinching the girth strap. Nothing was revealed on that pretty face. It was as blank as a churchyard angel's. As soon as the saddle was on, the man tied a lead rope to the mare's bridle and called to the young beauty.

For the first time, something other than anger showed on her face. Her eyes shimmered with telling moisture. The man called out again. She bit down on her lip, approaching the mare at a foot-dragging pace.

Once more he swept her up into his arms. Once more she went rigid, a shudder passing through her slight frame. And then, as if against her will, she flung her arms full around the man's neck. With a soft whimper, she pushed her face against his throat. Tears ran down her smooth cheeks. She clung to him like moss to a rock, her body—before so rigid and denying—now malleable and entreating.

The man froze, a slight check no longer than a heartbeat, before disentangling the girl's arms from his throat and lifting her into the saddle. He turned his back on her at once.

All the fight seeped from her posture; a lost and bewildered expression appeared on her face. And when she looked at the man, something bled from her eyes that the smithy recognized from long ago and that mostly from dreams, and troubled dreams at that.

How could the man rebuff this woman?

Then the dark stranger strode past the smithy to mount his own steed. His face was averted from the lady and the smithy saw him close his eyes, clenching them tight, and the smithy knew that the cost of his seeming callousness was immense.

They traveled north throughout the evening. Ash stopped once at a farm and bought some bread and cheese from the timid woman who answered the door.

Rhiannon did not speak. After forging that outrageous tale about someone deliberately maiming Stella and trying to kill her, Ash had made no attempt to speak, either.

For her part, she had no words to say to this . . . devil. He'd taken them in with his polished manners and ready laughter, his easy smile and amiable charm. They'd fed him, and sheltered him, allowing him time to regain his strength, unaware they'd harbored a predator in their midst.

Bitterly, she wondered what he wanted now. She'd already given him what men value most. Perhaps, the acrid thought occurred to her, he'd never considered allowing her to marry Phillip. Perhaps he'd merely taken the opportunity for a profitable holiday, all along planning on taking her to this Lord Carr. Perhaps her infatuation had merely been an agreeable happenstance.

Clearly, he no longer wanted her as his lover. He touched her, yes, but only to assert his strength and her comparative weakness, to show her, she was sure, how easily he could have of her whatever he wished. To frighten her.

He succeeded.

With no reins to clutch, her fingers had grown numb from gripping the rolled edge of the saddle. Her back ached with each step the mare took but she would not ask for mercy. Her thoughts swirled between a dream and waking state.

She had no idea how long he intended to ride. The moon had long since risen above the rutted country road. Its pale light smothered the landscape in a ghostly cowl. Crickets chimed from the grass, and an occasional night-dwelling predator rustled in the ditches, yellow eyes glowing flat and incurious. She'd seen their like before.

Images and sensations flicked through her mind. Memories were like wolves waiting for the door to open to come ravening in, and each mile forced the door open, inch by painful inch.

The sharp line of moonlight cresting the mountain. Muted voices whispering from the hiding hole in the clansman's croft. The staccato of hoofbeats. Scarlet coats made black by the night, suddenly illumined by torch fire. Discovery. Panic. Shouts . . .

No!

Her head snapped upright, her stomach roiling, the taste of bile thick on her tongue. Dizzy and disoriented she stared about her.

They were rounding a curve. Ahead, an inn squatted beside a crossroads. Bright light poured from small windows, and a curl of smoke stood pale against the indigo sky. Ash halted, waiting until she was alongside him to speak.

"We'll stop there for the night," he said. "You won't say anything or do anything to cause a . . . situation."

"Why won't I?" she muttered, head aching dully.

"Because it wouldn't do you any good," he replied. "I have papers naming me your guardian in my father's stead. No commoner is going to challenge the Earl of Carr's will or, by extension, mine. And if you should bedevil some half-drunk farmer into thinking himself Galahad to your damsel in distress, remember, his wounds would be your doing."

"No. Please."

No, please! Come out! The smoke . . .

"You wouldn't want more guilt on your tender conscience, would you, Rhiannon?"

She shivered.

"I would think that particular cup is full."

"Bastard."

"Unfortunately quite legitimate." He yanked on the lead rope.

At the inn, he dismounted and came to her side, lifting his arms. Weakly, she slapped his hands away. He stepped back and watched her pull her feet free of the stirrups and slide to the ground. Her legs, numbed from so long in the saddle, buckled.

He reached her as she collapsed, lifting her. "Don't be a fool. Hurting yourself isn't going to make me return you to Fair Badden."

"What will?" she asked weakly.

"Nothing." He clipped out a command to care for their horses to the tired boy who materialized beside them. Then he kicked open the inn's door and ducked beneath the low lintel.

A gristle-cheeked innkeeper blinked at their sudden appearance.

"I need a room," Ash said. "And the lady needs a basin of fresh water, towels. We'll eat now, while you prepare it."

Rhiannon squinted around the room, praying she would recognize someone of authority, someone who could stop this madman. There was no one. A pair of rough-looking travelers eyed her interestedly until their gazes fell on Ash.

"See them scars on his wrists? Manacles," she heard one mutter to the other. "Seen 'em before. Tattoo of the prisons."

Manacles? Prison?

"Now," Ash barked at the innkeeper.

"Yes, sir!" The man pattered off behind a door.

With a predatory smile at the two travelers, Ash moved to the fire. He set her down on a stool and dragged a small table in front of her, settling himself on a chair across from her, effectively penning her into the corner.

Heedless of him, she leaned her head against the wall. Her eyelids drifted shut until a rich, earthy aroma filled her nostrils. She opened her eyes. Two steaming bowls sat on the table beside a half loaf of dark bread and a bottle of wine. Her stomach rumbled loudly as she tried to focus her vision. A sickeningly familiar sensation of near-starvation swept over her with all its eviscerating power. Saliva drenched the interior of her mouth.

"For God's sake," she heard Ash say, "eat."

Shamelessly she lifted the wooden bowl and slurped down the thick, viscous liquid in great gulps. She *was* starving. Ravenous. Her hands shook as she tore into the stale bread and rammed a piece atop the mouthful of mutton stew.

She was breathing too fast, eating too fast, and the wine she sloshed into her mouth to chase down each mouthful of bread stifled the air from her throat.

Memory became present.

Time turned inside out.

Hunger. Excruciating hunger. She hadn't eaten in days. Nothing but berries and water. They hadn't dared poach a rabbit or build a fire. The redcoats would see.

Fear and flight. Hounded and hunted on roads, on foot, at night. The mocking moon made crossing the fields near suicidal. They skulked in the ditches, as the soldiers drove the roads, hunting down clansmen, all those men who'd answered the McClairen's call. The smell of gunpowder. The smell of blood. Men screaming. The mountains looming. *The Highlands*.

She stared wild-eyed at the cold-eyed stranger sitting opposite her. He was taking her back there.

Her head pounded. A rushing noise began in her ears, dimming the sound of the others' voices. Her vision swam and she stared into his eyes. Pale like the betraying moon, cold, like a Highland night, beautiful and uncompromising. She rose shakily to her feet, clutching for the edge of the table, spinning, out of breath—

Ash snuffed the guttering candle flame between his thumb and index finger, steeping the room in darkness except for the thin moonlight that trickled from the window and blanketed the slumbering woman on the mattress.

She'd fainted hours ago and had yet to come fully conscious. He'd seen the like in prisoners who'd gone too long without food and were finally fed.

He'd experienced it himself, his first night of freedom from the French gaol. A crease furrowed Ash's brow. Amongst prisoners such an occurrence might be commonplace but not in gently reared young ladies. Not that his experience with that breed was extensive.

Rhiannon had downed that vile broth as though it had been her only meal in a month. And when she'd risen to her feet, horror had clouded her eyes, a deeper, older horror than that which had blazed from her eyes since he'd taken her from Watt.

He pulled a chair near the narrow cot, cocking his head and studying her. Her lips parted on soft susurration. Not only was she exhausted, she was frightened.

It was his doing, of course. He'd pushed her too far. He should have recognized that earlier, but she wore bravery so well and he'd not much experience with fear, having become inured to it long, long ago. Yet he'd felt a lick of it earlier that day, when he'd recognized what had been done to the dog and realized a trap had been set for Rhiannon. And later, when they'd come out of

the forest and seen Watt's cheerful approach, that lick
had become a flail.

He reached over and tucked his jacket up around her
throat, taking care to wipe her square little chin. So
elegant a jaw, so proudly fashioned . . .

Abruptly he straightened, raking the black hair back
from his face. What the bloody hell was he going to
do?

He couldn't let her return to Fair Badden to be murdered, and murder was exactly what he feared had he
left her in Watt's suspect care. Granted, Watt's reason
for wanting to kill Rhiannon eluded him. He was not
satisfied that Watt's motives could be wholly ascribed
to his aversion to marriage—yet the attempts on her
life seemed to have begun with their proposed marriage. Nothing else had changed, or threatened to
change, the status she'd held in Fair Badden for ten
years.

But Watt had refused the excuse to withdraw his suit
that Ash had offered him. Yet his vow that he would
still marry Rhiannon hadn't been made by a besotted
man, nor even one too proud to acknowledge himself
cuckolded. A desperate man had made it. Which made
no sense.

And if Ash wouldn't allow Rhiannon to marry Watt,
he would not allow her to become one of his father's
short-lived brides, either. He couldn't marry her himself. Even if he could find some place to hide her until
she came of age and no longer needed Carr's permission to wed. Or if he could persuade her to marry him
in Scotland where Carr's permission wasn't needed.

He had nothing in this world: no friends, no holdings, and no future. What money he had was promised to his brother.

Abruptly he stood up, the chair scraping loudly in the hushed room. The only thing in this world that he owned was a promise he'd made to his mother on the day of her death: to watch out for Raine.

All his life it had seemed enough, been his lodestar. When Raine had been taken by that tattered Mc-Clairen mob, he'd fought and killed without remorse to free him.

He would not forsake his promise. He could not. It was the only thing he'd *not* forsaken, having abandoned faith, and hope, and lo—and everything else that romantics wept over and pious madmen preached. Nothing he'd done or become had diminished that obligation.

Nothing until Rhiannon Russell.

He stared down at her, and as he watched, she twisted her cheek into the deep velvet pile of his jacket collar, murmuring in distressed tones. Unable to help himself, he loosed a coil of hair that had caught against her lip and tucked it behind her ear.

She opened her eyes. For an instant they lightened with recognition but then the light died, killed by fear. She scooted up, heels drumming the mattress in her climb to the headboard.

"If you touch me, I'll kill you."

Well, yes. The thought was distant, like an echo in a cave, hollow and detached and having nothing to do with a body that seemed incapable of motion, a mouth that refused to speak the denial that clamored for expression.

Why, yes. If she refused to believe she'd been in danger, she could only think that that was why he'd taken her. It hurt. God help him, it hurt, and he nearly laughed at how ridiculous it was that such a little matter as a girl's misplaced fear could cause such immeasurable pain.

And was it so misplaced? Would she be wrong at that? All day he'd taken any excuse, however feeble, to hold her, embrace her, touch her; he wanted her so damned much.

And if something in him shriveled before the fearful suspicion in her eyes, well, it was a weak, trifling part of himself that succumbed, a part that he'd never even realized he'd owned, now happily dead.

He reached down, grabbed her arm, and yanked her to her knees.

He was better off without it.

Chapter 18

What little light came through the window did not reach Ash's face. He didn't say a word. He just stood over her, like a child's golem, a construct of darkness and earth, holding her like a child's cloth doll. Only the violence of his grip bespoke the deep well of anger his silence could not quite contain.

Well, Rhiannon, too, was angry. Years of obeisance fell from her like rusty shackles. Fair Badden had been an opiate, a sweet illusion of kindness and gentleness. But she'd only needed to pass beyond its borders to be wakened to the world she'd left behind, one of treachery, desperation, and deceit.

She pitched herself against his hold and he released her. She fell back on the bed on stiff arms.

"Is that what you think?" he whispered.

"What else?" she spat up at him. She was not half dead with fatigue now, not lost in a labyrinth of hellish, living memories. She knew where she was, what she was doing . . . what was being done to her. She'd fought once and survived. She would fight again.

"I'm taking you to my father's to keep you from being killed."

"You are too good." Even as she jeered, some misbegotten part of her wanted him to convince her that he believed what he said. Even if it was madness, madness she could forgive. But he was not mad, nor misguided. He was simply a devil.

He didn't expend the paltry effort of a reply.

"I don't know what you hope to accomplish by telling me this," she said, in spite of herself. "Why would someone want to hurt me or kill me? Why would *Phillip* want to kill me?"

His gaze slipped away from hers and she noted the involuntary act with bitter conviction. He would lie now. "Watt did not want this marriage. He may not even know why himself. Perhaps his father was forcing him to it and he saw no other way to escape."

She laughed. "Not want this marriage? I went to him yesterday, to tell him what I had done. He wouldn't let me, even though it was clear from what he said in the forest that he suspected. Is that the act of a man looking for a way out of a marriage?"

"You were going to tell Watt? Why?" He sounded shocked. "You asked me not to tell him."

"Of course." She bit off the words. "Because I feared you would say it in such a way that he had no recourse but to call you out—just as you *did*. You told him in the cruelest manner possible. I could not have gone to my marriage bed with that lie waiting to be discovered and I would not have deceived him. But you would have no understanding of that, would you, Lord Janus?"

A flinch? More likely contained laughter.

"None at all," he said. "I was going to advise you to prick your thumb as he slept and smear your thighs."

She felt the blood flee from her face, her skin grow cold, but she was stronger now. She ignored his crudeness.

"What I would like to know is why you have even bothered weaving this pitiful story," she said. "I would think a man of your talents would have at least come up with some better tale." Her lip curled back in as much contempt for herself as for him. "In fact, why fabricate this Banbury tale about assassins at all? I mean, you *have* the bloody letter naming you my surrogate guardian, don't you?"

She peered through the darkness, trying to find some sign she'd struck a human chord in that inhumanely still countenance. All she could see was moonlight shimmering over his black hair.

"You didn't really need an excuse to take me, did you?" she insisted.

"No," he finally answered in that cool, dead voice.

She could hear his breathing, the slight draw and exhalation, light, measured, as if he were consciously regulating it.

"So if you don't mean to rape me—and make no mistake, that is the only way you will ever again take your pleasure between my legs—what *do* you want?" With bitter satisfaction she heard the small, sharp inhalation of his breath. Pain or anger, it made no difference to her, as long as it discomforted him.

She waited for his answer, head up. A long moment passed.

"Don't you know?" he finally ground out.

"Money," she said flatly. It made sense. In hindsight his entire stay in Fair Badden had been one, long, well-orchestrated bit of dodgery: the charming, unsuccessful fumbler slowly transformed into a peerlessly lucky gamester.

"There'll be no money from Mrs. Fraiser," she promised. "The lands and everything on it are entailed to her son and he's far beyond the reach of your stratagems."

No reply.

She bent forward into the light from the window so that he could see her contempt, read her disdain.

"You've no chance of blackmailing *anyone* into paying for my return." A small satisfaction, but she would take what she could. "Whatever Phillip might want, Squire Watt will never accept me as his daughter-in-law now."

"So sure? I'm not."

She shook her head, and the long, tangled skeins of her hair settled around her cheeks and throat like a widow's webbed veil. "He might overlook the lack of a dowry but not the lack of a maidenhead."

"Oh, Rhiannon, I assure you, you've more to recommend to that particular marriage than a simple intact piece of skin."

"I loathe you."

"I know."

He would not be baited, nor pricked with the contempt she was wielding like a blade. His heart and soul were immutable if, indeed, he owned them at all. How could she have been so deceived?

"How lucrative was your stay in Fair Badden?"

The shadow shape shrugged, drifting back a pace, dissolving further into the gloom. "Four hundred pounds. More or less."

"You admit it?" she asked.

"Why not?" he countered. "You've already discovered me. I see no advantage in promoting your naïveté. If you could not stand to—how did you phrase it?—'go to your marriage bed with that lie waiting to be discovered,' how can I be any less noble? Only honesty between us now, eh, Rhiannon? Unless," his voice dropped, became low and mocking, "you'd rather we dispensed with even that inconvenience . . . ?"

She shrank back from its ugliness.

"No? Ah, well."

He was every bit as terrible as she conjectured. How much worse could he be? She had to know the extent of her gullibility.

"The song?" she asked. "Is that true, too?"

"Which song?" he asked.

" 'The Ride of the Demon Earl's Brood.' "

"St. John must have tripped in his haste to tell you that little tale."

"Is it true? Did you?"

"Why?" he countered. "Are you wondering just what sort of evil seed you received?"

She gasped at his crudity, at the calm passionless manner in which he delivered it.

"All right. Here it is. I slashed through a line of men armed with pikes and staves. I made my sword bright with their blood. I trampled them under my horse's hooves."

She wrapped her arms around herself.

"I aided redcoated Brits in killing Scottish peasants." And then, so quietly she barely heard him. "*I saved my brother from being killed.*"

She raised her eyes, speared the darkness that hid him with her gaze. "Those peasants were my clan. Mc-Clairen was my laird."

He stood as still and motionless as the night.

He'd seduced her on the eve of her wedding, killed her kinsmen, and stolen her from the home she'd so carefully fashioned, from the life she'd so carefully cultivated.

Well, she thought, she needn't be careful anymore. There was no one here whom she wished to please.

"You can't stay awake all the time," she whispered. "But you'd best try, Ash Merrick. For as soon as you're asleep, I'll be gone and you'll be lucky if I don't leave that silver blade of yours sheathed between your ribs."

"Trading threats, are we?" he mused softly. "Well, it's my turn now. Listen carefully. You're right. I can't stay awake until we reach Wanton's Blush. But if I catch you trying to run away, or trying to induce some poor fool into interfering with us, I'll not hesitate to punish you. Severely." Not a chord of warmth was revealed in his voice.

She huddled back on the mattress, glaring at him. She heard him take a deep breath.

"And as for your 'killing me' if I touch you—" His head shifted in the gloom and she caught the glint of his dark eyes. "Any time I want, anywhere I want."

* * *

For three days a tempestuous sky dogged their travel. It hounded them along faint, ancient drovers' paths up to high pastures and secret paddocks, the traditional hideouts of the raiders and thieves.

Ash did not try to break Rhiannon's silence. With her savage denunciation, she'd finally made him confront his own motives. His notion that Watt would want to kill her because he preferred the company of men was feeble and ridiculous. Her best interest hadn't been at the heart of his decision, his loins had been. He'd deluded himself, and that tortured him most of all. He'd always been honest with himself if with no one else.

With no reason to enjoin Rhiannon's good opinion, having repudiated it, he punished himself by seeking its opposite, her contempt—something she was more than obliged to give. It was a painful scourge. It was damn near killing him.

As for Rhiannon, she watched the rod-straight back before her with sullen hostility. She had little doubt Ash meant his threat to hurt her if she tried to flee. But it wasn't that or the bruising pace he set—or even the fact that in spite of his claim she'd yet to see him asleep—that kept her from trying to escape. She had no place to go.

Each night she met his mocking smile with a tilt of her chin but held her breath until he'd wound a blanket about his shoulders and settled with his back against the door of the inns where they'd overnighted. He ignored her then, his gaze fixed on the floorboards, leaving her to wonder what drove him now to complete whatever plot he'd devised.

She little cared. And if the haunted expression she

sometimes glimpsed upon his fierce, exhausted countenance might have once confounded her, bitterness left no room for such speculation. She simply welcomed whatever pain he felt. He'd destroyed her life.

During their travel her gaze slew cautiously about. It was all so intimately recognizable: the feel of the wet, cool air; the dark, drenched colors; the scent of flinty rock and gin-spiced conifers. It had been waiting for her return for a decade, like a witch's unwanted familiar.

The winnowing wind whispered a spurious greeting and the chill mist stretched milky fingers up to brush her legs in mock obeisance. Here the McClairens and all those sworn to support them—including the Russells—had returned from Culloden's bloody battlefield seeking sanctuary. Here Lord Cumberland's dragoons had found them. Here they'd been hunted down. Here massacred.

Even in moonlight the mountains seemed stained with blood, the ground, salted with her clansmen's deaths, forever inhospitable and barren. A thousand high, craggy acres of graveyard.

She shuddered and closed her eyes against it. They'd made her home a potter's field.

In such a manner they traveled for four more days and nights. On the fifth night they crested a high, tree-bereaved hill overlooking the sea. Below them and some miles off, a thin bridge of land connected the headland to a big, crescent-shaped island. It surged out of the sea, blocky and jagged with rock. At its inner curve it rose to a high shelf of land overlooking the sheer, dramatic cliffs facing east. On this apex perched a mansion, or castle, or fortress.

*   *   *

It was impossible to tell what exactly the place was, or had started out as, or looked to become, it was so rife with turrets and buttresses, cupolas and columns, friezes and pediments. A mad architect's maddest creation.

Lines of windows cast beacons across terraced lawns and pockmarked sweeping staircases. All about, pinpricks of light—lanterns?—swung and swayed about the massive fortress's base, like fairies dancing maniacally about the skirts of some mammoth, beleaguered matron.

Flitting in and out of the open doorways, through beams of light and patches of shadow, darting and settling in clusters and singly amidst the blackening lawn, were people, ladies and gentlemen, dozens and dozens of them.

Bemused and disconcerted by the spectacle, Rhiannon looked to Ash. His gaze was already on her, thoughtful and remote, his face stained with fatigue. He smiled tightly, and flung out his hand in a cavalier's overmannered gesture.

"Welcome to McClairen's Isle," he said, "and Wanton's Blush."

Chapter 19

They left the horses with a liveried servant and climbed the front stairs through the carved panels into a great hall ablaze with light and mirrors and gilt.

Beneath the beatific gaze of the plaster angels high overhead mingled dozens of people. They nibbled cakes and licked gloved fingers, spilt iced punch on Persian carpets, and laughed and posed and sweated in their rich gowns and piled wigs.

Ash led Rhiannon through the little queues of revelers and knots of gamers. Few noted their progress. Most had gone days without sleep, sun, or fresh food. They were swollen on wine and excitement, dull and fog-witted, groping through the mire of senseless spectacles and animal pleasures his father designed to keep them entertained . . . to keep them careless with their money. For, when all was said and done, Wanton's Blush was simply the most dissolute, the most licentious, the most sumptuous gaming hell in all the British Isles.

In a few minutes they had broken free of the crush in the main hall and stood in a narrow corridor behind the curved staircase. A laughing woman burst out of a nearby door, her gown slipping from one shoulder, a trio of flushed and hound-eyed men tumbling in pursuit. Ash snatched Rhiannon up and out of their way.

His arms tightened convulsively. The salty, musty scent of travel filled his nostrils. The feel of her body stoked the appetite he'd held in check into a veritable blaze. He looked down. She'd averted her face.

Temper surged through him. What did he care? He thought fiercely. He did not need her scorn to tell him who he was.

"Fa! Carr never said we were to have a masque tonight!"

Ash looked up. A pink-ribboned, satin-clad creature in a lavender wig leaned against the door frame.

"But 'struth, must be so for here's Little Red Ridy Hood herself!" The man's plucked and pencilled brows rose in twin semicircles above shallow, lashless eyes.

Smoothly, Ash lowered Rhiannon to the ground. She did not step back. Of course not. She'd never give him the satisfaction of showing fear. Neither did she say a word or rebuke him in any way. She did not need to. Her silence was eloquent enough. She expected he'd stolen her from Watt to satisfy his carnal appetite.

The lavender-headed fop's gaze drifted from his interested inspection of Rhiannon to Ash, sizing up the filth of travel, the five-day growth of beard, and the tangled tail of black hair.

"And this is either the woodsman or the wolf. I say, fellow, which are you supposed to be?"

"Pray commence trembling, Hurley, that's Merrick you're twitting." A gorgeous young girl appeared beside the plump, pink Hurley. Her young, pure face was absolutely smooth and her poise was unassailable. The gray of her elaborately powdered wig contrasted jarringly with her obvious youth, somehow making a mockery of both.

"Merrick?" the perplexed Hurley asked.

"My brother," the girl replied.

"Fia," Ash said, inclining his head. She was fifteen—or was it sixteen?—and having known so little of her mother, was utterly her father's creature. Ash trusted her less than anyone else, perhaps because in spite of himself he felt the bonds of blood between them, urging something different.

"Merrick? Carr's son?" Hurley stuttered.

"One of them," Ash allowed coolly.

"The ruthless one," Fia said with a small, practiced smile. She moved her salved lips close to one of Hurley's pink ears. Ash could practically see it quiver. "The dangerous one," she whispered loudly. "The passionate one."

Hurley's expression of perplexity gave way to a licentiousness. He reached out to tickle Fia beneath her chin. Calmly Fia slashed her fan across his knuckles. He snatched back his hand, staring at her in wounded wonder.

"Be gone, Lord Hurley. Before Merrick decides to misinterpret your attentions to his little sister." Her face was as smooth as a porcelain doll's and yet a little sneer curled around her words.

The white powder covering Hurley's face could not hide his flush, and with a mumbled adieu, he escaped. Fia ignored his departure.

Beside Ash Rhiannon stirred.

"What is this you've brought, brother?" Fia murmured. "Something for Carr? A new toy?"

"His ward," Ash returned shortly. Rhiannon's head remained bowed, her eyes downcast, her shoulders slumped. She looked as if she'd been beaten which, Ash decided, was probably just what she wanted to look like.

Fia, a little smile chasing cross her features, dipped her head and peeked up.

"He has a ward now, does he?" she said in a voice as gentle and dangerous as the sound of a snake slithering over a dry lawn. Calmly Ash stepped between them. Fia glanced at him in surprise. "Who'd have thought?"

"I would," a deep masculine voice with a distinct Scottish burr announced.

At the sound, Ash turned. Approaching him was a tall, broad-shouldered man. The chandelier light polished his dark mahogany head to a metallic sheen.

"Donne," Ash greeted him. He was surprised to see him here, at Wanton's Blush. Carr usually picked his guests carefully and while Donne was certainly rich enough to be admitted, he did not display the proper susceptibility to drinking, gambling, or wenching.

A smile carved deep dimples in each of Donne's lean

cheeks, mirroring the cleft in his chin. There was a watchfulness about the long, narrow eyes currently fixed on Fia. She'd straightened abruptly at his appearance but now stood regarding the Scot with the calm imperturbability she'd owned since childhood.

Rhiannon, like some damn silent statue, remained motionless at Ash's side. He needed to get her upstairs before Carr discovered them. He was tired and edgy, in no condition to deal with his father. Still, if Donne was here, perhaps he'd come with some interesting information.

"What the devil are you doing here, Donne?"

Donne shrugged. "I came along as part of a set. Hurley's house party, you know. I simply could not refuse the opportunity to game a bit and, of course, such charming company."

At his last words he bowed in Fia's direction, and though the movement was easy and elegant, a quality of practiced boredom robbed it of politeness and made it instead an actor's gesture, cruelly meaningless.

If possible, Fia's young, unnaturally beautiful face grew smoother; her large eyes went dark as obsidian in a black rill's bed.

Donne turned to Rhiannon, bowing again, and this time the movement was respectful, the gesture an acknowledgement rather than a caricature.

"Since Ash refuses to be civil, pray allow me to satisfy the amenities myself. Thomas Donne at your service, miss."

She lifted her face, her gaze latching on to Donne's handsome, lean visage, drawing Ash's cold consideration. She was pitifully easy to read.

In Thomas Donne's braw Scottish face she looked for a champion.

A sliver of pity touched Ash. Donne was the last man who would come to her aid. He knew little about Donne; he'd never asked, but what he did know was simple. Donne had been abroad and, in some mysterious place, had won, earned, or stolen a monstrously big fortune which he kept monstrously big by the simple expedience of not giving it away to any fool that came begging.

This apparently hadn't set well with his Highland cousins for, according to Donne, they'd long since blotted his name from the family Bible, an act that had in no way discomforted Donne. Instead, self-avowed coward and sybarite that he was, Donne simply eschewed the clan that had exiled him.

It would be a waste of time to seek an ally in Donne. Ash forced his gaze from Rhiannon. She would be living at Wanton's Blush. She'd learn soon enough that there would be no champions. Every person here had been handpicked because they possessed just exactly those characteristics that champions lacked: greed, self-interest, cowardice, insolence, and vanity.

His own sister was a prime example.

"I think Merrick has brought us a mute," Fia said. "Did you have to take her tongue to keep her from denouncing you, brother?"

This brought a swift glare from Rhiannon.

"I assure you, she is quite capable of denouncing me. Make your curtsey, Miss Russell," Ash said. "One of your Scottish baronets has introduced himself to you."

He may as well have spoken to stone, her disdain

and self-containment were so complete and so completely excluded him. Excluded them all. But then, he'd stolen her from her home and family under the most feeble of pretexts. He'd taken from her her good name and her maidenhead.

And if he'd twice now sought to convince her of his honest concern, twice now she'd refused to believe him. So how could he, he asked himself as he gazed at her averted profile, who had so little experience with honesty, fail to accept the verdict of one who understood it so well?

He was done with trying to realign his nature. He *was* as corrupt as she imagined.

"She won't speak to you, Donne."

"Not yet, perhaps," Donne said thoughtfully. "But, surely, as two Scots in a house full of Englishmen, we'll find in each other's company a wee bit of comfort, eh, Miss Russell?" His offer surprised Ash.

Donne's accent, a thing he slipped on and off as comfortably as a pair of slippers, had grown pronounced. Its music drew another of those grudging glances from Rhiannon and this time the light revealed her complete exhaustion, the pale mouth and ringed eyes. She wove where she stood.

She must be near to collapsing. He needed to get her out of here. Somewhere where she could wash and sleep.

"Not yet?" Donne said and Ash could not remember ever hearing such gentle tones from his mouth. "I can wait."

"I fear you wait in vain, Lord Donne," said Fia. "Perhaps the lady is discerning in her choice of companions and simply exhibits her good taste. Would that it extended to the matter of her attire."

The chance reference to her apparel caused Rhiannon's hands to flutter hesitantly about her heavy, muddied skirts.

"It looks as though Ash dragged you from a particularly feverish hunt."

"He did." These were the first words Rhiannon had spoken. Her glance slew up and speared Fia so that the younger girl, in spite of an upbringing that should have inured her to even the most violent of glares, stepped back.

Fia looked around, disconcerted by such honest animosity. "Let me send one of the servants for your trunks."

"There are no trunks," Ash said. "She has nothing."

"Odder and odder," said Fia. "Whatever is she here for?"

"That's easy," Donne said, without looking at Fia but instead studying Rhiannon. "Carr dotes on you so, Miss Fia, that he's imported a sister with whom you might trade girlish confidences."

The thought of Fia, even though still chronologically a girl, as anything in the least childish, was absurd, and well Donne knew it. But Fia refused to be baited. Her cool, silky gaze fastened on the tall baronet. "It's only fair," she said, "seeing how he's misplaced one sibling, that he replace it with another."

The reminder of Raine's whereabouts struck Ash painfully. With an effort, he kept his expression neutral, wondering whether Fia had chosen her words to hurt him, or rebuke Donne. It was impossible to tell with Fia. She kept her own counsel so completely.

"Still, new sister or not, Carr dislikes ugliness. He'll be horrified if he sees her like this," Fia said. "She looks to be near enough my size that she might borrow a dress. If she's to meet Carr, she'll need all the confidence she can find—or borrow."

Ash hadn't thought of that. Fia was right. Appearances were of the utmost importance to Carr. Gaining his approbation might prove prudent. The question was what Fia hoped to achieve by offering her aid.

Her face was as serene as a Madonna's, her eyes wells of unfathomable darkness. After an instant consideration Ash decided it didn't matter what she wanted.

This was Wanton's Blush. Subterfuge and treachery were the games of *his* childhood, and they were compulsory. There were only two rules here: Play at one level deeper than your opponent and never forget that everyone is your opponent.

He nodded. "Give her over to Gunna," he said, naming the white-haired woman who had been Fia's nanny since toddlerhood and the only bit of warmth any of them had encountered at Wanton's Blush since their mother's death.

"Yes."

"There's no need to rush an audience," he added casually. "She can see Carr tomorrow."

"Yes," Fia agreed once more. She moved to Rhiannon's side and linked her arm through hers, calmly ignoring Rhiannon's attempt to pull free. "Please come with me. I'll order a bath and we'll find you some clothes. Something to make you feel invincible," she said, drawing Rhiannon away.

"You won't run away will you?" Ash heard Fia ask as they left.

"No," Rhiannon replied without a single backward glance. "I've nowhere to go."

Chapter 20

The sun was full up when Fia slipped inside of the sumptuously appointed bedchamber where Rhiannon had slept. Though the girl entered on a light, furtive step Rhiannon came fully awake at once. She kept her breathing even and opened her eyelids to mere slits, studying the girl.

Today, Fia had eschewed last night's dramatic midnight hues in favor of an exquisitely worked butter yellow dress of astounding indecency. The tight, square bodice pushed her young breasts high above the décolletage, barely maintaining modesty. Pearls draped her slender throat and dangled from her earlobes. A tiny black patch flirted with one smooth white cheek and rosy salve coated her lips.

She looked like a dressmaker's mannequin, thought Rhiannon dispassionately, a dressmaker with a demimonde clientele.

A week ago a creature as exotic as Fia would have rendered Rhiannon tongue-tied. But when one was a prisoner such matters as another's demeanor ceased to be important. Or even very interesting.

Besides, Rhiannon thought with a brittle inner smile, it was so patently apparent that Fia expected to unnerve her—and everyone else. Last night Fia had perched herself on the foot of the bed and watched as a maid stripped the filthy riding habit from Rhiannon's back. In a tender, composed voice she had recited salacious stories about Carr and Ash and another brother named Raine. When her tales failed to invoke so much as a gasp, she'd become openly disconcerted. Her smooth white brow had knit with perplexity and she'd finally left Rhiannon alone.

It was a telling point and Rhiannon re-estimated Fia's age to be much younger than she'd originally surmised. A faint memory came back to her, her uncle advising her to "know well one's enemy."

Enemy, lover. Sanctuary, prison. Home and exile.

Now that exhaustion no longer kept such notions at bay, they prowled through Rhiannon's waking thoughts, mocking her with her own culpability. She'd succumbed to Ash's potent magnetism. She'd sought his company and flirted with him, burning with curiosity over what his kiss would be like. And after discovering that, she'd still not been content. Knowledge had only fed the craving, consumed her until she'd felt she'd *needed* to know passion—*his* passion. Well, she thought, biting hard upon her inner cheeks, she now had that knowledge, too.

If only it had been a shabby, tawdry thing, an act that *felt* as sordid as she knew it to be. But it *hadn't*. It hadn't felt like lust or rank sexual appetite. It had seemed her soul's imperative. It had been . . . wondrous.

If it hadn't, she wouldn't have hated him so much now.

It wasn't only that he'd deceived her but that she'd deceived Phillip, that he'd robbed her of the opportunity to confess what she couldn't explain. And though she knew that laying such blame on Ash's door was unfair, she no longer cared.

It was unfair that Ash had ridden into her life a scant three weeks before her wedding. It was unfair that his eyes were dark, his wrists scarred, and his soul as tattered and patched as a gypsy's cape—and that she recognized the cut.

A ruthless man, Fia had said. A dangerous one. Well, the Highlands had bred a rare, pure line of that sort. Hadn't she been ruthless in getting what she wanted, never thinking past the morrow, or of where her headlong dash into pleasure would lead her? Or anyone else. She turned her cheek into her pillow, sickened with guilt. She could see again the knowledge of her betrayal in Phillip's beautiful eyes, the disappointment, the hurt— She jerked upright in bed.

Startled by the sudden movement, Fia spun around. "You're awake."

Rhiannon seized on the distraction. "Yes. I'm sure you knew that, though. Otherwise you wouldn't have come in, would you have?"

The girl tipped her head in calm agreement. "Of course."

"You wished to see me?" Rhiannon settled back

against the thick bolster of pillows. *Calm. Breathe.* Yesterday she'd been a victim but today she needn't be.

"Gunna is outside. She wishes to see you."

"Gunna?" Rhiannon asked. "The nanny? Why would your nanny wish to see me and why would she need you to act as a vanguard to that fact, Miss Merrick?"

"She's brought some gowns for you to try on and I— Well, Gunna is most . . . unprepossessing. Actually quite hideous. But—" Fia hesitated. Whatever she'd been about to confide she decided against it. "She's served me faithfully. I would not want her hurt."

Fia smiled wryly at Rhiannon's obvious skepticism. "She still has her uses," she explained coldly.

"Bring her."

The young woman's eyes narrowed fractionally at the commanding tone and Rhiannon smiled. She was Rhiannon Russell and her distant cousin had been laird of McClairen. Ash had dragged her back to this place, rousing that long dormant knowledge. Let him see what he'd awakened. Whatever airs this hybrid English girl owned, she'd adopted. In Rhiannon's warrior heart five hundred years of pride and audacity churned for expression. "Now, Fia. Before I fall asleep again."

The girl smiled once more, this time an honest, rueful smile of such poignant charm and humor that in spite of every instinct that told her to beware of her, Rhiannon found herself warming toward the young girl.

Without a word, Fia drifted—there was simply no other term that adequately described Fia's modus of locomotion—toward the doorway and opened it. "Gunna!"

A moment later a bent and twisted figure in black wool crept in, a half-dozen gowns filling her arms. A mantillalike veil of black lace covered her head, pinned so that one side draped over the left portion of her face, concealing it. The open side exposed a deformed jaw, a large drooping eye, and a twisted caricature of a nose.

If poor Gunna had chosen this side of her face to present to the world, Rhiannon could only be moved to pity imagining what the rest of the veil concealed. The woman turned to Fia who hovered by her elbow in an oddly protective manner. "Jamie says yer father is looking fer you." Gunna's deep voice was thick with a Scottish accent. "Best be to him. Go on. Sooner gone; sooner back."

With a disgruntled sniff, Fia twirled and departed. The old nurse chuckled at her ward's flouncing departure before looking back at Rhiannon.

"Highlander, they said ye were, in the kitchens. What clan?" she asked, hobbling closer. Her tone was slightly brusque, the manner in which she regarded Rhiannon touched with enmity.

Rhiannon swung her feet over the sides of the bed and dropped lightly to the cold floor. "McClairen."

A flicker of surprise passed over the exposed side of Gunna's face. "McClairen? Ye don't have the look of the McClairen. They're a black-haired breed with white skin."

Rhiannon tugged the blanket from the bed and wrapped it around her shoulders. She didn't want to be reminded of those old clan affiliations. She'd left them behind a decade ago.

Wordlessly, she moved past the old woman and went

to the window. Below, a gunmetal gray sea battered the island's base.

"Forgive me, miss," she heard Gunna say. "I don't know my place and that's a fact."

Pride and coldness had replaced the woman's former grudging interest. Rhiannon felt ashamed. It wasn't Gunna's fault that she'd been brought here.

"I'm not a McClairen," she said. "My father was a chieftain in his own right but when McClairen called for men to fight in forty-five, my father answered." She closed her eyes. "And my brothers. And my uncles."

"Yer an orphan then," Gunna murmured, her manner thawing slightly. "No one left?"

"No," Rhiannon said. "They were all hunted down and murdered. Out there." She pointed at the bleak landscape outside the window. She stared at it unseeing. "Dear God, how I hate being here."

A light touch on her sleeve begged Rhiannon's attention. Gunna had moved to her side. Her hand was rough-skinned, the nails bitten down to the quick, but the long fingers were surprisingly elegant.

"Aye?"

"Of course," Rhiannon said impatiently. "Who wouldn't? This place is filled with ghosts and a bloodied lot they are."

Gunna sighed, her one eye following Rhiannon's gaze out over the sea. "I find," she said carefully, "that the ghosts that follow closest are those we've fled."

Rhiannon glanced at her and frowned. "There were no ghosts where I came from."

It wasn't strictly true, but those phantoms faded with the light. Not these. In one day she'd remembered more of her life in the Highlands than she'd thought about—or allowed herself to think about—in over ten years in Fair Badden.

The exposed corner of Gunna's mouth tucked into a smile. "Not all hauntings are hurtful."

She only meant to be kind and though Rhiannon doubted her wisdom, she appreciated her concern. "I hope so."

Gunna tugged on her arm, leading her back to the bed where she'd spread out the gowns she'd carried in. She scooped up one shimmering leaf-green damask and held it to Rhiannon's face.

"Ye'll be a beauty in this and that's a fact. Carr will be pleased." She watched Rhiannon carefully. It mattered little to Rhiannon what Carr thought of her appearance. Apparently Gunna read her lack of concern in her expression for she shook her head. "You seem a fair bit unconcerned what yer groom thinks of yer appearance."

"Groom?" she echoed dumbly, staring as the implications of that single word took hold. The woman's former disapproving attitude suddenly made sense, wringing a harsh laugh from Rhiannon. "I'm not going to marry Lord Carr."

"Truly?" Gunna asked.

"Truly," Rhiannon returned, regarding the old woman dryly.

"They say Mr. Ash brought you," Gunna said after a second's hesitation.

His name brought a flood of warmth sweeping up Rhiannon throat and face. "Yes."

"Carr's beast of burden." Both women spun around at the sound of Fia's voice. She was standing inside the door, leaning back against the panel. "Poor Ash."

Gunna ignored her charge's smooth, false tone, replying to the words rather than the timbre—a course of action that Rhiannon thought she might do well to emulate.

"Carr best have a care," Gunna said, returning the dress she held to the bed. "Methinks Lord Carr will get no more service out of that particular beastie until he gives up one of the carrots he's been danglin' in front of Mr. Ash's proud nose. Here, miss, let me take that blanket from you. We best get you dressed."

"Ash will do whatever he has to do," Fia replied, coming forward as Rhiannon complied and Gunna scuttled across the room to fetch a water pitcher and basin. "Ash would never do anything that might harm Raine."

"Raine? Carr's younger son?" Rhiannon could not help but ask. The one that was supposed to have raped the nun?

"Ye donna ken, do you, Miss Russell?" Gunna said. She dipped a soft towel into the water and rubbed it with soap and handed it to Rhiannon. "About Ash and Raine."

"No," Rhiannon said tersely, her voice muffled by the towel as she scrubbed at her face.

"It's an interestin' tale," Gunna went on. She took the dirtied towel and splashed more cold water in the basin in preparation for a cold, but much needed hip bath. Even with just her face clean Rhiannon felt better.

"And one we don't have time for right now," Fia interjected. "Carr wants her in the gallery before the hour."

"What?" Rhiannon asked, her gaze flying to the

mantel clock. It was barely fifteen minutes before the hour.

Fia shrugged. "I told him I thought that would be fine."

Rhiannon looked down. She still wore the same soiled chemise she'd had on for five days. She had no time to bathe now and Fia knew it. So much for last night's concern about Rhiannon making a good impression.

But then, Fia was a Merrick. Doubtless she had her own agenda. Well, let her.

Rhiannon may have been over ten years from this land, but being reared on a Highlands battlefield produces a pupil well versed in combat—of all kinds.

At the end of another long corridor the footman finally opened a door. Rhiannon swept back the green skirts of her borrowed dress and entered.

Ash Merrick stood in the center of the room, his hands clasped behind his back, his black hair tied negligently at the nape of his neck. He regarded her watchfully. His stance was broad and challenging.

At the sight of him her breath caught. She hadn't expected him and he was so damnably beautiful. "Your father sent for me. Where is he?" She sounded angry. Better than dazzled.

"Fia said you would have an audience with Carr. And so you shall."

"I have nothing to say to you." She forced the rising note of panic from her voice. "We have nothing to say to each other."

"I miss you." His words came out low, nearly inaudible, more whispered admission than declaration.

Her head snapped up in astonishment. Whatever she'd expected it had never been that.

Admission? Lie. He was a consummate opportunist. He simply wanted an accommodating prisoner, not a difficult one. Hadn't she proven already how susceptible she was to him?

No more.

She lifted hot, angry eyes to his light, unrevealing eyes. "How unpleasant for you."

"Tit for tat, eh?" His mouth tilted mockingly. "Standard practice in my family. I should tell you, in the interest of fair play, I've vast experience with payback." The smile dissolved, replaced by an intent, hungry look. "I never meant to hurt you, Rhiannon. Use you? Yes, I admit to that. Have you? Definitely. But I never wanted you hurt."

His eyes stayed locked on hers as he strove to convince her that he told the truth. She even half believed him. It didn't matter. In Fair Badden, her soft heart would have turned to warm wax with his confession. But the Highlands bred no soft hearts or weak resolves. Only those who would fight for their survival rather than allow themselves to be used and cast aside had survived.

"Too late." She watched for a telltale sign that she'd pricked his hard heart. "You should have gone away. I could have made some sort of recompense to Phillip."

"I told you. Someone tortured that damn dog of yours on purpose."

She felt the color bleed from her face.

"The same someone who scarred your face with a bullet and who hurled that knife at you at the Harquists' party," he went on in a cold biting voice.

She glared at him. "You misread Stella's accident," she insisted. "And as for the other incidents? Nonsense. And well you know it."

His gaze flickered away from hers, the tiny involuntary gesture justifying her suspicions. But instead of the vindication she might have expected, she only felt hollow, emptied, and lost.

He *had* manufactured the whole story for whatever covert purposes of his own. Purposes he had no intention of revealing to her.

"It's not too late," she heard herself saying in a dull voice. "You can send me back to Fair Badden."

His expression tightened. He sneered.

"No matter what Watt claimed, you would have ended an outcast. We were lovers and Phillip knows that. He'd never accept you now."

How could he speak of it so unemotionally? But then, she reminded herself, he'd only been involved in the physical act. He'd given her nothing of himself that he hadn't reclaimed the minute he'd left her.

"You didn't offer me any choice, did you? Or Phillip," she accused him. "You bludgeoned him with the knowledge of my betrayal. You lied to me in that, too."

His eyes clouded. "I thought I was keeping you safe. I thought to make it impossible for—"

"Phillip to marry me?" Rhiannon finished coldly. "Well, as you so kindly have explained, you did that."

"I thought to give him an *excuse* not to marry you."

"I still want to go back," she said, ignoring his fantastic rubbish. "You needn't do anything but get me to a coaching inn."

He shook his head. "There's nothing for you at Fair Badden. It's done."

Her breath felt hot in her nostrils but she made herself speak in a bell tone of coldness. "I do not know why you forced me here or why you even bedded me in the first place. Did the thought of a nameless orphan marrying into your English aristocracy so offend you?"

Amazingly, he laughed. "Now there's as fascinating a motive for deflowering a girl as ever I've heard."

She'd sought to shame him and instead he mocked her. Humor glinted in his dark eyes though his mouth remained hard. A mouth that had moved with exquisite tenderness over her skin, burnishing her nerves with pleasure.

"At least I've given you some plausible explanation for your actions. I have no excuse for willfully betraying my betrothed."

His nostrils flared slightly. "You don't consider lust motive enough? I assure you"—his gaze unraveled over her face, her mouth, her throat and bodice—"it's a most potent imperative."

He didn't move but she suddenly felt as though he'd surrounded her. She drew back a step. Her pulse tripped thickly in her veins. "But why bring me here then? Not for lust's sake. If forcing a woman could pleasure you, you would have forced me by now and you haven't."

Strangely, her words seemed to anger him. "I would not rely too much on such an assumption."

Once more she backed away from whatever emotion he strove so hard to suppress. His hands shivered at his sides.

"Let us say for the sake of argument that you are right," he grated out, "that I would find no ease in forcing myself on you. Now for one minute, just one, allow that I am astute enough to realize that in taking you from Fair Badden I could only secure your contempt." The very rigidity of his posture bespoke his fervor, forcing her to listen.

"Suspend your disbelief just a bit longer." He held out a supplicating hand—this man she doubted had ever been a supplicant—and confusion rippled through her resolve, shaking it.

"Say that I took you here for no other reason than the one I gave you. That I believed your life was in danger and that I suspected Watt of being responsible. If you can find no other reason for my act, could not that one, as fantastic as it might seem, be the truth?"

His voice remained firm, insistent. His eyes pleaded with her. But the notion of Phillip intentionally setting out to harm her, or that anyone could conceive him capable of such, was absurd.

"Please, Rhiannon." She'd never heard so raw a tone before. "Please."

But then, Ash did not know Phillip as well as she. He *might* mistake Phillip's nature. . . .

Her gaze raked his face, trying to see what his expression might betray. She moved closer, close enough to hear the ragged draw of his breath, so intent she was barely aware of a movement behind her.

A voice—cultivated, bored, and imperious—spoke. "Well, Ash, now that you've fetched her I suppose you'll want the money I promised you for your trouble."

Chapter 21

Ash saw the spark of uncertainty in her eyes die, snuffed out with Carr's words. She'd been searching for a reason for his actions; Carr had supplied one. Hatred of his father seethed in him. Carr's words left him nothing. Nothing but the rattail shreds of pride and Ash refused to lose those here, in front of him.

Rhiannon was lost to him. Her cold, appreciative smile flailed him with its lack of accusation. That was the worst of it. He'd done no less than what she'd expected. He'd almost duped her again.

He looked away. There was still Raine to consider. He would always have Raine.

Carr had sauntered into the room and begun a slow circle around Rhiannon, one perfectly manicured finger raised to his lips in concentration.

"Two thousand pounds, I believe," Ash said dully.

Carr ignored him, continuing his study of Rhiannon in her borrowed finery.

Fia's gown, like all the ladies' gowns at Wanton's Blush, was designed to titillate and impress, provoke and advertise. Rhiannon wore the borrowed finery with regal disdain for its provocative qualities. Layered over some sort of hoop contraption, the heavy leaf-green silk de Chine shimmered with little gold glass beads. Treble ruffles of lace were gathered at the elbows and cascaded over her forearms.

Under Carr's dispassionate stare, the faintest blush stained her slender throat and marked the upper curves of breasts uncovered by the low, square décolletage. She'd refused a wig. Her hair was coiled in a thick knot at the crown of her head.

The sight of her and of Carr studying her made Ash's mouth dry.

"What shall I do with you?" Carr murmured.

In spite of his calm tone, it struck Ash that Carr was upset. The lines fanning the corners of his eyes were pronounced as were the twin grooves bracketing his aquiline nose. His lips had thinned with discontent. Carr, whose life revolved around beauty and appearance, class and status, would never have willingly shown his ire.

He obviously regretted whatever impulse had led him to offer Ash money for his services. He must suspect how close Ash was to realizing Raine's ransom. Once Raine was out of prison Carr would be deprived of one of his more effective agents. He would hate that.

"Send me back, sir." Rhiannon's voice broke Carr's contemplation and caught him off guard.

Ash smiled. Carr was unused to young women

speaking in that tone to him. It was bound to exacerbate an already foul mood, and, indeed, the lines at the corners of his mouth deepened with displeasure but then smoothed.

"My dear," he said, "you have only just arrived."

"I have no desire to be here, Lord Carr." She did not look at Ash and her voice rose as she spoke. "Indeed, I am here much against my will."

"How is that?" Carr's brows rose.

"Your son *stole* me on the eve of my wedding!"

A heartbeat's pause while Carr absorbed this, then he gasped a melodramatic, "No!"

"Yes, sir!" Rhiannon said, nodding vigorously.

A wave of pity washed over Ash and he met her triumphant gaze wearily. She thought Carr had taken her part. She thought she'd horrified him with this tale of her son's ruthless perfidy.

"The blackguard!" Carr's tone rang with indignation and he spun on his boot heels to face Ash. Immediately the horrified indignation on his face was supplanted by indifference. He saw no reason to mask his real reaction from Ash. He looked up and saw Ash regarding him.

"What do you have to say for yourself?" Carr asked in a voice rife with displeasure, but his expression was incurious.

Ash refused to defend himself. It would only amuse Carr, and Rhiannon already thought the very worst of him. "You sent me for her. Here she is. You owe me two thousand pounds."

Carr composed his face to the proper aggrieved lines and turned back to face Rhiannon. "My dear, please forgive me. Had I known you were about to wed I would, of course, never have dreamt of tearing you from your foster home. I am amazed Ash was so fervent to do my bidding. Believe me, it is most uncharacteristic."

Ash watched Rhiannon eagerly examine Carr's benign countenance; saw the instant she perceived the tiny, false note of sympathy; saw her earnestness die and distrust replace it. Carr saw it, too, and for a second his eyes narrowed as he realized she did not wholly buy his act of sorrow, that she would not be, in fact, so easily gulled.

In spite of himself Ash felt proud of her.

"Why did you send your son for me after all these years?" she asked suddenly.

"I did not know where you were until most recently and then only by chance. A man who had come to Wanton's Blush with a party of my friends, some native son of your little hamlet, mentioned your surname and I recognized it as the same as my own dear wife's cousin."

"Which wife was that?" Ash asked sardonically and was rewarded by a lethal glance from his sire.

"My second wife."

"Why would anyone mention my name?" Rhiannon asked doubtfully.

Carr held up his hands before his eyes as though framing her. "My dear . . . such modesty is most becoming if a trifle, just the merest bit, *jeune fille.*"

Rhiannon colored and her gaze fell. Point for Carr. His smile was not without malice but Rhiannon, eyes still averted, did not see this.

"'Struth," Carr said, "You are a most beauti—"

"Why did you turn me away all those years ago?"

Her gaze flew up, discounting his flattery. He hadn't won her. Not at all. "We came to your front door," she went on. "My mother's old nurse and I. She had a letter, she gave it to the man there and he took it away. When he returned he refused to let us in—"

"He did?"

Ash had to credit Carr, his expression of amazement was superb, especially followed as it was by that convincing blend of indignation and sorrow.

"I . . . I had no idea! I swear on all that is sacred, until this moment I did not know you had ever come to my home." Carr moved closer to her and drew one of her hands up and between both of his, chafing it lightly. "I heard of what Cumberland was doing, of course. I knew your family would likely be punished for being dragged into taking a stance on the part of The Pretender—"

"My family *gave* their lives for him. Willingly!" Rhiannon burst out. "They were not coerced. They committed themselves with valor and honor and pride. And James Stuart is no 'pretender'!"

Her outburst seemed to startle Rhiannon as much as Carr for as soon as the words had escaped her, she bit hard on her lips and scowled. Carr looked briefly taken aback but then, seeing Rhiannon's discomfiture and confusion, he smiled sympathetically.

"Of course, my dear. Of course," he crooned. "And after I heard that Cumberland had satisfied his depraved need for vengeance, I sent men to search for my dear wife's relatives, most especially you, my wife's ward and thus mine. Alas, they returned empty-handed." He lifted one hand and with his fingertips tilted her chin up, so that she would be forced to meet his eyes.

It took all of Ash's self-control to stand still then, but if he were to indicate by word or deed that Rhiannon meant anything more to him than the two thousand pounds Carr had promised for her, Carr would use that to his advantage. And without a doubt Carr's advantage would be Rhiannon's disadvantage. So Ash stayed where he was even though the blood thickened in his veins and pounded in his temples and his hand shivered above where the stiletto hid in the top of his boot.

"What is this?" Carr suddenly said. "What is this scar on your face?"

"Nothing." Rhiannon said, jerking her head back. "A highwayman shot at a carriage in which I rode. The bullet grazed my cheek."

"Damn the bastard!" Carr's low words vibrated with anger.

Ash stared, confounded. He knew every gesture and expression in Carr's repertoire and the darkening of his sire's throat and cheeks was beyond even Carr's thespian talents. He was truly furious.

"I escaped, my lord," Rhiannon said evenly.

"And did *he*?" Carr spat. "This . . . this *highwayman*?"

"Yes."

"Damn!" Carr bit out. "Damn him to a painful death!"

"Really, sir. I suffered no great harm." Her tone was amazed.

Carr took a deep breath, releasing it slowly. "Yes. Yes. We must accept what we cannot change. You are here now. You are safe."

"I was safe in Fair Badden." Rhiannon kept her gaze locked on Carr, as though by ignoring Ash, she could somehow make him cease to exist. "I wish to return there."

Carr scowled, released her chin, and folded his hands behind his back. "Return there? But how would that look? I mean by dusk everyone at Wanton's Blush will know you are here, that you are my ward. How would it appear if I were to shun my obligations and ship you back?"

"Returning me to Fair Badden won't be a detriment to your good name, sir."

Poor Rhiannon, Ash thought, too honest by half. She hadn't been able to keep the sneer from her voice and Carr noted it. His eyes shot to her face, glittering. Gamely she continued. "You'll be returning a bride to her fiancé."

Carr pulled thoughtfully at his lip.

"Please," she urged him.

"Well, perhaps," Carr allowed.

Ash froze. Whoever endangered Rhiannon, it was someone in Fair Badden. She couldn't go back there. She mustn't be allowed.

"Put in such a manner, one could understand."

"Exactly! You'd be righting a wrong done to an innocent girl—"

"Not so innocent," Ash drawled, careful not to make any impression of urgency. "No, I don't think that will do. You see, Miss Russell's rather precipitate exit on the eve of her wedding will doubtless give rise to all sorts of sordid speculation. I fear her reputation is quite in tatters. As for her erstwhile bridegroom"—Ash paused and shook his head sadly—"I doubt he'll have her now."

"Bastard!" Rhiannon hissed.

Carr's pale gaze flickered back and forth between Rhiannon and Ash. He moved across the room to Ash's side and leaned forward. In a voice gauged so that Rhiannon could not overhear, he whispered, "Is that the way of it? I must say, she doesn't look so very fond of you. Perhaps you lacked finesse? What say, Ash? Wasn't she very good? Or weren't you?"

It was a ploy, Ash knew, a simple gambit to discover what Rhiannon meant to him. Still, he nearly betrayed himself. He wanted to choke Carr to silence so very, very much. Instead he kept his expression blank.

"What the people of Fair Badden speculate on and what is truth—" Ash shrugged eloquently. "Surely you know how interchangeable such notions are. Ruining Miss Russell's reputation was simply a matter of expedience. You wanted her. She wouldn't go and I doubted whether her bridegroom would release her without a reason. I provided a reason. But remember, one can ruin a reputation without troubling to ruin anything else."

Rhiannon, on the other side of the room, had lifted her chin proudly.

"Ruin?" Carr, his back still to Rhiannon, snickered. "Such vanity. I'll tell you a secret: Ladies love to be *ruined* and in truth are quite peevish if you stop at their reputations. Witness Miss Russell's ire."

"What of it?" Ash asked in bored tones. "I'm more interested in my fee."

Carr's humor evaporated. He stepped back. "I'll see

you're paid by day's end," he said, "then you can go wherever it is you go."

"No hurry," Ash replied, fervently pleading with a deity he no longer believed in that Carr would not send him away from Wanton's Blush—and Rhiannon. He would do whatever necessary to stay here and watch Rhiannon until he knew what Carr planned for her.

"I've seen your guests, Carr," Ash said. "Fat purse, rabid appetites. High stakes tables, I should imagine."

"You're a vile drunk, Ash. And a violent one. You could embarrass me or my guests."

Ash laughed humorlessly. "*Your* guests, Carr? Your guests would pay in gold for the titillation of my company. Their sort is so often drawn to the sordid for their entertainment."

Rhiannon flinched as though his words hurt her. Impossible. He was imagining things.

Carr considered him through narrowed eyes. "True," he finally murmured. "All right. You may stay. But for God's sake, find something decent to wear. I won't have you offending my eyes looking like that."

"Of course," Ash said.

"Now leave us," Carr said. "Miss Russell and I have much to discuss."

To hesitate now would be disastrous.

Ash walked out of the room smoothly and easily, without looking at Rhiannon.

"My dear Miss Russell," Carr said, "please be seated. Where are my manners?"

The young woman hesitated a second before taking the seat Carr had indicated and settling her dress about her. She was clearly unused to such extravagant skirts.

But having no experience in society did not mean she should be underestimated. Indeed, the sharp glances he'd already received from her were indicative of a keen perception.

"Sherry, m'dear?"

She nodded, watching him doubtfully. "Please."

In his youth such suspiciousness would have presented an irresistible challenge. To succeed in seducing a woman already on her guard would have been high entertainment. He busied himself pouring two glasses of sherry.

Unfortunately he was no longer so easily diverted. Even the piquant pleasure of bedding a girl his son wanted wasn't incentive enough to woo this girl. Not that he wouldn't do it at some future point if it profited him.

He'd seen the glimmer of possessiveness in Ash's eyes. The girl might be useful in manipulating his recalcitrant eldest son. But for right now, seducing the chit wasn't necessary, and he allowed finally, his mouth flattening, he was no longer so young that the idea roused him.

Only one thing still had the same power over him that it had always had: his ambition to return in full glory to his former position in society—a position from which he'd been exiled over twenty-five years ago. But if he didn't return soon he'd be too old to enjoy his triumph.

He handed the girl her glass. She accepted it with a mumbled thanks and took a delicate sip of the sherry; a flicker of appreciation appeared in her hazel eyes. Thank God they were not sherry-colored.

As *hers* had been.

Knowing Rhiannon shared McClairen blood, even diluted by half a dozen generations, Carr had been . . . anxious that she might have the McClairen eyes. Like Janet.

Thank God, Fia did not have her mother's eyes. He didn't think he could stand it. And Ash, too, cold as his eyes were, had little of Janet in him. Only the other boy, Raine, carried his mother's stamp in feature and character.

The thought brought with it a ripple of sentimentality, and for a brief moment Carr indulged it. Some, he knew, said he had no heart. If they only knew how still, to this day, he grieved for his first wife. If they only knew the truth about Raine's incarceration, they would not slander him so.

It was his younger son's resemblance to his mother and not his father's greed, as was widely reported, that kept Carr from ransoming Raine. Well, honesty forced him to admit, perhaps Raine's usefulness in bringing Ash to heel also contributed to his continued incarceration—but *mostly* it was his resemblance to Janet.

Was not that romantic? Was that not indicative of the power of his passion, that he let his son rot in jail because the look of him was too painful to bear?

Janet would think so. She was the only one who'd ever truly understood him. He gazed out the window at the lawns spread below. All the rooms he occupied and entertained in faced front. He disliked looking out over the cliffs where Janet had fallen. Indeed, he could barely bring himself to venture into those sea-facing rooms. Once, just before the break of dawn, when all his guests slept, he'd found himself in the back library overlooking the terraced gardens. He'd thought he'd heard Janet singing, her voice soft and light—

"Sir?"

He looked around. The girl—Rhiannon—was regarding him as though she'd spoken several times.

He pulled his thoughts together. He had other matters to consider. Like this girl. This Rhiannon who might, if things did not go as they needed to go, prove troublesome.

"Your son is wrong in his estimate of my situation," she said. "I am sure Mrs. Fraiser will not deny me the home I have known for over ten years."

She waited, her body angled forward in entreaty. He steepled his fingertips before his lips, regarding her intently, thinking.

He wanted to believe her. But if Ash had destroyed the girl's reputation to return her to Fair Badden and the stigma of being used and abandoned could only be seen as an act of cruelty. The Prime Minister's letter, ostensibly written to express his condolences on the death of his third wife, had made it clear that Carr dare not be delinquent toward this or any woman.

He remembered the pertinent parts by heart:

His Majesty has watched in amazement and deep grief as three of his subjects, all well endowed in feature, form, and fact, have died whilst in your care, Lord Carr. There are some who have suggested to His Majesty that your series of sorrows have benefited you materially. His Majesty is wroth with such slanderous talk. He is certain that no woman shall ever again come to grief or be caused sorrow while under your care. Indeed, he is most adamant.

He glanced at Rhiannon, doing little to disguise the dislike in his eyes. Not only could he not return her to Fair Badden, he must make certain that while she was here she enjoyed only the best of health. That meant keeping her from his guests who were apt to see her fresh innocence as part of the entertainment.

As for the other matter—that would have to wait. He had some time yet. Something would occur to him. It always did.

He slapped his hands down on the arms of the chair and pushed himself to his feet.

Rhiannon blinked at his sudden movement. "Lord Carr?"

"No, Miss Russell. I must, for your own sake, refuse you. You will stay here."

"But—"

"Perhaps later you can return to this place. I will think carefully on it, consider the ramifications of your return and the alternatives."

"Alternatives? Please!" She threw out a hand. "I don't want to stay here. I don't *belong* here!"

"Miss Russell," Carr took her hand and patted it, a gesture that seemed both awkward and unnatural, "the best I can do is to assure you, you will not be here too long."

Chapter 22

"*A*sh must look quite like one of the Russian *vampirs*," Fia said. As had become her custom in the nine days since Rhiannon had arrived at Wanton's Blush, Fia had arrived in Rhiannon's room just before dawn and perched herself on the edge of the bed. Rhiannon had recently vacated.

Rhiannon faced the young girl with a carefully bland expression. Fia's beautiful, still face was as cream in the half-light, her immodest, sumptuous gowns wilted by a night of carousal. Yet, fatigued though she must be, each day before retiring she appeared in Rhiannon's room to relate the evening's exploits and debauches. Too often they involved Ash.

"I have never heard the term," Rhiannon said now.

Fia's rare smile flashed and disappeared. "It's a folk legend of the Russian people. A count came to Wanton's Blush last year. He grew . . . fond of me and

being uncertain whether I would be more beguiled by
fairy tales or salacious palace intrigue, he amused me by
alternating the two." She leaned over, a spark of mischief in her dark eyes. "I preferred the fables. The Rus-
sians are quite savages, you know."

"Yes?" Rhiannon asked. "What exactly is this *vampir*
you compare your brother to?"

"A *vampir*, my dear Miss Russell," Fia instructed,
sitting back, "is a dead creature that rises at night to
dine on the blood of the living."

"Disgusting," Rhiannon said coldly. She shed her
nightgown and drew on a chemise and petticoats. It
would do no good to order Fia from the room while
she dressed. She would simply ignore the order and
none of the servants would dare put hand to her. Besides, Fia was the only person with whom Rhiannon
spoke, Carr having abandoned her whilst he "pon-
dered" what to do with her, and Ash, besides stalking
her with his gaze, having kept his distance.

Fia shrugged. "I simply report what is told me and
make the observation that Ash could be a model for
these creatures."

Rhiannon hesitated. She didn't want to ask. "Why
do you say that?"

"Because," Fia raised her eyes to the ornate plaster
ceiling for inspiration, "because he looks like such a
predator. And seeing him night after night hunt
through Carr's guests, I must own he *is* a predator. Not
that the ladies mind. I think any number of them would
like to be mauled by my brother."

Rhiannon ignored this statement, though she had no
doubt it was true. She'd seen the type of woman who
visited Wanton's Blush. Rapacious, hungry. Eyeing Ash

with the same expression she'd once seen in him regarding her a lifetime ago. It had thrilled her then. God help her, it still might.

"He looks . . . I don't know," Fia continued thoughtfully. "His eyes . . ." she made a circular motion in front of her own face. "They're barren, empty, as though he simply moves by instinct rather than sentient purpose. He drinks too much. He rarely eats."

Rhiannon inhaled sharply. It wasn't that she cared for him; it was just that she so hated a waste.

"He'll be a corpse in truth if he continues on his current path," Fia said glibly. "He burns from within. 'Tis quite a spectacle. You ought to come down from this tower of yours, Miss Russell, if only to witness Ash's last bright hours."

"Don't say that!" Rhiannon snapped, startling the young girl. "What sort of unnatural creature are you that you can speak so of your own brother?"

"Ach, Miss Fia, Miss Russell be right!" The reproach came from the doorway where Gunna stood. Fia turned to face her onetime nanny "Ye shouldna speak so. Miss Russell does not understand the ways of yer family."

"How could she?" Fia asked calmly, but the color was high in her smooth cheeks. "I don't understand them myself. You should have seen her, Gunna. She all but bit my head off simply because I told her what Ash was getting up to—"

"I don't wish to speak about him," Rhiannon said, trying to drive the image of Ash, burning and spent, from her mind.

"Then we won't," Gunna declared, crossing the room to the tall chest on which lay a comb and brush.

"Ye'll be going for yer morning walk as usual, Miss Russell?"

"Yes," Rhiannon answered gratefully.

"Then best let me comb out that tangle. And best ye be in bed, Miss Fia," she said pointedly. "Yer lookin' none too well yerself."

This news did not hasten Fia on her way. If nothing else, the girl was wholly lacking in vanity. She cared less for her looks than anyone Rhiannon knew, and in many ways even abused her beauty.

"Go on, Fia," Gunna urged more gently. "Ye can come back and talk to Miss Russell this evening, before ye go down."

"Oh, all right," Fia agreed, dropping lightly to her feet and sliding gracefully across the room. She did not turn at the door, nor did she give any gesture of farewell when she left.

Gunna watched her go and Rhiannon studied the old woman curiously. Gunna was genuinely fond of the unnatural witchling.

"She hasn't had yer advantages, miss," Gunna murmured, her eyes still on the door through which Fia had departed. "She canna be anythin' other than what she is and that's better than anyone has the right to expect, or anyone has the imagination to see."

Immediately Rhiannon felt ashamed of her lack of charity. Who knew what she would have become had she been raised in this odd, displaced pleasure palace?

"You shame me, Gunna. It is only that Fia seems not to feel any pain for . . . another and I find that unnatural."

"She feels pain, mark me she does," Gunna muttered and then turned her one good eye on Rhiannon. "As do you, miss. Fer *his* sake."

Rhiannon shook her head in violent denial. "I would have as much care for a mad dog."

"Tenderhearted are ye?" Gunna asked and cackled. "Then ye must have learned that trick in that wee small hamlet of yours fer no Russell I knew of was ever accused of being softhearted."

"You knew the Russells well enough to have marked their character?" Rhiannon seized on the change of topic, glad of the diversion.

"A bit," Gunna replied.

Several times now Gunna had made a casual mention of Rhiannon's family, and with each remark Rhiannon found her interest sharpening. A surname would sometimes bring with it an image from her childhood: Ross of Tilbridge with his great shelf of eyebrows; Jamie Culhane, an old man with impossibly red hair; and Lady Urquardt, a thin lady whom everyone knew by her retinue of wee spaniels.

Piece by piece, Rhiannon fit together a past she'd denied and a history she'd never been told.

"My father." The words slipped unthinkingly from Rhiannon's mouth.

"What of him?" Gunna asked combing out her hair.

"Did you . . . did you know him?" She heard the caution in her own voice.

"I knew *of* him."

"What was he like?"

"A fine, decent man," Gunna said shortly, frustrating Rhiannon.

The old woman shuffled over to the chest of drawers at the foot of the bed and opened the lid. She rummaged inside a second before withdrawing a pale blue wool gown. "This may keep ye warm on yer walk, miss. Though it be cold this morning. Ye should ask Miss Fia fer a cloak to wear if ye must go traipsin' out by the sea." She gave a little shiver. "Canna see what draws ye there."

Rhiannon stood up and let Gunna slip the bodice about her and fasten the ties. "What was he like? I don't remember much of him."

"Yer father?" Gunna asked. "I thought ye dinna *want* to remember. *Any* of it. That's what ye told me the morning after ye come here and that's more than a week gone by."

"I won't be remembering," Rhiannon whispered. "I dinna . . . I mean I do not think I ever knew him enough to remember him."

Faintly now, every now and again, she could hear a trace of her mother's soft rolling burr in her own voice. It disconcerted her. She belonged in Fair Badden, not here. Yet slowly, day by day, she felt her former self slipping away and a new creature emerging to take her place, a bold creature with a Highland accent and, if Fia Merrick were to be trusted—which she was not—a direct, impervious expression.

"Oh, then that's different," Gunna said mockingly, holding out her hand to support Rhiannon as she stepped into the pooled circle of wool on the floor.

"Gunna, please," Rhiannon said as the old woman drew the skirts up and over stiff petticoats, since Rhiannon eschewed hoops.

The old woman sighed heavily. "He was an honorable man and a loyal one, Miss Russell. When the Mc-

Clairen called, yer dad came forthwith and brought with him such men as he could muster."

"But what was he like?" Rhiannon urged.

"I dinna know him." Gunna shook her head.

It was no more than she'd expected. Where would an old serving woman become intimate with a minor Highland chieftain?

"Is there anyone here, anyone at Wanton's Blush who might remember him or my mother or brother? Anyone who could tell me some stories?"

Gunna shook her head. "This wasn't Russell land, dear. 'Twas McClairen."

Rhiannon caught Gunna's hand. "But my family was loyal to the McClairen. Perhaps there is a McClairen hereabouts who might have known my family?"

Gunna hesitated.

"Gunna? Please. I thought when I came here that I would be haunted by the souls of those murdered in the reprisals. But if there are ghosts here, they're a timid lot and must be lured from hiding to tell their tales."

"The McClairens are an outlawed breed, miss," Gunna said, gently pulling her hand free of Rhiannon's light clasp.

"I just want to hear the stories, Gunna." When had this become so important to her? "The stories my mother never had the chance to tell me."

Gunna stared at her a second then cleared her throat. "Will ye be walking with Mr. Donne this morning?"

Rhiannon's gaze fell in disappointment. Apparently Gunna had decided she was not to be trusted. She would have sworn that the old woman knew a Mc-

Clairen or two. Well, the only way to win her trust was not to force her confidences.

"No," she said. "Not today."

Thomas Donne had made it his habit to meet her after an early breakfast and escort her on her turn about the back garden. He was handsome, urbane, and his attentions were warm with consideration. But today she wouldn't be satisfied with a walk in the seaside gardens. Today she wanted to follow the path she'd spied from the far gate, a thin line that skirted the cliff tops.

Gunna said nothing more, simply finished fastening the waistband and then pinning the embroidered stomacher in place. Finished, she stepped back and eyed Rhiannon critically. "Be careful, miss," she said. "I dislike the thought of ye bein' out there alone."

"But I won't be," Rhiannon replied, her thoughts returning to Ash in his window, vigilantly watching over her.

Rhiannon swung open the old gate and picked her way cautiously along the narrow path that followed the cliffs. She'd gone some distance before she came upon a rocky outcrop jutting over the sea. Heedless of Fia's borrowed dress and her thin shoes she scrambled atop and stood up.

The wind blew heavily here, lashing her loosened hair across her cheeks and throat and whipping the heavy skirts back up and over her petticoats. Far below, the sea crashed against the jagged teeth edging the island's shore, the subsequent fine mist shimmering in the air below. Above this, a phalanx of pure white gulls had caught the updraft from the sea and hovered, suspended just beyond her reach.

Rhiannon closed her eyes and lifted her arms, letting the gusty wind buffet her body, pretending she too might fly. A sense of homecoming enveloped her. She'd done this before! She'd stood on some high point overlooking this same sea, spread her arms, and imagined she was flying.

She shivered, but not with the near panic with which she'd looked out at the sea on her arrival here. She shivered with emotion. She'd once loved the sea. She'd forgotten—

"Step back."

Her eyes flew open at the sound of his voice and she started to spin about but her shoe heel caught in the shale and she began to slip— Strong hands snatched her up, pulled her back tightly against a hard chest.

"Dear God, what were you thinking?" Ash's voice, warm and low, swept over her ear, his lips tangling in the loose hair at her temple.

The hands gripping her upper arms did not release her. Between her shoulder blades she could feel his heart pound against her back, the muscle of his thighs press against her rump.

And, God help her, God forgive her, that's all that was needed to bring a wave of longing rushing over her with such devastating power that she nearly turned in his embrace and wrapped her arms about him.

What was she that she longed to lay beneath this man? Mad or craven or as dissolute as the women whom Fia watched pant after him?

"You mustn't!" he grated out. His voice vibrated with anger. "You can't. God, *not here*. Not anywhere!"

She started at his unexpected words, tried to break free but his grip held fast, bruising her upper arms.

Abruptly she realized what he was saying. Dear Lord, he thought she'd been about to fling herself into the sea when in fact she'd been lusting after him!

A burble of hilarity escaped her and he shook her violently.

"Damn you! *Damn you*, if you think to escape me by such foul means."

She twisted but still he would not let her go, instead wheeling her violently and catching hold of her again. He grasped her chin, forcing her head up, forcing her to meet his eyes. His lips curled back over his teeth in a feral expression. "I will tie you to my bed and force food and drink down your throat and keep you there for all eternity before I will let you harm yourself."

He meant it. The violence he held in check scared her, and he'd never scared her before. Every vestige of the man who'd arrived in Fair Badden was gone, leaving this stranger with his burning eyes and punishing grip.

"I was not going to throw myself off," she said, and swallowed. "I swear it."

The fury stayed in his eyes a full minute as his gaze raked her face, searching her countenance. Slowly the fingers digging into her skin relaxed, the tautness about his mouth eased and with it her fear.

Anger took its place. He thought her so pitiful that she would kill herself rather than live here? That she was so undone by his betrayal that life no longer held any meaning for her?

God help her, she might be unable to banish the memory of his haunted, passion-filled eyes from her thoughts, or forget the soft touch of his hand caressing her, but she still owned her pride. She was still Rhiannon Russell.

"Nothing, *nothing*, you or your family could ever do to me could make me take my own life," she said in a voice quivering with ill-suppressed emotion.

He watched her intently.

"I watched my father bayoneted to death rather than give away the whereabouts of his men. I saw my uncle shot in the head still defiant even though he lay helpless on a frost-covered moor. I share their blood. How dare you think I'd kill myself over the likes of you?" she spat out.

"I beg your forgiveness," he said through stiff lips. "I should have known better."

"Yes." She raked him with her scorn. "Take your hands from me! They're filthy. I'm not one of your fascinated jades panting to discover if your embrace is as feral as your looks!"

His chin drew back sharply. He dropped his hands as if she'd scalded him and he tore his gaze from her, as though he found the sight of her painful. He looked down at the crashing sea, breathing heavily through his nostrils.

She regarded him angrily. The unkempt tangle of the black hair falling down his lean cheeks and beard-darkened jaw was dull and lank. Mauve stains marked his eyes, and an old bruise colored one brow.

She was about to look away when she discerned the faintest tremor in his hands hanging loose at his sides. She looked back up at his averted profile, studying it closer.

She saw now that his pallor hadn't been unhealthily white, the blood had literally drained from his face. She knew this because the hue was slowly returning. His lips were still chalky and the manner in which he held himself suggested a sudden overpowering enervation, not anger. My God, she realized with a sense of discovery, of wonder—he'd been afraid. Not merely afraid. Terrified. For her sake.

Confusion churned her emotions into an unrecognizable brew. She wanted to touch him, to smooth the fine lines from his forehead and the corners of his eyes. She wanted to shout at him and rail against what he'd done to her—to them.

She did neither. She drew back and had begun to move past him when she saw the long length of material on the rock behind him, a plaid woven in rich heather, gold, and emerald greens. She frowned and picked it up, turning to regard him askance, and found he was already watching her.

"What is this?" she asked.

A corner of his mouth turned up in mockery. "Gunna said you'd come out without a cloak. I'll not have you dead by any means, Rhiannon. Not by your hand or nature's ministrations. That's the McClairen plaid."

She stared down at it. He confounded her. She did not know what to expect from him next.

"Why?" she breathed.

"Gunna said as you'd been asking after your family. Your family's history and my mother's were interwoven." His voice was flat. "Take it. But don't let Carr see it. Any token of the McClairens enrages him."

With so few words he gave her a piece of her history, a piece of her past. Emotion clotted her throat. He could not know how important this was to her, how much it meant, and yet she could not rid herself of the notion that he *did* know. She carefully draped the tartan around her like a precious relic.

"Thank you." She touched his arm in a spontaneous gesture of gratitude. His lips curled derisively.

"Don't thank me. It's not but an old rag. And don't come out here again." His gaze shifted down toward the boulders at the cliff's base. A little tick jumped in his cheek. "It isn't safe."

Before she could reply, he brushed passed her and strode away. He did not look back.

Ash heard Carr speaking in the hall just outside the door. Quickly he shrugged out of his jacket and pulled his shirt free of his breeches. He flung himself into one of the gothic chairs that stood beside Carr's desk.

He would never have dared entered his father's office at all had he not noticed Carr leaving the gaming table in the adjoining room via the hall. The office door had remained unlocked.

Rifling through Carr's desk had been a risky venture, but since Ash's arrival it had been his first opportunity to discover the reason behind Carr's interest in Rhiannon Russell.

Now, when Carr opened the door, he would find Ash sprawled in one of his prize imports, his leg draped over the arm, his head lolling forward on his chest, his arm hanging bonelessly by his side, and his hand brushing the neck of a half-emptied wine bottle. The cool draft of an opening door filtered over Ash's hands. He strained his ears and heard the candles lighting the orderly surface of Carr's desk sputter irritably.

Ash opened his eyes to slits, taking the chance that it

would be a few seconds before Carr's eyes could adjust to the dim light. Carr's gaze darted about the room, falling on the position of the few papers on his desk, the surface of the drawers, and flicking, for just one telling instant, over the mantelpiece.

So, that was where Carr kept his treasures. The rigidity in his father's body eased, he turned his attention to Ash.

"What are you doing in here, Merrick?" Carr asked, his voice pitched low, testing.

Ash sighed deeply.

"Merrick!"

"Humph?" Ash grunted. "Say, what? Did I win then?"

"What are you doing in here?" Carr again demanded.

Ash peered woozily up at his sire as if he could not quite remember the name that went with the face. He pushed himself up a ways in the chair, grimacing, and looked around the room. "Ain't this the privy?"

"What?" Carr thundered.

Ash let an expression of confusion become dawning comprehension and finally drunken hilarity.

"Damme, sir," he sobbed through his laughter, "I *am* sorry. Bit foxed, you know. Had to leave the fellows midgame. Methinks I thought this chair was the privy! Sat on a few in London, don't you know." He leaned over and examined the baroque carved legs of the chair. "I swear I've never seen a more likely candidate."

Carr's face turned ruddy with rage. "You swine! I had that chair shipped here from a Moroccan seraglio! If you've soiled it I'll—"

He grabbed Ash's arm, hauling him to his feet. Ash

made himself hang loose in his father's vicious grip. He grinned foolishly. "Nah. Think I fell asleep first."

With a sound of disgust Carr shoved Ash away. Ash fell back heavily in the chair. The suspicion evaporated from Carr's face, leaving it blank as a reptile's.

And why should he be suspicious? Ash asked himself. He'd spent nearly two weeks convincing Carr he'd plumbed new depths of depravity—would take any bet, do anything to earn the sum needed for Raine's release. A glimpse in any mirror revealed a gray complexion and eyes red-rimmed with lack of sleep. Where other men scented their bodies with perfumes and powders, Ash anointed himself with stale beer and sweat.

"You're filthy with drink again, Merrick," Carr said. "Though I appreciate your efforts. I've acquired quite a tidy sum betting on just how many bottles you'll upend before passing out each evening."

"Care to split the winnings?" Ash asked cheekily. "No? Didn't think so." He fidgeted in his seat. "For a chair that ain't a privy chair, this is deuced uncomfortable."

"It's invaluable."

"Doubt that," Ash replied flatly. "I'd wager you can set a very exact price on it." He wrapped his arm over the back of the chair and hung his weight from it. "New, isn't it? Lots of new geegaws in the family manse—not our family manse, I realize, but who's to know?"

"I'm remodeling," Carr said coolly. "You never did understand what I was trying to do here. How could you?"

He wandered behind Ash's seat, his fingers caressing the back of the chair. "I need beauty like you need drink, Merrick. Life is a simple process of animal adaptation but Art is a controlled mutation that only a connoisseur is qualified to direct. . . ."

Ash had heard the speech before. Once launched into his discourse, little would stem Carr's flow of words. Ash kept his gaze fixed on Carr's face but allowed his thoughts to uncoil along their own path.

He'd had little time to rifle through Carr's desk. He'd scanned through his ledger discovering in the neatly penned columns two things: First, the refurbishment of Wanton's Blush was costing Carr far more money than he owned. Second, a large sum of unidentified origins was deposited quarterly in Carr's accounts.

As for the letters, Carr's communiqués had proven uninteresting if often sordid. Pleas for extension on debts outnumbered anglings for invitations to Wanton's Blush. Interspersed amongst these were detailed plans for plaster ceilings and marble friezes; bids and specifications from architects, artisans, and garden designers; payment demands from marble cutters and weavers.

Only one note had caught Ash's attention, a terse missive from one of his father's many victim-cum-debtors, none other than Lord Tunbridge. Of the pierced hand. After begging for a few more months in which to make good his debt, Tunbridge had closed his note: "I shall do all that I can to convince His Majesty that you are indeed reformed. This may take time and whilst I am engaged on your behalf, I adjure you to be in all matters circumspect."

Unfortunately, before Ash had had time to look for other letters carrying Tunbridge's seal, he'd heard Carr.

"—Donne might take her off my hands."

Ash's head snapped up before he could control the movement. His father's gaze was waiting. Carr smiled obliquely.

Ash swiped up the bottle of wine and took a long draught to mask his reaction. "Take who? Fia?"

He knew Carr was not speaking of Fia but of Rhiannon. She plagued his dreams and subverted his reason. Even whilst sunk in the deepest of carouses, he found himself reliving the moment when Carr had told her that Ash had been paid to bring her to Wanton's Blush. He saw again the frail promise of her trust shatter and become bitter cynicism; and when he was not drunk, he could not escape the contempt in her voice, telling him he was filthy and feral.

But most haunting of all was that moment on the cliffs when pitiful gratitude for his mother's torn tartan had overcome her natural, her so well-justified, revulsion and she'd whispered thank you and touched his arm. He still felt that touch as distinctly as if his flesh had been branded.

Like a fever that would not break, she lived in him, destroying his resolve and making mock of his intentions. He should be focused on winning enough money to ransom his brother. But he was in here, looking for clues as to why Carr had sent him to fetch her.

"Not Fia. My new ward."

"Donne has offered for Rhiannon Russell?" Ash mumbled, holding his wine bottle up and eyeing the three fingers of liquor disconsolately.

"Not yet," Carr answered. "But he dogs the girl's footsteps, or so I'm told. Weren't you?"

No, he wasn't and he should have been told. He'd

paid well for information about Rhiannon Russell and he'd received detailed reports for his coin: what hour she woke, what gown she wore, what book she read. But not that Donne courted her. Ash shrugged non-committally.

"Why do you want to get rid of Rhiannon Russell?" Ash asked as if just struck by the thought. "You just gave me a fat purse for bringing her here. Don't make sense."

"One can't be too forward-looking," Carr pronounced silkily. "I'm simply ascertaining my options."

"You've never so much as written the first word in a letter without already having planned the last line," Ash said. "So what I'm asking myself, is what you planned when you sent me for Rhiannon Russell?"

Carr's gaze met his. "Busy thinking, Merrick? Why is that?"

But Ash had found a dint in Carr's skin. He knew Carr's tactics; he would not be diverted by his questions. "What do you want with Rhiannon Russell?" He pressed the slight advantage.

Carr casually took a seat, settling and smoothing the satin cloth of his breeches before answering. "I really didn't know where she was until now," he explained in bored tones. "A man mentioned her name and said she lived in his village. I recognized it and asked him about her. It became clear she was the girl my valet had turned away from my London town house years ago."

Ash laughed nastily. "Don't try to tell me your conscience had been pricking you over her loss."

"Of course not," Carr said with a flash of annoyance. "I was *told* she was comely. I *knew* she was the last of a once wealthy family. I *assumed* that as such she would be heir to whatever trinkets and coin they had managed to hold. I gambled 'twas so."

"So simple?" Ash took another swig of wine. "Fascinating. Pray continue."

"The rest is, in hindsight, sloppy. But in my own defense remember I felt compelled by some urgency. Hoping to prevent some provincial boy from securing her inheritance by marrying the chit, I sent you for her. And, Merrick"—he looked up from the rings bedecking his pale hands—"had circumstances been different and Miss Russell an heiress, in fact, I would have been extremely upset had you returned with the news that she'd wed."

But Ash was more interested in how much Carr had divulged. Too much. Carr never explained anything to anyone. How much was lies and how much simple misdirection?"

"Alas," said Carr, "the girl doesn't own a thing. She's utterly a pauper. As I'm sure you know."

"Yes." Ash wiped the wine from his mouth with his sleeve. "Who did you say told you she was in Fair Badden?"

"I didn't. But since you ask, it was some blond Goliath named Watt. He came here with his fellow rurals in order to taste society." Carr smiled serenely. "They were quite surprised at the cost."

Watt? Ash remembered St. John saying he'd met Carr but no one had ever mentioned Watt being here. Certainly not Watt. Why the oversight?

"My turn," Carr said. "I find your interest in this girl inexplicable."

Ash was ready. "Not so inexplicable," he said. "I need money. I thought she had some. Put some effort into makin' meself pleasant, you know. Hate to see it go to waste."

"You *did* seduce her."

Ash waved his hand. "No. Though she might well think she's been seduced. You know how these sheltered little virgins are. You fumble 'neath their skirts a minute and they think they've been done."

"Indeed. Well, if Thomas Donne is overcome with patriotic fervor and decides to offer for the wench, I'm sure he'll appreciate your restraint." Carr's gaze lay carefully on Ash's face.

Donne's hand moving over Rhiannon's silken flesh. Her mouth opening beneath his. Her long, smooth thighs wrapped tight—

"That would be bloody convenient, wouldn't it?" Somehow Ash managed to smile disinterestedly.

"How long is it you're planning on staying at Wanton's Blush, Merrick?"

A vise tightened about Ash's throat. Carr *couldn't* send him away. He shrugged. "Don't know. Why? You can't spare the room?"

"The room yes but you've been winning more than losing and at *my* guests expense."

Ash snorted. "Didn't mean to encroach on your feeding grounds."

"But you have," Carr said. "I'm afraid I don't see any real advantage in having you here after all."

"I don't have anywhere to go," Ash said sullenly.

"If you'd like to remain here you'd best make yourself not only useful but lucrative," Carr said. "To me."

For a second, Ash held his father's gaze, clear gemlike blue eyes meeting cool, unfathomable dark ones. The orders were clear.

"Oh, I think I might be able to amuse you—*and* enrich you." With that Ash let his head fall back against the chair and his eyes drift shut.

"Make sure you do," Carr said.

Ash did not respond, playing the sulky mute. Five minutes passed before he heard Carr's footsteps retreating across the room. The door opened and shut.

He opened his eyes and pushed himself wearily to his feet. His head felt thick, his tongue dry, and his belly rebelled against too many days with too much wine and too little food. The sticky sheen of sleeplessness coated his skin, and he stank. He was burning himself out.

He should walk away. But he wouldn't. God help him, he couldn't leave her here. And the great jest of it was that staying would earn him nothing. Not even her smile. To her he was less than human. A rutting, sotted animal. Carr would never allow him to stay at Wanton's Blush if he weren't thus. As long as Ash appeared bestial and seemingly drunk, he was tolerated. Carr would never feel safe otherwise.

He longed to tell Rhiannon this but he dared not. She was too ingenuous, too candid. She didn't yet understand the layers upon layers of deception that were part of life at Wanton's Blush. Besides, she would never believe him. Carr was handsome, charming, and attentive.

Ash . . . Ash was the monster.

It was the price he paid to stay here with her. And as long as he did not have to witness her abhorrence, it was a price he was willing to pay. With that comfortless thought, Ash staggered to the door leading to the foyer and wrenched it open, blinking like some subterranean creature into the brilliant sunlight. He stretched out his hand, groping for the support of the wall.

It was then he saw her. The sunlight affixed itself to her smooth skin, shimmered in her hair, molded a warm shadow beneath the fullness of her lip, and picked out with exquisite detail the contents of her expression. Disgust. Pity. Revulsion.

It was too much.

"You," he rasped out. "Get out of here. Now!"

Chapter 23

"Up with you, you great stanking hound!"

Ash rolled over on the mattress, groped for some missile to hurl, and finding none, snarled, "Get out, Gunna! Your tender ministrations are not needed!"

The door slammed shut. Ash winced at the reverberating echo in his head. Good. He only wanted to be left alone. He'd stood just about all he was willing to stand—

A surprisingly strong hand grabbed a hank of his hair and jerked his head back. "Damme, witch! Are you seeking to tear my head off?" he gasped.

"I dunna want it," Gunna spat in disgust. "Many more days on yore present course and yer head will be so far pickled it'll be useful only as garnish. Ha!" She cackled.

"You're a witch, Gunna."

"Aye, and you're a knave. What are ye thinkin', Mr.

Ash? Destroyin' yerself like this isn't going to win the lassie's good opinion."

Ash went still. Gunna had always had uncanny insight into his mind and motives.

"I don't want her good opinion."

He heard Gunna click her tongue. "Her heart then, lad. And dunna bother to contest that, 'cause I'll not believe a word of any denial."

"You're getting cursed mawkish in your old age, Gunna." His ire had spent itself, leaving only overwhelming weariness. He smiled slightly. "Though you always did insist on finding the good in a thing. Surprising since you've spent so many years in his employ."

"He's not all bad," Gunna said and then added with the flat practicality that Ash had so needed during his early years, "though I'll allow he's *mostly* bad."

He laughed weakly. Gunna regarded him with something like fondness. "You'll do, Mr. Ash, if you'll just give yerself a fair chance. You're strong and hard, hot-forged and bright shining like that dirk ye carry. A passionate man. But there's no shame in that."

Her words eviscerated his laughter. "God! Look at me; think back on what you know me to have done. I am *not* 'bright shining'!"

"Aye, ye are, Ash," Gunna said softly, and touched her hand to the back of his head.

In reply he moaned.

"You probably think Raine a saint, too."

"*Too?*" Gunna echoed. "I dunna recall naming you 'saint,' Ash Merrick. Far from it. And no I dunna think Mr. Raine a saint. He's just reckless is all, as willing to let his emotions sweep him away as you are to keep yours hidden."

"Raine is a devil." He craned his head around and peered up at Gunna. She stood primly at the foot of his bed, her hands folded neatly at her waist, the ravaged side of her face composed. "If one pledges one's life to protecting a devil," he queried interestedly, "what does that make one? A demon?"

Gunna ignored him. "It's Miss Fia I fret most about. She's so vulnerable."

Ash rolled fully over. "Don't waste your time worrying about Fia. She's as self-possessed a little mannequin as ever I've seen. In a contest pitting my little sister against the world, I'd wager on Fia and give the world a ten-point lead. Carr dotes on her."

"Aye," Gunna murmured. "She's yet to see him for what he is. When she does, I fear what it will do to her."

"Give her a newfound appreciation of sin, I suspect."

Gunna's lopsided mouth creased in lines of disapproval. Though it was hard to gauge expression on that ruined mien, he'd long ago learned to read it in her eyes. He'd hurt her. She cared for Fia, honestly and deeply. Sometimes, however, a kind heart saw only what it expected to see.

"You might ask Rhiannon Russell about perception and reality," he muttered, flinging his arm over his eyes.

"Might I?" Gunna padded closer to the bed. "What did you do to her, Mr. Ash, that has you in such pain?"

Why bother to deny it? Gunna would only ignore any protestations to the contrary.

"Oh, destroyed a few of her illusions," he said. "You know, seduced her then trumped up some fantasy about her groom trying to kill her. Abducted her on the eve of her wedding. Dragged her here." He shrugged. "That sort of thing."

"Mr. Ash."

"Quite the bright-shining blade, aren't I, Gunna?" he asked calmly. He was not surprised when he heard her shuffling step carry her from the room.

"Come, lass. There's naught for it but to obey. Carr's made an edict and you'd best not cross him," Gunna said.

"I don't want to meet his guests," Rhiannon said, shaking her head.

It was late afternoon and Rhiannon had spent the day wandering through the seaward-facing bedchambers on the third floor. Most of them were unoccupied, draped in cobwebs and sheets.

Gunna had found her there, in the oldest part of the castle, a turreted tower that had been untouched during Carr's renovations. The walls were bare and the floor uncovered, but the cushioned window seat was soft and dry and the sunlight warmed Rhiannon's skin.

"Ye canna to hide up here forever, lassie," Gunna said gently.

"I'm not hiding," Rhiannon protested, knowing full well that she was. She could not see Ash again. Not as she'd last seen him. "Why should I hide?" she added weakly.

"There's been some idle gossip about the servants' hall."

"Really? And what do these gossips say?"

"You don't want to know it." Gunna took her hand and tried to pull her up. "Idle blather. I should know better than to open me mouth and spout such."

Rhiannon remained seated. Outside the sun sparkled on the sea. "I should like to know."

The sunken, drooping eye exposed by the draping of her veil regarded her cautiously. Rhiannon had the distinct impression the old Scotswoman was deferring judgment.

"They says in the servants' hall," the old woman finally began, "that Mr. Ash did ruin you and that's why ye'll have naught to do with him and that's why ye keep here by yerself. For fear of him."

Rhiannon drew back from Gunna's hold. They all knew. They all knew so much and so little.

"Others, however," Gunna continued carefully, "says yore breaking yer heart over him. I don't mean to be forward, miss, but I know how it can be. My sainted sister loved a man who broke her heart. He took from her everything a woman can offer and then he cast her aside. Is that what Ash Merrick has done to you?"

Rhiannon stared at her. Gunna's sister and she shared similar histories, but the man who'd used Rhiannon had not abandoned her. He'd done worse; he'd stolen her—and her heart.

With a start Rhiannon realized how much she wanted to confide in Gunna. She missed Edith so very much. Even though she'd never fretted Edith with her problems, her beloved foster mother had comforted Rhiannon just with her presence. Rhiannon glanced at Gunna. It had been long years since she'd confided in anyone. Ash alone had been the closest to breaching the high walls she'd built to keep others out and herself safe from her past.

"Did he, dearie?" Gunna repeated softly.

Perhaps it was time.

"If by 'ruin' you mean physically force me," Rhiannon said slowly, "no. He disguised his true nature, though, and I would not see past his beauty to his treachery. I betrayed myself."

Gunna's deeply lined forehead furrowed. "You could not . . . forgive him, of course."

"He doesn't *ask* for my forgiveness," she replied. "He'd do the same again. He told me so."

"Would *you*?" Gunna asked. "Would you be deceived a second time?"

Rhiannon stared at her hands, fingers lacing and unlacing, unable to answer. Would she? She'd like to have said "no, of course not," but her tenacious core of honesty did not allow equivocation.

The truth was she was deceived every time she looked at him. She still felt the pull of his attraction, the overwhelming lure of his masculinity.

"Do you love him?" A query so hushed it might have been Rhiannon's own heart asking the question.

"I don't *know* him. He fascinated me. But he was not what I thought." Was she telling Gunna or reminding herself? Gunna tugged on her hand and she stood up.

Leaning on Rhiannon's arm, Gunna began tottering toward the steep tower steps. "How's that?"

"He's cruel. And ruthless. He obtains what he wants and he wanted me. For one night."

Gunna began a cautious decent, leading Rhiannon. Her eyes stayed fixed on the stairs but after a moment she said, "I been here many years, lassie, and I dunna claim to know Ash Merrick well. He was more man than boy when I came to take care of Lady Fia, but while I might allow that he's ruthless, it's in my mind that that's what he's had to be. If he's ever wanted something, I have never seen him admit to it. He'd never give Lord Carr that sort of advantage. Carr already has too many ways to bend Mr. Ash to his will."

"Why?" she asked, trying hard to understand this man who'd so much power over her.

Gunna paused at the landing. "Carr's guests talk. They say that Ash Merrick is the best gambler in Scotland, England, or anywhere in between. And you must ken that Mr. Ash knows how to use that blade he carries. People are afraid of Mr. Ash.

"Now, lassie, wouldna such a man be useful to whisper a threat into an enemy's ear? Or issue a challenge? Or do any bit of a deed in London that Carr cannot because he's been made to live here?"

Despite the heat in the narrow spiraling stairwell, Rhiannon shivered. "I knew Ash was ruthless. I did not name him evil."

"Evil?" Gunna's lopsided mouth twined. "Mr. Ash isn't evil. Think on him as a fine Spanish blade and having about as much choice in where its owner plunges it."

"Carr."

"Aye," Gunna agreed. "And Carr would not like to lose that particular weapon."

Yes. She could see Ash as a weapon. Yesterday, storms blowing in from the ocean had kept her indoors. She'd been coming down the stairs to the main level searching for some way to occupy her time when a door had swung open.

Ash had reeled through it. He wore neither waistcoat nor jacket. His shirt was open halfway down his chest. A soiled stock fell like a noose about his neck.

He'd lifted his head, squinting against the weak light. His black hair fell across his soot-fringed eyes. He stumbled forward and only saved himself from falling by bracing his hand against the wall.

Then he'd seen her. His eyes had narrowed as though he had trouble focusing them and she realized he was drunk, debilitatingly drunk. "You," he'd said hoarsely. "Get out of here. Now!"

She'd needed no further encouragement. She'd fled like a hind from the hounds but she hadn't been able to flee the image of him. Yet she found herself deliberately thinking back over those few moments, just so she could evoke them.

"Best hurry, lass," Gunna said.

They'd come to the landing on the floor where her rooms were located. Impulsively, Gunna smoothed her hand down Rhiannon's cheek. Rhiannon flushed, deeply moved. "You're too good a listener, Gunna," she said.

"And you're too good a mute," Gunna murmured. "Now, Carr wants you and that's nothing to take lightly. Especially as his valet says he's been in a vexatious mood these past few days."

Rhiannon smiled ruefully. "I doubt Carr has even noted my absence."

"I would not count on that," Gunna said, opening the door to the stairwell and leading Rhiannon out into the wide, sunlit corridor. "Carr must fair dote on a beauty like you. What is it he plans for you, do you think, lassie?"

"I don't know," Rhiannon replied honestly. "I haven't spoken with him since my arrival."

"Ha!" Gunna straightened, her one exposed brow lifting in surprise. "Carr's not bothered with you at all?"

"Not a word."

"There's a wonder," Gunna murmured. "Why is Carr wanting you to be present today of all days?" She worried the slack portion of her lip with her teeth as she shuffled quickly toward Rhiannon's room. "Why would he want you to see Ash Merrick in such a state? Or maybe it's Mr. Ash he's wanting to do the seeing—"

"What are you talking about?" Rhiannon asked, scurrying to keep up with her.

The single eye gleamed with inspiration. "Carr might be using you to regain the use of his . . . Spanish blade. He knows Mr. Ash is taken with ye."

Rhiannon's curiosity faded. The old woman was a romantic after all, building fairy tales. Rhiannon would not make that same mistake. "Ash doesn't love me."

Gunna spared her a brusque glance. "Fa! He would'na lay with you lest he had feelings for ye, lassie."

An image of Ash's face stark with longing filled Rhiannon's mind's eye. Beltaine night. What she remembered may not have existed at all. She shook her head, willing it away. "He takes whatever appeals to him."

Gunna pulled her along. "He doesn't bed any of the ladies here. Last night Mrs. Quinton give me the key to her chambers to slip in Mr. Ash's hand, and he slipped it right back," she said impatiently. "There's somethin' in ye calls to him and I'm thinkin' he may not like it any more than ye."

Rhiannon *would not* let it happen again. And yet . . . God help her. "Why are you so sure he wasn't simply dallying with me?"

Gunna looked at her in patent disgust. "That's easy enough," she said. "Ash Merrick hates his father. He would never use a woman for mere sport if for no other reason than that his father would."

Chapter 24

The crowd gathering in the great hall for the midday entertainment vibrated with excitement. Titters of excited laughter rose from behind the agitated flutter of fans. The novelty of rising early these past few days still fascinated this jaded group. Besides, when the spectacle ended, nothing prevented them from returning to their beds, which they often did.

Thomas Donne stood near the bottom of the marble staircase and glanced up to where a flash of bronze satin on the landing high above had caught his eye.

So the Scottish fledgling had escaped her gilt cage, he thought. Perhaps when Carr's guests moved to the stable yard, she would descend, but not until then. She was as leery of human contact as a kestrel. Donne could not fault her. She was out of place in this cesspool.

After a second's hesitation, Donne stationed himself

at the foot of the stairs and waited, vexed by his un-likely concern.

Rhiannon Russell touched his heart, and Thomas Donne thought he'd long since mastered every bit of that organ. But her wild, fragile beauty and that loose, easy stride of hers recalled other girls with auburn hair and free-moving grace. Even all those English manners some matron had imposed on her could not mask her direct gaze or canny nature.

He'd forgotten how differently the Scottish raise their lassies. There was no falseness in Rhiannon. One got the notion that she saw every deceit a man perpetu-ated on others . . . and on himself. It was a compel-ling sensation and an unsettling one. He knew better than to rhapsodize over the past.

But in Rhiannon Russell he saw the best of Scotland. He looked at her and recalled brae heirs and valiant sons, killed or imprisoned or sent off to rot in En-gland's penal colonies. Aye, looking at Rhiannon Rus-sell was a bittersweet endeavor but one he could not deny himself.

A week ago he'd discovered that she woke early and moved about the castle freely while the rest of Carr's guests slept. Since he seldom found peace in slumber and even less here at Wanton's Blush, he'd made it a habit to seek her company.

She didn't seem to mind. Over the course of those short hours he'd discovered Rhiannon had other traits besides beauty and honesty. Each day she seemed to gain more of a singular strength, the sort of strength that comes from abandoning oneself to fate, of moving past fear. It was a characteristic with which he was well acquainted. He and Rhiannon Russell had much in common.

He leaned back against the newel and scanned the thinning company. Beneath their piled wigs, their faces were slack with witless hunger and numb desire. If he had a jot of red blood in his veins, he would take Rhiannon out of here this very night. No one would miss her until dawn. During the evenings she kept to herself and Carr never asked after her . . . Carr. Aye. That was the danger and the enigma.

Donne was not the only one who thought so. Several times, when the revelries had wound to a temporary end, Ash Merrick had sobered up and sought Donne out. Ash belabored Donne on every point he'd discovered about the Russell family and Rhiannon's hypothetical brother. Despite his penchant for debauchery—and just lately his wholehearted pursuit of it—Merrick still owned a subtle intelligence.

The reminder killed Donne's urge to chivalry. No one would notice if he took Rhiannon Russell—no one except Ash Merrick. A ruthless sort of gentleman, one a wise man would not lightly cross.

And Thomas Donne was a most wise man.

"Do you still pine for your bucolic home?" Fia looked over Rhiannon's shoulder and met her reflected gaze in the mirror.

"Yes," Rhiannon replied. "I miss Fair Badden very much."

Fia's heavy eyelids sank over her dark eyes. "Well, darling, you don't seem to be wasting away from the effects. You're in blooming good looks."

Rhiannon finished twisting her hair into a knot atop

her head and pushed herself away from the dressing table. "Thank you. I think."

"Why is that, do you suppose?" Fia asked silkily. "Do you suppose you were not as happy at Fair Badden as you claim? Or perhaps your heart was never as fully engaged as you thought?"

The little witch, Rhiannon thought with a sharp glance at the girl. Her expression softened when she saw that her glare had disconcerted the girl. That was the trouble with Fia; innocence and jaded knowledge inexorably twined together to form her character.

Most of the time Rhiannon couldn't decide whether Fia's questions were deliberately provocative and biting or astoundingly innocent and honest. And perhaps she was angered with Fia because Fia was in some small way right.

"I do not doubt, Miss Fia, that I loved well Mrs. Fraiser. Every day I think of her and miss her very much and hope that she does not grieve for me or worry." Fia was watching her fiercely, her brows puckered uncharacteristically in concentration.

"But, perhaps," Rhiannon went on, "Fair Badden does not hold the place in my heart I thought it did. Perhaps no place is anything more than what memory and experience make it."

The girl held Rhiannon's gaze for one long moment before Fia nodded shortly. "You should write a letter to your Mrs. Fraiser."

"I can do that?" Rhiannon asked in surprise.

"Of course," Fia said coolly. "This isn't Bedlam, Miss Russell, it's a castle. We do have servants for that sort of thing. Write her a letter—she can read? Good, and I'll have it delivered."

Nonplussed by Fia's detached magnanimity, Rhiannon rose to her feet and smiled tentatively. "Thank you . . . I will. Your kindness—"

"You really should let Gunna fit you with a wig. With your eye color a pale silver would be astonishing." Rhiannon quelled the impulse to smile. Fia was as disconcerted by having made the offer as Rhiannon had been on hearing it and she was seeking to cover her awkwardness. The least Rhiannon could do was to help her out.

"I dislike wigs," Rhiannon said. "Nits."

"I don't have lice!" Fia cried.

Rhiannon raised her brows. "Of course not."

Fia frowned. "We'd best be going. Have you finished? No powder, either? No beauty mark?"

"No." Rhiannon swept past the girl and through the door, smiling when she heard the trip of Fia's feet hastening to catch up. She was a tiny thing.

"Carr won't like your dress," Fia warned breathlessly on making Rhiannon's side. She eyed Rhiannon's gown as they began descending the stairs. "Too *jeune fille*."

Rhiannon was unconcerned with Carr's sartorial approval. Ash Merrick and Fia's curiosity about her family in Fair Badden occupied her thoughts. "You have another brother, do you not?"

"Yes. Raine. He's a few years younger than Ash. Big, rough-looking fellow."

"I don't believe I've met him."

"Well, darling, you wouldn't lest you'd been loitering about French prison yards," Fia said complacently.

Rhiannon halted. "Prison?"

Fia sighed and stopped also. "Yes. I thought you

knew. I thought everyone knew. Ash was imprisoned, too. Until Carr ransomed him almost a year ago."

. *Prison bracelets*. The scars he wore were from manacles. "What— But why—"

Fia *tch*ed gently. "Carr does not tolerate stuttering."

"Why were your brothers imprisoned in France?"

Fia shrugged with elegant unconcern. "My mother was Scottish, you know. She was quite the little Jacobite loyalist, I'm told. She sought to involve Carr in her dramas. Carr played along with her."

Did it not occur to the girl that she was Scottish, too? Rhiannon wondered.

"Her relatives eventually proved valuable during the rebellion of forty-five. Carr furnished the Duke of Cumberland with information he'd acquired through them. In return, Wanton's Blush was given to Carr."

Rhiannon barely heard the last part. *Cumberland*. The Butcher of Culloden. The floor dipped beneath her feet. She looked up, light-headed, and found Fia's lovely gaze fastened on her in puzzlement.

"Go on," Rhiannon said faintly.

"After Culloden, those of my mother's relatives still living discovered Carr's true allegiance."

His treachery, thought Rhiannon.

"They plotted to ambush and kill him. Only they caught my brothers instead." Fia's slight, childish shoulders lifted in a dismissive shrug. "Their captors didn't know what to do with them. For probably the only time in their lives my brothers had cause to bless their Scottish blood.

"For valueless as my mother had been to her relatives, they were a loyal lot. They disliked the thought of killing her sons. So, they handed them over to their

French allies to be used as hostages, thinking they would break Carr's back financially. Within days of their capture Ash and Raine were in a French gaol. The conspirators were, by the way, soon after rounded up and dispatched."

"Why is Raine still in prison?" Rhiannon asked in bewilderment. "Your clothes, the jewels, the food, this place . . . surely Carr can afford to ransom him?"

"He didn't try." Fia's elegant chin rose. "To give in to such demands would only encourage further tactics of that sort. He explained it to me."

Dear God, Rhiannon thought numbly, what manner of wasps' nest was this? A father who would not ransom his own sons long after the hostilities that had resulted in their captivity had ended? A cold, emotionless girl who supported such monstrous disloyalty?

"But Ash is free," Rhiannon said.

"Yes . . ." Fia's brow lined in perplexity. "Carr ransomed Ash. I must own, he never explained that to me. . . ." She glanced at Rhiannon and her brow once more smoothed. "Not that it matters. I'm sure Carr had excellent reasons. It's imperative that one see each situation for what it is without allowing sentiment to cloud one's judgment."

"Is that what paternal affection is, a clouding sentiment?"

"You don't understand."

"Don't you miss your brother?"

Color simmered beneath the smooth powdered surface covering Fia's face. "I don't know him. I don't know either of them. Carr said they had been too much under the influence of my mother as children and it has irrevocably marked them. He says they are unfit companions for me. Besides, Ash and Raine have never demonstrated any concern for me." A sliver of bitterness disturbed her usually suave voice.

"But still, they are your brothers," Rhiannon insisted. "Don't you wonder how Raine is? If he suffers? If he hopes for release and is doubly tormented in captivity by knowing his father refuses to pay for his freedom . . . perhaps even his life?"

"I don't wonder at all. What could such conjecture possibly accomplish?" Fia slowed her steps, as though she wished to draw away. "*You* are too emotional. An unfortunate characteristic Carr says is endemic in the Highland Scot.

"Besides, Ash will see that Raine is eventually freed. He's obsessed with the idea. Why do you think he agreed to waste all that time fetching you?"

Rhiannon could not answer. Her thoughts spun in a chaotic whirl.

"Money. To be used for Raine's ransom," Fia said in disgust.

Rhiannon stared at her unseeingly. "Are you sure?"

Fia lifted her shoulders indifferently. "I conjecture. What else is he spending his money on? Certainly not clothes!" She sniffed.

"Miss Russell!" A deep, masculine burr drew Rhiannon's stricken gaze from Fia's inimical one.

Thomas Donne strode up the stairs two at a time, his hard face softening at the sight of Rhiannon. Beside her Fia's expression grew guarded.

The girl drew back on Donne's approach, as though she could not bear for him to see her with her eyes bright and her skin flushed. Donne did not spare her a glance.

"You're not going to the fight, are you, Miss Russell?" he said to Rhiannon.

"I'm afraid I don't know what you mean," Rhiannon mumbled, the implications of what Fia had told her wheeling through her mind. "Lord Carr insisted that I attend some sort of entertainment. He said nothing about a fight. Not a cockfight? Or bear baiting. I can't abide either."

Donne glanced sharply at Fia. "No, Miss Russell. This is men fighting, bare-knuckled street savagery. Nothing a lady should witness."

"Carr specifically asked for her," Fia said calmly. "And many other ladies will be present, *have* been present all this week. It's not as abhorrent as you make out, Lord Donne. I doubt Miss Russell is so much more sensitive than the rest of us."

"Other ladies will be present?" Rhiannon asked doubtfully. She had no desire to see two men beat each other but if it provided the chance to press Carr about leaving here and, perhaps, discovering more about Ash and Raine, she would take that opportunity.

"Other *women* will be there," Donne allowed flatly. "But I would not place Miss Russell amongst their ilk. Refuse, Miss Russell," Donne urged. "Your attendance can only cause you distress. It's scandalous even for Carr. Even for this crowd."

"You've become a prude, Lord Donne," Fia said haughtily. "'Tis nothing more than an interesting demonstration. Personally, I agree with you that the thing should be called off, but only because it makes him so unprepossessing to face over the dining table. But why should Miss Russell care? If she really was kidnapped, as 'tis rumored, she might even enjoy seeing him receive a good thrashing."

Donne swung on Fia, his mouth smiling politely but his eyes flat with scorn. "Don't measure another's capacity for decency by what little you . . . see in others. Whatever Miss Russell has suffered at your family's hands, I cannot think she wishes to witness Merrick's crippling."

"Merrick?" Rhiannon echoed in unwilling alarm. "How is that?"

Donne stared at her. "But . . . didn't Fia or Carr tell you?"

"What?" Rhiannon asked.

"Ash Merrick is one of the combatants."

Chapter 25

*L*adies and gentlemen clad in last night's stained, rumpled silks, whey-faced and flabby-skinned in the unforgiving morning light, hung from the windows overlooking the stable courtyard and milled four deep around its border. A carnival mood infected them. By pitting an aristocrat against a commoner in a bare-knuckle fight, Carr had orchestrated a delicious scandal. And not just any aristocrat but Carr's own son, Merrick, and not a single fight but fisticuffs for three days running now.

They wouldn't have missed being part of this no matter how much it cost—and it had cost them plenty. London hadn't offered anything so infamous in a decade. And though they panted to be away to London to spread the tattle, they dare not leave lest something even more outrageous occur.

Their murmurs quieted as Baron Paughville's groom

entered the stable yard. He was stripped to the waist and oiled, his shorn head likewise greased to frustrate an opponent's handhold. Rumor had it he'd wrestled on the Continent. More telling, he was Scottish. The chance to break English bone and pound English flesh would have been enticement enough without the fat purse Carr offered for winning.

Ash Merrick stood chatting with the crowd at the rail with all the appearance of amiability. Surreptitiously, he noted the groom's long, thick arms and short, bowed legs and the forward tilt of his crouching gait. The Scot would be hard to get off his feet and onto the ground, where street brawls—and prison brawls—were won or lost.

Three days ago Ash would have been certain of his victory. If nothing else, he'd had the element of surprise to aid him. His opponents, all culled from the stables and fields hereabouts, were laborers. They did not imagine an aristocrat would deal violence so brutally or so expeditiously. Three days had taught them differently.

But it wasn't surprise alone that gave him an advantage. He'd learned to fight not only unscrupulously but also fearlessly. He could block out every external distraction including pain, narrowing his focus down until only he and his adversary existed.

What set today apart was simply his body. He was no longer physically up to the task. Though his spirit had risen to do battle through sheer instinct, spirit alone could no longer compensate for three days of brutal pummeling. The preceding victories had come at a price.

He suspected one rib was cracked. For a certainty

two fingers of his left hand had been broken. His left eye was swollen as a result of having become intimately acquainted yesterday with a combatant's boot heel, and purple welts tattooed his torso. Today would be his last fight, no matter what his father "urged."

The thought of Carr made Ash smile.

His father had lost a great deal of money betting against his son, while Ash had made a nice profit. His smile faded. Today, though . . . today Ash simply wanted to survive and have an end to it.

"What do we do now?" The Scots groom demanded of the crowd in general. He approached the cleared center of the stable yard and eyed Ash expectantly. "Is there anyone to make a beginning or end to it?"

Ash glanced about, looking for Donne. The elegant Scotsman had held Ash's bets for the past days. Not finding him, Ash tapped a nearby exquisite on the arm. The startled young man backed up. Ash grinned.

"Don't worry— Begad if it ain't Hurley!" Ash exclaimed. "Hurley, m'dear, be a fellow and make me a small wager, will you? Fifty pounds says I win." He seized Hurley's gloved hand and pried open the stiff lavender-sheathed fingers, slapping a fat purse into his palm and curling the fingers back over it. "There's a lad. And since you've been such an accommodating fellow, let me give you a tip. I wouldn't follow suit. My bet is only by way of incentive, don'tcha know."

"N-n-no," Hurley stammered. "I mean . . . y-y-y-yes. I mean, I am sure you'll win, Mr. Merrick."

"I did warn you." The small diversion palled and Ash dismissed Hurley without another thought. Best get on with it.

In a single motion he stripped off his jacket and then

pulled the cambric shirt over his head. Whispers of
female gratification sizzled beneath roars of masculine
approval. Ash faced the Scotsman still standing awkward and self-conscious in the center of a ring of beau-
tifully clad ladies and gentleman.

"No one starts and no one finishes it," Ash explained, approaching the other man, "save we two.
There are no rules. There is only one manner in which
to win and that is to leave here upright." He stopped
just out of arm's reach of the other man. "Exquisitely
simple, *n'est-ce pas?*"

"I gets it," the groom growled and launched himself
forward.

Ash had been right; the man had experience. He
came in low and aimed for the knees, seeking to take
Ash to the ground rather than battering haphazardly—
and ineffectually—at the head. Ash locked his fists together and swung down, chopping across the back of
the groom's oncoming neck.

Pain jolted through the broken fingers and thundered through his hand. The Scot tumbled and
sprawled flat under the blow. Ash wheeled back, curs-
ing and shaking his injured hand even as he felt arms
grapple him about his calves. Damn the man, he was
still conscious.

Ash kicked out and twisted sideways but the arms
about his legs tightened relentlessly. With a thick
grunt, the Scot heaved upward, pitching Ash into the
air.

The ground slammed into Ash's back like a smithy's
hammer. Pain drilled through his side with red-hot intensity, driving the air from his lungs, blackening the
edges of his vision. He gasped, rolling to his side and

curling up, protecting the injured ribs. The Scotsman recognized his agony and paused, his eye glinting with anticipation. It was only a second's gloating, but it was a second too much.

Savagely, Ash kicked out, his heel smashing into the groom's kneecap. A loud, sickening pop sounded above the shouts of bloodthirsty approval from the crowd. The Scot howled in agony, clasping his broken knee and stumbling backward.

Ash heaved himself to his hands and knees, shaking his head to clear the threatening mist from his vision, his ears roaring with the din of the crowd and the sobbed curses of his injured foe.

Stay focused. Stay with it. Two hundred pounds. Four-to-one odds. He needed to render the groom unconscious before the bastard did as much to him.

Ash found his feet and wheeled around, surprised to find the Scot, too, standing. The groom favored his injured leg, swaying from side to side. His mouth moved with a string of silent invective, flecks of red foam spraying from the corners of his broken lip.

The battered Scot charged again, coming at Ash with animallike tenacity, seemingly impervious to the blows Ash rained on his battered face. Time and again the Scotsman came at him, what he lacked in skill more than made up for by his sheer ability to endure. Time and again, Ash managed to dance out of reach of the huge swinging paws and deliver a series of unanswered punches.

By now both men were gasping for breath, filthy with grease and sweat and stable dirt. The crowd roared with approval as Ash staggered back once more from a glancing blow to his jaw, each minute using up precious breath, expending energy he did not own. He jabbed out over and over again but try as he might he could not deliver enough power to end the fight. His blows only seemed to enrage the man.

He was going to lose.

The Scot fought from passion and Ash had thought he was fighting for money but now he suspected he fought for something marginally more interesting . . . his life. Without a doubt the Scot would kill him if he could.

"Shall we finish, *mon ami*?" Ash panted. "I have a lady waiting and I would like to—"

With a strangled sound of fury, the Scotsman launched himself once more at Ash. This time Ash was ready. He met the onrushing figure with knees bent, arms flexed. When the groom's bull-like figure collided with him he did not try to stand up to the charge. He folded, letting his opponent propel him backward and adding his own weight to the impetus by digging in his heels and grasping the Scot's thick arms. With a huge grunt, Ash jerked the Scot into him rather than thrusting him away.

Ash's shoulders hit the ground and he heaved back, pulling the groom down as hard as he could. The groom's face crashed into the unyielding ground. His thick body cartwheeled heel-over-head. The arms around Ash went slack and the heavy body completed its loose-limbed tumble, dropping into the dust with a powdery thud.

Clenching his teeth against the pain, Ash lay flat, waiting for the Scot to rise again like some bloody phoenix and kill him. He couldn't have stopped him. Not an ounce of energy remained in his body. It was all he could do to breathe, his chest heaving up and down, his eyes staring in bewildered appreciation at the obscenely clear blue sky overhead, the dust settling like Pentecostal ash on his trembling limbs.

The Scot did not move.

For a long second there was absolute silence. The crowd began to murmur with delighted scorn. He heard a plunk beside his head and glanced over. A bitter smile curved his lips. They were tossing coins at him. Gold coins. God bless them.

The he heard the familiar voice.

"For God's sake, get up, Merrick, or we shall be forced to declare a miscontest," his father said, "and from the look of her, I doubt my dear ward would be able to stomach another bout."

The pain in his side and hands and lungs evaporated before the wretchedness welling through him. He'd thought he understood his father's game. He hadn't even begun to understand.

Unable to help himself, he turned his head. His gaze found her figure with unerring accuracy. She stood between Carr and Thomas Donne. Carr held her arm, his long fingers stroking her hand comfortingly as he whispered in her ear.

She was not listening. Her head was erect, her posture poised for flight. Dark red-gold coils of hair gleamed in contrast to a face as pale as bleached linen. Absolute horror suffused every feature.

Ash's lids drifted shut. Against the black tapestry of his lids he saw himself through her eyes, bloody and broken, covered with stinking dirt and rancid grease, a body he'd rendered unconscious—or worse—laying

half across his legs along with that for which he'd
beaten him. A few gold coins.

"Well, to give the lad his due, he fought inge-
niously," Carr said.

Rhiannon had been so transfixed by the hideous
spectacle that she'd failed to note when Carr had taken
her hand. She pulled it back.

No matter what depths she imagined Ash to have
reached, he always managed to find a more profound
debasement. The crowd was flinging coins at the two
inert bodies. A redheaded wench dashed into the make-
shift arena and knelt by the Scot. She grasped his upper
body and tried to heave him upright, at the same time
scraping the guineas and shillings into her skirts. The
crowd roared with laughter.

"I have never seen anything so degrading," Rhiannon said.

"I daresay Ash would agree," Carr replied. "But everyone at Wanton's Blush must pay for the privilege of
being here, by whatever means they can."

"You mean that you asked him to fight? You risked
your own son's life against that mountain of flesh?"

"*Asked?* I don't *ask*, Miss Russell." Carr said. He was
not trying to charm her today. In fact, it seemed as
though he was deliberately provocative, trying to alien-
ate her. "I command. King George may rule in London, but I rule here. I may be exiled, but I still have my
court." He made a sweeping gesture around the crowd.
"I don't suppose I can let Merrick fight again tomorrow. Who would bet on him?" He scowled, displeased,
but then his expression cleared. "But if he were by

some miracle to win, think of the odds he'd have overcome! At least twenty to one—"

"You're hateful." As she spoke she saw Ash turn his
head toward her and open his eyes. Something so raw
passed between them that she had to look away. When
she looked back, he'd lurched to his hands and knees,
his head hanging low.

"Isn't someone going to go to him?" Rhiannon
swung on Carr.

He met her gaze disinterestedly. "Such concern. You
have a soft heart, m'dear. But to answer your question,
no. There are very few rules in this sort of thing but
one of them does require the victor to leave the arena
under his own power."

"He needs attention," she insisted.

"Does he? Well, I don't know where he'll find it. As
far as I know there are no quacks in my castle."

Rhiannon looked at her companions. Beside her
Thomas Donne maintained his enigmatic composure.
She glanced at Fia, expecting nothing from that quarter, and was surprised to find the girl looking greenish,
her gaze flickering unwillingly toward the dirt in which
her brother lay.

"I'll go to him," Fia murmured.

Carr's head snapped around. "What?"

"I can clean him up. If you will just have some of the
servants—"

"You will not!" Carr hissed before recovering his
poise. "Absolutely not. Don't forget, you are my hostess. Can't have you coming to the table smelling of
vomit and"—he glanced once more at Ash—"whatever
other excrement Merrick has rolled in."

He was all the monster Gunna had suggested and

Fia had unintentionally substantiated. The charm Carr had exercised on their first meeting hid a soulless fiend. Even Fia looked startled by Carr's venomous tone. And though Rhiannon was suspicious of why he would suddenly reveal himself to her, she was too concerned about Ash to pursue such thoughts.

A small cheer from the crowd drew Rhiannon's attention. Ash had made it upright. He lurched toward the ring of spectators. They opened before him and swallowed his figure, closing behind. Now that a victor had been established, voices rose as wagers were claimed and satisfied.

"I'm going to him," Rhiannon said. "You can't stop me. You may rule here, Lord Carr, but you do not rule me."

"Just as I feared." Carr sighed. "As you will, Miss Russell. Come along, Lord Donne."

He secured Donne's arm and led him off through the crowd. "I believe you actually bet on my son? How perceptive of you—"

Rhiannon looked toward Fia. "Where can I find Gunna?" she asked.

"She'll be in my rooms," the girl murmured distractedly. "How odd—"

But Rhiannon did not stay to hear what Fia found odd.

Carr looked too well satisfied. Few others besides Fia would have realized it. Rhiannon had just challenged his edict. Her disobedience should have been like a spark to tinder but Carr had left calmly, a buoyancy to his stride that bespoke complacency.

It made no sense. For days now Carr's temper had

been building. She'd heard him pacing in his office several times. Once, when she'd cracked the door thinking to offer him her company, she'd discovered him scribbling on a piece of paper, stabbing it with his pen. He'd been so involved that he hadn't even realized she'd entered—in itself a telling sign. Carr noted everything.

Finally he'd thrown the writing instrument down and balled the paper up in his hand, hurling it to the floor. "How? Under what excuse? Simply have a change of heart and send her back? No. Someone must take her back, or forward. Or any bloody where but here."

Fia had been too long under Carr's tutelage to ignore the import of such a rare outburst just as she was too wise to let Carr know she'd heard it. She'd closed the door as quietly as possible and run to her room.

Now, watching Rhiannon stride off in the opposite direction from Carr, for the first time in her life Fia felt the pull of divided loyalties.

The problem was Fia liked Rhiannon. Of all her acquaintances the Scotswoman alone—with the exception of Gunna—treated her in the manner Fia imagined other fifteen-year-old girls were treated. At least, Fia amended, Rhiannon didn't treat her like the polished and precocious woman everyone else assumed Lord Carr's daughter must be.

Since her twelfth year Fia had been presented not as a child but as an unnatural hybrid—part woman, part doll. She'd been bribed with toys she was too old for and offered experiences she was too young for.

Rhiannon Russell did not flatter or patronize her. True, Rhiannon also neither trusted nor particularly liked her, but even this Fia found refreshingly candid. She was as close to a friend as Fia had ever known.

She didn't want Rhiannon hurt.

She was being silly she supposed. She knew Carr had a reputation as a diabolical fiend. It had always amused her. Carr was no monster. He was a genius who chose not to be governed by the irrational emotions or the asinine laws made by lesser men for lesser people. It made perfect sense.

Or, Fia thought, her young face troubled, it always had before.

Chapter 26

*A*sh couldn't make it up the servants' stairs and he refused to ask the snickering footmen to carry him. By gritting his teeth and concentrating very hard, he managed to stumble into one of the small antechambers behind the great hall—a mean, dark room, presently unused and therefore as devoid of furnishings as it was of light.

Gratefully, Ash sank to the floor, his back against the wall. His ribs throbbed dully. He forced himself to twist and was pleased when it hurt no great deal worse than before, indicating that just perhaps his ribs weren't broken. Scant comfort but all he was likely to get. His hand felt as though it were being crushed in a vise. His skin stung where the sweat and grease ground into innumerable abrasions.

He would have lain on the floor and allowed sweet oblivion to overcome his senses but each time he closed his eyes he saw her face and read again her horror. The pain in his body faded, becoming faint compared to the pain of that recollection.

From his earliest years he'd understood what he was. He'd never wasted a moment regretting it. A wise father may well know his child, but it was more important that the child recognize not only his sire but those parts of himself his sire had bequeathed.

Somehow he'd forgotten that. Indeed, it seemed lately that he'd lost the part of himself he knew best. Well, he'd bloody well remember, because this pain— this pain was unendurable. It had to end. It *would* end.

He'd finally accrued enough money to ransom Raine. He'd even written to the French demanding particulars of how and where the trade would occur.

The door opened and a bar of light fell across his injured eye. He winced, flinging up one hand against the intrusion and placing the other palm flat against the floor. He heaved himself to a crouching position, facing whoever entered.

He squinted against the bright rectangle of the door frame. "Another challenger?" he asked with a bitter laugh. "Why not? It might not be a very interesting confrontation but it might prove satisfying—for you. Hell, for both of us. Though being a gentleman I should ask you to take your place at the end of the queue."

"Ash."

It was *her* voice. Ragged and low and it nearly undid him.

He swallowed hard. Had his father sent her as a special reminder of the many ways in which he could bring his eldest son to heel or had she sought him for her own purposes?

"What, Rhiannon?" A small pleasure to speak her Christian name, but one he wouldn't cede. "Have you come to condemn me for my chosen path, my ill-gotten gains, the depth to which I have sunk? Don't waste your breath or my time. I don't give a damn what you think."

Liar.

"No." She turned and spoke to someone in the hall. He climbed to his feet, weaving slightly. His little speech had cost him dearly.

"I'll need more water than this and hot," she was saying to whomever waited without. "Very hot. And bandages and he'll need a shirt."

"You're not going to clean me up," he ground out, sickened by the thought of her hands sloughing the filth from his limbs.

She ignored him, hefting a pail from the floor outside and setting it inside the room. She closed the door behind her, sinking the room into twilight.

"Where are you hurt worst?"

"What the hell are you doing here?"

"You already know that. I've come to patch up your wounds."

"The hell you say." He made himself stand away from the wall. Sweating with concentration, he moved toward her. She did not back away and as he drew near and his eyes adjusted to the murky lighting he saw that she wore one of those new gowns Carr had insisted she don, a shimmering bronze striped through with rich green.

She looked elegant and regal, no longer the modest

little beauty. No, quite evolved now. Quite different from that pretty wench.

This gown dipped low, far lower than anything she'd ever worn in Fair Badden. Her bound breasts, pushed up by the constricting bodice, trembled in an agitation delicious to behold. He'd never had the time nor inclination to lechery, owning a full complement of sins that already commanded his attention. But even battered and broken, just the sight of Rhiannon made him grow hard.

Yet it was not *his* hand that reached out and hovered inches above naked flesh. It was hers. Incredulously, Ash realized she meant to touch his naked chest. Like a wild thing unused to human contact, his stared at her in startled wariness.

Rhiannon shivered before the threat she read in his hot, smoke-dark eyes. He looked cornered, dangerous, and unpredictable. If she had sense she would leave. Whatever he was to his brother, he was her enemy, a scoundrel who'd used her, lied to her, and stolen her from her home for money. She began to move back toward the door and safety but her gaze, released from his, fell on the purpled skin sheathing his ribs.

He hadn't wanted to fight the Scotsman. Carr had forced him to it.

Her hand rose, closed the distance, and gently, carefully, traced a deep gash across his breast. His eyelids fluttered shut. She sidled closer, her touch feather light, warily watching his face for signs of—

He grabbed her wrist, spinning her round and catching her by the throat with his free hand, shoving her violently against the wall, hissing as his swollen hand, cushioning her wrist, slammed into the wall. His eyes opened on a blaze.

"You've changed, little Rhiannon," he muttered thickly. He angled his head sideways. Around her throat his fingers tightened. "You've grown bold and headstrong. What happened to the sweet, obedient young woman I met? Don't you remember, Rhiannon *alainn*? Or is that it? You want a reminder of her fate?"

There was nothing of kindness in him. She'd been wrong. Wrong to stay. Wrong to be moved by his pride and his plight—

"Remember now?" he whispered, the soft rough music of his voice mocking his violent actions. He pushed his body flat against hers, dominating her slighter frame. Even through the layers of thin silk petticoats and draped satin skirts she could feel the swollen part of him brand the outside of her thigh.

"Or now?" He thrust his hips graphically against hers. Her courage wavered. Eyes wide with stricken, mute appeal she stared at him. A muffled word—a curse? an endearment?—escaped him and then his mouth closed on hers, punishing and brutal.

His tongue dove between her lips, thrust deeply within her mouth, and stroked her tongue, seeking the warm sleek side of interior cheeks. Passion exploded within him.

Rhiannon.

He felt the weight of her breasts flattened against his chest. Her throat was a silky column in his palm. Her wrist was as delicate as a bird wing.

He could have her. Here. Now. Pain speared his side and throbbed in his hand. Pain sat like a vise in his chest and burned like acid in his thoughts. He knew only one way to make it stop—

He fumbled low at her knees, bunching the heavy satin up, savoring the long, smooth slide of his knuckles up her thighs. He dragged the skirt higher, and cupped the softly rounded swell of her buttocks, lifting her, pressing her even more tightly to the wall, vaguely aware that she was clutching his shoulders.

His gaze devoured the sight of all the ivory skin he uncovered, remarked the dark stain left by his dirty hands as they traveled up the long lines of her lovely milk white thighs. She'd been clean.

He laughed softly and laughed again when he saw her face go still with apprehension.

Cleanliness. He'd never been clean. He'd no experience with anything unpolluted. Until her. She was fresh and sweet and innocent. In spite of her nightmares. In spite of being stained by the blood of battle. *In spite of him.*

The scent of her filled his nostrils. The cool polished feel of her hair slipped in silky waves over his forearm. Why should he not have her when she'd wrung from him the one thing he'd always had—the knowledge of who he was.

He dipped, bending at the knees. She could not resist. Her body was imprisoned between his and the wall. He rocked forward against the hidden delta he'd exposed. Erotic pleasure surged through his limbs, pooling in his groin. He couldn't stop, would not stop, he would take her, use her, pitch and flux and drown in the sin of ravishing her. He *wanted* to overpower her, force her to pliancy, punish her for making him—

Through the thundering of his heartbeat he felt a

faint vibration, a shiver no stronger than the pulse racing in her throat. She was sobbing.

Not the sweet sob of abandonment he'd heard on that warm, cursed Beltaine Eve. Not the sound of newly discovered passion, of pure desire. It was not a pleasured sob like the one she'd offered to the night sky when she'd so artlessly, so ravishingly given herself to him. It was a pitiful gasp for a breath he would not allow.

Dear God, let me rape her, he prayed. Let me be done with her. With a thick sound, he wrenched his mouth from hers.

Rhiannon breathed.

She opened her eyes and found Ash's thick-lashed eyes inches away, fierce and alien. Had she once thought them cold? Impossible. Molten lead and green wood smoke, heat and ash, nothing cold here. Nothing recognizable.

His hand about her throat tightened fractionally as if he read in her pleading expression something he would not endure. Anchored only by her hands braced on his shoulders, her hips jammed to the wall by his, she stared at him. For a long second their gazes locked. Fury roiled just beyond expression in Ash's battered face. She took a deep, shuddering breath.

"Let me go," she commanded him.

The edges of his nails dug deeper into her throat.

"Why should I?" he sneered.

She wanted to whimper, to claw at the hand on her throat. It would be futile. She'd seen Ash's expression on the faces of the soldiers who'd bayoneted her cousins. The redcoats had been ordered to commit acts that none of them would have willingly done in the normal course of their lives. But because it was war, because Cumberland said to, they'd obeyed, burned crofts, shot men like wild dogs, bayoneted boys.

They couldn't stop. Their brutalized minds wouldn't let them. They wouldn't stop for even an instant and consider that the Highlanders were people. And *nothing* must remind them elsewise. When her youngest cousin had shed a tear, a soldier shot him, furious that the boy had reminded the redcoat that he was murdering a child.

She saw in Ash's embattled countenance that same frantic need to kill an overburdened conscience with one heinous, unforgivable act. To finally take that last step over the line and free-fall into an abyss of moral blackness, a place where choices and options no longer tortured him.

And yet, in spite of all she knew of him, she did not think he had been brought to that place. She locked her hand about his strong supple wrist, praying she was right.

"Because," she said very clearly, very firmly, "you are hurting me. You are frightening me."

He stared at her a second as if he could not comprehend her words. Slowly the fingers around her throat loosened. He released the skirts he held crumpled at her hip. He did not say a word, only stepped back, a single step, just enough for her to move away.

Swallowing, keeping her gaze fixed on his, she slipped sideways, skirting the room's edge. He watched her stonily, mutely, his hands loose at his sides, his eyes bleak and exhausted and terrifying. Fumbling behind her she found the door latch and twisted it, pushing the door open. Only then did she dare turn her back and leave.

Fia found Gunna lugging a heavy-looking pail down a corridor. The old woman puffed as she staggered under the weight. With a quick glance around, Fia hastened forward. The startled old woman dropped the bucket the few inches she held it above the floor and snatched her veil before her face. Seeing it was Fia, she relaxed.

"What are you doing?" Fia hissed. "If Carr sees you downstairs, you know he'll dismiss you."

"Ach! He'd naught do so," Gunna snickered. "He couldna replace me and well he knows it. Dinna worry, darlin', I'm just heading in there." She jerked her head toward a half-ajar door. "I must bandage up the lad is all."

Fia glanced at the door. "Ash is in there?"

"Aye, most likely unconscious. But, hold lassie. If he ain't, I'd no be entering that particular lion's den just now. He's like in as black a mood as Lucifer in sunlight."

"Why?"

Gunna shrugged as Fia latched her fingers around the bucket's handle and lifted it. "I dunno. Perhaps he's in no mood to have his lover become his stepmother."

Fia stopped. The water in the bucket sloshed, soaking the bottom of her skirts. She barely noticed. "His lover?"

"Aye," Gunna said, *tch*ing gently and bending down to dab at Fia's jonquil-colored skirts.

Fia watched her in surprise. Gunna seldom gossiped and did not encourage it in Fia.

She shouldn't ask Gunna more. But Carr had taught her the import of knowing about everything that affected one's life.

"What?" Gunna said, reading Fia's wide eyes. "Did you think that all Mr. Ash's drinking and carousing was for the hilarity of it? I had it from the lassie herself that Mr. Ash and she were lovers. Only once, 'tis true, but I'm thinkin' Mr. Ash would like to make it twice. Mayhaps even more." She winked at Fia.

"But," Gunna went on, "Carr must have other ideas. Why else would he send Mr. Ash to bring the lassie here if not to marry her himself? No matter *what* the lassie herself believes." Gunna chortled and picked up the bucket. "It's no wonder Mr. Ash is in so foul a temper, is it?"

"But Carr *didn't* bring her here to marry her," Fia murmured, following Gunna's bent form down the hall. "He can't."

Rhiannon and Ash were lovers? Yet Carr had commanded Ash to bring her here and Ash had done so. Why? And if Carr had wanted Rhiannon here badly enough to send Ash for her, why was he now pacing the floor and muttering about finding someone to take Rhiannon Russell away?

"Why can't he marry Miss Rhiannon?" Gunna asked casually, stopping outside the door.

"Because," Fia answered distractedly, still trying to sort through what she'd learned, "the Prime Minister gave an edict to Carr years ago, after the death of Lady Beatrice. He said that if one more of Carr's wives died, no matter what the cause, Carr would answer to the king and he would answer with his life. Upon hearing this, Carr swore he would never marry again—no matter what the inducement."

The old woman frowned and pushed the door to the darkened room open farther. A hiss of pain from the darkness just inside greeted them.

Gunna turned to Fia. "Best you be gone now, dear. Afore yore father comes seeking you and finds you here, with him."

Before she could reply Gunna slipped into the room leaving Fia to hasten back the way she'd come, her thoughts in a whirl.

Chapter 27

.

His arms were strong and sheltering, his body a rock-hard instrument of pleasure. Rhiannon moaned softly and Ash lifted her with big, warm hands on either hip, sliding deep within—

A sudden wild clattering brought Rhiannon upright in her bed. She looked wildly about but there was no lover, phantom or otherwise, beside her. With a little moan of distress, she sank forward, bracing her forehead against her upraised knees and rocking back and forth.

Two days now since Ash had so nearly raped her and yet it was not her escape from so heinous an act that occupied her thoughts. No. She remembered instead the blue-black welts marring his beautiful body, and his pain-filled eyes. Even when she managed to push him from her waking thoughts, he found other ways to come to her, at night, in her dreams, as the lover with whom she'd shared such passion on Beltaine night.

A light tapping on her door brought her head up. The sun had just crested the sea, unraveling strands of rosy light across her bedroom carpet. It was early, far too early for even the servants to be about. Another soft rap preceded a sound of wild scrabbling.

"Miss Russell?" A young male voice queried desperately. It was vaguely familiar. "Please, Miss Russell! Answer soon! I can't keep her still!"

Rhiannon swung her legs off the bed and slipped to the floor. Donning a dressing gown, she crossed the room and opened the door.

A huge yellow monster erupted from the floor, launching itself directly at Rhiannon, dragging the thick linked chains that leashed it clean out of its handler's hands. The creature hit Rhiannon square in the chest, knocking her flat to her back.

Like a lion over its prey, the huge animal stood over her, curled lips exposing huge ivory canines.

"Stella!" Rhiannon cried.

The grinning gazehound dropped its enormous head and swiped Rhiannon's entire face with a tongue the size of a small hand cloth.

"Oh, Stella!" Rhiannon wrapped her arms around the hound's thick neck and hugged.

In the doorway the young man shuffled uncomfortably, drawing Rhiannon's attention. She recognized him as Andrew Payne from The Ploughman in Fair Badden.

"However did she get here? Did Mrs. Fraiser send her?" Rhiannon asked.

"Nah, Miss Russell," the young man said. "It was

Mr. Merrick. Some weeks back Mr. Watt hurtles up to the front of the inn driving a wagon hitched to a wind-broke horse, as furious as ever I've seen a man. He's shouting about how Mr. Merrick has taken off with you and swearing he'll find Merrick and kill him and get you back. He's in such a lather that me father calls some fellows from the public room to see that Watt doesn't hurts himself. Off they hauls him, leaving me to the wagon."

The sound of rattling dishes drew Rhiannon's attention. Still on the floor with her arms linked around Stella's neck, she motioned the boy inside. "Come, Andy. Now tell me the rest."

Andrew entered, snatching his hat from his head, twisting the woven wool between his hands. "Well, I sees Stella here." He nodded at the beast. She wagged her tail in delighted recognition of her name. "She's covered in blood and breathing weak and her hind leg is crooked."

Rhiannon ran her hands over the dog and sure enough, found a thickened lump on her hind leg.

"I always liked her, useless though she be," the boy admitted gruffly, "so I takes her back to Mrs. Fraiser with the rest of the story."

"How did Mrs. Fraiser take it?" Rhiannon asked softly.

The boy shuffled uncomfortably, his gaze skittering away. "She shed some tears, miss, but she sees Stella and she sets right out to patching her up and setting her leg. A few days later, Mr. Merrick's letter arrives and that gave her some comfort."

"What letter?" Rhiannon asked.

"A letter *and* a purse. The letter says how he would

not take you without good cause and asks Mrs. Fraiser to fix up Stella."

"What did she do? Was she sad?" Rhiannon asked anxiously.

"Ach," Andy said. "She's a touch melancholy but greatly eased. She says as any man that takes time out of an abduction to write a letter askin' that a no-good bitch be patched and brought across the entire country just to keep a lady company must have a powerful care for the lady.

"And then, well, you know Mrs. Fraiser. She says what's done is done and that ye'll do fine. You're a survivor."

"What do you mean, brought across the country?"

"The money," Andy explained patiently. "Mr. Merrick sent it so someone could bring Stella to Mc-Clairen's Isle. I volunteered and glad I am of it. Never seen nuthin' like this place."

He grinned widely, staring around the sumptuous bedchamber and letting out a long, low whistle. Rhiannon stared at him unseeing. *Ash* had caused Stella to be tended and brought here? Ash, the blackhearted deceiver, her would-be rapist? But also, the man who'd brought her an old tartan so she might have something of her family's history. Dear Lord.

"I got in an hour ago," Andy said, his gaze still wandering around the room. "Mr. Merrick saw me straight off, right there in the kitchen while he made sure me and Stella had something in our bellies."

Stella promptly flopped down and rolled to her back, her great dinner plate–sized paws waggling in the air in an attempt to elicit a belly scratch.

"He doesn't look so good, Mr. Merrick don't. And

his eyes look a great bit of empty. And— Oh I am thick-headed!"

With a *tch* of self-disgust, Andy fumbled in his pocket and withdrew a folded piece of paper. He handed it to her. "He sent this to you, miss." He grinned at Stella. "And don't you worry, you great sweet-eyed tart, I gots something for you, too."

Once more Andy shoved a hand in his pocket, this time pulling out a beef's knucklebone. He tossed it to Stella and her jaws closed on it in midair. "Got that from one of the scullery maids," he explained. "Nice girl. Accommodating, if you know what I mean."

A considering expression stole over Andy's young face. He slapped his thighs suddenly. "Well then, I . . . I, ah, I best be off. I . . . I left something in the scullery. I'll stop back afore I leave for Fair Badden to see if you've anything you'd like me to take to Mrs. Fraiser."

He plunked his abused cap back on his head and, with a cheeky nod, opened the door. He looked up and down the deserted hall. "Not much for morning activities round here, are they?"

He disappeared, closing the door behind him.

With trembling hands, Rhiannon unfolded the paper. The words were few, the handwriting angular and harsh, without any softening or embellishments—much like Ash himself. She blinked away the sudden moisture in her eyes and read:

Forgive me and accept this dog by way of my apology. Please. I didn't mean to frighten you. Please.

                                           Merrick

But he'd sent for Stella long before the scene in that dimly lit room, before they'd even reached Wanton's Blush. He'd done what he could to see that Stella's wounds were treated and then he'd arranged to have her brought here, so that Rhiannon might not be alone. Because Ash understood what it was to be alone, without allies or confidants.

Or love.

But he'd tasted that emotion in Fair Badden. She was sure of it. He simply hadn't experience enough to recognize it.

He may not be the charming bon vivant who'd first captivated her in Fair Badden. But neither was he an unfeeling monster who'd seduced her only to discard her. He was a hard man in desperate need of tenderness, roughly used by fate and father, seeking a moment's respite from constant strife.

The realization burned through her heart like a dry field afire, illuminating the darkest corners, the cautious frightened places she'd tended and hidden in for over ten years. The safe places.

But Ash Merrick was not safe, and loving Ash Merrick would never be safe— She stopped, her hand stilled in Stella's thick, smooth coat.

Loving Ash Merrick.

She rose smoothly, strongly, sure of herself and her destination. At last.

Ash slouched forward over the writing desk in the corner of his room, staring at a column of numbers he'd written from memory. If he remembered correctly the numbers from Carr's ledger went back seven or eight years. They had no notations associated with them, only dates.

But what, if anything, had they to do with Rhiannon Russell? He sighed heavily, rubbing his palms over his beard-roughened cheeks. By now that lad would have delivered that useless hound to her. They'd be rolling about her bedroom floor in an ecstatic reunion. The thought brought a smile to his harsh countenance and he kept the image there, in his mind's eye, for a minute, savoring the pure sweetness of it before straightening and raking his hair back from his forehead.

He'd more important things to consider. He'd overheard Fia telling Gunna that King George, not content merely to exile Carr to the Highlands for his habit of losing wives, had gone one further, promising to extract retribution if yet another of England's daughters succumbed while in his care.

That must have been what Tunbridge's letter had alluded to—Carr's obsession with his "place" in society. Tunbridge must have been sent to pave the way toward some sort of reconciliation between the king and Carr.

And there was more. Last night Ash had managed to corner Carr's man of business in a bout of intense drinking, a small triumph in itself since Carr had hired for that post a man of nearly pathological discretion.

Ash had spent hours weaving lurid and grossly exaggerated tales about his days in Paris. Under the influence of drink and bonhomie, the wizened little man had finally begun to nod sympathetically. Bit by bit he'd disclosed his secrets. After relating the expense of running the castle, the little fellow had placed his finger alongside his nose and let one rheumy eye close in a careful wink.

"Carr has income near enough to make it all work," he'd whispered. "Information is always worth gold to some. Plus there's the gaming. Certain gentlemen, and I'm sure you can figure out at least one of them, since Lord Carr says you speared his hand, pay His Lordship for the privilege of being invited to his tables. Then there's bonds and banknotes and that property overseas . . ."

Then, as if suddenly aware of just how much he'd divulged, the little man had clapped a hand over his mouth, risen unsteadily to his feet, and fled.

Overseas property? The Americas? Australia?

Ash rose from behind the desk and walked to the window. Ever since Rhiannon's arrival Carr had grown daily more tense. But in the past few days his irritability had given way to a certain expectancy. It boded ill for someone and that person mustn't be Rhiannon.

Lost in contemplation, Ash was only vaguely aware of the door opening behind him. Assuming it was a servant bringing a pot of strong black coffee, Ash gestured toward the desk without turning. "Put it there, please, and don't bother to stay and tidy up. I'll be gone from here soon enough."

He stared out at the sea. The dim, hushed predawn light soothed his burning eyes. It was like Fair Badden's pure sweet dawns. He would have liked to have gone for a walk this morning as he had so many mornings there. He would have liked to have stridden through the dew-shimmered grass with that fool hound Stella gamboling behind him and Rhiannon at his side.

With an exhausted sigh, he rested his forearm on the

window above his head and leaned wearily into it. No such pastoral pleasures for him. He had an image to maintain, a reputation at stake.

"No. No sunlit vagaries for me," he murmured to himself. "Not when an entire night beckons me with the promise of untold amusements."

"Ash Merrick, you're a liar."

He wheeled around. She stood in a soft wash of paling light, a cloud of silky lace pooling about her bared feet, her shoulders rising from the froth of her night garment like an alabaster Venus rising from the waves.

He swallowed. It was all he could do. He was too tired and she was too beautiful and he'd tried, God knows he'd tried, to keep her safe from Watt and Carr and most especially himself.

But he hadn't any reserves left; he'd been wrung out of his last drop of self-restraint and he'd never owned any good intentions anyway. He'd wanted her, lusted after her, desired her, and *needed* her and she was here, in his bedchamber with cloudy dawn molding itself to her skin and a haze of soft slumber muzzying her soft, rich mouth.

But he tried. He still tried.

"If you take another step into this room," he advised her, "I will not let you leave until I've had you on your back."

She took a step into the room.

Chapter 28

*A*sh met her before she took another step. He reached her and dipped, sweeping her up in his embrace as easily as if she'd been feather down. Jaw set, he strode across the room and kicked open the door to the adjoining suite, stopping in the door frame.

Little light came through the long, tall windows facing out over the sea. A storm rushed down from the north, steeping dawn in a clotted blue-gray, making the room twilight. A great canopied bed, counterpane pristine as a sacrificial altar, stood in the center.

The windows rattled with a sudden gust of wind, breaking Ash's stillness. He carried Rhiannon to the bed, laid her in its center, and followed her down, imprisoning her between his arms. Trepidation clouded her exquisite gold-green eyes. Too late. He braced himself above her on shuddering arms.

His gaze devoured her, roving greedily over her

shadowed eyes, touching on the mane spread across the counterpane, and moving lower to the deep, lace-edged vee of her sheer nightgown. It exposed the creamy column of her throat, the delicate collarbones spread like wings beneath fragile flesh, and the velvety shadowed valley between her breasts. She'd grown thinner in the last month.

"Oh, Ash," she said, reaching up and delicately touching the bruised flesh beneath his injured eye.

She ruined him. She saved him. He turned his face into her palm, branding it with a hot, fervid kiss.

He didn't want to rape her or rut with her . . . he wanted to make love with her.

He lowered himself, pressing her body into the thick feather mattress, intent on simply kissing her. He bent forward; his lips touched hers.

His head spun with light-headed pleasure. Her lips were as cushioned and warm as he remembered, but softer now, slightly, shyly, breathlessly opening for him. He sipped in her breath, tasting the corners of her mouth with his tongue with feigned languor.

"Kiss me, Rhiannon," he whispered, hopelessly vulnerable now, wretchedly aware that petitioning her favors guaranteed his rejection. How could she do anything else? She'd been someone else's bride-to-be and he'd seduced her.

"A kiss." He brushed his lips over the velvety shell of her ear, hoarding sensations, pleading with gentleness, begging with restraint. Her fragrance intoxicated him: warm and clouded floral, the sharp tang of sea and pine, the musk of arousal . . . *arousal*.

He angled his head, licking the base of her throat. Her pulse fluttered beneath his tongue.

Carefully, he slipped one hand beneath her waist, crept his arm up her back between her shoulder blades, and cradled the back of her head in his palm, lifting her body up. The thick satin mass of hair fell down over his arm.

"Rhiannon."

She kissed him. She lifted her head and molded her lips to his. He shivered with the unexpected voluptuousness of it, his body growing hard with burgeoning desire. The tip of her tongue teased just within his mouth, both bold and hesitant, untutored and wise.

His mind teemed with gratification, overwhelmed by every exquisite detail: her softness, her graceful curves, the beat of her heart. A beautiful female body lay beneath him, vibrant and glowing with slowly awakening appetite. But all this could not explain his total absorption, because he was involved with so much more than the body that yearned beneath his hands and lips.

Rhiannon. Rhiannon's heart, flesh, and bone. Rhiannon revealed to him, beneath him, surging up to cling to him. It had been Rhiannon since Beltaine night. He could no longer fight that knowledge.

She undid him.

He settled his hips against hers, rocking into her with little irrepressible jerks. Her thighs relaxed, she tilted her hips. He shivered, fighting for control, fearful of crushing her. Mouths still melded, hand still cupping her delicate skull, he shifted away and swept his hand between them, encountering fragile silk and gossamer lace. He no longer thought, he reacted instinctively. The material that kept her from him hissed as it tore.

Startled, her eyes flew wide. Her hands instinctively flew up to brace against his chest.

He cursed himself. He'd no graces, no art, nothing but this devastating desire growing each moment, and each moment shredding his tenuous mastery of it.

He released her mouth, overwhelmed. His heartbeat raced out of control. He closed his eyes, fighting the imperatives of pure want, forcing his breath to a quieter tempo, chaining desire to his will.

He had not meant to frighten her.

"I won't hurt you," he promised thickly. He bracketed her face between his forearms and, with as much gentleness as he possessed, touched her cheek, her temples, lining one silky-smooth brow and feathering her eyelashes with the back of his forefinger, trying to show her what he could not say.

Beautiful. Lovely and sweet and impossibly desirable. His gaze roved over all the grace notes of her countenance: the slight dilation of her pupils, the thin white scar on her cheek, the delicate blue tracery of veins on the whiteness of her breasts.

Slowly, the taut line of her mouth relaxed as he plied her with soothing caresses. He brushed her shoulder in slow, ever-widening circles, moving gradually to her breast. She sighed, a sweet sound of abandonment. He found the tip of one breast and rolled the nub between his thumb and fingers, watching her face intently.

She inhaled sharply. Her shoulders arched off the bed; her breasts rose in an unvoiced overture. He made no attempt to withstand the offer. His mouth closed on her dark, ripe nipple, sucking gently at first but then more greedily, lifting and kneading the other plump breast.

It was more than Rhiannon could bear. All the words, the terrible names, the warnings and castigations she had been chanting like a charm against his enchantment could not save her. She did not want to be saved.

His mouth pulled forbidden sensations from her while his hand fondled her other breast into peaked and ready arousal. The hardness pressed against the vee at the top of her thighs rubbed with intimate promise, swirling into a rush of titillation.

Unable to resist, she combed her fingers through his long, tangled black hair, stroked his face, and felt the rasp of his unshaven cheeks. He drew harder, deeper. A throaty purr vibrated from deep in her throat.

The sound caused him to release her. His eyes flashed up to meet hers, black and unreadable. For a timeless moment she stared into their depths and then he lowered her shoulders to the bed. Slowly, like a prowling beast, he moved up over her, his legs on either side of her hips. He braced himself on his arms, suspended above her, his hair falling forward, masking his features. The only sounds she could hear were the pelted spatter of rain on glass and her own harsh breath.

He suddenly pushed back, knees spread wide, and rested on his heels. His gaze locked on her mouth. He grasped his shirt bottom and pulled it from his breeches and over his head.

It had been dark on Beltaine night and thus she'd never fully seen what she'd clutched and stroked and petted and strained to join. And when he'd fought he'd been filthy and battered. Now, finally, she did.

For the first time she saw how beautiful he was, more beautiful than her imagination had allowed. His hips were narrow and his shoulders broad, his body taut and lean. His clear skin sheathed hard muscle and long, clean bone. Her gaze dropped and fled. The evidence of his arousal strained the fabric of his breeches.

His gaze followed her own. "Yes, *boidheach*, readied, hard and urgent, for pleasuring you, for pleasuring myself. For passion's sake."

"No other reason?" she whispered, trying to ignore the sliver of uneasiness his words had caused.

If he heard he gave no indication. His eyes were nearly black with arousal, focused and intense. He stretched out his hand. Purposefully, he ran his knuckles in a long, drawn out caress starting from the base of her throat, moving slowly between her breasts down over her belly to the thicket of soft curls between her thighs. She writhed beneath the gentle contact, trying to remember what she'd asked and why.

"Need there be another?" he whispered hoarsely.

She did not answer, for his fingers had found her nether lips and were gently stroking the silky interiors. Moments and hours, he played upon her body, stroking and urging, nibbling and licking, tender kiss and sharp nips ending just the pleasure side of pain. She lost herself in the vortex of sensation, liquid with want, the agitated sounds of constricted pleasure humming from her throat, foretelling her crisis.

Finally she could take no more, she held up her arms, her eyes wide and unseeing. He fell upon her like a sea eagle on a dove, jerking his strained breeches away, unerringly finding the moist cove he'd so thoroughly prepared. He entered in one long, sense-shattering slide.

She caught her breath, instinct and need supplying what befuddled memory withheld, and shifted her hips to accommodate the length of him. She would surely die. It felt that good; it promised that much.

"Rhiannon," he gasped, grasping her hips in his big calloused hands, the scarred wrists shining like a strand of milky pearls in the dim light. "This time it counts." His gaze held hers until finally she surrendered.

"Aye. It does."

He began moving, his teeth grinding together and his eyes clenched in extremity. Unbearable stimulation, too rich a broth, too heady a brew, her body riding waves of increasing desire, pulling her muscles tight with anticipation, forcing her hips to rise, to accommodate more, to welcome the increasing power of his thrusts. Her back arched, her hips bucked, and her mouth opened on soundless supplication as her hands flew up to seek purchase against the storm of sensation buffeting her from within.

They found Ash's rock-hard body. A sound like a growl vibrated from his throat. The muscles of his arms and chest and throat stood out, straining and corded-over with dark veins. He thrust forcefully, caught up in the intensifying rhythm, aggressive, masculine, moving in her, taking her.

There. And there. All the swirling sensations condensed and telescoped with dizzying speed to a single center.

Then it exploded.

Every inch of her skin, every fiber, every bone flooded with rich, boundless pleasure.

There. There. She panted, riding the tidal wave of feeling, absorbing it, shivering with its aftermath. She clung to him, dimly becoming aware of the runaway thunder of his heartbeat beneath her ear. He flung his head back, lifting her and clamping her to him.

"Rhiannon. *Chan urrainn dhomh ruith tuilleadh.*" *I cannot run anymore.* "For my heart's sake. It always has been."

Words had no meaning here, the only truths were his arms and body, his kisses and his strength. His words barely penetrated her thoughts, sweet verbal caresses when her whole body was being stroked.

"Rhiannon!" He thrust into her one last time.

His whole body shuddered. A low cry of triumph surged from his throat. He froze, holding himself deep within her, straining and raw and beautiful in the act of completion.

Gradually the rigidity melted from his body. His face fell forward into the lee of her throat. His breath sounded harsh in her ear. With a small groan, he set his shoulder to the mattress and rolled, pulling her over onto him. His forearm looped about her waist, keeping her there.

He was hot and damp and solid and she'd never felt anything so good, so perfect. Lush with completion, she drifted, disjointed and detached from time and memory, his chest her pillow, his body her bed.

"Sleep, Rhiannon," he murmured, stroking her hair from her temples. His breath was warm. "The day will wait."

She sighed, utterly content, and nuzzled her cheek against the rising plane of his chest and, beyond all expectation, fell asleep.

Rhiannon woke slowly. The warm skin beneath her cheek rose and fell in measured cadence. *Ash.* She opened her eyes. It was still early, the room was still dark. A glance at the boiling gray sky outside the window told her why. A storm had taken hold of the coast. It might be days before it blew over.

She lifted her gaze to Ash, studying him as he slept. She was startled by what she saw.

She'd always thought of Ash as a man, fully mature and well into his prime years. But now, with slumber erasing the jaded sophistication from his face, and his eyelids hiding his bleak, world-weary soul, she realized that Ash Merrick was a young man, a *very* young man. Perhaps no more than a few years her senior. Tenderness filled her.

Being careful not to disturb him, she swung her legs over the edge of the bed and sat up. He sighed in his sleep and flung one long, tapering arm out across the bed, as though even in his sleep he searched for something. She leaned forward, intent on bestowing a kiss on his bluish-cast cheek, but thought better of it.

She had to leave him, before someone discovered her in his bed and told Lord Carr. She'd no doubt that Ash's father would use the information in some hurtful way. She did not want to be another flail Carr wielded over his son. She wanted only to love Ash.

She smiled sadly. She'd been correct in Fair Badden to think she'd been prey to a girlish infatuation. She'd been besotted by Ash's black and white good looks, by the forbidden danger suggested by his scarred wrists, and by a susceptibility to his glib tongue and urbane manners. She'd been enamored of a mask, a character Ash had created to hide the real man, a man so much more complex, so much more vulnerable, and yet so much stronger than that play actor. A man in need of love.

Well, Rhiannon thought, he had her love if he wished it and even if he didn't. She loved Ash Merrick.

How sad, she thought, that she'd spent so many years amongst loving, gentle people and never learned the simplest truth of that emotion—that the heart does not need reasons to love, only the opportunity.

She'd never had to earn Richard or Edith Fraiser's love. She'd never had to be careful in securing Phillip's affection.

The thought of Phillip ambushed her. How ill she'd used him! How grievously she'd wronged him! She could never begin to make up to him what she owed— but she must. She would never know peace until she tried.

She stood and gathered her ruined nightgown about her as best she could. With one last, lingering glance at Ash, she slipped from his room and down the dark corridor.

Chapter 29

The stable was warm, the dawn was cooled by sheets of rain, and young Andy Payne was as hot and cocky as only a sixteen-year-old male newly initiated into the world of carnal pleasure can be. His darlin', Cathy? Carly? had left earlier and he'd dozed a bit—this tupping business was most strenuous play—but now he felt quite up to a cup of milk and a bit of beef.

Whistling happily, Andy clambered down the ladder from the hayloft, leaving the stables and heading for the kitchen building. The smell of baking bread was just beginning to ride the gusting east wind. He followed it down the path between the alehouse and the icehouse, and in doing so ran smack dab into a human mountain.

Andy staggered back, staring up into a once handsome visage now ravaged by sleeplessness and pain.

"Mr. Watt!" Andy cried.

Phillip clamped his hand over the boy's mouth, hushing him in a low urgent voice before half dragging him into some scrub larch fifty feet away. A half-dozen men materialized from the brush and encircled Andy. Their faces were grim, their clothes hard worn, their boots scuffed with travel.

Andy counted three he knew besides Phillip Watt: John Fortnum, Ben Hobson, and Edward St. John. The other two men were vaguely familiar but the glint of excitement in their eyes he knew all too well from his years working his Dad's tavern. Troublemakers, this lot. Up to no good. He'd stake the guinea in his pocket on it.

"What are you doing here, Mr. Watt?" Andy asked, though he suspected he already knew, and that knowledge lodged in the pit of his stomach and made it ache. "Where'd you come from?"

"We've been here three days, boy," Phillip said tightly, "waiting for the chance to get word to Rhiannon. Thank God you've come along."

"But all you'd have had to do is write her a letter and send it by courier. Or give it to her yourself," Andy said in bafflement. "She walks out on the cliffs each morning. They aren't keeping her prisoner, you know."

"Ha!" Phillip's laughter was bitter, and bitterness from this man, whom Andy had always known as a jovial, fine chap, was as odd as summer snow. "She's watched day and night. I've seen her guards. We all have." He looked around at the others; they nodded in curt concurrence.

"Is . . . is she all right?" Phillip asked gruffly.

"Miss Russell?" Andy asked. "Aye. She maybe lost

some weight but she's not being mistreated. I think she's mayhap lonely."

Phillip's lip curled back in a sneer. "What? Even with Merrick—"

He bit off whatever he'd been about to say and grabbed Andy's hand. He thrust a single folded and sealed piece of paper into it. "Take this to her. Give it into her hand and hers alone."

The look on Phillip's face sent Andy stumbling back. The others watched approvingly.

"Aye, sir." Andy gulped audibly. "Aye. Right away, sir."

He knuckled his forehead and backed away, scooting clear of the larch, apprehension chasing him. Apprehension not only for himself, but for Phillip Watt, who looked as changed as a man can be, and even more apprehension for Rhiannon Russell. Andy hadn't liked the look in Phillip's eye when he'd asked after her.

Andy peered back over his shoulders. The men from Fair Badden had vanished and— For the second time that morning Andy ran directly into the tall broad figure of a man. Strong hands steadied him and a smooth Scottish voice spoke from the darkness, "Now, then, lad. Why don't you be tellin' me about your friends out yonder?"

Donne saw Rhiannon walking swiftly toward the conservatory, a cape over her arm and a huge, lanky yellow hound pacing beside her.

"You're not thinkin' of going out today, Miss Russell?" Donne called after her.

She looked round in surprise and smiled doubtfully as he approached. This morning she wore her beauty full open, a lush highland rose radiant with youth and promise. He only wished his heart allowed room for something so fresh and honest. Alas, it was too full with the need for revenge.

"Well, yes . . . I was," Rhiannon said.

"You'll be blown from the cliffs, Miss Russell. But if go you must, allow me to accompany you."

"That is most kind of you, Lord Donne," Rhiannon said, "but I confess today I would most enjoy my own company."

"But I insist," Donne said. He moved close to her and looked down at her shining cap of unpowdered hair. "I have a note for you from a friend of yours."

"A friend?" she repeated.

"Aye. A friend from Fair Badden." He offered her his arm, and after that first startled hesitation, she placed her hand upon his forearm. "Not another word, Miss Russell. Carr was quite right to term Wanton's Blush his kingdom and he the king. A despotic king. He rules through many means, intimidation and blackmail being but two. Whenever you speak, whatever you say, I advise you to be oblique."

"Lord Donne, pray remember that Lord Carr is my guardian," she said uncomfortably, her eyes searching his face.

Yes, he thought, during her short stay at Wanton's Blush she'd learned to be wary, to trust no one. Pray God she wouldn't have to stay and learn harder lessons still.

"So he is," Donne said smoothly. They'd reached the conservatory doors. He took her cape from her arm, spread it wide, and settled it gently on her shoulders. Once more he offered her his arm. "Shall we walk?"

She nodded and he drew her outside. The rain fell in fits and starts, stripping the petals from the flowers. The small ornamental trees in the formal gardens danced with each gust, the creak of their branches underscoring the rushing sound of wind.

He drew her close to him, angling himself to protect her as best he could. He led her out onto the terrace and from there down the stairs, ducking beneath the arch that gave entry to the kitchen gardens and from there the sea.

At the seagate he finally stopped and positioned himself so that he acted as a barrier. He handed her the letter. She stepped back, half turning for privacy, and broke the seal. She read and as she read her fine, gold-buffed skin paled, the color bled from her lips, and her hands shook.

"I would go to him, Miss Russell," he said.

Her eyes snapped up.

"I intercepted the messenger your fiancé sent, a boy named Payne. I convinced him I had only your best interest at heart. He was scared. The young should never be burdened with such responsibility," he murmured, his gaze distant. He gave himself a little shake and looked toward her. She was watching him closely. "He told me about it. About Phillip Watt, and Merrick kidnapping you."

"You don't understand."

He shook his head gravely. "I do. Ash Merrick is a ruthless man. I know him. I understand him and in some ways," he admitted with a wry smile, "I even admire him. And because I understand him, because we are in some ways but different sides of the same coin, I tell you this, Miss Russell. There's no room in his heart for anything so fragile as affection or so nebulous as honor.

"There is nothing for you on McClairen's Isle but pain, Miss Russell. If you stay you will end up being a pawn. Carr already has an interest in you, which is frightening enough. Add to that Merrick's interest and you have a very unprepossessing future. Did you know that Merrick specifically asked me to discover how your death could benefit someone?"

Her head snapped up at this, her gaze unreadable but intent.

"Yes," Donne said gravely, unwilling to hurt her but knowing he could not spare her, "Merrick, too, is trying to determine your worth in this mad chess game being played."

"Thank you for your concern, Lord Donne." She sounded breathless. "It is much appreciated."

The fear he'd hoped to engender was nowhere to be seen in her lovely, composed face. Only a deep sorrow and, oddly, something like peace. Frustrated Donne tried again. "You don't understand. This isn't simply a rather nasty family. It's evil.

"Carr *killed* his first wife and then killed the next two. No one says it, especially those dependent on him for their gambling. Who would dare? But in London everyone knows it, accepts it as fact—including the king.

"Carr is not living here because the air suits him, Rhiannon. He's here because he's been *exiled* here. The king will not have him in London and what's more, the king has promised to separate his head from his shoulders should any other heiresses die under his care.

"That's what your guardian is, Miss Russell! He left his sons to rot in God knows what form of hell rather than spend his precious money to ransom them.

"*And Merrick is his son*. The same blood runs thick in his veins, believe me. I've seen him skewer a man's hand for cheating and you saw him fighting—"

"He had to," Rhiannon broke in. Her eyes had grown cold and her face frozen. "He has to do what he does in order to free his brother."

"His *brother* raped a nun! He is as bad as his sire. They all are." Donne shouted, infuriated by her inconceivable faith in Merrick, her abysmal naïveté. "Fia is nothing but Carr's whore, groomed to fetch the largest marriage settlement possible!"

"Lord Donne," Rhiannon said, the mist beading on her lashes and coating her lips in salty spray, "I . . . I am so sorry."

"I don't want your condolences. I want your promise that you will go to Watt. That you will leave this cursed place." He grabbed her upper arms, unable to keep himself from shaking her. "I am *trying* to *help* you, Miss Russell!"

She lifted her chin, her gaze scouring his face, a slow dawning inspiration turning her expression first to amazement and then to consternation. "Yes," she swallowed. "I promise. I will go to him."

He released her and she turned, the wind catching her cape and sending it billowing out behind her as she retraced her path, leaving him behind in the heightening wind.

* * *

Fia heard the receding crunch of Donne's boots on the gravel path. He was leaving.

Her knees buckled and she slid down the outside of the garden wall, her sodden cloak pooling around her on the muddy grass. She closed her eyes.

Murder. Whore. Mad.

That small child who still dwelt, hidden and secret beneath Fia's sumptuous, worldly exterior whimpered. She wished she'd not come here. She wished she could forget what she'd heard.

She'd come down the stairs and seen Donne approach Rhiannon and speak. Whatever he'd said had arrested Rhiannon and with every appearance of consternation, she'd allowed him to lead her off.

Mindful of Carr's instruction to gather whatever information one could, she'd slipped along the outside of the kitchen garden wall until she'd heard them speaking.

It had not been hard. Donne's voice had risen above the rush of heightening wind. She'd heard every word.

She wished she had a knife like Ash's. When Rhiannon had left Donne she would have met him at the terrace bottom and pierced his black, lying heart. But she didn't have a knife and Donne was large and strong and harder than any man she knew, harder even than Ash.

She had thought Thomas Donne was perfect: polished, hard, yet with a core of something immutably . . . compassionate. She rolled her head against the hard, gray stone, sobbing on laughter. Compassionate.

She'd fallen in love with him two years ago, the first day she'd seen him, when he'd come to Wanton's Blush with friends and stayed a weekend. Since then she had loved him with all the intensity of her passionate young heart, doing whatever she could think of to attract his notice, to secure his regard.

It had been hard. Every day she'd had to fight to overcome the shyness that drowned her whenever she was in his presence. Too often she'd succumbed to the insecurities that made her flee a room he'd entered rather than risk making a fool of herself in his presence.

She'd adopted every artifice and embellishment that instructors and governesses, artists and dressmakers, perfumers and wig makers could provide. For him. And he hated her. Hated them all.

Because—she bit her lip until it bled—because, or so he said, her father had murdered her mother. And Ash was evil and manipulative, and Raine had raped a nun, and she? A little keening sound rose from deep in her chest. She was a whore. Carr was her procurer.

For the first time in years, tears sprang to her eyes. They spilled from her lids and streamed down her face mingling with the pouring rain. More and more of them, a torrent of them, all the tears she'd never shed and all the ones she would never allow again. And when she had spent them all, when she was exhausted and soaked with rain and shivering with nausea and cold, she planted her fists wrist-deep in the muddy ground and pushed herself upright and made herself walk through the storm back to Wanton's Blush.

To her father's office.

Chapter 30

"What do you mean you're not coming with me?" Phillip's voice rose. Rhiannon met his gaze sadly. The rain had faded to a soft misting drizzle. Her eyes were as calm and impenetrable as an autumn pool. She did not look like Rhiannon. She looked like a stranger, a sad, pitying stranger both older and wiser than the Rhiannon of Fair Badden. Too wise. He wanted to erase that wisdom from her eyes.

"I can't go back, Phillip," she said. "I came because I owed you more than a note, not because I intended to leave with you. I'm so sorry, Phillip. I appreciate it so much that you came here. I only wish I could have spared you the journey."

"Appreciate?" He shoved his hand through his wet hair. "You *appreciate* my coming here? That's all?"

She didn't reply and he felt the fury that now always seemed to be simmering just beneath the surface of his thoughts boiling forth. "What will you do? Go back to that," he flung his hand in the direction of the castle, "*brothel*, and whore for Merrick? Is that what you choose over me?"

If his words hurt her he could find no evidence of it. Her lovely face only grew sadder; her pity became more pronounced.

"It's no use, Phillip," she whispered. "Even if I agreed—which I never would—your father would never let us marry and you'd be thankful. Because in your heart, you do not want to marry me."

"Don't say that!" His glance slewed back to where his companions waited beneath the dripping trees. Even from a distance, he caught St. John's disgusted expression and Fortnum's miserable one. "We can find a way round my father. He'll come round. As long as we live in Fair Badden, he'll come to accept it. Why, for God's sake, he all but chose you to be my bride in the first place!" He tried to deliver a laugh and failed.

She shook her head.

He ignored her rejection, anger overwhelming cautionary reason. The moment Ash Merrick had entered his life, he'd begun destroying it.

God, how he hated the man! thought Phillip. Merrick had turned his world upside down, charmed and mesmerized him, and then betrayed him in the most basic sense. Betrayed them all, Phillip thought, looking back at the others who'd lost money and peace of mind to that dark prince.

Merrick would demonize them no longer.

Phillip grabbed Rhiannon's arms, hauling her close, vaguely aware that she winced, but too overwrought to care.

"We don't need to get married in a church," he said. "We're in Scotland, dammit. We have only to say the words before a proper witness. We can return to Fair Badden with the deed already done."

"But I won't say the words," Rhiannon answered softly.

He shook her hard, a terrier with a rag, unable to stop himself. "What is it, Rhiannon? Do you think to become mistress of that castle? Don't you know what Wanton's Blush is? It's a byword for perversion."

She squirmed in his hands. "Phillip, please. You're hurting me."

"I don't care!" he thundered, his roar rising above the gusting wind. "I don't care. I have been hurt, too!"

She stilled. Her head dipped, but with sadness not shame.

"I know," she said. "I know. But this isn't the way, Phillip. This isn't going to make it stop hurting."

"Maybe not," he ground out, "but I won't let you throw yourself away on him. I couldn't live with myself if I allowed you to become his creature."

"Oh, Phillip—"

"He won't marry you, Rhiannon." Phillip shook her again, trying to reason with her, well acquainted with the strength of the spell she was under. "He'll just play with you for as long as you amuse him and then he'll betray you."

Her eyes lifted to his, no longer a girl's unlearned gaze, but one filled with compassionate understanding. He could not look at them. He drew a deep breath through his nostrils.

"I won't let him have you."

He dipped and caught her under her hips, tossing her over his shoulder.

"Phillip! No!"

Jaw bulging with determination, he strode back to the others, ignoring her pleas and her vindictives, her flaying arms and thrashing legs. He was a decent man, a good man, and he'd offered her his name. She'd been promised to him. He'd only to get her away from that devil's influence and everything would return to the way it had been before Merrick. The way it should be.

In front of him, his companions broke from their awed observation and scurried for their mounts, trading roguish smiles and excited murmurs.

And if Phillip felt more ill than victorious, they needn't know and would never suspect. They'd only know that Rhiannon was his and he would not let her go.

It was late afternoon when Thomas Donne found Ash Merrick and his father outside Carr's office. Ash's voice was low, Carr's expression flat with animosity. No other guests were present. They were readying themselves for the nightly bacchanal.

Donne's smile thinned with satisfaction. He could not have asked better. He wanted to see Carr's face when the bastard realized that whatever plan he'd had for Rhiannon had been thwarted. And, Donne admitted, he would not be averse to witnessing some small pain on Ash's proud, dark countenance when he discovered she'd rejected him in favor of another.

It was little enough revenge against the family that had decimated his own, but small satisfactions were all he would allow himself until he found the means to bring this house down in its entirety. Watt had been a gift, a bit of unanticipated pleasure. How piquant that the situation allowed Donne to maintain his role of pretended friendship even as he delivered the blow.

"Merrick! Lord Carr!" he hailed.

Ash looked up. Carr's brows rose questioningly.

Donne hastened to their sides, taking care to compose his features into lines of concern. He pulled Watt's note from his hand pocket. "I just returned from Miss Russell's suite. I had gone there to ask her if she would care to walk in the conservatory. Her door was ajar. I entered and found this on the floor. I know it does not speak well of me, but I read it. I think you had best read it, too, sir, seeing as how you're her guardian."

He held the missive out. With a frown, Carr took it. As he read it, his frown disappeared and was replaced by an expression of surprise. Donne waited, his heartbeat thickening with anticipation, careful to reveal none of it. And then—and then—Carr's face bloomed with pure, unfettered exultation.

Carr looked up, his eyes shimmering with satisfaction. And relief. Stupefied, Donne stared at him, aware that Ash, too, was regarding his father with consternation. Ash snagged the letter from his father's hands.

"Bloody well good for her." Carr had managed to rid his expression of pleasure, but he could not erase the gloating quality in his voice. "This is what comes of offering foundling brats a home. Ungrateful baggage." His gaze settled on Donne. "You saw, didn't you, Donne? I offered her a home, dressed her like a princess, introduced her to my friends, and she turned her back on it. There was nothing more I could do, was there?"

Donne was so completely offset by Carr's reaction, he could not think of a reply.

"I couldn't stop her, could I?" Carr insisted.

"No," Donne answered.

Carr's head bobbed up and down. "Well, that's that then. She's gone and I still have guests who require my attention." Carr clapped his hands together, only just refraining from rubbing them together. He strode away on a buoyant step.

Donne watched him go, trying to account for Carr's reaction. He would have staked his life on the fact that Carr had plotted some ill use for Rhiannon Russell.

He glanced at Ash. His glance stayed and became a stare, riveted by what he saw.

Some small pain. That's what he had told himself when he'd devised this scene. If Carr's reaction had lacked evidence of his being injured, Donne's wishes in regard to Ash had been answered tenfold, a hundred, no, a thousand.

Donne had never before witnessed such raw anguish on a man's face, a pain so extreme that no mask, no experience with torture, no instruction in endurance, *nothing* could hide its eviscerating power. It turned Merrick's eyes to arctic ice and then ashes and then emptiness. Merrick's hands hung loose at his sides as though he had no power to lift them, as if just the act of standing tested him beyond his measure.

"She's gone, you say?" Ash's voice was quiet, empty.

"Yes. Gunna says she walked out early this morning. Hours ago. I found the boy who delivered this message to her."

"Boy?"

"Andy. Yes."

He glanced up as though he was having trouble forming cohesive thought. "But you just came from her room," Ash murmured. "You didn't mention questioning the boy."

Donne cursed himself for a fool. "I did not think it advisable to let your father know any more than necessary about her whereabouts. And that's not the point. Listen, Ash. The lad says Watt was with a great number of men. That they'd camped on the far side of the island. There's no good going after her. And no point."

"Yes. I know."

God help him, he had no stomach for this sport. Ash had been gutted, sure and proper, and Donne saw no sense in playing with the entrails. "She's out of Carr's grasp, Ash. That was all you *really* wanted, wasn't it?"

Ash turned his head slowly, seeking Donne's gaze and pithing him with such sudden searing understanding that Donne knew he'd given himself away and revealed himself as an enemy. And he also knew it made no difference to Ash, that nothing made any difference anymore.

Ash turned without a word and walked away, leaving Donne standing alone. He decided then to leave this place and to stay away until his resolve returned, because the long-lost hereditary laird of the McClairen's did not feel any of his anticipated pleasure in revenge.

Dressed in sumptuous, scandalous scarlet and gold, face painted in a mask of unrivaled beauty, Fia threw herself into that night's festivities. Abandoned and scintillating, she danced with countless nameless men and flirted with as many more. Throughout Wanton's Blush, at gaming tables and in back corridors, masculine and feminine voices alike remarked her extreme behavior. She shone with a fascinating sharpness, a diamond newly cut.

When the meat of the night was being served, when strong heads and weak had been plied with their nightly opiate of wine and titillation, Fia heard dimly, like a cricket's song beneath the squall of a storm, the great clock in the center hall chime the eleventh hour. Calmly, disinterestedly, she removed Lord Hurley's hand from her naked shoulder and without bothering to explain herself, left him panting and red-faced in a shadowed corner of the conservatory. She walked to her father's office.

Once there, she looked around to make sure she was alone and then unlocked the door with the key she had stolen earlier that day. She entered. It was dark but she knew this room well. She struck the tinderbox beside the door and lit a lamp on a nearby table.

She did not waste time going over the items lying on Carr's desk. Instead she moved to the ornate marble mantel and pried her nails into a seam on its top. A thin square of marble came up in her hands, revealing the deep niche where Carr kept his most valued papers.

She did not know what she looked for. Proof, she supposed. One way or another an answer to Donne's accusation.

Carr had once told Fia that her mother, Janet McClairen, for all her insane loyalties, had been the one woman he'd loved. Fia had believed him for the simple fact that he obviously hadn't *liked* loving the woman.

Love, he'd said, clouded the judgment, absconded

with reason, and diminished a man's effectiveness. This was so in keeping with everything she knew about Carr that she'd believed him. But perhaps he'd been a better play-actor than she'd imagined.

She'd always adored her father, even as she feared him, because cold and analytical as he'd been, he'd always been direct with her. Honest. He'd made it their especial bond. Others could be lied to, manipulated, occasionally—and necessarily—hurt through deceit, but he would *never* use her in such a way. Certainly he would never barter her to the highest bidder like . . . *like a whore.*

But perhaps Carr *had* lied. Perhaps everything he'd told her had been deceits, equivocations, and sophistry told to keep her malleable, to distance her from her brothers because they knew the truth, to keep her shut away from the world while he groomed her for her future . . . sale.

Perhaps Carr had killed Janet McClairen.

Her mother.

Carefully Fia removed a thick packet of letters and papers and returned to the desk. Carr would be occupied for hours with "subjects."

She had time to discover the truth. God help her . . . and perhaps Carr.

Chapter 31

*R*hiannon sat huddled against one of the boulders ringing the small clearing. She drew her knees up, folded her arms, and waited. The men from Fair Badden were sleeping.

As she watched, a curl of smoke floated up from the smoldering campfire like a phantom fleur de lis and dissolved into the black night. No moon or stars shown in the ebony sky. It was a good night for prey animals to be afoot. A good night to walk away.

Phillip had not bothered to set a guard. He'd assumed that a woman alone would never dare flee into this desolate wilderness. He'd been mistaken. She was a daughter of these unforgiving mountains. Whatever they threatened her with could be no more painful than that which Phillip had already done to her: taken her from Ash.

Rhiannon waited another fifteen minutes before

gathering her damp skirts and creeping forward. Nearby—too near to chance saddling—the tethered horses nickered softly. Silently, she rifled through the belongings scattered about and found a skein of water. She slipped its leather thong across her shoulders, anger thrumming through her.

Her entire life had been a series of fear-inspired flights: the escape from the Highlands, her abduction from Fair Badden, and now Phillip's "rescue." She'd been taken from her home and then from her adopted home and now from Ash, always for the same reason: so she would be *safe*. And in the process she'd left behind those people and things she loved.

No more.

She would stay in the Highlands and if by staying she was destroyed, then she would be destroyed fighting for what she wanted, not fleeing what she feared. True, Ash Merrick was dangerous and passionate and complicated. Perhaps he would even be the death of her. But she loved him, with all her heart she loved him, and she would fight to stay at his side.

At the edge of the campsite, she lifted her hem and sprinted into the woods, her eyes riveted on the east. And Ash.

There was not much to pack, but then there never had been. A shirt, an extra pair of breeches, woolen socks. Ash thrust them into a leather satchel atop the belt stuffed with the money for Raine's ransom.

He still had his promise. He must hold on to that. It was all he had now. All he'd ever had, really, except for those brief incandescent hours before she'd left.

He understood. He did not fault her choice. Whatever magic they'd wrought as lovers had dissolved with Watt's note and sanity's return. She'd weighed Ash's poverty—not merely a paucity of coin—against all Watt had and represented. Watt had won. How could it be different? What could Ash offer her that could compare with friends, family, security, and home?

He'd thought of going after her—but it was a brief madness, the desperate last measures of an injured heart. He wanted her happiness too much to delude himself any longer. He couldn't pretend Phillip wanted her dead. That wretched giant would never harm Rhiannon.

Ash's gaze strayed to the adjoining room and the bed that still held their fragrance, the unique perfume of their lovemaking.

He'd made love with Rhiannon. He allowed the words to sweep over him with all their sweet, shattering power. He'd loved Rhiannon.

He braced his arms atop the satchel, his head falling forward. He'd loved Rhiannon and he'd never told her. In a life rife with misadventure and iniquity he knew that was the one act for which he would never forgive himself.

He threw his head up, inhaling through clenched teeth. It was as well for her that he'd never told her. It would have only added to her confusion. She loved Fair Badden. She cared for Phillip. If she would never again know such passion—he stopped, forcing himself to bitter honesty—if *he* never again knew that passion, many lived without it.

If this emptiness held at its core a hurt that threatened any second to erupt and consume him, he would survive that, too. It need only take time to heal. Say, a few eternities.

Yet, he thought, he would not have traded a second in her arms, a single word, not one of her smiles in order to extinguish all his anguish. Whatever pain it cost him was well worth the remembrance of her.

He released a long, shuddering breath and forced himself to buckle the satchel's straps. France waited.

He threw the pack over his shoulder and without looking back, walked away from the room, along the empty corridors, past the silent servants' furtive glances, down the filth-littered staircase, and out into the bleak morning light. He headed across the moss-slick cobbles toward the stables.

A dog's plaintive yip echoed through the yard. Dully, he looked about. A big yellow hound had been tied to the rail. Though the rope bit into her muscular throat she strained against her bounds. A prime case of Wanton's Blush tenderness, he thought bitterly, and went to the beast, bending down and unknotting the choking noose.

"Best leave," he muttered. "Take your chances in the mountains. Wanton's Blush is no place for man or beast."

The dog tucked tail and loped off, it's stiff hind leg in no manner impeding its speed. Ash stared after it. "Stella?"

The hound stopped at the stable yard entrance and looked back.

"Stella," Ash spoke quietly. "Come."

The hound turned its great head in the direction of the mountains, black nostrils quivering.

"Come."

Reluctantly, the dog returned to him. It was Stella. A tiny fire seeped through Ash's numb heart. Rhiannon would never have left Stella at Wanton's Blush. Whatever she'd intended when she'd gone to meet Phillip, she'd planned on returning. She had not willingly left here. Joy mingled inexorably with anxiety. He needed to find her. He started for the stables at a trot.

"Ash!"

He looked back. Fia was hastening across the courtyard, her cape whipping in the swirling wind. "Wait!" she called again.

He paused, anxious to be off, but he waited until she'd reached his side.

"You're leaving," she said.

"Yes." He was eager to go, but Fia obviously wanted a few words, and he knew that even if Rhiannon was an unwilling companion, she was in no danger from Watt.

"You were not going to bid father a fond adieu?" Her smile was bright and mocking. "Or your little sister?"

His own raw vulnerability identified the subtle disappointment in Fia's young voice. He regarded her sadly. Whatever Fia was, she had been made that way through no offices of her own. "Fia, do you want to leave here?"

His words took her aback. Her smooth face softened with astonishment. She searched his face warily, as if suspecting a trick. "No, no . . . I can't." The words tumbled out. "Where would I go? What would I do?" She lifted her chin. "Why would I want to leave, anyway?"

"I can't take you with me now," Ash said, reading

the distrust in her gaze. "Not now. But if you wish, I will come back for you, Fia."

She opened her lips to frame some stinging reply but her mouth snapped shut without uttering it.

"Think on it, Fia. I'll write. I promise."

He called the dog to his side and had started past Fia, when she caught at his sleeve. "Where are you going?"

"Rhiannon," he said shortly.

Her brow puckered. "She's gone?"

"Yes."

"But she can't. She mustn't." Fia's silky voice had roughened with such fear that Ash halted in the act of uncurling her fingers from his sleeve.

"What is it you know, Fia?" Ash asked. She hesitated. "Fia!"

"I think Rhiannon is in danger from Carr. I read his letters last night, all of—"

"What did you find, Fia?" Ash cut in.

"Her brother, Ian Russell, he's alive. He lives on one of the French-owned islands by the Americas."

"Still alive?" Ash's tension eased. "Then Rhiannon is not an heiress. She should be safe. Unless Carr has hired someone to kill her brother."

He threw the consideration out without thought and was shocked when he saw Fia blanch. Dear God, he thought in astonishment, she had not known what Carr was capable of and was only now discovering it.

"Yes," she said in a distant, hushed voice. "I don't think . . . Russell has been sending Carr money for Rhiannon's support and a substantial dower. Over the last ten years Russell has sent Carr thousands of pounds. Money Rhiannon never saw."

The quarterly entry in Carr's ledger. The overseas property Carr's little man of business had mentioned. Of course.

"There's more," Fia went on, lifting her face and speaking calmly now, too calmly. "I found a letter from this Ian Russell. Though he's a Jacobite fugitive, he grows homesick. Ash, he's coming here for one day, to see Rhiannon and then return to his island. I think Carr plans to have him arrested or . . . or killed."

One day. Realization swept over Ash in a cold, tidal wave of fear.

"No, Fia," he said. "Carr would never allow his association with a known Jacobite to become public or Russell to testify; it would end any hope Carr has of returning to society, if not forfeit his own life. And Carr can't take the chance that a hired assassin might fail. Russell is an unknown quantity, an adult, a battle-tested man who may well arrive with his own complement of companions."

He turned from Fia and began moving away, but Fia caught his arm again. "Why do you look like that?" she demanded. "What does he plan?"

He jerked his arm from her hold. "He plans to kill Rhiannon." He threw the words over his shoulder as he broke into a trot, his thoughts racing. That is why Carr had sent him to Fair Badden. Ash had been sent not to retrieve Rhiannon, but Rhiannon's corpse.

Ash ran faster, the king's edict ringing in his head: "No flower of England must die while under Carr's care." Carr had made sure that Rhiannon wasn't under his care, that she was miles away, that she had, in fact, never even met Lord Carr. Why, Ash himself would provide witness to that fact.

He burst through the stable doors and raced to his horse's stall, snatching it open and entering. Carr had planned it so perfectly. Ash would return with the body. Carr would strip the rings from Rhiannon's cold fingers and give them to Ian Russell, who would be too overwhelmed by grief to ask questions, and soon after gone forever, never realizing that not a penny of his money had reached Rhiannon. Should Russell find out otherwise, there was no telling what retribution he would seek, what he would do.

Hands flying Ash bridled and saddled his horse and leapt into the saddle, grabbing for the reins. No wonder Carr had been so stricken when he'd arrived at Wanton's Blush with Rhiannon. It was the one place on earth Carr could not allow her to die.

But now she'd left, and Carr's agent, whoever he'd hired or blackmailed into killing her, could finish the job.

Ash dug his heels into his horse's sides, flaying it with his hand and calling out loudly as the steed launched itself from the stable doors.

He had to get to Rhiannon before the assassin did.

"Where the bloody hell has she gone?" Phillip roared. His voice sent the starlings shrieking from the pine branches.

"Back to her lover," St. John sneered, crawling to his feet.

"I'll get her back," Phillip declared. His fury was a living thing. Merrick had taken her not once, but twice now. This last time Merrick might not have dragged her off, but she hadn't left here of her own volition.

She'd become Merrick's doxy, chained to him by carnal desire.

"Nay, Phillip," John Fortnum said gravely. "Nay. The lass doesn't want to be rescued. It's clear to see."

Phillip swung on him, his hands balling into fists at his side. "She doesn't know what's good for her. She's fascinated, under his spell. I'll break the hold he has on her when I break his filthy neck."

The others gained their feet and traded cautious glances.

"I didn't come here to commit murder," Ben Hobson finally said.

"Is it murder to rid the world of a devil?" Phillip demanded. "He taints whatever he touches and destroys what he seduces. He deserves nothing less than death!"

"No, Phillip," Fortnum pleaded. "Think what you're saying. He's a man, Phillip, like any other man. No demon."

Phillip ignored him, ignored them all, stalking past the shuffling, muttering men and slinging his saddle over his mount. He laced the cinch straps and tightened the girth, the air hot in his lungs as he put on the bridle. Finished, he swung into the saddle, yanking back on the reins and spinning the horse around.

The men had not moved and Phillip scoured them with his glare. "Go then! Tuck tails and run! I'll find him without you!"

Chapter 32

"*H*ie on!" Ash shouted.

The great, yellow bitch darted about the cold campfire with increasing agitation, her hackles rising and foam spattering the huge muzzle sweeping the ground. At the edge of the clearing she suddenly lifted her head and shot into the brush, angling back the way they'd come. Ash hesitated. There would be no reason for Watt to take Rhiannon back toward Wanton's Blush. Nothing lay between here and there but rough wilderness.

He bent over in his saddle, studying the ground. The majority of hoof prints clearly led south and to the west, yet Stella's attitude had been nearly frantic, as though the scent had been thick in her nose. She'd not led him wrong yet.

Ash spurred his horse, plunging down the rocky slide of land after the hound.

The beast had been misplayed, he thought watching her. She was no gazehound, but a scent hound. She'd taken the lead from the beginning, quartering in sharp angles ahead of him, her nose to the earth, following a trail only she could discern. It was almost enough to make Ash believe in a benevolent deity, one who'd sent Stella to him as guide, for without her he would never have been able to pick up Rhiannon's trail in this unmarked wasteland.

But the hound had been crippled and the day had worn perilously hard on her injured leg. Except for sporadic bursts of speed, she lagged now, loping on three legs.

With increasing regularity Ash had circled the failing dog in ever widening rings, stopping often to rise in the stirrups and call Rhiannon's name. Each minute now portended a coming crisis, a fatal meeting between Rhiannon and Carr's assassin.

Around noon Rhiannon reached a high pasture. She sat down and pulled off her half boot. She tore another strip of silk from her underskirt and replaced the bandage covering the open blister on her ankle. A shiver racked her body and she shrugged out of her damp jacket, hoping that the weak sun would warm her.

She shouldn't be stopping at all, but she was beyond tired—wet and still cold from her night out on the mountain. Twice now she'd thought she'd heard the sound of pursuit. Once she'd glimpsed a lone rider on the lower slopes of the mountain. But that had been early and she'd kept to the steep upper slopes since then, eschewing the easier footing below.

All of her years as mistress of the hunt stood her in

good stead. She knew the tricks of backtracking, the importance of moving with the wind through the densest brush and of staying away from the open places. Each time she utilized these lessons, she swore she would never again chase down an animal for sport. She understood too well now what it was to be the prey.

She forced her swollen foot back into the half boot and stood, looking cautiously down the long, empty pasture. The storm had blown over at dawn, leaving only a thin fog that the sun had quickly burned away. Before her the field grasses bowed low, fanned by a chastising breeze.

It would be criminally easy to spot a dark-clad figure moving across that flat green expanse but the alternative of climbing through the steep banks flanking the narrow valley would cost her hours. Hours Phillip would put to good use. He had the advantage. He knew where she was going and he must know she dared not spend another night exposed to the elements on the open mountains. Her only hope lay in reaching McClairen's Isle before he found her.

Once more she looked around, peering intently at the edges of the pasture, straining her ears to hear any sound of pursuit. She crouched down and hobbled into the sea of grass.

Stella's heart was more able than her body. She limped now with painful determination, no longer capable of loping. She held her head up, nostrils quivering but moving on a direct if painfully slow course, as if pulled by an invisible string. Driven by a sense of foreboding, Ash left her behind. He cantered in the direction she traveled, soon far outdistancing her.

Whatever path Rhiannon had taken had obviously been the most torturous route possible. Several times Ash had to dismount and lead his horse up a shale-slick incline or around a series of jagged outcrops.

The sun was high overhead when he entered a narrow valley a half-mile long. He pulled his mount to halt, scanning the rocky walls embracing the glen. He saw nothing. He carefully surveyed the swaying grasses before him. Again, nothing. His heart thudded dully.

Stella could easily have switched directions and even now closed in on Rhiannon while he floundered about in an ocean of grass. He'd lost not only Rhiannon but also the hound that had been leading him to her.

He stood in his stirrups and cupped his hands and called out, "Rhiannon!"

He would not give up. She was somewhere. Perhaps not here, but near. He could bloody *feel* her.

"Rhiannon!"

He waited, his body stiff with tension, every nerve stretched. He would find her. He would search the entire damn country if need be, but he would find her. His voice rose, filled the valley, echoed off the stony mountain walls. "Rhiannon!"

Far away, near the end of the glen a slender figure rose from the spring green grasses, a wood sylph called by a mortal's implacable summons. The sun blazed off her rich, dark mane.

"Rhiannon!" He spurred his horse forward and galloped like a madman across the field. He'd almost reached her. Joy animated her wholly beautiful face—vanished, became terror.

She stared past him, shouted words made unintel-

ligible by the rushing wind. He leaned forward, only
one thought driving him now; he had to reach—

A blow like thunder caught his side, throwing him
from the saddle. He hit the ground hard, his momen-
tum catapulting him sideways and tumbling him yards
before he settled. Blackness swam in manic circles
around the edges of his vision. A woman was shouting.
Rhiannon.

He slew about and caught back an agonized cry as a
sharp, lacerating pain drove through him. He peered
down, trying desperately to focus. His right arm was
trapped at an awkward angle beneath his body, and a
dark, warm stain was seeping through his shirt. He
didn't have time for this.

He shoved his good arm into the ground, pushing up
on his knees. The world spun madly. Arms swept
around him, the scent of pine tar and sweat and *her*. He
clenched his teeth, fighting the enveloping void.

"My God!" he heard her say. "Dear God, Phillip,
what have you done? Help me!"

Watt. Of course. How well he'd courted that man's
hatred. . . .

Rhiannon eased Ash down to her lap, cradling his
head, sheltering him as well as she could. He gritted his
teeth at the movement. Tears sprang to her eyes that
she was hurting him more than he'd already been hurt.

A shadow fell over his face and she looked around,
crouching lower over Ash's body. Phillip Watt stood
above them, the pistol still smoking in his hand. His
face was white, his eyes startled and empty, like a
dreamer who'd been awakened too abruptly from a
nightmare.

"Is he dead?" His voice was numb with disbelief.

"Dead?" She spat the word. "If he were dead, Phillip, then either you or I would be, too, for surely I would lose my life in trying to see that you lost yours!"

The low, intense venom in her voice took him aback. The hand holding the pistol dropped to his side. He lurched forward a single step. "I didn't know. I didn't realize. God help me, there's so much blood—"

"Get your horse," she commanded. "We need to find help for him."

"Yes," Phillip mumbled.

Ash stirred in Rhiannon's arms. She returned her attention to him, hovering over him in a protective attitude, her eyes searching his white countenance. With shaking hands, she brushed the long black hair from his temples. "Quiet, my own, my heart. Easy. Be still, my love."

"Well, what are you waiting for Phillip? Kill the bastard."

At the sound of that smooth voice, Rhiannon's head snapped up. Edward St. John sat his horse a few yards behind Phillip. One fist rested on his hip; the other held a primed pistol.

Phillip spun around, like a child being called by too many voices, his expression confused and miserable.

"Kill him," St. John urged calmly. Rhiannon tensed, her arms tightening around Ash.

"I . . . I can't!" Phillip burst out.

"Of course you can," St. John said. "He really is a devil, you know. Or if not the devil, the son of one. At least a devil with cards. I can testify to that with some authority. Carr quite, quite has me in his debt. Indeed, in my short two weeks at that hellish Eden called Wanton's Blush I lost every bit of money I owned. Plus quite a bit I did not own. In fact, I lost my entire inheritance."

A flash of deep, burning hatred revealed itself in the trembling of St. John's smiling lips. "You aren't going to shoot the bastard, are you, Phillip?"

Dully, Phillip shook his head. With a disappointed sigh, St. John reached down with his free hand and withdrew another pistol from his belt. "I thought not. You really are Milquetoast under all that manly bluster, aren't you, Phillip? No matter. I would have had to kill you anyway. I was simply hoping you might accomplish at least one decisive act before your death. It was to be my gift to you. For old time's sake, don't you know."

"But why?" Phillip asked.

"Because you're a witness," Ash said. Rhiannon looked down at him. His gaze went past her, fixing on St. John with cold enmity. "A witness to Rhiannon's murder."

"True." St. John laughed and Phillip lurched forward a step. St. John jerked the pistol barrel around, aiming it directly at Phillip's chest. Phillip checked.

"Now, now, Phillip." St. John suddenly grinned. "Really, this has worked out so much better than I'd hoped. I shall kill the girl and then you, Phillip. When I send Fortnum and the others—oh, yes, our companions are still staggering about these godforsaken mountains somewhere—they shall find this little tragedy. Merrick, you *will* do me the favor of dying shortly? That's an awful lot of blood you're spilling."

Ash's hands groped feebly down his side and over his hip. His fingers grew red with his blood.

"Yes," Ash murmured. "I think I can promise you my cooperation."

Ash's gaze met Rhiannon's and she realized what he was seeking. She sobbed, doubling forward over him, her hands aiding his search. "Leave him alone!"

"Good!" St. John said, ignoring Rhiannon's rocking figure. "Because you simply must die. I'd shoot you myself but I haven't got an extra bullet. But perhaps I should keep you company whilst you expire."

"You're too kind," Ash said weakly.

"Not at all. Of course, I could just—move things along a bit." His eyes were flat and cold.

"I don't understand," Phillip said.

"The cornerstone of your character, Phillip." St. John shook his head, his gun still trained on Phillip. "Allow me to explain. With my help our sad friends shall piece together an entire unsavory tableau: A rapist—Merrick—shoots his rival—you. When his slut, having finally come to her senses, objects, he shoots her, too. Phillip, you get to be a hero. Because before you die you manage to get off the shot that ultimately kills Merrick. All very tragic, what?"

"But why?" Phillip asked again.

St. John's smile disappeared. "Carr promised to forgive my debt if I did this thing for him."

"Carr will never forgive your debt," Ash laughed weakly.

"We shall see—or rather, *I* shall see." St. John aimed the pistol at Rhiannon's back.

"Nothing personal, my dear," St. John muttered, "but as I said, Carr is a devil and the devil must have his due—"

The stiletto flashed from behind Rhiannon's concealing skirts. Hurled by a master hand, it flew straight, but the eyes guiding it were clouded and so rather than

St. John's heart it pierced his shoulder, shattering the bone. One pistol dropped from his nerveless fingers; the other discharged into the ground and fell from his hand as he clutched for the knife buried in his shoulder.

"Bedamn!" St. John gasped.

Phillip leapt forward but St. John was too quick. He groped for his reins with his good hand and caught them up. Digging his spurs into the mare's flanks, he sawed back on the bit. The horse reared, her hooves flailing out, striking at Phillip. Then she shot forward and tore across the field.

Phillip watched St. John flee, torn by the need to pursue him and his debt to the man who was attempting to rise from Rhiannon's arms.

"No." She wrapped her arms around Ash and held on grimly. He closed his eyes and sank once more in her embrace, finally allowing the beckoning darkness to take him. "Go, Phillip," Rhiannon said to him. "Find the others. Now!"

There was nothing for it. Catching his horse's reins Phillip swung into the saddle. He knew what honor demanded. He rode for help.

At the far end of the glen, a scent filled Stella's nostrils. Not *her* scent. That was nearer now, but still some distance. Her scent was a promise.

This scent was a threat.

She knew it well. Her hackles rose in response, and a growl rumbled from deep in her powerful chest. It was the one who'd tied her so she could not move and twisted her leg until it hadn't worked and then twisted it more until she'd howled.

His odor rushed toward her on a warm, driving

wind. She lifted her head and saw a man on the horse coming toward her, oblique and at an angle. Her stamina had failed her hours ago and she had no vigor left on which to draw. She was a kennel dog, a lady's coddled companion. But hatred is a power in itself and of that she had plenty.

Deep within Stella's heart a feral beast still reigned, its ferocity held hostage by kindness, its savageness imprisoned by love.

The scent that filled her nostrils set it free.

If anyone had been watching, they would have seen the mounted man reach the glen's far end and look back over his shoulder. They would have witnessed his relief as he realized he was not being pursued and so stemmed his mount's headlong dash to a slower gait. They would have seen him smile with malicious triumph as he entered the forest.

And if they had watched a bit longer they would have seen a long, muscular form racing with all the speed of vengeance through the winnowing grass and vanishing in the same spot.

Ash felt tears falling on his cheeks and lips. Woozily, he opened his eyes. The afternoon sun swam in golden pools above him, blinding him, and he turned his head away. Stella's huge head swam into focus, her tongue lolling clownishly. Good beast, Ash thought vaguely, she'd found them.

"Ash?" He peered up at the shadowed face above him. Worry and grief marked her voice. She turned her head slightly. The sun caught and caressed her features, limning her cheek and throat with light and tipping her eyelashes in gold. Her hazel eyes glinted with green fire. She was beautiful and courageous and everything to him. Everything.

He'd almost lost her and he hadn't told her he loved her and he had to correct that. She had to know.

"Rhiannon."

"Hush," she murmured. "The others will be here soon. You'll be fine. I've washed the wound and stopped the bleeding. It really—you *have* to be fine."

"So pretty. I never . . . said." He raised his hand and brushed the tears from her cheeks. She *would* weep silently, he thought. She'd done so as a child when she'd first come to Fair Badden. He remembered, a story told mostly by her omissions. "I need . . . to tell you."

She smiled down at him, her trembling lips soft and musing. "I know," she whispered, her fingers caressing his jaw.

He rested quietly a minute, savoring her soft caresses, the fragrance of spring grass and sun-heated skin, his gaze roving her features with calm deliberation until a thought occurred to him. "Where were you going?" he asked. "Where were you heading when I found you?"

A look of exquisite tenderness came over her face. "To you, Ash."

Once more he nodded, commanding himself to be content with that answer. But he was a passionate man and he was starved for an answering passion, *her* passion, her heart, her love, starved for words he could not ever remember hearing, and so, though he knew he was being greedy and taking shameless advantage of her tender heart, he did not hesitate before asking, "Why?"

This time her smile was fuller, richer, more certain,

hearing in his commanding tone a promise of a future that had only hours ago seemed an uncertain thing.

She thought of all the years ahead in which she would tell him she loved him and all the ways in which she would demonstrate it. And because for the first time in her life she felt sure of another's love, of owning it purely and wholly, she could afford to be the slightest bit roguish. And so she gave him back his answer with the same words he'd used when he'd first told her he loved her.

"For my heart's sake, beloved. For my heart's sake."

Epilogue

*C*arr watched his daughter. She stood at the end of the servants' hall facing a small group of men—dirty, mud-coated peasants. He'd come upon them quite by accident. Usually he gave up the redoubtable pleasures of the servants' quarters altogether but this afternoon he'd needed to talk to his wine steward.

The men fidgeted, eyes downcast, faces sullen with the universal expression of the yeoman. Fia's face, as always, remained composed, as unrevealing as a sphinx. She said something and with much bobbing of heads the men disappeared, shuffling backward through the servants' door.

Fia turned and saw him, hesitated a second. Something bright flickered in her black eyes and then she sailed gracefully toward him. For a second she looked just like Janet. He shivered.

"What did those men want?" Carr asked her when she'd reached his side.

"They've found a body about fifteen miles west," she said calmly, "on the mainland."

"In the mountains?"

"Yes."

"So?" Carr asked. "What of it?"

"It's apparently a nobleman. The clothes, or what are left of them, are fine and there was an expensive wig."

There must be more to the story. "Yes?"

"He looks to have been savaged by a wolf."

"Impossible." Carr snorted, his interest in the tale fast fading. "There haven't been any wolves in Scotland for over a hundred years."

"As you say."

He began to turn, intent on finding the wine steward, but something about her complacence made him uncomfortable. She'd ever been cool, like a beautiful ice princess. Now she was hard as ice as well. And no longer cool, but cold. That type of coldness that burns. "Who was the man, did they say?"

"Edward St. John." Her eyes stayed on his face, soft and intent as a cat's mesmerizing gaze. "You look upset. Did you know him? Ah, yes. I recall. He was here last year, was he not? He lost a great deal of money to you. Losing money to you must surely be the way to your heart, for upon my faith, Father, you are pale with the news."

"Was he alone?" Carr demanded.

"Quite alone."

The bloody, bloody bungler. Carr had all but handed the Russell bitch to him. He deserved to die.

Now he would have to make another plan before Russell arrived, find some other puppet whose strings he could pull. . . .

"I wonder why he was traveling alone in those mountains?" Fia smiled.

She was toying with him! The realization struck him like a slap across the face. The audacious chit! How dare she? Anger clotted his cheeks with high color. His mouth compressed. He wheeled and began stalking away from her.

"Oh, Father?"

He looked around. She stood exactly where he'd left her. Her hands were clasped lightly before her.

"What?"

"I forgot to mention earlier but a messenger came for you last night."

He scowled. "What is it, Fia?"

"'Twas a message from a Mr. Ian Russell." She tilted her head. "I don't recall knowing anyone named Ian Russell. And I have quite a memory for names."

Russell. No! He wasn't suppose to arrive until late summer!

Carr's heart leapt to his throat. A thick, dull pain lanced through his side. His throat constricted and his fingertips tingled. The blood surged and boiled to his face.

"What?" he demanded in a choked voice. It was hard to breathe. His hands felt dulled, numbed. "What about Ian Russell?"

"Odd message," Fia said slowly.

"Damn it, Fia," he gasped, "what . . . did . . . it . . . say?"

"Oh, only something about the political climate not

being favorable for sailing and that he must delay his trip indefinitely. Isn't that odd?"

Carr closed his eyes. Relief washed through him, but the cost of his momentary panic was high. The vise around his chest eased only slowly, the feeling returning to his fingertips in increments. When he finally opened his eyes, Fia was gone.

Le Havre France
July 1760

It was a nice inn, relatively new, and very nearly clean, particularly the private room in which the dark young man had carefully ensconced the pretty young woman. The innkeeper's wife, an earthy practical woman had winked at the handsome fellow when he'd demanded the room have a lock and he the only key, and remarked that a fine stud had no need of a tethered mare.

He'd laughed, returning a sally in coarse Parisian patois. Surprising because the gentleman looked a good measure better than his gutter speech declared him. And certainly the little mademoiselle looked patrician with her red glinting hair and wide hazel eyes and her blushes. . . .

Ah well, he was certainly handsome enough to lure a decent girl of good family and she was certainly beautiful enough for him to risk that patrician family's wrath. And the way they watched each other . . . ! The innkeeper's wife smiled and shook her head. It had been many a year since something so small as a look passing between a man and a woman had had the power to awaken her imagination. But these two!

Still smiling, she banged on the door to the private room, balancing a tray in the other hand. It contained the meal the man had ordered. The door opened and the beautiful woman stepped back, motioning toward the table. She did not speak. In fact, the innkeeper's wife had yet to hear the girl utter a word. She shrugged. Perhaps she was a mute and perhaps that was why she settled for a coarse-spoken beau. No matter how powerfully built or how passionately he watched her, a girl like this . . . she should be in a castle. Unless something was wrong with her.

Ah, well. It was no concern of hers. They'd paid in coin. She set the tray down and, after bobbing a little curtsey, left.

Rhiannon glanced at the steaming plate of stewed chicken and returned to the chair she'd pulled up beside the window. She knew the innkeeper's wife wondered at her lack of speech but she hadn't the "advantage" of Ash's years in a French gaol to teach her the nuances of an accent. She smiled tenderly, as always impressed that Ash could recall any part of his years in prison and find value in it.

Outside in the little seaport town the late summer sun was finally giving up the sky and sinking into the horizon. Ash should be back by now. He'd left yesterday at daybreak, making her promise not to open the door to anyone save the innkeeper and swearing he would return with Raine by nightfall the following day.

She'd begged to go with him but he'd refused. Rightfully so, she suspected. She could only be a burden to him on his covert mission to ransom his brother. England and France were at war and her speech marked her nationality quite clearly. If she was caught, well, even though born Scot, Rhiannon now owned an English surname—Merrick.

Rhiannon Merrick. Nearly a month had passed since they'd stood with Edith Fraiser and John Fortnum just north of the Scottish border and declared themselves husband and wife. Edith had cried. Rhiannon had never been so happy. She was still happy, deliciously so. Each day revealed more of the depth of honor and integrity the man she'd wed owned; each day proved the depth of his love for her. It was there in the care he took with her, in the passion and tenderness with which they made love, and in the worry that he could not quite hide. They had nothing. Except Raine's ransom.

Then, a week ago, he'd offered even that to her. It was, he said gravely, a fair princely sum. With it they could live wherever they wanted, anywhere in the world. His eyes had been still, his face composed, the offer utterly sincere—but she knew him now. She saw the haunted shadow behind the tender smile.

She knew then that he'd do anything for her, be anything she asked him to be—but all she wanted him to be was Ash Merrick. And Ash Merrick had vowed to ransom his brother. So here they were.

The sound of a carriage clattering on the cobblestones outside the window drew Rhiannon's attention. She pushed open the window and hung her head out. The carriage pulled to a halt before the inn's front entrance and the driver clambered from his seat. Before he could descend and pop open the door, it swung open and a lean dark figure leapt unaided to the ground. Rhiannon held her breath waiting for a second figure to emerge.

The driver went to the solitary man's side and held

up his lantern; the swinging garish light swept over Ash's face as he counted out coin into the driver's outstretched palm. His expression was bemused, taut, his brows dipping low over his eyes. He glanced up and saw her. A wave of pure pleasure lit his whole dark countenance. He swung away from the driver, heading for the entrance, and Rhiannon slammed the window, hastening into the hall.

A moment later he strode down the narrow corridor toward her. She stretched out her arms and flew to meet him. His strong arms caught her up in his embrace, his head bent, and his mouth closed greedily on hers. She scraped her fingers through his hair, held his beloved face between her palms, and returned his kiss.

He pushed the door behind her open, still kissing her, and carried her into the room, kicking the door shut behind him. Finally he raised his head.

"Raine?" she said, unable to keep from lifting her hand and stroking his cheek.

Slowly he set her down. He shook his head. "I don't know, Rhiannon. I don't know."

She gazed at him questioningly.

"I went first to the prison to speak to the head gaoler. I wanted to make specific arrangements as to the time of Raine's release before I *visited*"—his lips curled back in a sneer—"the politician who was to accept Raine's ransom."

"Yes?"

"I went to the prison. I spoke to the head gaoler. Rhiannon, Raine is not there."

"What do you mean, not there?" Rhiannon asked, a dull sense of horror growing within. "Dead? Oh, Ash, did he die?"

"No!" Ash shook his head violently. "Not dead. Of that I am certain. I even 'interviewed' a few of the guards late last night at a local tavern they frequent in order to make certain."

"Then where is he?"

"I don't know. No one seems to know. He simply seems to have disappeared. If there were someone else who might have ransomed him I would suspect the French already released him."

"Your father?"

"Carr?" Ash's glance was incredulous but then, seeing her anxiety, his gaze softened. "No, Rhiannon. I forget your soft heart. But no. Not Carr. There is no one."

"Then he escaped," Rhiannon said.

"To where?" Ash asked.

Rhiannon touched his cheek gently. "He wouldn't go to Wanton's Blush, would he?"

"Not unless he'd a very good reason."

"Then perhaps he's just . . . looking for his life," she suggested softly.

He scowled and then sighed and finally moved his hand over her temples, brushing back the soft tendrils with infinite tenderness. "What a wise creature you are, Rhiannon Merrick. How much I love you."

She turned her face into his open palm and pressed a kiss against its center. "What are we to do now?"

He stared at her and then suddenly smiled, his expression far lighter than she'd ever seen it, free of shadows, obligation, or the past, filled only with love and anticipation.

He reached beneath his cloak and withdrew a long, heavy belt of double stitched leather. He held it up.

"My dear, it seems we're suddenly quite rich—indeed, heirs to a fair princely sum."

She stared at the money belt in bemusement. Though all that money meant little to her, she knew his inability to assure she would have a comfortable future had troubled Ash greatly, so she smiled, too. "But what do we do with it?" she asked.

"Why, my beloved, we find our happy ending."

Turn the page for an introduction to Raine Merrick,

The
Reckless One

The second novel in Connie Brockway's breathtakingly romantic McClairen's Isle trilogy will be available from Dell in January 2000.

The Reckless One

*R*aine Merrick watched a black-clad figure step through the cell door. Hidden beneath an opaque ebony veil and layers of midnight-hued silk, she moved with an odd, hesitant grace. A black velvet cape covered her shoulders and long black gloves encased the slender hands holding her skirts above the stagnant puddles on the floor. Madame Noir had arrived to make her selection for her evening's entertainment.

The prison guard, Armand, followed her, his face flushed and his ridged brows lowered in displeasure. Beside him shuffled a huge monolith of a man bundled against the cold, a thick cape draped over his massive shoulders and a woolen scarf wrapped about a thick neck. The eyes beneath the brim of his hat were sharp and piercing.

Silently, Raine cursed the Fates. Why couldn't she

be accompanied by someone big, but dull-witted and slow.

As she turned and spoke to her man she moved in front of the rush of torches. The backlighting revealed her profile through the mantilla-like covering: a slender throat, a sharp-angled jaw, a patrician nose. The men who returned from a night in her "care" swore she never removed that veil. No one had ever seen her face—not even Armand—and no one knew her real name. She always registered under the pseudonym Madame Noir at the hotel she used for her trysts.

She'd finished her whispered conversation and turned toward the prisoners. With what looked like a conscious gathering of purpose, she crossed the room toward them, her attendant shadowing her. She stopped before the colonist.

"Too old," she murmured in exquisite, aristocratic French.

She continued circling the room. She paused before the Prussian, who lifted his still wet head and gazed at her with dull, hopeless eyes. She paused before saying, "This man will die if he is not made warm."

"Yes," Armand agreed disinterestedly. "But he is Prussian."

She remained studying the shivering man.

"But I might have a desire for a Prussian someday," she said quite calmly, and moved on.

Immediately Armand barked out an order that the Prussian be taken down, dried off, and fed. In another situation, one might possibly mistake Madame Noir's comments for compassion, Raine thought cynically. She'd moved toward the English youth.

Armand scuttled to her side. "He's new, Madame.

English. Young. Feel. Touch him," he chattered as though the panicked-looking boy was an animal being auctioned. Which he was, Raine reminded himself. Which they all were.

"Please! I come from a noble family. I cannot be used so!" the youth sobbed. "I am not the one you want! I am not the one—"

"I am."

Madame's head snapped around at the sound of Raine's calm voice, her veil swirling about her shoulders and settling like the dark wings of a nighthawk. She cocked her head sideways, increasing her resemblance to a small, sleek bird of prey.

"Monsieur is English?" she asked, her interest revealed in the sharpening inflection of her voice.

"Aye." He watched her carefully. "English. You have a . . . taste for Englishmen, Madame?"

Behind the heavy veil he thought he saw the glimmer of her eyes as her gaze traveled over him. He forced himself to stand still and turned his palms up, inviting her inspection. "I'm your man."

"Perhaps."

Armand hurried over. He grabbed a handful of Raine's hair and jerked his head back.

"Here, Madame. Come. Examine. Look. I know Madame is most careful in making her selection."

She came within a few feet of him. Her warm scent filled his nostrils, unexpectedly stirring his senses. Without warning, sensual images from his all-but-forgotten past ambushed him, flooding his mind, filling his thoughts.

Musk and flowers, cleanliness and dark promise. Womanly and virginal all at once. Straining bodies, a sweet aftermath. The sudden sensual memory stunned him with its eviscerating force.

He closed his eyes, breathing in deeply through his mouth, tasting as well as scenting her.

He hadn't been in the same room with a woman in five years.

"Touch him," Armand urged.

Did she hesitate before reaching out? Did she note the uncontrollable forward cant of his body in anticipation of her hand? Her hand brushed his naked skin. He forgot everything else.

His breath caught and he flinched back. Not because he abhorred her touch. Just the opposite. Because he wanted it. Her fingertips flowed down his naked chest to his belly, to where his breeches hung low on his hips. He shivered, willing her hand to slip lower still, waiting, aching with arousal, for that intimate touch, heedless of the spectators.

He felt her gaze drop to the evidence of his arousal. Abruptly, she snatched her hand back, like a maiden.

"Madame wished a challenge?" Armand was asking. "Here is such a one. Arrogant. Young. Healthy."

"I don't think—"

"Forgive me, Madame." Her man lumbered forward.

"Yes, Jacques?" she said.

"I believe this one would suit very well."

Raine glanced sharply at the mountainous man. Since when did a servant advise his mistress on her sexual requisites? She did not reprimand him, however. She merely hesitated. Raine ground his teeth in frustration. She had to pick him. She *must*.

"I will be whatever Madame wishes me to be." He

forced the words out between his lips, surprised at how easily they came, how facilely he abdicated the last shreds of his pride. "I will do whatever Madame wishes me to do."

He held his breath.

She seemed to be holding hers.

"All right," she finally said. "I'll take him."

Jacques nodded approvingly.

"Very good," Armand said. "I'll send two guards with you."

"Not necessary," Jacques said, handing Armand a heavy-looking velvet pouch. Raine blessed the man's self-assurance.

Armand shot a telling glance at Raine. "But it is, Monsieur. I know this man."

Madame, who'd held herself aloof, made a dismissive movement with her hands. "I do not wish spectators at my sport. I desire privacy with him."

"I understand, but Madame, you must see that if this man should escape—"

"Do you dare to press me?"

"Non, Madame!" Armand assured her, hauling a thick set of keys from his belt and opening the lock that held Raine manacled to the wall. "But *certainment*! Still, I fear this one." He fastened a length of chain between Raine's manacles. "The guards will ride post, on the back of the carriage. You will have privacy. I will have peace of mind. This is sensible, yes?" Armand looped the chain around his fist and jerked Raine forward.

Madame swung around, irritation vibrating from her slender form. "If you insist."

His ruddy face wreathed in smiles, Armand held Raine's chain out for Jacques, who accepted the heavy links. Madame stalked from the cell, her skirts rustling.

Jacques shoved Raine between the shoulder blades, propelling him through the door and down the low corridor toward a flight of stairs leading up to the prison's receiving yard. There, just outside of the gates, waited a closed carriage. The guards were already perched on the footmen's steps at the back. Armand stood beside the open door.

Raine's gaze darted about, looking for any chance to break away. As if he'd read his thoughts, Jacques shoved him again, causing Raine to stumble over his chains. He swung around with a growl. The behemoth met his glare blandly. "I wouldn't be testing me quite so early."

Forcing down his ire, Raine shuffled across the yard through the open gates. Once outside he stopped, unable to help himself, and lifted his face to the weeping sky. For the first time in five years he drew breath outside the prison. He closed his eyes, vowing never to return.

"Go on, son." Jacques's voice was surprisingly mild. "Get in."

Raine hefted his chains and flung them in onto the floor of the carriage. Jacques reached past him, snapping a padlock through the chains, locking it to a bolt on the floor. Damn the man's caution! He'd have to find another opportunity to escape.

Unceremoniously, Raine climbed into the carriage. From across the carriage, boot heels scrabbled against the floorboards. Of course, she'd already entered. He peered around the dimly lit interior.

She was almost indiscernible in her black gown and heavy veils, being tucked as she was as far back into the corner as possible.

As though, he realized, he scared her to death.

Mindful of how his shoulders crowded the doorway and blocked the light, Raine slouched down in the seat opposite her, angling himself in such a way that he did not threaten her in any manner. The side of the carriage dipped as Jacques climbed into the driver's seat. Raine kept his gaze carefully averted.

He could hear her short, agitated breaths, feel her tension. Jacques called out, and the horses plunged forward with unexpected alacrity, pitching her across the slick leather seat. Raine flung out a hand, his fingers closing around her upper arm.

"Take your hands off of me," she whispered.

She was not commanding him. She was pleading. There could be no mistaking the imploring quality in her voice. As false as he suspected it to be, her performance changed things, her simulated fear working on him insidiously, potently.

His body reacted instinctively to the implicit submissiveness in her appeal. She was pretending that he held the whip hand, that she was some sort of anxious virgin closeted with a ravening beast. Her fantasy marched closer to the truth than she could know.

Her heat soaked through the gown, warming his palm. Even chained and at her mercy, even knowing that this was all a contrivance to aid her arousal, that none of it was real, he could not deny his own sexual response.

Role-playing be damned. He wanted her.

"Madame," he said softly, lifting his arms and spreading open Jacques' cape, displaying his shackled wrists and his naked chest, "as you can see, I am at your disposal, to do with as you please."

She shrank back against the deep tufted leather seats. "You don't understand," she whispered.

"*Oui*. I do not. You will teach me, though. What *is* your pleasure, petite Madame? You touch; I am not allowed to touch? You arouse and then withhold the culmination of the arousal? Is that how you achieve satisfaction? Pray, do your damnedest by me. I am in a lather to be victimized."

"Quiet!"

"Just tell me the rules of the game, Madame," he said tersely, more than willing to pay whatever price freedom demanded.

He leaned forward and gently grasped her wrist, drawing her palm forth until it lay flat and low on his belly. He drew his breath in with a hiss of undeniable pleasure. "Can you feel my muscles clench with the promise of that which you withhold?"

She tried to snatch her hand back, but he kept it there, desperately trying to gauge the nature of his role. How much to ravish, how much to seduce. His very life depended on his ability to gauge her reactions. Once, a lifetime ago, he'd been well on his way to being a master of such sensual expertise.

"I was resigned to my celibacy, Madame," he said grimly, "having long since purged myself of the tormenting memories of a woman's soft body, a woman's sweet mouth, a woman's ardent embrace. You've resurrected those chimerical images. Given them substance, teased me with hope." His voice grew fervent and low. She tried to tug away, but her efforts lacked conviction. She wanted to hear this.

"I am a condemned man." He secured her other wrist, and heedless of her resistance, abruptly yanked her forth, tumbling her into his embrace. He hauled her into the vee created by his widespread legs. His arm snaked about her waist. She gasped, her hands pushing at his cold, damp chest. The feel of her velvet fingers against him stroked his nerve endings. His heart thundered in his chest with equal parts fear and arousal.

"Let me service you," he growled, the line between playacting and reality blurring with the heady feel of her pressed against him. His patience with the game abruptly wore thin. She would find herself ravished in fact, if he played this part much longer. "Let me touch you. Fondle you. Inflame in you a fire to equal my own. Yield to me, Madame. Enjoy me."

He tilted his hips forward, rocking lightly against her, while striving to keep the anger from his voice. Anger as much at himself as with her. For his body betrayed him, mind and spirit. "Here. Now," he grated out urgently. "Let me take you. I cannot wait. Only unchain me," he ground out in a low, harsh voice, "and I will swive you as thoroughly as a spring stallion at his first mare."

"Let me go!" The veiled face jerked away and Raine cursed his impetuousness.

He'd read her incorrectly. He could ill afford so grave a mistake. He released her arms immediately.

Trembling she scrambled back into the seat opposite him.

"Forgive me," he began in a hard, far-from-humble tone. But he'd been stretched a bit far, worn a bit thin. "I should not have allowed my desires to make me so bold." His hot eyes lifted contemptuously to her concealed face. "But then, I thought you liked your captives vulgar and base."

He waited for the inevitable: a blow across his face, an imperious call to turn the carriage around.

It did not come. Amazingly, she only squeezed herself further back against the seat. "Sir. Please. Be still. Be quiet. The guards might hear you. Only wait, I pray you," she said urgently.

They drove a quarter hour longer in silence before the carriage lurched to a halt. Raine peered outside. They had stopped in the yard of an inn. Beyond the three-story building, Raine could see only the occasional light in the distance. They were near the outskirts of the city. Good.

The carriage door swung open. Jacques stuck his massive head in, eyeing Raine suspiciously as he fit a key into the padlock that secured Raine's chain to the floor bolt. He unlocked it, wrapping the links around his fist and jerking Raine across the carriage.

With a snarl, Raine stumbled out.

"I will take him up," one of the prison guards said. "Once he is in the hotel room, he is your responsibility. You best make sure he is returned by first light tomorrow."

Jacques eyed the bloated French gaoler with ill-disguised disgust. "Has Madame ever neglected her part of the bargain?"

"No, make sure she does not grow lax in her . . . satiation. This one is wily. Reckless."

Without waiting for a reply, the guard yanked Raine after him, leading the way around the back of the well-equipped hotel to the servants' entrance and from there up a flight of stairs to the suites.

"Which room?" he demanded.

Jacques pointed to a linen-paneled door a few feet down the hallway. They were almost to it when it swung open and Madame appeared in the doorway.

Jacques grabbed Raine's arm and thrust him bodily into the shabbily ornate room. A four-poster, hung with dull blue satin drapes, stood in the center.

"Madame," Jacques said, handing her a pistol. "This will only take a few minutes. I will pay the guard and his partner and return. I would do so here, but I do not trust him to give his partner his portion, and I would not have . . . you interrupted. In the meantime, keep this pistol trained on him." Jacques nodded toward Raine. "If he moves, shoot him."

She took the gun, leveling it at Raine.

"I *will* kill him if he tries anything," Jacques said tersely, and then, with one more worried glance at Raine, he stomped from the room, slamming the door shut behind him.

Raine stared at the gun. The pistol bore looked as cavernous as the entrance to hell, which, Raine allowed fleetingly, it just might be.

Without a second's more hesitation, he acted.

His hand flew out, snatching the barrel and twisting it viciously. With a cry, she released it. He grabbed her wrist, spinning her around and slamming her back into his chest, pinning her free arm to her side.

His forearm pressed under her chin. With one hand he manacled her wrist; with the other he held the gun. Carefully he released the hammer and shoved the pistol into the waistband of his breeches.

"Scream now, Madame, and you will die now," he whispered into the veiled ear so close to his lips.

In response she began struggling fiercely, her free hand tearing at his wrist. She kicked violently, but her movement was hampered by the thick layers of skirt. Still, one booted heel found his foot, crunching down on the instep and drawing from him a hiss of pain.

Savagely, he wrenched her chin back against his shoulder, bringing the veiled face near his mouth.

"Cease!" He heard her whimper, but her struggles abated. Immediately he became aware of her buttocks pressed intimately against his loins. He smiled humorlessly at his body's heated response.

Since the moment she'd stepped into that damned cell, she'd bewitched him. Perhaps his years in prison had perverted his sexuality because, 'struth, she aroused him more than had a thousand fantasies he'd devised to keep him company over the long months.

"Please," she rasped. "Please. Listen to me!"

"No, Madame," he whispered. "You listen. Heed me well. I will never return to that place. Not alive. And you are the means for me to keep that vow. You are *my* prisoner now."

She moaned, her face twisting away from his, the silky veil slipping against his lips. "Please—"

"Shut up," he growled, as a sudden realization overwhelmed him.

He needed to kill her.

Without his doing so his chances of his gambit succeeding were well-nigh nil. Should he actually make it alive out of the hotel, he would not last an hour if he had to drag her along with him. And if he left her behind, she'd raise an immediate cry. He should kill her now: quickly, silently, *now*.

But he couldn't. As much as every instinct for survival demanded it, he could not kill her. In more frustration than anger, his arm tightened around her throat. She began kicking again and he lifted her, hitching her against his hip, filling his arms with the firm, supple woman.

The simple act awoke memories of cool Scottish nights and passionate, yearning Scottish lassies striving towards fulfillment, struggling not to free themselves but to find a closer union, their arms wrapped about his throat, their thighs about his hips.

Aye. Not everything about Wanton's Blush had been unpleasant. And that thought, the old devil-may-care humor that had once been the hallmark of his character awoke. The rash, heedless boy who'd died, unredeemed and unransomed in a French prison, was resurrected. At least one thing he would have of this night, one small victory he would claim.

Damned if he wouldn't see Madame Noir's face.

He grasped a fistful of dense, gauzy material. "Madame, you are revealed," he said. "Voilà!"

He wrenched the veil from her head. Pins scattered at their feet, followed by the soft, soundless flutter of her veil falling to the floor. Loosened tresses, soft and heavy as damask silk, cascaded over his bare forearm in shimmering waves. Gold. Antique gold, healthy and luxuriant.

Confounded, he grasped a handful of the silky stuff and jerked her head back.

Fine skin. Creamy and utterly smooth. Blue eyes, dark blue. Near indigo. Frightened. Young. Very young.

Too young.

"Madame," he said, easing his forearm's pressure from her throat, "who the hell are you?"